Romantic Suspense

Danger. Passion. Drama.

Christmas Cold Case
Maggie K. Black

Taken At Christmas
Jodie Bailey

MILLS & BOON

CHRISTMAS COLD CASE
© 2024 by Mags Storey
Philippine Copyright 2024
Australian Copyright 2024
New Zealand Copyright 2024

First Published 2024
First Australian Paperback Edition 2024
ISBN 978 1 038 93556 4

TAKEN AT CHRISTMAS
© 2024 by Jodie Bailey
Philippine Copyright 2024
Australian Copyright 2024
New Zealand Copyright 2024

First Published 2024
First Australian Paperback Edition 2024
ISBN 978 1 038 93556 4

MIX
Paper | Supporting
responsible forestry
FSC www.fsc.org FSC® C001695

Published by
Harlequin Mills & Boon
An imprint of Harlequin Enterprises (Australia) Pty Limited
(ABN 47 001 180 918), a subsidiary of HarperCollins
Publishers Australia Pty Limited
(ABN 36 009 913 517)
Level 19, 201 Elizabeth Street
SYDNEY NSW 2000 AUSTRALIA

Cover art used by arrangement with Harlequin Books S.A.. All rights reserved.

Printed and bound in Australia by McPherson's Printing Group

Christmas Cold Case

Maggie K. Black

MILLS & BOON

Maggie K. Black is an award-winning journalist and romantic suspense author with an insatiable love of traveling the world. She has lived in the American South, Europe and the Middle East. She now makes her home in Canada with her history-teacher husband, their two beautiful girls and a small but mighty dog. Maggie enjoys connecting with her readers at maggiekblack.com.

Books by Maggie K. Black

Undercover Protection
Surviving the Wilderness
Her Forgotten Life
Cold Case Chase
Undercover Baby Rescue

Mountain Country K-9 Unit

Crime Scene Secrets

Unsolved Case Files

Cold Case Tracker
Christmas Cold Case

Visit the Author Profile page at millsandboon.com.au for more titles.

And thou shalt have joy and gladness;
and many shall rejoice at his birth.
—*Luke* 1:14

To Kripke and Bernadette
of Sonora

and their photographer
Teresa Anne Murphy

For all the joy your pictures have brought to my life

Chapter One

It was like driving through a thick, vanilla milkshake that was somehow still in the blender. Inspector Ethan Finnick navigated his pickup van through the storm, as thick globs of snow pelted from the darkness and splattered his windshield. He drove slowly across the narrow, one-lane swing bridge that connected Manitoulin Island to the mainland. Narrow iron bars rose on either side.

"Doesn't exactly feel safe, does it?" Finnick asked, glancing in the rearview mirror at his constant back seat companion, an elderly black Labrador retriever named Nippy.

Nippy—short for Nipissing—had technically retired from his job as a K-9 cadaver dog six weeks ago when Finnick had stepped down as head of the RCMP's Ontario K-9 Unit to head up the country's first Cold Case Task Force. But as far as Finnick was concerned, the two of them were partners for life. The vehicle shuddered over a bump and Nippy woofed in complaint before lying his grizzled snout back down on his paws.

Finnick snorted. Then he prayed for strength and wisdom to face what awaited him on the other side of the bridge.

Casey Thompson.

Unbidden, the beautiful heart-shaped face and fierce hazel

eyes he'd last seen some ten years ago filled his mind. Instinctively, he pushed the memory away as quickly and ineffectually as the wipers currently trying to keep the snow off his windshield. Casey's former husband, Tim, was suspected of murdering a college student named Stella Neilson a decade ago, and Casey was the potential key to solving the cold case now. The Ontario police commissioner himself had asked that Finnick's new team make this case a top priority due to how police had bungled the original investigation.

Finnick eased the van off the single-lane swing bridge and drove past a long line of other drivers waiting to cross in the other direction and get off the island once the light changed. Hopefully, he'd be headed that way too before long. He turned south toward the small town of Juniper Cove.

Finnick had been in his late thirties when he'd first met Casey. His hair had already been going gray back then, and he'd gone by *Finnick* for so long, he'd almost forgotten that technically his first name was Ethan. Casey had been in her late twenties, with somehow both the idealism of a person half her age and the wisdom of someone twice it. Needless to say, he'd liked being around her. Nippy had just been a pup fresh out of K-9 training when they'd been sent up from Toronto for a few days. They'd been tasked with searching Casey's sprawling Manitoulin property for any trace of her missing husband and nineteen-year-old Stella, who'd last been seen leaving the island together. They'd found nothing.

When, seven years after Tim and Stella's disappearance, Casey had successfully petitioned the court to declare Tim dead so that she could collect his life insurance, a lot of people in law enforcement cried foul.

But, so help me, Lord, there's something about this case that's stuck under my skin like a splinter I can't reach. When we met ten years ago, she'd seemed so strong in her conviction that Tim couldn't be a killer. Not to mention her faith that You'd see justice done, despite the chaos battering her life.

Show me the truth beneath the lies. Help me convince Casey to assist us in finally solving what happened to Tim and Stella.

It had hardly been Finnick and Nippy's first case and they'd worked countless ones since.

Yet when he'd learned the case was being reopened and that Casey was reluctant to talk, he'd felt the urge to jump into his van and drive the six-hour trek from Toronto to try for himself.

"So now I'm going to drop by and talk to her in person," Finnick told the dog in the back seat, as if Nippy had been listening in on his conflicted thoughts. "Worse she can do is slam the door in my face, right?"

He was less than twenty minutes away, and maybe he should give her an opportunity to slam the phone down before he showed up at her house unannounced. He was about to instruct his hand's-free feature to call Casey's number when his phone rang, shattering the silence.

He punched the accept button. "Hello?"

"It's Jackson," came a deep male voice. "Hudson and I are calling you to give you some really good news. We've decided to take up your offer to join the team."

K-9 Officer Jackson Locke and his German shepherd partner, Hudson, had served with Finnick for years and had been among the first job offers he'd made for the new Cold Case Task Force. Formerly of the RCMP, Jackson made five, joining his sister, private eye Gemma Locke, Constable Caleb Perry and K-9 Officer Lucas Harper of the special investigations unit along with his arson-detecting yellow Lab, Michigan.

Thank You, Lord. My team is coming together.

Finnick had always taken an interest in cold cases, wanting justice for victims and families who were still waiting for it. It had been a long-held dream of his to form this unit, and now that dream was becoming a reality.

"So, brief me," Jackson said. "Gemma said you've already started on our first case?"

Finnick replied, "Nippy and I just arrived on Manitoulin

Island and I'm on my way to talk to Casey Thompson since the cold case involves her late husband… She may be reluctant to help though."

"Can't really blame her," Gemma's voice echoed down the line, and Finnick realized he was on speaker. "We're basically asking her to go before the courts and announce she just might be wrong about whether or not her late husband is dead. The past ten and a half years can't have been easy for her. A lot of amateur online sleuths think Casey helped Tim kill a woman and cover up the crime, and then killed him too."

"And the internet is never wrong about anything," Jackson said, dryly.

Gemma snorted. While Jackson was a cop through and through, Gemma was the team's lone civilian, a PI and a meticulously focused researcher who matched her brother's talent beat for beat. She was Finnick's first hire for the new task force.

"Long story short," Gemma said, "eleven years ago, Stella Neilson was living on Manitoulin Island and engaged to marry the island's golden boy, Drew Thatcher. He now runs a real estate business."

Finnick slowed the van to a crawl and rounded a curve. He was less than fifteen minutes away from Casey's home now. In between the sheets of blowing snow, he could now see Juniper Cove spread out below him in a blurry tapestry of Christmas lights. He blinked and still saw colored dots dancing before his eyes. A brightly decorated sign loomed above him. "Welcome to Juniper Cove, Finalist for Canada's Most Whimsical Christmas Village. Sponsored by Thatcher Family Real Estate, the Perfect Home for the Perfect Family."

Speaking of Drew Thatcher… Despite that Stella's fiancé might normally be a person of interest in a case like this, Drew's supervisor at work had provided him with an iron-clad alibi back then and he'd been cleared of any wrongdoing.

"Stella and Tim worked together at the local hardware

store," Gemma went on, filling her brother in. "He was her supervisor. Stella disappeared a few months before the wedding, and the last time she was seen alive was leaving the island in the front seat of Tim's car. Apparently, it was bright red and hard to miss."

The snow was growing even thicker in front of his eyes now. He slowed further, not wanting to miss his next turn.

"They both vanished," Gemma said. "There was a rumored sighting of the pair in Sudbury a few weeks later, but it was never proved to be them."

"And what about the original detective assigned to the case?" Jackson asked.

"He died a few years ago and the case was just left to gather dust," Finnick said. "We've got his files and they're really weak. He was convinced Stella ran away with Tim. I barely met the man. My only involvement in the case was a search of Casey's property with Nippy. And that was a full year after Tim and Stella had gone missing."

Which was how he'd ended up sitting across from Casey in her farmhouse kitchen, touching her hand and feeling like he'd just somehow found something special buried deep in her eyes that he'd never even known that he'd wanted to find.

And that he wasn't about to let himself act on.

"Now, you are coming for Christmas Eve dinner, right, Finnick?" Gemma asked, breaking into his thoughts. "Because both Caleb and Lucas have confirmed, and with Jackson here, we'll have the full team."

"Sure," Finnick said, making a right onto Casey's street. He wasn't really in the habit of celebrating Christmas, but it would be good to get the team together before the task force launched in January. "The storm's getting worse by the second and I'm nearly there. I'll call you back." They said their goodbyes and he disconnected.

Finnick still wanted to give Casey the heads-up he was coming. He commanded his hand's-free app to select her number.

"Finnick," Casey said. She'd answered before it even finished ringing once. "I'm on the roof of my barn, trying to fix a twisted string of Christmas lights. Can I call you back?"

She's on the roof fixing Christmas lights in this weather?

"What?" The word exploded from his lungs more as an exclamation than a question.

He could hear the wind rushing down the phone line, echoing the wail of it outside his van, along with some kind of rattling sound. He had no doubt she was telling the truth.

"I'm on the roof—"

"—of your barn, I heard!" he said and remembered that Casey ran an online business making handmade soaps and candles out of her converted barn-slash-garage. "Climb down and I'll talk to you on the ground."

For a moment, there was no answer but the whistling wind and a clattering sound he guessed was the twisted string of lights. In all the time he'd thought about one day talking to Casey again, this had never once been how he'd imagined it.

"Hang on," she said. "I'm just making my way to the trap door. Don't worry, I made sure I was tethered to the drop ladder before I came out."

Well, at least she hadn't climbed a ladder up the side of the building.

"Why did you even answer the phone if you're on the roof?" he asked.

"Because I saw your name on the screen," she said, "I was afraid the call would drop, and I don't know how long it's going to be before we lose cell service in this storm. Phone service isn't exactly reliable here and it's actually best at the top of the barn."

But his personal number was unlisted and so it shouldn't have shown up on call display. Then it hit him. She must've kept it saved in her phone all these years.

His heart skipped an unfamiliar beat. She'd answered *because* it was him.

"Nippy and I are on our way to see you," he started.

"If this is about this new Cold Case Task Force thing, I need more time to think about it. It's a really big decision."

"I'm the head of the task force thing," he said. "I'm looking into Tim and Stella's disappearance, and the Ontario police commissioner has personally asked me to see if we can overturn Tim's death."

"Tim's dead!" Her voice rose above the wind. "He didn't hurt Stella and I'm not going to help you prove otherwise. Besides, I used the insurance money to pay off his family's debts. This farm has been in his family for four generations. If I declare him alive now, the insurance company will sue me and I'll lose Tim's family's farm."

Well, regrettably, it wasn't up to her.

"Hey! Hey! Get away from there!" she shouted suddenly, her voice aimed away from the phone now, and it took him a moment to register that he wasn't the one she was shouting at. "Finnick, I've got to go, I think there's a trespasser on my property trying to break into my shed—"

A loud banging noise cut off the final word from her lips.

"Casey!" he shouted, feeling something lurch in his chest as her name exploded from his lips. "Are you okay?"

But the phone had gone dead, and when he tried back over and over again, all he got was the incessant beeping sound of an incomplete call. His heart seemed to thud along with the sound.

Lord, please help Casey! Take care and keep her safe until I can get there.

Wind beat harder against the side of the van, colluding with the ice beneath his tires to try to send him flying into a ditch. Everything inside him wanted to speed to Casey's farm to find out why the call had dropped and make sure she was okay. Instead, he gritted his teeth and focused on keeping his vehicle on the road. He must be close now.

The snow fell harder, but finally, he glimpsed Casey's farm.

Her house and barn were wrapped in lights. What appeared to be a life-size nativity scene stretched across the entire front of her property.

All of a sudden, a young woman who he'd never seen before dashed out in front of his van so abruptly that Finnick cried out to God for help and smashed his foot on the brake. The van slid, trying to gain traction as the woman stood in shock, like a rabbit caught in headlights.

Fragile—with long pale hair tossed by the wind and eyes huge with fear. His eyes darted to the small bundle she was clutching to her chest.

Hang on, is she holding a baby?

His brakes locked. His van spun wildly.

He was careening toward her with no way to stop.

His phone flew free from its dashboard mount and clattered somewhere behind him.

"Get down, Nippy!" he shouted to his K-9 partner. "Brace for impact!"

Finnick gripped the steering wheel so hard his knuckles ached.

Save us, Lord! Please don't let me hit her!

Then he was flying off the road through a field and into the snow. He heard a thud and realized he'd hit something, just in time to catch a fleeting glimpse of a large, four-legged creature bouncing off his windshield. A wall of snow rushed up to meet him. Then came a bone-shattering crunch as the van smashed into something hard hidden under the snow. He was thrown against the seat belt. The airbags deployed. His windshield cracked and caved in.

And then it was over and silence fell. He couldn't hear the woman he'd nearly hit or the child she might've been holding.

"Nippy!" he called. "Are you okay?"

As for himself, he was sure to have aches and pains later, but nothing worth worrying about now. He wrestled with his seat belt, it fell free and then he twisted around to look into the back seat. Nippy scrambled up from the floor and licked his hand reassuringly. Finnick yanked his hood up, shoved the door open, then stepped out into the storm. He sunk into snow up to his knees. Nippy leaped into the front seat and climbed out, appearing unharmed. Sparkling Christmas lights that seemed to cover every inch of Casey's farmhouse and barn cast an odd ethereal glow over the snow. Thankfully, the object that had bounced off his van was some kind of camel that'd been part of a sprawling nativity scene. He didn't see the young woman with the baby anywhere.

"Hello?" he turned toward the road and shouted into the darkness. "Is anybody out there?"

The barn door flew open. There, in the golden light, stood the dark silhouette of Casey Thompson.

Tall and lithe, with her arms crossed and shoulder-length hair flying around her face.

"Finnick, is that you?" Casey's voice rang out through the darkness, brave and strong with only the tiniest hint of fear. "Are you all right?"

But as he opened his mouth to answer, a dark shadow moved behind her.

Then he heard Casey scream.

The figure had come out of nowhere, leaping from the shadows of the barn from somewhere behind her van, slamming into her body and throwing her back. Her feet slipped out from under her. Her body hit the floor. Then her attacker was on top of her. She couldn't make out his form, let alone his face. Strong hands clamped around her throat and squeezed. She grabbed at them, trying desperately to ease his grip on her neck as she thrashed about, struggling to throw him off her. A second scream for help ripped through her lungs, even as she felt her attacker squeezing her throat again.

"Finnick!" She shouted the name of the man she hoped had

just crashed onto her property, throwing all the fear, strength and hope she had into the word. "Help!"

Help me, Lord! Save my life!

Her attacker's grip heightened until it hurt to breath. Darkness swam before her eyes. A second male voice shouted now, from somewhere on the edges of her consciousness. She couldn't make out his words. Then another sound reached her ears. A dog was barking, furiously.

"Shut up, sweet pea, or I'll kill you!" Her attacker leaned toward her. His voice was harsh and artificially deep, like he was afraid she'd recognize it. "Where is he? Is he here?"

He? He who?

Is he looking for Tim?

"No..." She tried to shout the word but all she could manage was to whisper, "He's...dead..."

The faint light of the Christmas bulbs outside the barn swam before her, and she finally saw the face of the man attacking her. It was a mask, rubbery and loose, of a shepherd with a supersized grin and yellow beard molded to his face. She blinked. He was wearing the very mask and robes she'd decked her scarecrow out in just a few days ago.

Her older sister had complained it was creepy.

Now, it was downright terrifying.

"If you're hiding him, Casey," the man hissed, "I will find him and kill you both."

The barking rose to a fever pitch.

"Get away from her!" Finnick's voice reached her ears.

The man in the creepy shepherd mask leaped off her. He ran into the dark recesses of her barn, no doubt to escape through the back door. She sat up and gasped quick and painful breaths, as her wobbly limbs struggled to let her stand.

"Casey! Are you okay?" Finnick's voice sounded toward her.

Within seconds, he'd burst through the open barn door with a black Labrador retriever at his heels. And for the first time in a decade, she looked up into the face of Inspector Ethan Finnick.

He'd had sandy blond hair that was lightening prematurely ten years ago. Now it was full gray and peppered with fresh snow. There were new lines on his handsome face.

Worry pooled in the depths of his eyes.

A snowmobile roared from behind the barn. Her attacker was escaping.

"Are you okay?" Finnick asked.

"I—I think so..."

Her breathing was getting stronger and steadier by the moment, and nothing felt bruised or broken. Finnick crouched beside her and reached for her hand. She reached up toward him. His strong fingers held hers tightly and pulled her up to her feet. Despite the fact he was wearing gloves, she could feel warmth radiating through his palm into hers. She remembered a moment like it ten years ago, when they'd sat at her kitchen table talking and his fingers had suddenly grazed hers. They stood there in the barn for a moment, face-to-face, with his hand still holding hers, as if to make sure she was steady before letting go.

"Casey, who attacked you?"

"I—I don't know," she said. "A man...in a shepherd mask and robes...that he stole off my scarecrow."

"Where is he?" Finnick asked.

"Gone... He ran." She watched as Finnick whispered a prayer thanking God that she was safe, and Casey felt the warmth in her hand move up into her chest. "I thought I saw someone when I was up on the roof, and I dropped my phone. When I climbed down I couldn't see anyone, then he jumped me."

"Okay," he said, "give me a second."

He stepped back and placed a quick call to the island's police chief, Rupert Wiig, who seemed to know exactly who Finnick was, and who she remembered he'd worked with before. She listened as Finnick relayed what she'd told him about her attacker.

The elderly black Labrador poked his head out from behind Finnick's legs. The dog's soft, black snout butted against her hand. He was Jackson's partner, Nippy, she remembered. She ran her fingers over his silky ears, brushing the snow from his fur. Nippy licked her fingers and his tail thumped on the wooden floor.

Finnick stepped away and exchanged a few more words with Wiig that she couldn't hear. Then he ended the call and turned back.

"Nippy remembers you," Finnick said.

There was an odd tone to his voice that she couldn't quite place.

"Wiig said he'd get his team looking out for the man who attacked you," he went on. "I told him I'd take your statement and relay any pertinent information to him. I'm afraid my van crashed on your lawn and the windshield is shattered. Also, I should tell you that a young woman ran out in front of my van and I had to swerve to avoid her. I don't know where she is now or if she's okay. So, I gave her description to the chief as well and he said he'd have people looking for her too."

Casey looked past him at the dark and blowing snow.

"I know it doesn't look like it, but there are houses five minutes' walk in all directions," Casey said. "And the center of town is twenty minutes on foot. She won't have to walk long for help. Thankfully, we have a really good neighborhood watch, organized by my big sister, Eileen."

The same sister who'd told her to take the creepy costume off the scarecrow. She fished her cell phone from her pocket, pulled up a text to her sister and handed it to him.

"Here, input all the details," she said, "and in a flash, Eileen will have every person on the island looking out for her. What did she look like?"

"Young, with long hair, and scared," Finnick said, as he

typed. "She was holding something. It might've been a baby, but I can't be sure."

"A baby?" Casey repeated.

"I'm afraid so."

The text swooshed away from her phone and within a second, it pinged again as Eileen sent out an all-island alert about the woman.

He handed the phone back. "That's a handy neighborhood-watch thing to have."

"Eileen set it up after Stella and Tim vanished," Casey said. "I know everyone thinks that Tim killed Stella and then vanished, but—"

The piercing and panicked sound of a baby's cry rose suddenly on the wind.

Casey's heart lurched. Was this the baby Finnick had seen?

But even as she was about to ask, it was like something instantly snapped inside Finnick. Immediately, he turned without hesitation and sprinted through the snow toward the sound, even while her brain was still scrambling to process what was happening. Nippy ran after him and so did she.

Lord, help us find and save the child!

The plaintive cries seemed to be coming from the center of her nativity scene.

Then she saw the baby.

A real, live infant, no more than a month or two old, was lying in the manger, in between the figures of Mary and Joseph, with a note pinned to its chest.

SAVE ME.

Chapter Two

Finnick whipped off his thick winter coat. Immediately, he felt the cold and wet weather smack his body. But he gritted his teeth and ignored it. If it was this bad for him, he couldn't imagine how bad it was for the tiny child. Thankfully, the kid was still bellowing.

Keep fighting. Stay strong. Stay alive. I've got you.

Carefully, he picked the child up, swaddled the infant in his coat and clutched the bundle to him. The baby snuggled against him as if craving Finnick's warmth. Something fluttered in his chest.

Then he glanced up. Casey and Nippy were by his side.

"Whose baby is this?" he asked.

Worry pooled in Casey's eyes. "I've got no idea."

"We need to get this kid inside. Now."

Casey didn't even answer. She just turned and ran toward the house. Finnick raced after her and Nippy stuck close to his side as if to help protect the child. They all arrived at the front door at once. Casey flung it open and then stepped back so Finnick could rush in first. The living room was just like he remembered, with a well-worn but comfortable couch and two chairs, an old steamer trunk as a coffee table, a kitchen to his right and a hallway straight ahead. Despite the abundance of Christmas decorations outside, there wasn't so much as a sprig of holly inside. Casey didn't even have a Christmas tree. Or any presents.

A fire smoldered in the fireplace. He knelt down in front of it and carefully laid the squalling baby down on a rug. Gently he unzipped the child's snowsuit, while Casey and Nippy hovered over him. It was soaked through, as was the white onesie underneath.

"Hang on." Casey turned, dashed down the hallway and disappeared through the door of what, if he remembered right, was her spare bedroom. An instant later she was back with a huge armful of red, yellow, blue and green onesies. They tumbled from her hands onto the floor beside him. His head shook. There must've been every size from preemie to toddler.

"How do you have—" he started.

But he stopped when he realized she'd already turned and dashed down the hall again, only to return with diapers, wipes and blankets. Casey vanished down the hall a third time. Nippy stood between the baby and the doorway. The dog's head was bowed in worry and his tail waved protectively. Gingerly, Finnick eased the child out of the wet clothes, checked the vitals as best he could and gently massaged the baby's tiny arms and legs with his fingertips to bring circulation back.

Strong heartbeat. Good breathing. No obvious injuries. *Thank You, God.*

Then Casey was back, lugging a bassinet full of baby blankets over one arm and a folded wooden stand for it over the other.

"The tall cupboard in the kitchen has a few cans of formula and there are two bottles on the shelf above the counter," she said. "Sadly, only enough to get us through the first twenty-four hours. But at least it's something."

But why do you have all this baby gear on hand?

There'd been nothing about her having children in any of

the research into Casey that his team had done. The question burned at the front of Finnick's mind. But it froze on his tongue as he saw the ache of sadness that pooled in Casey's eyes as she looked down at the child. Her chin quivered. And Finnick's instincts told him that whatever the answer to his question was, it was a tragic one.

Lord, whatever Casey's feeling right now, please hold her in Your hands. I need her to be strong right now. I can't do this alone.

"I'll get the formula," he said, quickly. "You get the baby changed. Thankfully, the kid is strong and healthy."

What looked like a silent prayer of thanksgiving crossed her lips, and tears filled her eyes. Casey nodded, set the bassinet down and knelt beside the child.

"Don't worry, Honey Bun," she murmured to the child softly. "You're safe now."

Finnick stood slowly and watched as she tenderly eased the infant onto a changing mat. He added an extra log to the fire, then turned and walked into the kitchen. Nippy, he noticed, stayed at his post by the baby's side. As he opened the cupboard, he found just three plates, two bowls and half a dozen cups…and an entire box of brand-new bottles and a bottle warmer that had clearly never been used.

The baby's cries finally stilled, and a sweet and gentle hush came from the other room.

When he emerged from the kitchen, he found Casey sitting on the chair closest to the fire, with the baby nestled in her arms.

"He's a boy," she said, softly. Casey looked up at him and her dazzling hazel eyes seemed to shine in the firelight. The child's own blue-eyed gaze also looked up at Finnick, curiously. "I'm guessing he's about six weeks old."

Finnick opened his mouth to speak, only to feel some unexpected emotion block his throat. So instead, he just handed her the bottle in silence and busied himself with setting up the bassinet and stand. Then he cleared his throat.

"Also, my sister texted to let me know the woman you nearly hit with your van has been found, safe and sound," Casey said. "She was seen getting into a white van at a gas station about ten minutes' walk from here and leaving the island."

"And leaving her baby behind," Finnick said. "The note pinned to his snowsuit said 'save me.' Why does this child need saving and who does he need saving from?"

To his surprise, thick tears welled suddenly in Casey's hazel eyes, slipping from the edges of her beautiful lashes. Finnick found himself dropping down to the floor and kneeling beside her chair.

"Hey," he said softly. "It's okay."

His fingers brushed her arm. But she stiffened under his touch. She shook her head and he pulled back.

"I didn't tell you everything that happened in the barn," Casey said. "I meant to, but there was so much happening at once—"

"Hey, it's okay," Finnick cut her off. "Don't beat yourself up for what you didn't say. Just tell me what I need to know now."

A look of relief flashed across her face, as if she'd been expecting him to berate her. While he wasn't exactly sure what to make of that, he mentally filed it away for later.

Casey ran her free hand over her face. Then her eyes met his, clear and direct.

"The man in the mask said, 'Where is he?'" she murmured slowly, as if trying to remember the exact words. "'Tell me where he is. Or I'll find him and kill you both.'"

He sucked in a painful breath.

"And you think he meant the baby?" Finnick asked.

"I don't know," she said. "I thought he meant Tim and that he was just another conspiracy theorist here to harass me."

He looked from her heart-shaped face down to the tiny bundle in her arms.

Lord, please give me the strength, power and wisdom that I need to protect them with my life.

"I had absolutely no idea he might've been talking about this baby," Casey added. "Like I said, a lot of people have written to me or called me with their crackpot theories about what happened to Tim and Stella."

Nippy sighed loudly, and even though Finnick logically knew it had everything to do with the warmth of the fire and nothing to do with the conversation that the humans were having, he felt the sigh with every fiber of his being.

"Stuff like *this* is why the Cold Case Task Force is so important," Finnick said. His voice was louder and more emphatic than he intended, and though the baby didn't stir, he could almost feel it reverberate through the room. "You've gotten used to being harassed. Nobody should have to get accustomed to that. And if we solve this case—"

He stopped and caught himself, feeling a stronger determination than he'd ever felt before move through him.

"—*when* we solve this case," he corrected himself, "then there won't be the same uncertainty hanging over what happened before." He sighed. "Look, I think it's a really normal and human thing to want answers when something bad and confusing happens." Like, he guessed, having a husband drive off with a coworker and never be seen again. "But you've got to trust me that all I want to do is figure out what really happened to Tim and to Stella."

"Tim didn't kill Stella," Casey said. "I don't know where he is, where he went the day he disappeared or what happened to him. But I know he's dead."

"I hear you," Finnick said, "and if you're right and he's dead, I promise I'll do everything in my power to prove it."

Lord, I don't think I've ever wished that anyone was dead before. And I don't have it in me to hope for that now. So, I just pray that You help me find the truth. Wherever it leads.

"Okay," he asked her again, "so you have no idea who

this baby is, where he's from or why someone left him in your manger?"

"None at all," Casey said. Her eyes locked on the child who was gulping down the bottle.

"I believe you," he said. And he did.

"Manitoulin Island isn't that big," Casey went on. "There's only one high school and a handful of churches. Juniper Cove itself has a population of six hundred and eight." Six hundred and ten, Finnick thought, counting himself and the infant. "Everyone knows everybody else's business on an island like this. I'm not saying I've met everybody, but you tend to hear when somebody's having a baby and I can't think of anyone who had a child in the past three months."

Finnick sighed and ran his hand over the back of his neck.

"We're going to have to call Child Protective Services," he said.

"The number is posted next to the phone in the kitchen," Casey said, "along with the extension of the social worker I've been working with. The closest office is on the mainland and it normally takes them a little over an hour to get here, when the weather's good."

"And you know this, how?" Finnick asked.

For that matter, he was still curious why she had a mountain of new baby clothes.

"They've got my home on file for emergency foster care," Casey said.

"You're a foster mother," Finnick said, slowly. A fact that had been missing from his briefing. "Do people know this about you? And are you the only one in Juniper Cove?"

"Yes to both," Casey said. "I'm the only safe location listed as an emergency place to drop off a foundling on the island."

"So, it's possible this woman was desperate," Finnick said, "and decided to take the baby somewhere she knew he would be safe. Have you ever had a child placed with you full-time?"

"Not yet," Casey said. "I've been qualified for three years.

But each time one has come up, I've failed to pass the final background check. I think because someone in town who holds a grudge against me for what they think Tim did has been lodging anonymous complaints against me."

Her tone was light as she said the words, but still they hit him like a punch in the gut.

"I'm so sorry," Finnick said.

"It's fine," Casey said. "It just means going through a fresh batch of questioning and background checks. Every time I pass and get back on the list. But by the time it's all cleared up, the child who was supposed to be placed with me has ended up with another family."

She smiled sadly. Her gaze was still locked on the baby in her arms.

The tiny boy had finished his bottle. His eyelids closed and his little nose was scrunched in what seemed like sleep.

"Looks like he's dozed off," Finnick said.

"I think so too," Casey said. She shifted him deeper into the crook of her arms and dropped the bottle beside her on the chair. "Poor thing must be exhausted. Normally, the protocol for a foundling is to take them to the closest police station, and from there, CPS will place them in a foster home. I can't just keep him here without first going through the proper custodial steps. But considering the storm and the fact the closest police station on the island will still probably take us almost an hour to get to, hopefully they'll agree to release him into our care, what with my being cleared as a foster parent and you being a cop and all."

Our care. Jointly. As in hers and his together.

Casey looked from the sleeping baby to Finnick and shrugged slightly.

"Do you mind calling CPS?" she asked, with a small laugh. "I should, but I don't want to wake him up."

Finnick felt himself grin.

"Yeah," he said, "no problem."

"You'll also find the number for the island mechanic and the one on the mainland by the phone, so you can get someone out to fix your windshield," she added. "The island one is closed over the holidays, so you'll have to call the mainland shop."

Nippy raised his head as Finnick passed, but when the inspector didn't signal him to join, Nippy sighed and laid his head back down on his paws. Finnick felt his grin tighten in determination. If the Child Protective Services rep did express any concern about leaving the baby in Casey's care, Finnick would be all too happy to assure them that he was certain, from everything he'd seen, he had absolutely no doubt that Casey would take excellent care of the child.

Finnick added the fact that someone had apparently wrecked her dream of being a parent by lodging anonymous complaints against her to the mental file he was compiling on Casey.

Who would do such a thing? Was it really someone with a grudge—holding Casey accountable for her husband's crimes? Or did some of the locals think Casey was involved in what happened to Stella?

He placed the call to Child Protective Services on the kind of old-fashioned landline he hadn't used himself in years. He ended up on hold longer than he liked, but when he finally got through to a live person, gave his name and badge identification and explained the situation, it turned out Casey's prediction about the child being released into their joint care had been absolutely right. In fact, he had the impression the rep would've still preferred that Finnick and Casey take him to the closest mainland station, to go through the regular steps, if it hadn't been for the storm. Instead, Child Protective Services would be sending a representative out in the morning to take the baby into their care. They were expecting the rep to arrive between ten and eleven. Until then, he was released into Finnick and Casey's care as their joint responsibility.

He then reached the mainland mechanic, who said he was

facing a long backlog of emergency repairs but would have someone out to fix his windshield by lunch tomorrow.

All right. So until then, the cop and the witness would be raising a child together in a winter storm.

He placed a quick call to Jackson's cell phone, got his voicemail and left a message saying that he and Nippy were fine, but he'd been in a minor fender bender so was spending the night on the island.

Filling Jackson and Gemma in on Casey and the baby could wait until they were actually talking on the phone. In fact, he should probably arrange a full team briefing.

He walked back into the living room to find Casey curled up on the chair with her feet tucked up beside her, and the baby still asleep in her arms. Nippy was stretched out in front of the fire. The old dog seemed to be sleeping too. Casey met Finnick's eyes silently, and for the first time since he'd crashed onto her property, he watched as a tired but genuine smile crossed her lips. Heat rose to the back of his neck. He broke her gaze and busied himself with picking up the baby's wet clothes off the floor.

"You were right about CPS," he said, keeping his voice low so as not to wake the sleeping child. "They've released him into our joint care until a rep can get here from the mainland tomorrow. You were right about the mechanic too. I decided not to tell him I'm a cop, mostly because I'm not certain I want people in this town knowing there's an investigator here looking into Tim and Stella's disappearance yet. Sometimes, the longer we can keep the lid on what we're doing, the easier it is to get the information we need. So, for now, if anyone asks, I'd appreciate it if you tell them that my name's Ethan, I'm a friend of yours and I'm buying a box of your soaps and candles as last-minute gifts for a Christmas Eve dinner I've somehow gotten roped into. Which is true, actually."

Despite the warmth of the house, the baby's clothes were

cold to the touch and the note that had been pinned to the baby's chest was so soaked it fell apart in his hands.

"Sadly, we're not going to be getting any DNA or fingerprints off of any of this," he went on. "And considering the storm, I doubt we're going to find any footprints."

He glanced out the window. Already their own tracks from the manger to the house were being erased. He turned his attention back to the baby's clothes. There was a smudge of blue ink on the label of his onesie. Finnick held it up and squinted.

"Joey," he read. "Apparently, our little visitor has a name. Does the name Joey mean anything to you?"

The question was light as it crossed his lips. But then he glanced at Casey and watched as the color drained from her face.

Immediately, he sat down across from her on the metal trunk that served as a coffee table.

"What's wrong?" he asked. "Do you know who this baby is?"

Their knees were so close they were almost touching, and as he looked down he couldn't help but notice that her legs were shaking. So were her arms.

"No," she said. "I don't know. Maybe."

Quickly, she stood, crossed over to the bassinet and set Joey down amid the soft blankets.

Then she turned and looked at Finnick. Her mouth opened and then closed again, as if she was afraid of the words that were about to cross her lips. He watched as she whispered a prayer for wisdom.

"Hey, it's okay," he said, softly. "Whatever it is, you can tell me."

"I get a lot of unbelievable letters from people claiming to know the truth about what happened to Tim and Stella," she said, her voice barely rising above a whisper. "I don't take them seriously, but..." She trailed off. Her gaze looked past him to the sleeping child. "I recently got a letter from a woman named Ally, claiming to have given birth to a baby named Joey." Then her hazel eyes finally met Finnick's. Fear, doubt and determination all battled in their green-and-brown depths. "Ally wrote that Tim is still alive, and that Joey is his son."

"Joey is Tim's son?" Finnick repeated. The detective shot to his feet and began to pace. "You're telling me you got credible information that Tim Thompson, your former husband, might still be alive and have a son, and this is the first I'm hearing of it?"

Casey felt her head shake. At the end of the day, Finnick wasn't there to be her friend. No matter how good he seemed at listening, or how sweet his dog was. He was a cop, and he always would be.

Lord, I don't even know what to pray for right now, I just know I need Your help.

And so does Joey.

"It's not like you're making it sound," Casey said. Her arms crossed and although her voice was low, she packed every bit as much feeling into it as if she'd been on the verge of yelling. "I told you and your colleague, I've gotten hundreds of letters from people trying to scam, threaten or blackmail me."

She swept everything off the steamer trunk that served as her coffee table onto her couch. Books, mugs and unused baby clothes tumbled onto the cushions. Then she yanked the lid open and gestured for him to look.

Finnick stepped forward and glanced inside. Six topless boxes formed a makeshift filing system. So far, she'd filled five and a half of them, with hundreds of letters, each one of them in its own transparent plastic sleeve. Finnick frowned and sighed. But he didn't look surprised.

"Don't worry," she said. "I always wear gloves when I open them and slide them into a plastic sleeve immediately, in case some cop ever wants to see them."

"You might've done more work to solve this case than the

original investigator who was assigned to it," Finnick muttered. "Not that I worked the case beyond the search Nippy and I did of your property. But we have his files and they're definitely lacking. Can I take that with me?"

"You can take all of it if you want," Casey said, "if it'll help you figure out what happened to Tim and Stella. But these aren't leads. They're letters from kooks trying to get money from me. Trust me, anything that contained anything resembling an actionable fact was turned over to police immediately. As for the rest, years ago, I dutifully reported each and every one to the police. People would claim they had seen him alive, knew who killed him or could prove his innocence—for a price. Each time my heart would be filled with all this foolish hope and I'd run to the police with it. Until eventually, an officer told me that sending letters wasn't a crime, unless they contained a clearly stated threat of violence, and that if police chased down every letter-writing nutjob in Canada, they wouldn't have time to go after real criminals."

Finnick's frown deepened and his brows knit.

"Well, whichever cop said that, it was 60 percent untrue," he said. "Depending on the volume of letters sent by any one individual, this could most definitely count as criminal harassment. But it is a hard case to make stick, and all too often results in a warning the first instance. So, the fact that you've been keeping track of them is probably the best thing you could do." He shook his head as he scanned the trunk. "I'm going to take a picture of this for my team. So they can see what some of our cold case victims might be dealing with and be understanding of that."

She felt oddly comforted that Finnick had just called her a victim.

"You got the baby Joey letter?" he asked.

"Absolutely." She was already scanning for it. A moment later, she pulled it from the trunk and handed it to him.

"This isn't even the first letter I received from someone

claiming to have Tim's child," she said. "I've probably had over a hundred about secret babies alone. Not to mention all the other outlandish claims." That was the reason she'd filed Ally's letter away without thought. But now they'd actually found a baby named Joey...

Finnick pulled it gently from her hands, took it by the very edges and scanned it for a moment. Then he read it out loud. "'Hi Casey, You don't know me. But my name is Ally, I'm twenty years old and I've been romantically involved with your husband, Tim Thompson, on and off for months. I just gave birth to Tim's son. His name is Joey. Send me twenty thousand dollars or I'll sell my story to the media. Ally.'"

Finnick turned the paper over as if hoping to find something more written on the back. Then he blew out a breath and ran his hand over the back of his neck.

"Wow," he said. "Not much to go on and she was trying to blackmail you. I can see why you didn't rush to the police with this one."

He sat down on the far end of the couch, away from all the stuff that had once been on her coffee table. She hesitated, then sat down on the opposite end, letting all the mugs, books and random items pool between them.

"Or think somebody was going to drop a baby off outside my house," Casey said, "with a note begging me to save him."

The question Finnick had asked earlier flickered in her mind.

Why does this child need saving and who does he need saving from?

"We can't assume that this baby is the same Joey from the letter," Finnick said. "I mean, it would be a pretty big coincidence if this Joey and the Joey in the letter aren't connected. But we can't just guess at it." He shook his head. "I hate to ask you this," he said, "but how can you be so certain that Tim's dead?"

Casey squeezed her eyes closed so tightly she felt tears building under the edges of her eyelids.

"Because I didn't marry an evil monster," she said. Her eyes opened and she could feel the tears now clinging to her lashes and hoped they wouldn't fall. "I'm sure you've heard that kind of thing over and over again, from people who can't admit their loved ones are criminals. But Tim was a real-life guy with a personality and faults, not the stereotype people want to make him out to be."

"Then, what was he like?"

"A goofball," Casey said. "A lovable, easygoing guy who'd spend twenty minutes chatting up elderly customers and would give people the shirt off his back."

There'd been something so safe and comfortable about being around Tim. His arms had felt like home. And his cheerful spontaneity had seemed like the perfect fit for a woman like her who'd felt perpetually stressed and who overplanned everything.

"Don't get me wrong," she went on, "I'm not saying he was perfect. He lent money generously, even when we couldn't afford it. He picked up hitchhikers and would be two hours late for dinner because someone he barely knew asked him to help move a couch."

And sometimes, despite having a good heart, Tim had made her feel like the least important person in his life. Because he'd been too busy chasing after everybody else's needs—whether they truly needed him or not—and he was never there to just hold her hand or sit on the couch together.

"He let people take advantage of him," Casey added.

"And how did that make you feel?" Finnick asked.

"Resentful," Casey admitted. "Then guilty for feeling that way. Because I knew he was a good guy who loved me and his heart was always in the right place."

"So, your theory of the case is that it was a random act of violence?" Finnick asked.

"I don't know," Casey said. "Maybe. I can't imagine anyone wanting to hurt Tim. All I can think is that Stella was in some kind of trouble, Tim leaped in to help her and he got caught up in whatever was going on. Wrong place at the wrong time, kind of thing. For all I know, it was a spur-of-the-moment decision on his part to take her wherever they were going."

"Can you think of anyone who'd have wanted to hurt Stella?"

Casey shrugged. "She was engaged to Drew Thatcher," she said. "But they seemed happy. Stella always seemed kind of withdrawn to me, and Drew was—well, he still is—a really outgoing, charming guy. Plus, he was at work and had an alibi."

She ran both her fingers through her hair.

"I wish people had looked harder at Patrick Craft," she added.

"Who's he?"

"Back then?" she asked. "He was Drew's best friend and the last person to see Stella and Tim together. He had a baby with his girlfriend, and she left him shortly after Stella and Tim vanished, leaving him to raise the kid alone."

"And where is Patrick now?" Finnick asked.

"Still on the island," Casey said. "He's the owner of Craft and Son Construction, which he inherited from his father. He's also the chief of our voluntary firefighters. I know you didn't get that good a look at my garage, but my soap-and-candle workshop is in the back and there's a loft bedroom in the rafters. He designed and built that. Did a similar one at my sister's house for my nephew. It may seem odd to a non-islander, but in a place this small, you can't afford not to get along with someone."

"And why do you wish police had dug deeper into him?" Finnick asked.

"Because I know Tim is innocent," she said, "and it seemed awfully convenient that Patrick just happened to see them leave the island together. I don't know, I just get a weird and unsettling feeling whenever I see him. He never really meets my eye. It's like he knows something he's not telling me."

Then again, going over a decade without answers had given her a lot of time to try to come up with alternative explanations for what might've happened. For all she knew, her suspicion of Patrick was no different than other people's suspicion of her.

Finnick nodded. "What happened to his kid?"

"Patrick's still a single dad. His son's name is Tristan and he's twelve now."

Finnick didn't answer. Instead, he went over to the fireplace, added a fresh log and then moved the wood around slowly with a poker, as if trying to get the positioning just right. Everything about Tim had been fast. The way he talked, the pace he walked, the speed at which he leaped into things without thinking, even the way he waved his hands around to punctuate whatever he was saying.

Finnick was the opposite of that.

Nippy had repositioned himself by the baby, with his snout on his paws, facing the child. For a long moment, silence fell around them, punctuated only by the crackling of the fire, the snow beating against the windows and the gentle wheezing sounds of Nippy's low snores and Joey's high-pitched ones mingling together.

"If you told me that Tim picked up a hitchhiker who'd murdered him and Stella, I'd believe you," Casey added, feeling the need to say something to fill the silence, "or that he'd been talked into driving her four hours roundtrip to Sudbury."

"But not that he was having an affair or that he killed anybody," Finnick said finally, still crouched by the fireplace. He hadn't made it sound like a question.

"No way."

Finnick turned and looked at her. The orange flames danced in his dark eyes.

"I believe you," he said. "At least, I believe you're telling me the truth as best you know it. But there might be things about Tim that you don't know. And if so, it's my job to find that out."

But what if the keen-eyed inspector and his gentle dog found out things she didn't want to know?

Finnick went back to the fire. And she wondered if he was strategically using the silence to give her time alone with her troubled thoughts. Or if Finnick was naturally just a quiet guy of few words at heart.

After a long moment, Casey turned toward the window and stared out at the night. She'd left the Christmas lights on and at least four inches of snow had fallen since Finnick had crashed his car.

She watched as snow moved past the windows in waves of white, punctuated by bursts of color from her changing Christmas lights.

"I noticed earlier that you've got a whole panorama of Christmas lights and displays outside your home," Finnick said. "But nothing inside. Not even a tree. Why is that?"

Until he spoke, she didn't realize that Finnick must've been following her gaze out the window.

"Juniper Cove is trying to win this competition to be named the Most Whimsical Christmas Village in Canada," Casey said. "My big sister, Eileen, is head of the committee. Her husband, David Wilks, is the pastor of the local church. This competition is a really big deal for Eileen—for everyone here, really—because the increase of tourists and publicity, not to mention the prize money, could make a huge difference to the town and the whole island. So it was important I do my part."

She glanced back at the window and her heart stopped as she saw a dark figure moving through the lights like a shadow. The man in the ski mask froze momentarily, standing there in the front yard, staring right at the windows as if trying to see who was inside. She covered her mouth to stop from screaming and waking the baby. But Nippy barked sharply, as if the dog had been suddenly jolted awake. She glanced at the Lab, who was now on his feet.

"What's wrong?" Finnick rose from his seat and crossed over to the window.

She looked out again, just in time to see the figure dash into the darkness and slip around the side of the house.

"There's someone outside. I think he was watching us."

over to the window.

Chapter Three

The figure had vanished from her view.

"What did you see?" Finnick asked.

She looked up him and watched as his gaze darted from the
window to his K-9 partner, to the baby who'd already begun
settling, before finally resting back on Casey's face.

"A man in a winter ski mask was standing right there." She
pointed to the empty spot where she'd seen him. "I thought he
was looking right at me. Then he disappeared around the side
of the house, toward the barn."

"I'm going to go check it out," he said. His words and tone
were comforting, as if his focus was on trying to keep her
calm. But he didn't manage to hide the worry and concern she
saw in his dark eyes. "Hopefully, it's nothing to worry about
and just some guy who was walking in the storm and stopped
to take shelter. But you stay here, just in case."

He quickly crossed the floor toward Nippy, who was still
on his feet, signaling to the retired K-9 as he went. Joey was
still fussing softly but seemed to be drifting back off to sleep.
Casey glanced outside again and saw nothing but lights and
snow.

"Why did Nippy alert?" she asked.

"Oh, that wasn't a K-9 alert." Finnick shoved his feet into his boots. "Just a regular bark letting me know he heard something outside." He grabbed his coat and was still putting it on as he opened the door. "He only alerts to the smell of a dead body, and let's both hope you never witness that."

Finnick and Nippy ran outside and into the snow. He pulled the door closed behind him as they went, but the winter wind caught it and slammed it back open. She could vaguely hear Finnick calling back to her to close and lock it again, as he disappeared around the side of the house. But instead, she checked the sleeping child, then pulled the door only partially closed and stood in the doorway, looking out at the stormy night.

For a moment, she couldn't see anything but the usual lights of her Christmas display being tossed and pelted by the wind. The sound of Finnick shouting for someone to stop and Nippy's loud barks rose from the darkness.

Then she saw the man dash out from behind her house. His long legs were almost flailing as they churned up the deep snow, as if he was too frightened to remember how running worked. And even from behind, in the dark and in the winter clothes, she thought she recognized his shape or maybe just something about the way he was moving.

Cameron? Her nephew—Eileen's only child.

She'd always been incredibly fond of the twenty-two-year-old and was happy to see him whenever he sporadically dropped by. This was despite the fact she knew his general lack of responsibility tended to worry his parents to death.

No idea what he'd been thinking lurking around her property in a ski mask at night—if he'd even been thinking at all. But regardless for the reason for this foolishness, the consequences were about to catch up with him fast. In an instant, Finnick and Nippy were on his tail, chasing after him with such determination and speed it was as if they didn't even notice the snow.

"Cam!" Casey raised her hands to her mouth and shouted. "Cameron Joseph Wilks! Stop!"

The figure hesitated and glanced back, only to catch himself on one of the extension cords powering her lights. He lost his footing and tumbled headfirst into the snow. Yeah, it was her nephew all right. She pushed her feet into her boots without lacing them, yanked a blanket off the back of the chair and wrapped it around her shoulders, and then stepped out onto her front steps, just in time to see Finnick give Nippy a subtle and silent hand signal.

Nippy stopped running and stood in the snow, his tail suddenly wagging. Finnick stopped too, the pair maybe ten feet away from Cameron, and even from a side view she could see a warm and disarming smile cross Finnick's face.

Cameron pulled his ski mask up. His oval face was pale in the flickering Christmas lights. She hadn't seen him in almost a year, but he had that same expression in his eyes that somehow always looked hungry, despite the fact he'd packed on a couple of pounds while he'd been away at college.

"Auntie Casey!" he called as he scrambled to his feet. "I just dropped by to say hi and…and see if you had a pair of cross-country skis I could borrow. But when I saw you had company, I figured I'd just see if I could get them for myself."

Instinctively, she glanced at her watch. It was a quarter after ten.

"You could've just knocked and asked if you could check in the garage," Casey called back.

Finnick faced her and seemed to read her in an instant. She wondered what he'd seen there. But he was already turning back toward Cameron.

"I'm sorry, man." Finnick reached down and offered him a hand. The warm and disarming smile on Finnick's face seemed to radiate through his voice. "Nippy and I didn't mean to startle you."

Nippy waved his tail as if in agreement. Cameron took his hand and Finnick helped him to his feet.

"You doing okay?" Finnick asked Cameron. "All good? Nothing broken?"

"Yeah, I'm okay," Cameron said. He brushed snow off his legs and jacket. "I didn't look where I was going and just slipped over an extension cord."

"There are a lot of them out here," Finnick conceded.

"When did you arrive on the island?" Casey called. "Your mom said you weren't coming home for Christmas. She said you were photographing a wedding."

And Eileen had sounded royally annoyed about it too.

"Got here a few hours ago," Cameron called back. "The wedding party canceled on me last minute and Mom really wanted me here to help take pictures of her Whimsical Christmas competition."

"Well, sorry for getting off on the wrong foot." Finnick chuckled. "My name's Ethan. I'm a friend of your aunt's and accidentally spun out when I was on my way to see her. Just got invited to a Christmas Eve shindig at a friend's house and figured Casey's candles and soaps would make some great gifts."

He patted Cameron gently on the shoulder. It was a reassuring, almost fatherly gesture. But Casey couldn't help but notice that he hadn't identified himself as a cop, and for the first time that she could remember, he'd introduced himself by just his first name. He told her he'd done the same with the mechanic.

Suddenly the eerie Creepy Shepherd mask flickered in the back of her mind again. Her breath stuttered as she remembered the feeling of his hands around her throat.

Lord, why am I hesitant to ask Cameron about that?

"Oh, you haven't seen the shepherd robe and mask my scarecrow was wearing around here anywhere, have you?" Casey asked, keeping her voice as light as she could. "Your mom gave me grief for it. Said it looked creepy. Well, somebody stole it earlier and jumped out at me wearing it. He scared me half to death. Then he took off on a snowmobile before we could stop him."

She paused and waited for his answer. But Cameron just shook his head.

"No," he said. "But I'll be on the lookout. What happened to the van?"

"A woman ran out in front of me and my tires lost traction," Finnick said. "Your mom sent out a message about her to the neighborhood watch. She was your age or a little younger. Blond hair. Looked lost... You see her?"

"No." Cameron shook his head. "But Mom mentioned she'd been picked up by someone and left town."

He wasn't meeting her eyes or Finnick's. But where to start on what Cameron might be hiding?

"You want to come inside and warm up?" Casey asked. "I've got hot chocolate. We can catch up and then I can give you a ride home."

But her nephew was already shaking his head.

"Nah, I should get home before the snow gets worse," Cameron said. He took a step backward. "Plus at this rate, I'll be able to run home faster than you'll be able to shovel your vehicle out of the barn."

He wasn't wrong about that. A few more inches of snow had fallen since Finnick's arrival. She glanced up at the continuing snow and hoped the tow van would still be able to get through in the morning.

"Okay, well, I'll hopefully see you tomorrow!" Casey called.

Cameron had already turned and started back toward the road.

"Absolutely!" Cameron called. "Don't let my folks know that I was here. I think Mom wanted to tell you about it tomorrow."

He jogged back to the road, and for a moment Casey, Finnick and Nippy just stood and watched as her nephew disappeared from view. Then, even once he'd gone, Finnick stared into the empty space where the young man had vanished, before turning and starting back toward Casey and the house, with Nippy at his side.

Casey stepped back inside the house as he approached, thankful to see Joey was still asleep in his bassinet. She slid off her boots as Finnick and Nippy entered the house behind her.

"Well, that was suspicious," Finnick said dryly. "I can't remember the last time I saw a less convincing performance. Do you know what that was all about?"

"Not exactly." She shrugged the blanket off her shoulders and dropped it back over the chair. But Finnick stayed at the door and didn't take his coat off.

Okay, now how to explain her particular family dynamics to someone she barely knew?

"Cameron is a good kid," Casey said. "Well, I guess he's not really a kid anymore. But he's had some problems with money and responsibility. And I guess you could say that his mom—Eileen—is kind of controlling. But only because she thinks she knows the right way that everything should be done. Which is something she got from our mom."

"That must've been fun to grow up with," Finnick said.

Casey laughed. "As the younger sibling who never could do anything right? Yeah, it was a blast." She sat on the arm of a chair, her legs suddenly feeling too tired to hold her up anymore. "Anyway, she's probably got Cameron on some kind of curfew, and he snuck out to see me, then looked in the window, saw you were here and decided to leave in case you were someone who'd tell his mom. Which, granted, does not explain why he ran around toward the barn instead of just taking off."

Finnick ran his hand over the back of his neck.

"I have so many questions," he admitted. "Cameron is in his twenties, right?"

"Twenty-two," Casey said. "He was born when I was fifteen. I was his first and only babysitter."

A smile crossed her lips. She'd liked Cameron from the

start. For once, it had felt like there was someone in the family she could relate to. Somebody else who was too loud, too clumsy, awkward and never did anything Eileen or her mother thought was good enough.

"He always drops by to see me when he's in town," she added, "and never thinks to call and tell me he's coming."

"Do you think he'd ever steal from you?" Finnick pressed.

"I hope not," Casey said. "But I could see him borrowing something and forgetting to ever tell me. He's a bit irresponsible, not malicious."

Finnick's brows knit.

"And you said he had a curfew," he said. "At twenty-two."

"Well, Eileen would never call it that," Casey said. "That's my word for it. She probably just told him that it would 'mean a lot' to her and Cameron's father if he could 'see his way' to being in the house 'by ten, so that everyone gets a good night's sleep.' Or something like that."

She realized she was unconsciously mimicking her older sister.

"Any criminal history?" Finnick asked.

"I don't think so," Casey said. "He used to skip school and once got caught smoking behind the church when he was, like, thirteen. When he was eighteen somebody called his folks to let them know he'd been seen sitting inside the bar in the next town over. And they've never let him live it down. More recently he got into some financial trouble. I think he was gambling online and racked up some bills. Eileen is helping him out financially, so she tends to keep a pretty close eye on him when he's visiting. Don't get me wrong. They're really loving parents. They just hold him to a ridiculously high standard that he can never live up to."

And I've never had a hope of living up to Eileen's standards either.

Finnick nodded and there was something in his eyes that

made her think he was hearing more in her words than she was saying.

"What did Eileen think of Tim?" he asked.

"That he wasn't good enough for me," Casey admitted, "and that I was making a mistake by marrying him. But once he disappeared, she was nothing but protective. Maybe even overprotective."

"And if she wanted to say 'I told you so,' she never came out and said it?" Finnick asked.

"Yeah, pretty much," Casey said. Joey was beginning to stir now. She'd have to make him another bottle and see about settling him in the crib in the spare room.

When she looked back at Finnick, his eyes were also on the child.

"Do you think Cameron had anything to do with what happened here tonight?" he asked.

His voice was so calm it was almost emotionless. But that didn't stop her lungs from tightening in her chest.

"No," she said. "I don't think so. Why? What are you suggesting?"

"I'm not suggesting anything," Finnick said. "I'm keeping an open mind about everything. Maybe your nephew and your family have something to do with this child. Or with the 'Creepy Shepherd' who attacked you. Maybe they even have something to do with Tim and Stella's disappearance. Or maybe nothing at all. By my math, Cameron would've been about eleven when it happened."

He pushed the door back open again and a cold gust swept into the room, sending a shiver down her arms.

"I'm going to go get my stuff from my van, and then we're going to head to the barn," Finnick said. "You said we could use the loft?"

Casey nodded.

"It's actually pretty comfortable," she said, "and it's heated, because I can't let the ingredients I use to make my soaps and candles freeze. But I've got to warn you, some of the soaps and candles smell so sugary it's put me off sweet things like candy for good. There's a cot set up and sleeping bags. And it's got clear sightlines to the house. Or do you want me to set up a bed in the living room for you?"

Finnick hesitated for a moment. Then shook his head. "Thanks, but I need some privacy to check in with my team," he said. "Plus you said the cell signal was strongest out there. Just flash the house lights if you need us and we'll be right over."

"Will do," she said. "Hold on, I'll give you a set of keys so you're not locked out." She popped into the kitchen, pulled her spare key ring from her junk drawer and then came back. "The square one is for the barn's side door and the circular one is for the house."

"Thank you." He took the keys from her. His gloved fingers touched her bare ones for just an instant, and somehow, she felt an odd sort of warmth move through his hand into hers. His dark and handsome eyes met hers, and she had to bite the inside of her lip to stop herself from leaning closer and hugging him good-night. "Thanks again for letting me stay," he said. "Here's hoping everything will look a lot better and clearer in the morning. You sleep well."

"You too."

Then Finnick and Nippy disappeared out her front door and back into the snow. She shut it behind them, turned the lock and leaned back against the door, wondering why her heart was racing.

The barn was dark, but as Finnick and Nippy stepped inside, he felt a gentle warmth surround them, along with the smell of cinnamon, peppermint, lavender, clementines and a dozen other spicy, fruity and flowery scents he couldn't place. Casey had told him that the smell had put her off sweets. Now he could see how that could happen. He felt along the walls, found a light switch and turned it on. A gentle yellow glow filled the barn. It was large, with a garage for her van and tools in the front, and a workshop full of colorful wax and soap in the back. A narrow set of steps led up to the loft, with a railing on one side.

He started for it, but Nippy beat him to the stairs. Finnick glanced down at the black Lab.

"I'll carry the stuff up," Finnick said, "and then I'll come back to get you."

But already the dog was climbing up to the loft, slowly and stubbornly. Finnick snorted, tossed his bags higher over his shoulder and started after him, bracing his hand against the railing and his legs on the steps, in case the dog faltered and tumbled back down into him. The dog made it to the top, slowly but surely. Finnick dropped his bags and looked around. There was a cot against the wall, a cooler, a kettle, a lamp and more than enough blankets for an army. He spread one on the floor and Nippy promptly lay down on it.

Finnick sat on the edge of the cot and plugged his phone into an extension cord that poked out from underneath the bed. Within moments it sprung to life. He called Gemma, and she answered before it'd even rung once.

"Finnick, hi!" Gemma's voice came through the phone, sounding slightly worried but also like she was smiling. "We got your message. How are you? Are you still at Casey Thompson's?"

"I am and I'm good," Finnick said. "I'm staying on her farm. I'm sorry I kept you up."

"It's fine," Gemma said. "I don't normally go to bed until eleven. Do you want me to wake up Jackson? I doubt he's getting much sleep lately anyway. Between you and me, I expect Amy and Jackson to give up trying to plan a wedding and just elope any day now," Gemma went on. "He and Hudson are up here at the cottage almost every weekend, and now he's going to be with the team in Toronto, I'm guessing that'll play a role in where they buy a house."

Finnick prayed and silently thanked God yet again that Jackson would be joining them. While Finnick and Jackson hadn't always seen eye to eye, the K-9 officer and his search and rescue dog, Hudson, were one of the very best teams Finnick had ever had the privilege of working with. Finnick added an extra prayer of thanks for Gemma, Caleb and Lucas.

He filled Gemma in quickly about baby Joey, the man in the Creepy Shepherd mask who'd attacked Casey, the fact that a woman named Ally had sent a letter claiming that Tim was still alive and that Joey was his child, and the various other things that had happened and that he'd discovered since they'd last checked in.

"Got all that?" he asked, when he was done.

"I think so," Gemma said. He could hear the sound of her laptop keyboard clacking through the phone. "It's a lot. I have so many questions."

"I'm sure you do," Finnick said, "but I doubt I have many answers for you."

"So, where do we start?" Gemma asked.

Now, that was the right question. The sound of her keystrokes stopped, as if Gemma was waiting for further instruction. Finnick took a deep breath and blew it out, overwhelmed for a moment by the sheer size of the case and the number of potential leads. Then he decided to just lay everything out and trust his fledgling team.

"Contact Caleb and Lucas," Finnick said. "Make sure that they get a copy of the original police file on Tim and Stella's disappearances. I'm not going to assign specific tasks to each of you because it's a busy time of year, both for you all and the people you might be trying to contact to chase down leads."

Besides, by laying out the work and letting the team decide

what each of them wanted to take on, it would give him an interesting perspective on them all and how they worked together.

"First priority is seeing if there are any missing person reports that match Joey or the woman I think I saw carrying him," Finnick said. "For now, I'm going to assume that she's his mother—Ally—who wrote to Casey, claiming that Tim was the baby's father. But we can't know any of that for certain."

"Got it," Gemma said. The sound of typing resumed.

"Then I want to pull together any recent suspicious activity we can find by anyone using the name Tim or Timothy Thompson," Finnick said, inwardly groaning as he did so at the realization of just how much work that would be. "Assume he's in Ontario, start at the island and move outward. But again, I don't want the team wasting their time investigating everyone in Ontario named Tim Thompson."

"I know," Gemma said, confidently. "Don't worry, I got it. We're not looking into everyone named Tim Thompson who bought a house, landed a job or got married. We're after people who used his name at some rundown motel whose IDs were dodgy, credit cards were fake, or stories didn't match up. If Tim Thompson's still alive, he's done a really good job of hiding under the radar so far. And the kind of people who have come across him aren't the type to run to the police about it."

Finnick exhaled and thanked God the private investigator had agreed to join his team. He suspected there'd be more than a few cold cases coming up where her civilian perspective would come in handy.

"But if Tim is still out there," Gemma added, after a long pause, "why would he use his real name? Why not give Ally a fake name?"

"No clue," Finnick said. "Some criminals like bragging about who they are and what they've done, especially when they're trying to impress or intimidate someone."

Although nothing Casey had told him about Tim lined up with that.

"When I asked Casey who she thought police failed to look into properly she mentioned Patrick Craft, Drew's best friend, who was the last person to see Tim and Stella alive, and the only one who places them in Tim's car together. Also, see if you can find out who at Drew's work provided him with an alibi for when Tim and Stella vanished. Maybe there's something we can shake loose."

"Will do."

Then, instinctively, Finnick lowered his voice, as if Casey could somehow hear him all the way from her house.

"Also, I want someone to take a look into Casey's family," he added, "specifically her older sister, Eileen Wilks, who's married to the local pastor, David Wilks, and her son, Cameron, who's twenty-two."

Gemma's chair squeaked and he had the distinct impression that she'd just sat up straight. "Any special reason why?"

"Casey's nephew was skulking around the house earlier tonight," he said, "and when he was caught he made up some nonsense story about borrowing skis. Casey said he'd had some money problems and I wondered if he was trying to steal from her."

He didn't hear the sound of typing.

"And do you think this has something to do with the case?" Gemma asked.

Or was he asking his team to look into something entirely unrelated to the case because of his personal feelings, worry and general need to make sure Casey was okay?

"I don't know," he admitted. Both to Gemma and to the question in his own mind. "So don't put a lot of time into it. Just a quick look to rule it out."

"Got it," Gemma said. "Anything else?"

"Isn't that enough?" Finnick asked. She laughed and so did he. "Okay, so today's the twenty-second," he went on, "which makes tomorrow the twenty-third. I'm expecting the mechanic from the mainland to be here around lunch, but I'm not going to leave until the social worker comes to pick up Joey, which I'm expecting to be sometime between ten and eleven. I'd like you to arrange a team meeting over the phone for eleven thirty. I'm not sure how good the connection is going to be here for a group call, but even if I get my windshield sorted and the van back on the road before noon, I won't be home until after six."

"You could come straight here tomorrow if you want," Gemma said, "and get here a day early."

"Thanks," Finnick said. "I appreciate that. Really, I do. But I think I'll just come up Christmas Eve for dinner. It'll be good to see everyone together in person."

And despite that he'd prefer to return home first to regroup, there was no way he was going to miss his team's very first meal together.

The call ended soon afterward, and by then, Nippy was already snoring. Finnick found a light switch in the loft, which plunged the barn back into darkness again. Then lay back, looked through the window at the darkened farmhouse and prayed for Casey, for Joey and his mother, Ally, and that God would help him and his team discover what had really happened to Stella and Tim.

Help me, Lord, and guide me. This whole case feels like that kind of tangled mess Christmas lights are in when you pull them out of the box. I can't find the end or the beginning. I can't tell how many different strands to this there are and if they even fit together. I don't even know where to start.

Hopefully, his van would be fixed quickly, and Joey would be taken into care, giving him a few minutes to say goodbye to Casey and tell her that he'd be in touch with anything new about the case.

An odd pang of something that almost felt like sadness twinged in his chest at the thought of saying goodbye to Casey.

It surprised him. It had only been a matter of hours since he'd crashed into Casey's life, and before then, he hadn't seen her in a decade. How could he even be thinking about missing her when he left?

Chapter Four

The first thing Finnick noticed when he awoke was the glare of the brightest sun he'd ever seen, shining through the windows and illuminating the wood around him like a spotlight. The second thing he noticed was that his nose was cold and all the comforting warmth the barn had been filled with the night before had somehow vanished in his sleep.

He glanced through the window at the farmhouse. Casey's silhouette was dancing around the kitchen with Joey in her arms. Although he couldn't hear her, something told him that she was singing.

Casey was such a beautiful, brave and incredible woman.

He added a final thought to the prayer that had filled his heart when he fell asleep.

And, Lord, please help me finally find her the justice and happy ending to this tragedy that she deserves.

Instinctively, he reached for his phone, which told him both that it was a quarter after eight and that the cell phone service was down. Next, he flicked the light switch up and down. The power was down too, and judging from what he could see out his window, Casey didn't have any lights on in the house either.

Finnick stood slowly and stretched, feeling his old bones

creak slowly to life. Then he heard Nippy whimper. The dog was standing at the top of the stairs, wagging his tail nervously.

"Don't even think about it," Finnick said. "It's too steep for your arthritis. Stay there and I'll help you."

He pondered his options for a moment, then just went with the easiest solution—picking the dog up and carrying him down slowly. Nippy sighed at the indignation but laid his head on Finnick's shoulder. When they reached the ground, Finnick set him on the ground and opened the barn door. A thick wall of snow tumbled toward them. At least another foot had fallen in the night, adding to the several feet already on the ground. The road had been erased under a perfect sheet of white that ran from field to field; his van was buried up to the hood and the nativity figures were wading in snow up to their knees. But the sky was cloudless and almost impossibly blue, and bright morning sun beat down on the snow.

Nippy bounded out the door with a joyous woof only to disappear into a cloud of powder and vanish under the white blanket. A second later the dog leaped out of the drifts and tumbled back into them, like he was a dolphin and the snow was his ocean. Finnick laughed. Man, he loved that dog. He grabbed a large shovel from inside the barn door and started to dig a path from the garage to the street.

He was just finishing up when he heard the roar of snow-mobiles, and looked to see three of them slowly making their way toward him. The man on the front vehicle waved. Finnick waved back and then walked over as the machines came to a stop at the end of Casey's driveway. The drivers cut their engines and pulled their helmets off.

On the first sat a man in his thirties with a huge mop of curly hair sticking out from under his red pom-pom hat, wearing a giant, charming grin. The second held a tall, muscular man with an angular face, short hair, a bushy mustache and a more cautious smile. Behind him, on the back of his snow-mobile, sat a boy who looked to be about twelve who was the spitting image of his father, but with a quicker smile and more relaxed shoulders. It wasn't until the young man on the third turned to face Finnick that he realized it was Cameron. Casey's nephew had a camera slung around his neck.

Nippy sniffed the air as the old dog followed Finnick toward the trio. For a moment, Finnick felt the faintest warning at the back of his spine telling him that the K-9 detected something on one of the men. Then Nippy's snout dipped back down and his tail started to wag.

Whatever he'd sensed, he'd either decided it wasn't important enough to tell Finnick about or it was too faint to trace.

"Good morning!" the tall man said. "We're just going door to door to make sure everyone's okay and see if anyone needs help, what with the power out, the roads closed and everything."

"Why, that's really nice of you," Finnick said. "I'm Ethan. This here is Nippy."

"Welcome to Juniper Cove," the tall man added. "I'm Patrick Craft, head of Craft and Son Construction, and also the fire chief of Juniper Cove's all-volunteer fire department."

"Well, that would explain the mustache," Finnick said.

Everyone laughed. The boy louder than the rest, as if he was the kind of kid who enjoyed good-natured joking at his dad's expense.

"Nice to meet you." Finnick turned to the young man sitting behind Patrick. "And this must be the son?"

The kid grinned. "I'm Tristan."

"Nice to meet you, Tristan."

"And I'm Drew Thatcher." The curly-haired man extended a gloved hand and Finnick shook it. "I own Thatcher Family Real Estate."

"'The perfect home for the perfect family,'" Finnick said, "I saw your sign on the way into town."

So, that would be Drew, Stella's ex-fiancé, and Patrick, the man who saw Tim and Stella leaving town together. Was it just a coincidence that the two of them, along with Cameron, were the designated welcome committee checking up on Casey? After all, it was a pretty small town. While she may have suspected the police didn't do a good enough job looking into Patrick years ago, she'd also hired him to renovate her garage.

"We just wanted to remind everyone that there's plenty of fuel in town for those wanting to top up their generators," Drew went on, "and the town's shops are all still open for anyone needing last-minute gifts or supplies. The roads should be open in about an hour and we're hoping the phones will be back up before too long as well."

"That's wonderful," Finnick said. At this rate, the social worker would still make her appointment to pick up Joey and he might manage to get his van fixed and back on the road by lunch.

"We're also distributing flyers for the Christmas events in town," Cameron added. He reached inside his jacket pocket, pulled out a yellow sheet on paper and handed it to Finnick, who took it and thanked him. "Mom says to tell everyone that they're all still running and nothing will be canceled due to the weather."

"That's quite the spin out you managed to do with your van last night," Patrick said, glancing at the vehicle. He shook his head. "You know the island mechanic is away over the holidays and the mainland guy is pretty backed up. It might be a few days until he can get to this. I'm still waiting for him to get snow tires on my delivery van. Apparently, he ran out of the right size and they're on backorder."

"Well, I've got a mechanic from the mainland coming to fix my van this morning," Finnick said.

"Not if he's planning to cross the bridge he's not," Drew said. "Bridge to the mainland is down. There was a major accident last night when a van crashed through the barrier. Who knows how long it will take to fix. For now, nobody is getting on or off this island."

* * *

Joey's big blue eyes looked around with curiosity as Casey carried him through the kitchen and stopped in front of the large front window. The tyke had been babbling and chattering nonsense at her nonstop, ever since she'd changed him that morning. Despite the traumatic events of the night before, and the fact he'd been separated from his mother, Joey was a happy little guy and something about him tugged at her heartstrings, just as hard as his tiny fist tugged at handfuls of her hair.

Then Casey felt the shiver of a warning brush her spine as she glanced out to where Finnick and Nippy stood, talking to the group of guys gathered in front of her house. Something was wrong. She couldn't even begin to guess what it was. But even with Finnick's back to her, she could somehow read it in the way his shoulders tightened and his back arched slightly, as if Drew, Patrick or Cameron had just told him something that Finnick didn't want to hear.

Or maybe it was something he'd been able to read in one of their faces.

Her arms tightened around the small baby, now bundled up in her arms. But she kept her tone cheerful and light.

"You and I are not going to worry about what's going on outside, Honey Bun," she said. "Because we're cozy and safe, and that's all that matters."

Ever since she'd first laid eyes on Joey, she'd felt the instinctual need to protect him.

But from what? She didn't know. Let alone whether it had anything to do with what had happened to Tim and Stella.

But, Lord, whatever it is. Please give me the strength I need to keep Joey safe.

She wrenched her eyes away from the window, despite how much everything inside her wanted to keep her gaze on the handsome inspector now talking to her nephew and the two men who were inexorably linked to the cold case that had ruined her life. Not to mention the impulse inside her to walk outside and hear what the men were saying.

Lord, help me trust in You. Help me trust Finnick and his team too. And also help me trust that the truth about what really happened to Tim and Stella will come out in Your time.

But, please, if it be Your will, make it soon.

What people didn't get about living in a small town was that, once you'd lived through a tragedy, it was impossible to ever escape the reminders of it. Stella's parents hadn't been islanders and didn't have any community roots. They'd retired and left the island in the year after their youngest child disappeared, to be closer to their other children and grandchildren. Last she'd heard, they'd never forgiven the police or the town for what had happened to Stella.

But everyone else involved in the strange disappearances had stayed.

After all, Patrick, whose eyewitness testimony had placed Stella in Tim's bright red car, had also been the man who'd renovated her garage, because hiring someone off-island would've sent tongues wagging. Drew had worked at the town's local ice cream and hamburger joint back then, alongside the woman he'd since married, and was raising three beautiful daughters with. Not to mention all of their families and friends attended the Juniper Cove Community Church, where Casey's brother-in-law officiated Sunday service. Or the fact Eileen ran the neighborhood watch and had a hand in every community event the island had ever held.

For all the songs that had been written about how hard it was to go through a romantic breakup in a small town where everyone knew everybody else's business, all those heartaches had nothing on what it was like to have a former husband who'd vanished and was suspected of murder.

A sudden jolt of pain yanked her head to the right, and her mind out of the past, as Joey managed to snag another fistful of her hair in his tiny grasp.

Casey laughed, feeling oddly thankful for the tug back into reality.

"Joey, be gentle please," she said to him, as she eased her blond hair out of his fingers and tucked the wisp behind her ear. "I'm making your breakfast now. It'll be ready in a moment."

Then she turned back to the stove, where oatmeal was bubbling in a pot on one burner, a bottle of formula was warming in a pan of water on a second and a kettle of water for coffee was boiling on a third. Thankfully, it was gas, which meant she still had heat to cook, despite the fact the power had gone out. The roads would be covered too, but she'd never known them to be closed for more than an hour or two.

Soon the oatmeal was ready, the bottle was warmed and the smell of fresh coffee filled the air. Thanks to the heavy winds and excessive winter wonderland outside, the case worker might arrive a little later than planned. But as a fellow northerner, Casey was sure that the social worker wouldn't let a bit of snow stop her entirely, even if she had tried to call ahead and found the phones down.

"Not that it wouldn't be nice to get a little more time with you," she told Joey.

He squealed and waved his hands in response, and Casey felt an unexpected lump form in her throat. She swallowed it back.

"Breakfast is ready, Honey," she said, playfully, keeping her voice light. "Now, your options are formula or coffee."

Footsteps creaked on the floorboards behind her. She turned and met Finnick's dark eyes. They were wide with surprise. His lips parted, and then closed again, as if she'd somehow knocked the words right out of his mouth.

But for a long moment, she didn't actually realize what she'd just said or done that had surprised him. Nippy stood by his knee, with his head bowed slightly and his tail wagging slowly as if he could tell his partner had been thrown by something, but the K-9 didn't know what. Neither did Casey.

Finnick recovered his voice first.

"I'll take the coffee, thanks," Finnick said, with a weak smile.

A hot flush moved across her cheeks.

Did the Inspector Ethan Finnick, Head of the Ontario Cold Case Task Force think she'd just playfully called him *Honey*?

"Oh, um, I'm sorry," she started, without having any idea how her sentence was going to end. "I... I..."

But before she could find her words, Joey let out a loud and frustrated cry. His tiny fists waved.

"He's hungry," she said and quickly passed the baby into Finnick's arms, even as he opened them to reach for him.

She turned back to the counter, plucked the warmed bottle of formula from the pot and let a couple of drips fall on the inside of her wrist to check the temperature. Then she turned back. "The snow might slow the social worker down a little bit," she added, "but I still want to get him fed, changed and ready."

"The bridge is shut down," Finnick said. "A major accident, and won't reopen for hours. Maybe not even until tomorrow or Christmas."

And tomorrow was Christmas Eve.

"You're kidding." She blinked.

"I wish I was," Finnick said and frowned. "Because I was really counting on getting my windshield in and getting off this island this afternoon. And you weren't kidding about the mechanic being slow. Apparently, Patrick's still waiting on snow tires for his delivery van, which is nuts considering the snow up here." Joey squawked loudly in protest. "I'll fill you in more in a second. Let's get the kid eating first."

He took the bottle from her outstretched hand, and his fingers brushed against hers. Finnick tucked Joey into the crook of his arm and repeated the same temperature test on his wrist that she had on hers.

"So, you really do investigate everything," she said.

"I wouldn't be much of an inspector if I didn't." He grinned almost sheepishly and gestured to the tiny drip of formula now running into his sleeve. "But truth is, I did that instinctively."

His comment had been light and so was hers. But internally she was reeling from everything he'd just told her.

The bridge to the mainland had been out of use before, especially during the summer when it swung up to let boats through. But it had never been shut for more than an hour. Let alone a day.

Just how long were Finnick and Joey going to be staying?

Finnick offered Joey the bottle, but despite how loudly he'd squawked for it just moments earlier, the baby's lips now stayed stubbornly closed.

"Come on, little man," Finnick said. "I know I'm not as sweet or nice smelling as Casey, but don't hold that against me."

He chuckled softly as Joey hesitated for another moment, then took the bottle and began wolfing it down, with loud and determined sucks.

"By the sound of things, it's a pretty big accident," Finnick told Casey. "A van jackknifed on the ice. It needs to be removed before they can fix the bridge. And then they'll have to worry about the lineup of people trying to get on and off the island."

Especially considering the bridge was so narrow, traffic could only go in one direction at a time.

"Internal island roads should be open in an hour or so," Finnick added. "It's just a matter of mobilizing snowplows."

"Thankfully the island has several of those," Casey said.

"They're also hopeful that electricity, cell phones and landlines will be fixed soon," Finnick said.

"Presuming none of the damage is so serious they need a repair crew from the mainland, right?" Casey said.

"Exactly," Finnick said and frowned. "But for now, I'm stuck here."

Stuck on the island? Stuck with her? Or both.

Casey sighed, and Nippy walked over to her and butted his head against her leg, as if wanting to help. She reached down, ran her hand over the back of the dog's head and scratched behind his ears. His fur was wet from the snow.

"I'm sorry, pupper," she said. "I don't have any dog food. The best I can do is cut up some lunchmeat for you. Unless you like oatmeal."

"Actually, he likes root vegetables," Finnick said. "Carrots or squash are his favorites, if you have anything like that."

"I have some chunks of pumpkin in my freezer," Casey said, "fresh from my garden." She pulled them out and put some of the veggies in a pan to warm.

"Perfect," Finnick said. "Thankfully, according to our visitors, most of the main stores in Juniper Cove are still open and running on backup generators. Plus there's an indoor Christmas market in the town hall. Apparently, all the Whimsical Christmas events are still on."

"There's a Christmas Eve nativity pageant scheduled for tomorrow with the island's children," she said, "followed by outdoor ice-skating. The volunteer firefighters turned a shallow part of the cove into a rink."

Casey grabbed a pad and pen off the counter and began writing a shopping list.

"I'm going to get some extra baby food in town," she said, "and of course dog food for Nippy."

"Do you have a generator?" Finnick asked.

"In the barn," Casey said, "but I'll need to get it hooked up to the house. Usually I just ride out blackouts with my fireplace and gas oven."

Because for the past ten years, she'd only had herself. Casey hadn't had a man, his dog and a baby to worry about too. A mismatched and unexpected family of sorts, who were now cut off from the mainland and would be hunkering down together.

Casey spooned ladles of oatmeal into two bowls and set some warmed pumpkin in a third bowl on the floor. She then poured two cups of hot coffee while Finnick finished feeding the baby and burped him.

Next, she got a car seat and set it in the middle of her small kitchen table. Finnick placed Joey in there. Then Finnick, Casey and Nippy ate a simple, peaceful breakfast together while Joey sat in the middle, his wide eyes watching them all.

It was a quiet meal—but a soft, safe and comfortable kind of quiet. The kind filled with silent glances and simple smiles.

This was the place where Finnick had lived in her memory. Ten years ago, he'd been sitting across from her in the same chair at the same table. She'd been talking about Tim and started to cry. Partly it had been because she'd been sad and she missed him. But there were other feelings too, all muddled up together. She had been frustrated at the fact it had been almost a year with no answers, and angry at Tim for being the kind of guy who'd randomly leave the island without telling her. She'd been scared that she was now going to be alone for the rest of her life. Then, silently, Finnick's dark eyes had met hers. He had reached across the table for her hand and squeezed it, filling her with more comfort, understanding and strength than any hug she'd ever had. Over the years, as the memory had flickered across her mind, she'd tried to underplay the images and convince herself it had been meaningless, or even an accidental touch somehow.

Maybe because something about the memory was too powerful to let herself believe it was real.

But now, face-to-face with Finnick, sitting in the same places they'd been before, she knew without a doubt that Inspector Ethan Finnick would never have taken her hand like that if he hadn't meant something by it. Even if it was just to let her know that he was sorry for what she'd been through and that she wasn't alone.

Twenty minutes later, breakfast was done, the dishes were tidied and the foursome was getting dressed in their winter gear to head out across the thick snow toward Juniper Cove.

Casey wore Joey close to her heart in a chest harness, which she then zipped up inside her puffy, oversize, white ski jacket so that only his little head—decked in a fuzzy green hat—stuck out the top. Joey could watch the world go by as they went.

To her amusement, Finnick dressed Nippy in a smart black-and-red-plaid jacket, which pretty closely matched Finnick's own faded plaid winter jacket. Then Nippy stood stoically and allowed Finnick to slide bright red doggie boots onto each of his paws.

"I know you don't like wearing them, bud," Finnick said. "But we're both getting older and bundling up will help with your arthritis."

They made their way down the narrow path that Finnick had dug from her front door to the road. Then they tramped down the road itself, following various snowmobile tracks. The night before, the snow had been blowing so heavily they'd barely been able to see across the street, let alone all the way down the hill to Juniper Cove's Main Street. No wonder Finnick had been worried about how far Joey's mother would have to walk to find shelter. Now, in the bright morning sun, they could clearly see the surrounding farmhouses, each wrapped in a virtual spiderweb of unlit multicolored bulbs, with lawns full of large dormant figures of snowmen, reindeer and other animals made out of lights, waiting to come to life when the power came back.

Canada's Whimsical Christmas competition was supposed to be sending at least one secret undercover judge to each community over the holidays—not that Casey imagined any undercover judges would be able to make it onto the island with the bridge closed. Although, along with decorating their houses, Eileen had specifically requested that everyone dress as Christmassy as possible. Which Casey had completely forgotten about until she started noticing just how many townspeople they greeted on their walk to town were decked out in hats with pom-poms and antlers, brightly patterned scarves and even some Christmas sweaters gamely pulled on overtop of their coats. Suddenly her own red hat and gloves, which had always helped put her in the Christmas spirit, felt downright grinchy.

As they approached the center of town, the sound of carolers rose to greet them from the live choir that stood on the steps of Juniper Cove's community center. They were dressed in their Dickensian best, including top hats, bonnets, flowing skirts and an abundance of ribbon. She spotted Cameron down the street taking pictures of the choir from a distance. He waved and then returned to shooting.

Garlands were wrapped around every lamppost, wreaths hung from every light, and it was like each and every shop had tried to outdo their neighbors with the sheer volume of stars, trees, snowflakes and holiday greetings that bedecked their windows.

As they drew closer to the town square, she heard Finnick suck in a breath.

"What's up?" she asked.

Finnick bent his head close to hers as if he was afraid the throngs of carolers and well-wishers would overhear him.

"I haven't attended a Christmas event in over twenty years," he admitted. "When I joined the force, my father was dead and my mom was in a retirement community and never minded if I came to visit her a day before or after the holidays. So I always volunteered to work so that those with families and kids could spend Christmas with their loved ones." He chuckled, softly. "Now it feels like two decades of Christmas celebrations have caught up with me and tried to trap me inside a giant snow globe."

Their footsteps grew closer to the carolers and now Casey could see her older sister leading the choir. Chestnut curls stuck out from under the brim of Eileen's bonnet and she wore green gloves that buttoned up to her elbows. When she spotted Casey, Eileen quickly brought "O Come All Ye Faithful" to a rousing end and then handed her baton to Drew's wife, Jessica. A soft-spoken woman, Jessica had had a well-known and hopeless crush on Drew for years before they were brought together by Stella's tragic disappearance. Jessica carefully tucked her sleeves into her own long gloves and took the baton.

Casey quickly pointed them out to Finnick as Eileen crossed the street toward them.

"That's my sister," she said. "The woman who's just taken over for her is Drew's wife, Jessica, and the three blonde girls in the blue bonnets, in the front row, are their kids, Sophie, Lily and Molly."

"Why aren't you in the choir?" Finnick asked.

"Eileen says I've got a voice like nails-on-a-chalkboard—"

"Cassandra!" Eileen called before Casey could even finish the thought. "I'm so glad you could make it!" Her arms opened wide for a hug, then she hesitated as she saw the small bundle against Casey's chest. "Oh, you have a baby?"

"Yes, he was abandoned at my house last night," Casey said, "and I'm keeping him safe until the social worker can collect him. We think his name is Joey."

Eileen tutted affectionately and then sighed.

"No doubt left by the girl you texted me about," Eileen said. "I don't know what this world is coming to. Babies having babies, and then abandoning them! I blame the parents. David and I told Cameron that if we ever caught so much as a whiff of him getting involved in nonsense with the wrong type of girl, or going to parties or bars, we'd cut him off financially in a heartbeat."

She shook her head again, then turned to Finnick and smiled. "I don't believe we've met." Eileen stretched out her hand toward him. "I'm Casey's big sister, Eileen. My husband is the pastor here in town and that's my son, Cameron, taking the pictures. He's studying photography in Toronto."

"Nice to meet you," Finnick said. He took her hand and shook it warmly. "My name's Ethan. This is Nippy, short for Nipissing. I was hoping to buy some last-minute Christmas gifts from your sister. Sadly, my van spun out on the ice and I busted my windshield."

Eileen's eyes widened, as if a light had suddenly dawned and it was flashing at her in warning.

"I'm so sorry to hear about your van," she said. "If you could please excuse me for a moment, I need to steal my little sister away for a few moments to discuss a Christmas thing."

"Of course," Finnick said.

To Casey's surprise, Eileen took hold of her arm and led her a few paces away down the sidewalk.

"How well do you know this man?" Eileen whispered, urgently.

"Not that well," Casey admitted. *He's a cop investigating Tim and Stella's disappearance, actually.* The words crossed her mind but stopped at her lips. After all, Finnick had asked her to keep that information under her hat for now. "I met him once, briefly, when he visited the island a long time ago. He crashed his van on my property last night during the storm and I let him stay in my barn until he could get it fixed."

"In your *barn*?" Eileen sounded horrified. "Casey! He could be an undercover judge! We have to get him set up in the Candy Cane Bed and Breakfast. They've got gingerbread muffins and peppermint coffee. Not to mention fresh, tree-patterned down quilts on all the beds."

Casey bit the inside of her lips to keep from laughing. She looked back at the street to where Finnick and Nippy were still watching the carolers.

"It's okay," Casey said. "Ethan is not a judge."

"Like he'd tell you the truth about that!" Eileen said. "The competition rules clearly state that incognito judges will be making undercover visits over the holidays to evaluate us on hospitality, ambience and overall expression of the Christmas spirit. Now, I'm sure whatever you did for him last night was as adequate as you could manage, but it's important that you encourage him to visit the town center to see everything Juniper Cove has to offer."

Joey cooed softly as if trying to get her attention. She wrapped her arms around him over the top of her jacket and pulled him closer to her.

Was it really the worst thing, if Eileen was convinced that Finnick was there to judge how Christmassy the town was? This Whimsical Christmas competition meant so much to her sister. Casey couldn't imagine how distressed she'd be if she knew a detective had shown up to investigate a cold case in the middle of it.

"That's not what I think," Casey said. "But you can talk to him for yourself."

After all, once Eileen had her mind made up it was almost impossible to change.

"You go on ahead into the Christmas market," Eileen said, "and I'll give him a quick tour of the town. I'll introduce him to everyone and make sure he gets to see the best side of Juniper Cove." Casey opened her mouth to respond, but before she could get a word in, Eileen was patting her arm. "I'm going to go tell Jessica to take over the choir. Don't worry, I'm sure everything will be fine."

Eileen hurried back across the street to the singers. Finnick sauntered over.

"What was that all about?" he asked.

"My sister thinks you might be an undercover judge, here to evaluate the Christmas competition."

Finnick snorted.

"She wants to give you a tour of the town while I'm in the indoor market," Casey added.

Finnick ran his hand over his jaw.

"That's not the worst idea," he said. "People will be a lot more eager to talk to me if they think I'm a judge."

Eileen was already walking back toward them. Finnick fixed his eyes on Casey's face.

"Are you going to be okay?" he asked.

"Yeah, the market's pretty awesome and half the town will be in there. Eileen also wants you to move into the bed-and-breakfast. She's impossible to say no to, which is why I never do," Casey said, with a self-conscious laugh.

"Well, I'll be the one saying no to her, not you," he said. "Stay safe and I'll meet you in the market when I'm done."

Finnick looked down at Joey and something softened behind his eyes as he ran his hand over the baby's back. Then, before they could talk any further, Eileen was there and enthusiastically offering to give Finnick the grand tour. Goodbyes were said, and then Eileen led Finnick and Nippy down the street.

As Casey watched them go, she felt an almost sour feeling begin to rise. Eileen had never taken her seriously. Or thought she did anything right.

Casey headed into the Christmas market. Immediately, she was surrounded by the warmth, sounds and smells of the holidays. She unzipped her coat so Joey wouldn't get overheated then moved through the stalls. She bought a quiche, a meat pie, soup and fresh bread for easy meals. Then she added a couple of sweet handmade outfits for Joey and some simple baby toys. On impulse, she also bought a soft green scarf for Finnick along with a matching dog scarf for Nippy.

Yet no matter how many beautiful stalls she visited and Christmas greetings she exchanged, the memories of how Eileen's thoughtless and critical words after Tim left filled her mind and wouldn't let her rest.

If only you'd paid more attention to your husband, Casey,

*maybe Tim wouldn't have left the island without telling you
where he was going. Then we'd all know what happened to
him and Stella.*

And now, Casey was at risk of losing the farm that had been
in Tim's family for four generations.

Suddenly the hall seemed to be getting hotter. The chattering around her seemed to grow louder. An emergency exit
caught her eye to the right. She pushed through the door and
found herself out in a narrow alley behind the community
center.

Silence surrounded her. Cold air filled her lungs. Light snow
fell down soft and gently around her. She zipped her coat back
up around Joey and discovered the baby had fallen asleep. She
cuddled him close as a sudden cry for help filled her heart.

Help me, Lord, I'm so overwhelmed.

Had she ever asked God to help her before? Except of course
for desperate prayers when in an emergency. Casey wasn't
sure. She'd spent countless hours beseeching God to help Tim,
Stella, the police and all those touched by the cold case. But
she couldn't remember if she'd ever specifically asked God to
help *her*. Maybe she hadn't thought she deserved it?

Casey turned to go back inside, only to find the handle
locked. She knocked, and when she got no response, she turned
and walked through the quiet alley back toward the front of
the building. The faint sound of carolers rose on the air.

Too late she heard the crunch of footsteps behind her. Then,
before she could swing around, a strong hand clamped over
her mouth. What felt like the muzzle of a gun pressed hard
into the small of her back.

"Hello, sweet pea," a harsh and artificially deep male voice
whispered in her ear. "I don't want to have to kill you. I'm just
here for the kid."

Chapter Five

Panicked tears filled Casey's eyes and froze in her lashes, as the unseen menace behind her tightened his grip on her mouth. Her shopping bags fell from her hands. The muzzle of the gun dug painfully into the small of her back.

"Now you're going to take me straight to wherever you've got the kid," the man hissed, "and you're not going to do anything to stop me. Got it?"

And just like that a slight and fleeting hope crossed her heart.

He didn't realize she was carrying Joey, hidden safely inside her jacket, with only the top of his tiny head showing. The moment he realized Joey was there, he'd try to snatch the baby from her. Or maybe even kill them both. But for now, Casey had one tiny chance to get Joey to safety.

She had to get him to Finnick.

"Now, nod so I know that you've heard me," her attacker said.

She nodded slowly to show she was listening. Her hands crept up to the tiny baby strapped inside her coat, and she cradled him close to her chest, silently begging Joey to stay quiet. Slowly, she pulled up the zipper as far as she dared while still allowing him space to breathe. As long as Joey didn't make a sound, and her attacker didn't realize he was there, she still had hope of saving him.

Desperate prayers filled her heart.

Guide me, Lord. Help me save Joey's life. I cannot let this man lay a hand on him.

The man pushed her forward and they started walking slowly toward the back of the building. He was taking her to an even more isolated area. The sound of carolers began to fade. A window loomed ahead on the opposite building. But the blinds were down on the inside and there was no way to signal for help. She waited until they drew level, then risked a quick glance sideways, hoping to catch the reflection of the man holding them captive. For a fleeing moment, all she saw was her own terrified eyes looking back at her over a black leather glove. Then they took another step and there, in the glass, was the distorted reflection of the rubbery Creepy Shepherd mask and green robes she'd seen the day before.

His gloved hand moved from her mouth to her throat and squeezed just enough to send the fear of what he'd do if she didn't cooperate coursing through her. She opened her mouth, wanting to scream, but she could barely manage a whisper.

"Tell me where to find the child!" His unsettling voice filled her ear.

"Candy Cane—" she sucked in a pain-filled breath "—Bed and Breakfast."

The hand snapped back to her mouth. He started leading her behind the buildings to the inn, taking a path where nobody would see her, until she could no longer hear the sound of the carolers singing or the hustle and bustle of the noise on the street. All she could hear was her own ragged breathing and their footsteps crunching in the snow. What would happen when they reached the bed-and-breakfast? Would he send her in alone to get the baby? What would happen if she tried to scream for help?

Would Finnick and Nippy even still be there?

Joey stirred softly, with a tiny whimper, like he couldn't decide whether or not to wake.

Please, stay quiet, Joey! Please stay asleep. If he realizes you're here I don't know if I'll be able to stop him from hurting you.

The Creepy Shepherd pushed her forward roughly, one step at a time. Casey could feel the desire to fight rising up inside her. She wanted to reel around and elbow him hard in the face, risking that he wouldn't be able to get a shot off that fast. But if she fought back, she'd be putting Joey in danger, and she couldn't do anything that would risk his life.

She had to stay calm and focused. She had to make it to Finnick.

Joey whimpered again, louder this time. Casey tried to cough to cover the sound.

Please, Joey! Just a few more moments!

But it was too late. Suddenly she felt the Creepy Shepherd's hands snap roughly to her shoulders and fling her around roughly to face him. Her foot slipped on the snowy ground and she fell back. Her hands shot out behind her, desperate to break her fall and protect the baby strapped to her chest.

A long, loud and plaintive wail rose from Joey's lungs as Casey felt her body hit the snow, shattering any lingering hope that she might be able to hide the child.

The Creepy Shepherd loomed over her. Angry, swear-laden words and syllables spilled incoherently from his lips. For a moment, he seemed too apoplectic at the realization she'd just fooled him to even form his vile threats into anything understandable. The gun shook violently in his hand as if he was too enraged to steady it. Then he dropped it somewhere in his billowing robes and lunged at her.

"Give him to me!" he shouted.

The Creepy Shepherd yanked the zipper down and grabbed at Joey, trying to pull him out of the carrier. Joey howled louder.

A yell ripped from Casey's lungs, so powerful it was like it'd come from somewhere deep inside her.

"You. Will. Not. Hurt. Him!"

She continued to scream for help, both in the hope that anyone might hear her and run to her rescue and also to God above. She fought back as hard as she could, desperately pushing the man's hands away before he could succeed in stealing Joey from her, and trying to rip off his mask.

But she was still down on the ground and he was standing above her. The Creepy Shepherd grabbed for the child again and she could hear the Velcro on the carrier begin to rip. Her attacker was bigger than she was, she was short of breath and he still had a gun. It was only a matter of time before he overpowered her and took Joey.

Help me, Lord! Please! I need You now!

Suddenly she heard the faint sound of a dog barking. It was followed by the sound of a man's voice shouting.

Nippy and Finnick! They'd heard their cries and were coming to their rescue.

For a moment, the Creepy Shepherd hesitated, as if debating whether to just wait until they arrived and kill them all. Then he turned and dashed off between the buildings in a blur of green fabric.

Casey gasped a breath—*Thank You, God*—and tried to push her shaky legs to stand. Before she'd even made it up, she heard Finnick call her name and then felt his strong, hands reaching for her. She stumbled to her feet, but he still held on to her, as if knowing somehow that his grip was the only thing keeping her quivering legs from collapsing.

"Are you okay?" Finnick asked softly.

Casey opened her mouth to speak, but no words came out. Instead, she shook her head, and then found herself tumbling into his arms and starting to cry. Finnick held her gently, creating space for the whimpering child still strapped to her chest. Nippy pressed up against her legs, filling her with his warmth.

Why was Finnick holding her and comforting her? Why wasn't he chasing after her attacker? Why wasn't he letting her fall? Making sure that she was all right wasn't important, was it?

Why is he putting me first?

Questions cascaded through her mind. But she hadn't cried in front of anyone in years, let alone sobbed on a shoulder, and now that she'd started, it was like she couldn't stop. Joey's cries faded and the baby began to coo softly, as if comforted by the warmth of both Casey's and Finnick's arms around him. She glanced down to see his huge blue eyes looking up at her. Then Joey smiled.

She laughed through her sob, then slowly pulled back out of Finnick's arms.

"Are you okay?" he asked again. "What happened?"

She nodded and this time she was able to find her words.

"The Creepy Shepherd just tried to kidnap Joey."

Concern filled his dark eyes. "Same man as last night?"

"Yeah," she said. "Same disguise and deep, distorted voice."

Finnick let her go, and then reached down to run a gentle hand over Joey's back.

"Did he hurt you? Either of you?"

"No," Casey said. "I tried to lure him to the Candy Cane in the hopes of reaching you. Then when Joey started to cry, he tried to yank him out of the carrier. Thankfully, you heard us."

"Nippy heard you," Finnick said and finally broke his gaze on Joey to look down at his K-9 partner. "We were standing outside the bed-and-breakfast. His ears just perked, he woofed and started running. I took off after him, not even knowing what he was on about. I just mumbled something like, 'I'm sorry. Nippy says we've got to go.' Your sister and the other people I was talking to must have thought I'd lost my mind. I'm sure nobody could hear you. I couldn't even hear you for a while." He chuckled in amazement. "Nippy is a very good dog."

He ran his hand over the elderly animal's head. Nippy's snout rose happily, as if he could hear the pride in Finnick's voice.

"A decade ago, Nippy was cross-trained in search and rescue," Finnick went on. "But he wasn't quite as good at it as he was at tracking cadavers, and since there were already a lot of dogs in search and rescue, we decided to drop it. I guess he didn't forget. They only retired him due to his age, and some arthritis in his hips. You never want to risk having a dog on the case who's not up to the task."

Finnick closed his eyes and took a deep breath, and she wondered if he was praying. Casey shivered, as if her exhausted body had finally registered the cold. Finnick exhaled and opened his eyes again.

"Okay, I'm going to call this in to my police contact on the island and ask people to look out for someone dressed as a creepy shepherd in case that brings in any leads," he said. "I do not think the general public is in danger right now, and I'm not going to release the fact he was after Joey." Finally, his eyes met hers again. "Also, I'm not going to let you and Joey out of my sight again until this is over. Unless you're safely at home, with the doors locked, or in the company of somebody else we trust to keep you safe, you're with me. Got it?"

Something tightened in her chest. "Got it."

She could tell that Finnick wanted to carry Joey on the walk home. But she wasn't ready to let him go, so instead, he just helped her tighten the straps of her carrier and then, as they walked, stuck so close to her side that the hems of their jackets might as well have been stitched together. First they collected Casey's shopping bags from where she'd dropped them in the snow. Then they doubled back to the Candy Cane Bed and Breakfast, taking Main Street this time, although the sights and sounds of Christmas moved past Casey in a blur. The choir was still singing and now Drew had joined his wife and daughters in belting out carols. The family smiled and waved to them as they passed. Sweet smiles beamed on the three girls' rosy faces. Farther down the road, Patrick and his son, Tristan, were diligently tackling a block of ice together with hammers and chisels for an ice-carving competition. Casey's brother-in-law, David, stood in front of the community church, handing out candy canes and flyers reminding people of the Christmas Eve nativity play and Christmas morning service. Eileen was still in front of the bed-and-breakfast—now berating Cameron for wandering off at the wrong moment and missing the unveiling of a new gingerbread house. But she abruptly stopped when she saw Casey and Finnick approach.

Eileen ran over. Her hands fluttered as she asked Finnick if he was ready to resume the tour, if he'd decided to take a room at Candy Cane, and what Nippy had gone off running after.

"A rat." Finnick said, answering her last question and ignoring the other two. "And if you'll excuse me, I'm going to walk Casey home."

Casey expected her sister to argue, having never once known Eileen to back down. But it must've been the fact she still suspected Finnick was a judge, the authority in Finnick's voice, or a combination of both, that had her flapping her hands some more and telling Casey to bring him to all the events. She told them she'd see them later.

As Casey, Finnick, Joey and Nippy were walking out of town, a roar of cheers rose behind them, and it took her a second to realize why. The power had come back on. Christmas lights flickered to life on houses ahead of them. A snowplow approached them at a crawl, clearing the road as it passed and moving toward town.

The wind picked up too and blew through the freshly plowed road toward them, leaving powder in its wake. Nippy raised his snout and sniffed the wind. They kept walking, and a few minutes later, she heard something buzz in Finnick's pocket. He yanked out his phone and smiled.

"Good news," he said. "The phones are back. Hopefully, that means we'll have the bridge to the mainland back too."

"Hopefully," she said and tried to smile. But the word felt hollow on her tongue.

When the bridge was open, Joey would leave, followed by Finnick and Nippy, and she'd be alone again. Which was fine. She was used to being alone, and they had their lives to live without her.

Still. The thought sat heavy in her heart.

Finnick placed a quick call to the police chief and filled him in on what had happened to Casey. After some back and forth, they decided not to alert the public that there was a man running around dressed like a shepherd.

"The costume isn't the threat," Finnick explained to Casey after he ended the call. "The man is. And if we get the whole island looking for that specific outfit, he'll just ditch it and switch to wearing something else. It's to our advantage that he keeps wearing that outfit as long as possible and doesn't switch disguises on us, assuming both attacks were done by the same man."

"It definitely seemed like the same guy," Casey said. "His voice was distorted, like he was using something to make it deeper than usual. But I definitely recognized it."

They kept walking through the snow, back toward her house, and they found themselves having to slow their steps every few moments to keep pace with Nippy. The dog was still sniffing the wind, and more deliberately, with his ears perked. It seemed there was some scent on the air he was able to detect now, which he hadn't smelled before. Finnick glanced at the K-9.

"Everything okay?" he asked the dog.

Nippy whimpered slightly and tossed his head in frustration.

"That means he's not sure what he smells," Finnick said. "Or the scent is too faint to detect. There might be a dead raccoon nearby."

Finnick turned back to his phone, and because Casey hadn't brought hers, she had nothing to check as he scrolled through messages.

"I missed a meeting with the team," he said. "I'm going to have to try to reschedule it, and of course we're going to have to call the social worker. But my team has started chasing some leads and are reporting in what they've found." He scrolled a few more moments, then stopped short and grabbed her hand. "I think we've found Ally."

"Really?" Casey asked. "That was fast."

She turned toward him, and for a moment, his finger lingered on hers as he held his phone up between them with his other hand. There on the screen was the smiling picture of a young, blonde woman, with a baby who looked an awful lot like Joey in her arms.

"Her name is Ally Wilson," Finnick said, and they kept walking. "She works as a waitress at a dive bar near a Sudbury casino. Seven weeks ago, she gave birth to a baby boy named Joey. No father on the birth certificate, but she told fellow waitresses it was a customer. She didn't make it home last night and didn't show up for her shift today."

Casey's mouth gaped.

"How could someone on your team find all that out so fast?" she demanded. "It took police months and months before they were even convinced that Tim and Stella's disappearance might've been foul play. You didn't even search my property with Nippy until he'd been gone almost a year. And now your team finds all this out overnight?"

Finnick's jaw tightened and for a moment it looked like he was trying to swallow something that tasted bad.

"My first hire for the Cold Case Task Force," he said, "is a private investigator named Gemma. She doesn't think like a cop and can get through the kind of doors that are reluctant to let police in. She figured that if Tim was still alive, he'd be frequenting some pretty lousy dumps full of the kind of people who don't call the cops, so she started calling around to a bunch of them, asking about Ally. She was at it all night and eventually she called the right dive at four in the morning and a worried friend of Ally's answered the phone."

Casey blinked.

"That's incredible," she said. "Where was she when Tim and Stella went missing?"

"High school," Finnick said. "My team are all in their twenties."

They'd reached Casey's farmhouse. She turned and started down the path Finnick had dug in the snow, back to her front door. Finnick began to follow.

Nippy barked loudly, and they turned around. The dog's nose was straining toward the road ahead of them. His paws were dancing on the snow. Then Nippy barked again, this time more urgently than before.

Finnick's face paled.

"What is it?" Casey asked.

"Nippy detects something," Finnick said. "Not a raccoon, a person. And whoever it is, they're dead."

A chill ran down Finnick's spine that had nothing to do with the cold, and for a moment he almost found himself hoping that the K-9's keen senses were wrong.

Nippy whimpered and pawed the ground impatiently.

"I hear you," Finnick told him. His gaze followed the direction the dog was indicating and saw what looked like a cabin in the distance. Its wood was gray and faded with age.

"What's that?" he asked Casey.

"That's the original one-room cabin that Tim's great-grandfather lived in while he was building the main house and barn," she said. "There have been Thompsons living on this property for over a hundred years. When Tim's father was a kid, apparently he and the other kids used to all camp out there in sleeping bags. But now the roof is mostly missing and the floorboards are rotten. Tim always said we'd restore it when we had the money, for our own kids."

Her voice hitched and Nippy barked again. Seemed the K-9 was certain there was something in that cabin now that he wanted Finnick to see. And what they found there wasn't going to be good. He glanced down at Joey. The little boy had fallen asleep again with his head nestled peacefully against Casey's heart, and Finnick suspected the child could hear it beating.

"All right, I'm torn about what we do," Finnick said. "I want you to go in the house and lock the door. But I also don't want to leave you alone in there until I've had a few moments to search it and make sure there's nothing to worry about—"

"I'm going with you to see what's in the cabin," Casey cut him off firmly. "It's on my property and I can tell you if anything's off since the last time I was there."

"Okay," Finnick said and nodded. "But promise me you'll stay back."

"I will."

They left the path that Finnick had shoveled earlier and cut through the deep snow, single file, following Nippy's lead. After a few minutes they were able to see indents in the snow, letting them know that somebody had made their way to the cabin, by taking a different path from the road hours earlier, dragging something behind them. But so much snow had fallen since then, it was impossible to make out any distinct footprints or know exactly what they'd dragged. The door to the cabin lay open, sideways on broken hinges. Finnick called Nippy to heel and then stepped inside.

A woman lay on the floor, huddled up in a ball. Blond hair fell over her face. Her hands cradled a bloody gunshot wound to her stomach, which he was sure had been fatal. His heart lurched.

"Hello?" he called softly, even as he knew he wasn't going to get an answer. "I'm here to help you."

Finnick took a deep breath, walked toward her. Behind him,

he could hear a soft gasp leave Casey's lips and her footsteps falter on the wooden floor, but he didn't let himself look back. He had a job to do—one of the hardest he ever had to do.

Nippy whimpered, his head bowed.

"Good job," Finnick said sadly and ran his hand down the K-9's side. "Good dog."

Then Finnick crouched down, gently reached out a gloved hand and touched the woman's arm. It was cold and stiff to the touch. He brushed the hair back from her face.

It was Ally.

The woman whose face he'd seen for a fleeting second the night before in his van headlights and then again in the picture Gemma had sent. She now lay dead on the cabin floor. A wallet bulged from her jacket pocket. He eased it loose to double-check he was right and found her employee identification card from work alongside her driver's license. He sighed. Just moments ago, he'd found a lead and now she was already gone.

Lord, please have mercy on all those who loved her, and help me bring the one who hurt her to justice.

He stood up slowly and turned to Casey again. Her arms were wrapped around Joey, holding him tightly to her. Finnick walked toward her and gestured for her to step outside.

"It's Joey's mother, Ally," he said. "She's been dead for hours."

"I don't understand," Casey said. "She was seen getting into a van driving out of Juniper Cove."

Casey's eyes were still locked on Ally's body. Finnick reached out his hand, took Casey's arm gently and led her through the snow toward the house.

"I don't know what happened," Finnick said. "I'm guessing the person whose vehicle she got into killed her and dumped her here."

Finnick wondered if the killer was trying to frame Tim. Although, he wasn't sure how that fit with Ally thinking that Tim was the father of her child. He could feel Casey shaking under his touch and reminded himself of his promise to keep an open mind about everything.

"There's a lot we don't know right now," he said. He steered her back onto the path he'd dug. "So we've just got to focus on putting one foot ahead of the other, and on taking the next step. Right now, you're going to get Joey inside, change him, feed him, play with him and make sure he's all good. And I'm going to call the police and get them here to process the scene and take care of Ally. I'm also going to call the social worker from CPS and let them know that Joey's mother has passed away."

Casey nodded again and he watched as her chin rose in determination.

Everything looked exactly as they'd left it inside the farmhouse, down to the streaks of water the dishes had left on the counter. Still, Finnick did a complete sweep of the house, double-checking each room, window and door lock, before leaving Casey inside to take care of Joey.

He stepped out, called the chief of police and quickly filled him in. Finnick placed a call to Child Protective Services next and then fired off a message to his team letting them know about Ally. After, he and Nippy walked back to the cabin and stood in the doorway, keeping watch over Ally's fallen form. Finnick prayed until he finally saw two police cars and a third unmarked vehicle pull up.

Moments later, Chief of Police Rupert Wiig, stepped out of the unmarked car and headed across the snow toward him. The old man's hair and full beard seemed even whiter than the snow. He had the build of a man who had been a force to be reckoned with in his youth and had since spent many years eating an abundance of good food and sitting in a very comfortable armchair. If Finnick were to guess, he'd have pegged his age at least a decade, or even two, past when he could've retired. He was soon followed by two young men and a young woman in their twenties. Two police officers and a crime scene investigator, judging by their uniforms. They reminded Finnick of his own new team. There was a slight jog in Rupert's step, like he was determined to reach Finnick before the younger trio did.

"Hello, my old friend!" Rupert called, with only the slightest sign of exertion in his breath. "I'm so sorry about all this. I'm sure this isn't the kind of scene you expected to stumble into when you decided to visit the island to do some last-minute Christmas shopping."

So, did that mean that Rupert had opted not to tell the rest of the team that there was another senior cop visiting the island?

Either way, Finnick was going to go with it.

"No indeedy!" Finnick called back.

"We've got an ambulance on the way too," Rupert said, "but I won't call for it until we're ready to move the body. The island only has two ambulances, and the island's tiny hospital is completely overloaded, with the people who've spun out on the ice driving or fallen while shoveling. They can't get any backup in because the bridge to the mainland is still closed and not expected to reopen until tomorrow now."

So that meant neither he nor Joey were going anywhere soon.

Nippy wagged his tail and woofed loudly at Rupert in greeting.

"Why, is that Nippy?" Rupert exclaimed. "You were just a tiny pup when I saw you last."

"Well, now he's getting old like the rest of us," Finnick said.

"Speak for yourself!" Rupert retorted. The two veteran police officers clasped each other's hands in a warm two-handed shake. Then Rupert stepped back as the three younger people arrived and stood smartly behind him, waiting for instruction.

"What can you tell us?" the cop who'd reached them first asked. He was about twenty-four with snow in his black curly hair. And since the officer hadn't offered up his name, Finnick didn't feel like he had to offer his.

"We were walking back from town when the dog started fussing that he smelled something," Finnick said. "I wondered if it was a raccoon. We wandered over here and found the body."

"Did you touch her or disrupt the scene in any way?" the female crime scene investigator asked.

Finnick noted both cops had now pulled pads from their pockets and had begun taking notes.

"Just her wrist to confirm she was dead and her wallet to get her name," Finnick said. "Ally Wilson. I was wearing gloves the entire time."

"And what brought you to Juniper Cove?" the first cop followed up.

"Well, it's definitely not because I was roped in to judge Juniper Cove for the Whimsical Christmas competition," Finnick said, and faked what he hoped was a realistic-looking nervous-civilian grin. "So, anyone who tells you that has got their wires crossed."

Nods spread between the law enforcement officers, then the trio moved inside to process the scene. Finnick's forced smile faded as they walked into the cabin.

He raised an eyebrow at Rupert, who gestured him away from the cabin.

"Nice save," Rupert said. "If I didn't know any better I'd have believed you were a rattled civilian who'd just stumbled upon his first corpse."

"I didn't know we were keeping law enforcement in the dark," Finnick said.

"Don't misunderstand. They're all amazingly talented." Rupert crossed his arms. "But the biggest threat law enforcement faces on an island like this is gossip. And I've learned not to take any unnecessary risks after how badly we bungled the Stella Neilson and Tim Thompson disappearance."

"So, you blame the cops for the fact the case went cold?" Finnick asked.

"Wouldn't be much of a cop if I didn't blame myself for the cases that don't get solved," Rupert said. "I wish you and your task force all the best. But from my point of view, the biggest obstacle you're going to be up against is what 'everybody already knows' about the case." He released his arms just enough to make air quotes. "Because whenever 'everybody knows' something to be true, it usually turns out that nobody actually knows a fool thing about what they actually witnessed or saw for themselves. They're just repeating what they've heard. If forty-nine people see a barn cat went walking through town this afternoon, but one particularly gifted storyteller thinks they see a leopard, by tomorrow morning, my phone will be ringing off the hook with a hundred people who'll pledge on their lives they saw spots, claws and fangs." Rupert snorted. "Do I sound jaded?"

"No, this is helpful," Finnick said, "and a timely reminder that for the cases my team tackles, public opinion will probably be already baked in. So, what does everybody know about Tim and Stella's disappearance?"

"According to my wife, what 'everybody knows' and no one will tell you, is that Stella was never good enough for our golden boy, Drew," Rupert said. "Her parents were mainlanders who moved here, but Drew's a third-generation islander. He's much better off with Jessica, and their three girls are precious. Also that Stella was trouble. She was heard fighting with Drew before she took off with another man. They're just surprised it was Tim she left with and not Patrick."

"Drew and Stella had a fight before she disappeared with Tim?" Finnick asked. "Why have I not heard that before?"

"Because you're a mainlander and a cop," Rupert said. "Nobody's going to admit to a cop that they're glad Stella left the island. That would look heartless or suspicious. Especially if it turns out that the reason she's gone is that something bad happened to her. But they'll gossip to an old cop's wife."

"And what does island gossip say about Tim?" Finnick pressed.

"Some say that Stella manipulated him," Rupert said. "Some say Tim took advantage of her. Most think she was cheating on Drew with him. And everybody loved Drew."

"And some think she was cheating with Patrick too?" Finnick asked.

"Some do," Rupert said. "The young man had a reputation."

"What kind of reputation?" Finnick pressed.

"Patrick and his former girlfriend had a baby outside of wedlock," Rupert said, "which people thought showed a lack of morals on his part." Finnick remembered what Casey's sister, Eileen, had said about Joey's mother. "Fair or not, a man doesn't shake a reputation like that in a place like this. Again, this is just island gossip. I'm not claiming for one moment there's any truth to any of it. Take it with a big grain of salt."

"Will do."

There was a flurry of exclamations coming from the cabin behind them. Seemed the investigation team had found something important.

"Hey, Chief," a cop called. "We've found something."

Rupert turned and walked into the cabin, with Finnick and Nippy a step behind him.

"She had this in her pocket," the crime scene investigator said. She held up a white, rectangular piece of plastic.

On the front was a picture of Tim Thompson with his name under the name of a hardware store.

It was Tim Thompson's employee key card.

Chapter Six

Casey gently lowered a drowsy Joey into his crib, eased her hands away from his tiny body and then stood back, hoping he wouldn't wake up. It had been almost an hour since Finnick had left her alone in the house and headed back to the cabin. Since then, she'd fed Joey, changed him, and then gave him time to wriggle and kick on his play mat while she made herself a simple lunch of soup and bread, then wrapped the Christmas presents she'd bought in town and set them on the mantel. Soon, the small baby's eyes had begun to close again. No doubt he was tired out from all the fresh air and excitement of the morning.

Casey stepped back, waiting to see if he'd settle into a deeper sleep. Instead, his blue eyes snapped open, his face scrunched into a grimace, and he began to wail.

"Shh shh shh shh shh..." Casey hushed the babe softly and laid one hand on his chest. "Everything's okay, Honey Bun. I'm here."

She stood there for a long moment, keeping her breath gentle and her voice soothing until finally Joey's cries quieted and his eyes began to close again. Casey exhaled slowly and pulled away. She dropped down onto the rug, curled up beside him and watched him sleep, not quite ready to leave him.

How much longer would this precious baby be in her life?

She'd called the social worker while Joey had been playing. Thankfully, Finnick had already called her to fill her in about Ally's death. At the time, she'd been too busy caring for the baby to really let herself dwell on what the social worker had been saying. But now, alone in the silence of the darkened bedroom, the social worker's words ran relentlessly through her mind.

To Casey's surprise, according to the social worker, their local broken swing bridge had made both national and international news, with dramatic pictures of the jackknifed transport van hanging half-off the bridge, with the beautiful frozen lake below and snowy island behind it. Although the ice near the shore on each side was thick enough for ice fishing and ice-skating, it wasn't strong enough for people to cross all the way from one side to the other. And a dramatic buildup of cars had formed on both sides of the bridge with people desperate to get on to be the first to cross when it reopened.

"It's expected to reopen in the middle of the night or early tomorrow," the social worker had said, "at the earliest. So, I'm just going to hold tight here until traffic is moving smoothly again. In the meantime, I'm looking for a more permanent home for Joey. Now that we know his full name and that his mother is dead, we can see if there's a relative on either his mother's or his father's side who can take him, or we can plan to relocate him into a foster home near his remaining family."

Presuming CPS was able to identify the father. There were a lot of kids in the system, and even many who were put up for adoption, who's fathers were never known or identified. Often for tragic and criminal reasons.

"I know you'd probably happily keep the little tyke forever," she added and at this, the social worker's voice had softened, "but there's a lengthy process we need to go through, including first ruling out if both families are potential caregivers for him, and confirming they don't intend to be actively involved in his life."

Casey had told the social worker that she understood, and of course, she had. Social services always tried to place children with family. It was a slow process on purpose. When one of the parents was still alive, even if they were in prison for the worst of crimes, if that parent didn't voluntarily give up parental rights, it could take years for the courts to strip them and make a child available for adoption.

"The mother was from Sudbury and there are a lot of good foster families there," the social worker had reassured her, "as well as an excellent team of pediatricians we work with. Joey will be well cared for."

"You will be well cared for," Casey whispered to the sleeping child.

She clung to the promise of those words, closed her eyes and began to pray.

Lord, this precious child has been abandoned by a mother who he's now lost forever. Please, keep Joey safe. Empower Finnick and I to keep him safe for as long as he's in our care. Prepare the family You have planned to raise him as their own. May it be filled with wonderful people who love You, love each other, and will love Joey and protect him as I would.

And please, when the time comes, give me the strength and peace I need to let them go.

Casey hadn't meant to fall asleep there on a rug, on the floor of her spare bedroom. She didn't even realize that she had until she slowly opened her eyes again to find that she felt more rested, renewed and invigorated than she had when she'd drifted off. The door she'd left open had been closed. A pillow had been placed under her head while she'd been sleeping and a soft quilt tucked around her body, enveloping her in its cocoon. Her watch told her almost forty minutes had passed since she brought Joey in to sleep.

Finnick must've checked on her and found her there.

More than that, he'd taken care of her.

An odd and unfamiliar warmth filled her body—not just from the quilt itself but from the knowledge that someone cared enough to gently tuck it around her.

She stood slowly and crept to the door as quietly as she could so as not to wake the still sleeping child. She eased the door open silently and closed it behind her.

Faint voices trickled down the hallway from the living room.

"I don't know why you guys are all dancing around the fact that we have a clear and obvious suspect here." The voice was male, frustrated and unfamiliar. "The victim, Ally Wilson herself, wrote Casey Thompson a letter claiming that Tom Thompson was her child's father. We have evidence, motive and a clear pattern."

"How do you figure that, Caleb?" This new voice was female and equally frustrated.

Casey began to creep down the hallway toward the living room.

"Ally Wilson and Stella Neilson were both young women," the male voice argued. "Both have a connection to Tim Thompson—"

"Allegedly," the female voice cut in.

"—and both are either dead or vanished," he went on. "They were about the same age. Stella was last seen with Tim. Ally tried to blackmail Casey Thompson with the fact that she had a baby with Tim. Casey is attacked by a man claiming to be Joey's father."

Casey reached the end of the hallway. Nippy was stretched out on his side in front of the fireplace with his eyes closed. Finnick was sitting on the couch with his back to her and his laptop open on the trunk that served as a coffee table. Four video chat boxes were open on the screen showing three men and one woman.

"Clearly, there's a pattern here." The voice came from a blond man in the upper-right corner of the screen, who she assumed was Caleb. "For all we know, Stella was also pregnant with Tim's child and planning on blackmailing him or Casey."

"Now you're just pulling theories out of a hat!" The woman's voice rose. She had short brown hair and was waving both hands at the screen for emphasis. "Jackson, Lucas, Finnick. Somebody back me up here!"

A man with brown hair and a beard chuckled. "I know better than to cut in when you're on a roll, sis."

Finnick hit the volume button to turn them down, no doubt thinking she was still asleep. But Casey had already been eavesdropping longer than she should have. She cleared her throat and Nippy's head rose in her direction, but Finnick's eyes were still focused on the screen.

"Gemma, she had Tim's key card on her!"

"That means nothing!"

"Who had Tim's key card?" Casey asked.

Finnick leaped up quickly and shut the laptop, cutting off the conversation.

"Casey, hi!" Finnick looked flustered, almost apologetic. "I was just talking to my team."

He turned back to the laptop as if noticing for the first time he'd accidentally shut it. His eyes closed for a long moment as if praying silently. Then when he opened them again, they were clear and unflinching. And somehow she knew that he wasn't going to beat around the bush in what he told her, which was both scary and comforting.

"Come sit." He patted the empty space on the couch beside him. "I'll show you what we found, get your thoughts on it and then I'll reconnect to the team call and introduce you to everyone."

He moved over on the couch as she sat down beside him.

Finnick opened a picture on his phone and then handed the device to Casey. She stared down at the laminated key card in the picture for a long moment. Every little detail brought back a flood of memories, from the slightly goofy smile that showed Tim had been caught off guard when his picture was taken, to the way the last few letters of his last name were scrunched on the signature line when he ran out of space, to the way the top loop of the card was torn from how he'd kept ripping the lanyard clip off and duct-taping it back together.

"I also took a picture of the back if you'd like to see it," Finnick said, "but it's nothing but a scratched-up magnetic strip."

"No need," Casey said. "It's definitely his. He used to leave it behind all the time and then call me to come bring it to him." She handed the phone back to him. "Where was it?"

"In Ally's pocket."

Casey gasped in a painful breath that seemed to sting all the way down to her core.

No wonder someone on Finnick's team would assume that Ally was telling the truth about Tim being Joey's father.

Finnick's phone began to ring, alerting him that his team was trying to reconnect him to the video call. Casey wondered if they'd been politely giving him time before calling back. Or if they'd been so locked in their debate about the potential significance of Tim's key card it had taken them this long to notice the call had dropped.

Finnick hesitated.

"Go ahead," she said. "No need to keep them waiting."

Finnick opened the laptop and accepted the call on his computer app. The four faces she'd seen earlier flickered back to life in separate boxes. Although now she could see that the young woman in the top left corner had the same brown hair and expressive blue eyes as the man in the box beneath her, who'd called her sis. On closer inspection, they seemed to be sitting on opposite ends of the same couch.

"Hi, guys, this is Casey," Finnick said. She waved in greeting and they waved back. "Going clockwise around the circle, top left is Gemma Locke, the best private detective I've ever met and the one who was up at four in the morning tracking down Ally's identity for us.

"The man in the square beside her is Officer Caleb Perry, who spent years as a beat cop before I met him as a rookie K-9 officer."

And whose brow was still knit in frustration over something.

"Below him is Lucas Harper." Finnick gestured to a man with a dark beard and even darker eyes, who Casey realized was the only one who hadn't spoken up during the banter earlier. "He used to work with the special victims unit and that yellow Lab rolling around behind him on the floor is his arson K-9, Michigan. Lucas actually contacted me and asked if he could join the team when he heard a rumor about the task force being founded.

"Which brings us back to Jackson Locke—" Finnick pointed to the last square "—brother of Gemma and one of the finest K-9 officers I've ever had the privilege of working with. He's not officially part of the team yet and is still getting up to speed."

They all exchanged a fresh round of hellos.

"I've asked Casey to look at a picture of the key card," Finnick went on, "and she identified it as Tim's. While we have her here, do any of you have any questions for her about it?"

"Is it possible Tim didn't have his key card with him on the day he disappeared?" Lucas asked. His voice was calm, and although he wasn't smiling, there was something reassuring about the steadiness of his tone. "Could he have left it at work?"

Casey shook her head. "He would've needed it to lock up that night."

Caleb leaned forward and rested his elbows on an unseen table.

"I'm sorry if you were offended if you overheard me say

something about your husband being our obvious suspect—"
he started.

"Late husband," Casey interjected.

"Former husband who has been legally declared dead,"
Caleb corrected himself, and his tone softened, "but, believe
it or not, I'm not unsympathetic to what you've been through.
I once dated a woman who I was warned about, and I refused
to believe it. Then she murdered someone, and I've always
blamed myself for not seeing it sooner." His gaze moved from
Casey to Finnick. "I just want to make sure we're not being
blind to the obvious truth of what's going on here, just because
it's uncomfortable for some people to believe."

"I hear you," Finnick said, "and you're right that we all
need to keep an open mind about this until it's solved. In the
meantime, I want you to track down every possible shred of
evidence you can find that Ally was involved in a relationship
with Tim, and anyone else she might've been involved with.
I'm still hopeful I'll see you all at Gemma's tomorrow night.
But first I need to get off this island and get a new windshield
installed in my van."

"If you were here, I'd be able to pop out the old windshield
and install a new one for you myself," Lucas said. "I worked
at my grandpa's garage all throughout high school."

"I thought he was fire chief," Caleb asked.

"That was my dad," Lucas said, with a grin.

A cheerful squeal sounded somewhere off-screen. Jackson
reached down, scooped something up into his arms and sat
back up with the baby on his lap. She was about six or seven
months old, with short curls and a giant smile.

"This is Skye, my fiancée Amy's daughter," Jackson said.
His smile grew as wide as the child's. "Amy and I have already
started the adoption paperwork so we can finalize it as soon
as we get married. Amy's working at the bookstore right now
but wanted me to tell you she's looking forward to seeing you
all at Christmas too."

Cheerful exchanges about upcoming Christmas plans went around the group, and the call ended shortly afterward in a fresh flurry of goodbyes. Finnick closed the laptop again. He leaned his elbows on his knees and clasped his hands together, as if silently praying. Once again, she had the sense Finnick was choosing the next words he was about to speak carefully.

"I'm not going to go into the depths of somebody else's business," Finnick said after a long moment, "because it's not my story to tell. But Amy's ex-husband, Skye's father, was a criminal and a pretty nasty piece of work. I know it's hard to look at a beautiful child, like Skye or Joey, and imagine there's a sad history behind how they came into the world. But I believe God can create beauty and hope out of every human tragedy. If I didn't, I wouldn't have the strength I need to do this job."

"Does that mean you really are keeping an open mind about the fact Tim might've killed Stella and Ally?" she asked.

"I'm honestly doing my best to keep an open mind to everything," Finnick said, carefully, "including the fact Tim might still be alive."

"Well, I can't," Casey said.

She stared down at her own knees. They were barely an inch away from Finnick's. Their hands were so close it would take nothing for either of them to reach out and take the other's. And yet, it felt like there was a huge, impassable gap between them.

Lord, am I wrong to cling so tightly to what I believe is true? Having an open mind feels impossible right now. But help me be open and willing to see whatever You want to show me.

"I want you to know that regardless of what you overheard, I am confident my entire team is also keeping an open mind," Finnick added. "I have, and might, ask them to try to prove or disprove certain theories. But I have faith in them and I know they won't let bias impact their work."

The team seemed both very competent and very close. She wasn't completely sure what they thought of her though.

"Not even the square-chinned blond cop who looked like the obvious secret villain on a police procedural?" Casey asked bitterly and then immediately regretted saying something so unkind.

"Caleb?" Finnick chuckled suddenly, as if she'd managed to surprise him so thoroughly the laugh just exploded out of his lungs. "I hope when this is all over, you'll give me permission to tell him that. Because, again when this is all over, he'll probably get a kick out of someone saying he looks like a secret villain. Caleb can be a bit stubborn about his views on things, but he has a pretty good sense of humor about himself and has to put up with the others teasing him about being the team's 'handsome hero cop' cliché."

He seemed so confident that not only would everything they were going through be solved one day but that they'd all still be able to smile. It was almost comforting.

"Well, he's not my idea of handsome," Casey said, "but I'm definitely not going to hold that against him."

Finnick turned to face her and ran a hand over his jaw. "And what is your idea of handsome?"

You.

The single word crossed her mind so quickly it startled her.

But it was true. Sure, she'd been really attracted to Tim's youthful energy and eager grin. But there was something so specifically handsome about Ethan Finnick that went deeper than the strong lines of his jaw, the echo of his earlier laughter, which glinted like gold in his dark eyes, and the way his fingers traced the curve of his smile. Finnick was attractive in a way that tugged at something inside her chest that she hadn't felt in years, like the chain of an old dusty lamp being pulled with just the right touch to bring the light back to life.

Finnick's smile faded slightly, but the warmth in his eyes seemed to deepen.

Heat rose to her cheeks as she desperately tried to think of a flippant answer to his question or even find a way out of the conversation.

Could he read her mind? Did he know she felt this way?

Then Finnick shot to his feet as if he'd suddenly realized he'd sat on a beehive.

"I noticed you wrapped some Christmas presents," he said, walking around the trunk and looking at the fireplace, leaving her to stare at his back. "Did you do that while I was talking to the police at the cabin?"

"Yeah, I did." Casey stood too and walked the opposite way around the trunk. "I bought a few little things for Joey from the Christmas market. I know he'll probably be long gone by Christmas Day, and that he's too young to even remember his first one, but I still want him to know that he's loved. Even if I don't have a tree to put them under."

"Do you want to go cut one down?" Finnick turned back.

The suggestion was so sudden she laughed.

"You mean right now?" Casey asked.

"Why not?" Finnick asked.

"Because Joey's asleep and the Douglas fir grove we get our Christmas trees from is clear on the other side of the property."

"But there are pine trees not fifteen feet from the back door," Finnick said. "We can go chop one of those down and still be close enough to Joey that we'll be able to listen out for him. I can even park Nippy right in between the back door and bedroom door and ask him to alert if Joey stirs."

Casey bit her lip. The thought was more tempting than he knew. Thompson family tradition was they cut down a tree from the exact same spot every year. Due to the amount of work involved in trekking out there, cutting one down and dragging it back, she hadn't actually had a tree since Tim's disappearance. But cutting down one of the hundreds of others on the property felt like betraying relatives of Tim's who'd died before she was born.

Yet at the same time, it would be nice to have a tree. Especially for Joey's first Christmas.

"Okay," she said. "As long as we give up if Joey starts calling."

"Absolutely," Finnick said and grinned. "I'm going to go get something from my van. I'll meet you out back."

Not ten minutes later, Casey was standing on her back porch, in her winter boots, coat, hat and mitts, having confirmed not only that Joey was asleep but that the eight-foot pine tree she'd had her eyes on for years was less than twelve paces from Joey's window.

She heard Finnick behind her in the hallway, directing Nippy to lie down across Joey's bedroom door and keep watch, then he appeared in the doorway behind her.

"Ready to do this?" he asked.

She looked down in disbelief at the object in his hand. It was an old-fashioned metal axe with a wooden handle, so small it was probably more accurate to call it a hatchet. He twirled it like a lumberjack.

"I have a chainsaw in the garage," she said.

"Yeah, but it's not the same," Finnick said. "Have you picked out a tree?"

"That one." She pointed. "Unless you think it's too big."

"I think it's perfect."

They walked out into the snow and approached the tree. He handed the axe to her, handle first, and she took it. It was heavier than she expected.

"Have you never chopped down a tree?" he asked.

She thought for a moment.

"No. Come to think of it though," she said, "I've done a lot of carpentry and built my own worktable."

"Okay," he said. "Well, square off to where you want to hit the tree, grip it with both hands, take a step backward and then swing from your hips. Trust me, this will help."

Help what? she wondered.

But she stepped back as instructed and swung. The blade sliced cleanly into the tree trunk and stuck there with a satisfying *thwack*. She yanked it back hard, almost slipped but managed to maintain her balance and then steadied herself to swing again.

"I wouldn't admit this to most people," Finnick said. "I don't even think anyone on my team knows this about me. But when I'm overwhelmed and frustrated with everything at work, I go to my local gym and punch the heavy bag."

Another swing. Another *thwack*.

"I know a lot of people jog, walk or swim to clear their minds," Finnick went on, "and honestly, sometimes I feel like the oldest and slowest guy hitting a punching bag in a room full of twenty-year-olds. But something about the physical exertion helps. Even better when I can see myself accomplishing something."

"I get it." She swung again, watching as the axe cut deeper and deeper through the trunk. It was almost like the combination of rhythmic motion and physical effort was helping release the frustrations inside her. "I feel so trapped by all this sometimes." She swung again. "Like my life has been put on hold by something out of my control, and I'm forever going to be seen as the woman whose husband both vanished and might be a criminal."

The axe wedged so deep into the tree, it'd almost made it all the way through.

"For whatever it's worth, I don't see you that way," Finnick said. "I think…" He took a deep breath. "I think you're amazing, Casey."

She tried to yank the axe back, but it stayed firmly stuck within the trunk.

"You are unbelievably strong," Finnick continued, "and you've been through so much, and yet you still have such a kind and generous heart. You're just a beautiful—"

Casey braced one foot against the trunk and yanked again.

The tree toppled over backward in front of her. The axe slipped from her hands. Casey lost her footing and tumbled backward, into Finnick's chest. His strong arms wrapped around her and held her close. His heartbeat thumped against her back. She turned her head to thank him, only to find his lips barely a breath away from hers.

"You're just a beautiful person, Casey," Finnick finished, and his voice grew husky in his throat. She could feel the heat of his breath on her face. "At least, that's who I see."

The sweet smell of Casey's hair filled Finnick's lungs as he held her tightly against his chest.

"Thank you," she whispered, and he felt her lips brush up against his cheek. "You're a pretty special person too."

She turned toward him. But he didn't step back and his arms didn't let her go. Instead, he just stood here, holding her to him. He could see her hazel eyes looking up into his and feel how the small of her back fit perfectly against his hands.

Casey leaned toward him. He leaned toward her too. And Finnick knew in that moment that, just as his van had careened off the road the night before, he was about to send his own heart and common sense into an equally unadvised tailspin.

He was about to kiss Casey Thompson. He was going to envelop her in his arms and let their lips finally meet in that kiss he'd first imagined when he'd grabbed her hand back in her kitchen over a decade before.

But before their lips could meet, Casey tucked her head into the crook of his neck and hugged him back tightly. "I'm so glad you're here and that I have you as a friend."

He swallowed hard, firmly shoving the reckless thought of kissing her away into the furthest recesses of his mind.

"Yeah," he said. "Me too."

And then all at once, Nippy began to bark, Joey began to cry and Casey pulled away and ran toward the house. Moments later when he stepped inside, he heard the sweet sound of Casey soothing Joey's tears and the baby calming in her arms.

He had almost kissed Casey.

Right. Now, that had almost been the most foolish thing he'd ever done.

Even though she'd never given him any indication that she wanted him to kiss her or that she would've kissed him back. Let alone the fact he'd never been the kind the guy who went doing things like that, even when he'd been in his twenties, no matter how attracted he was to someone.

And Casey was beyond attractive.

Lord, what's going on inside me? I've never been the kind of guy who let his heart get all tangled up in a woman. My team is looking to me for leadership. Help me get this case wrapped up and back to my team.

Whatever was going on inside him was beyond ridiculous. Casey's life was here on this island. His was with his team, running his task force, which was going to be based on the outskirts of Toronto. That was over six hours' drive away in good weather. Casey wasn't asking him to stick around on the island for her. And even if she ever did, there was no way he could stay.

I have prayed so long to open a cold case unit and I'm so confident that this new task force was Your answer to my prayer. Please, help me stay focused on the work You've called me to do.

Finnick turned and went back out to the tree, picked up the axe and gave it one final swing to sever the trunk from its stump. Then he dragged it through the snow to the back porch, where he set it up under the awning to dry off a bit before he'd bring it inside. Nippy was waiting for him, just inside the door, with his tail wagging.

Casey was in the bathroom. He watched, as he passed, as Casey ran a bath for Joey, singing to the baby as the water filled the small tub. Finnick went into the kitchen and ate the remnants of the soup and bread that Casey had left on the counter for him. He tidied the dishes, wiped the counter down, then sat at the kitchen table with his laptop and went back to working the case.

Gemma was still chasing down Ally's friends to see what more she could find out about Joey's father and the past few months of Ally's life. It seemed the young woman wasn't one for steady, long-term relationships, but she'd started dating what her friends called an "older man" recently, when the "cute younger guy" she'd been with had ended their relationship. Not much to go on, but Ally was still digging. Caleb and Lucas meanwhile had divided up the area around the bar where Ally worked and were checking local businesses for any sign of Tim Thompson. And while Jackson wasn't yet an official member of the task force, Finnick had gotten an email from the inspector who'd taken over from Finnick as head of the RCMP's Ontario K-9 Unit, letting him know Jackson had officially requested a transfer to join Finnick's team.

Disappointingly, Rupert and the local police hadn't been able to pull any usable fingerprints or DNA from Ally's body or where it was found. And while the team had been canvassing the area between Casey's cabin and where Ally was seen getting into a vehicle, they were still no closer to figuring out who had picked her up and how she'd gotten onto Casey's property.

Finnick looked over at his old, faithful partner. Nippy had repositioned himself next to Joey's play mat, with his snout on his paws, likely waiting for his new little friend to arrive after his bath. As if sensing Finnick's gaze on him, Nippy raised his head and fixed his dark eyes on Finnick, waiting for direction.

Rupert and his team might not be able to trace whoever had killed Ally and deposited her in the shed on Casey's property.

But Nippy could.

The smell of death could linger on fabric for a good twenty-four hours, including car interiors. If he took Nippy for a slow walk though Juniper Cove, maybe he could get the dog to track the vehicle the killer had used.

Finnick heard the sound of Casey's footsteps coming down the hallway. She was humming softly under her breath and from the patter of her steps on the wooden floorboards it sounded as if she was dancing. And he could feel something in his heart almost skip in time to the melody. He'd been back in her life less than a full day, and already, he'd become way too invested in whatever she was thinking or feeling.

Truth was his first impulse was always to tell her about whatever new lead or idea he had about the case. But she wasn't on his team and she wasn't law enforcement. And despite how incredibly comfortable he felt around her, she wasn't the person he rushed home to at night to tell about his day.

And he couldn't afford to let himself get distracted with thoughts about her now. That would have to wait. And he'd summon the self-control to make it wait. Because, for now, he needed to untangle her from this case. And from constantly being front and center in his thinking about it.

A moment later, Casey appeared, with a freshly bathed Joey in her arms. He was dressed in a bright red onesie with smiling snowmen on it.

"I bought this for him at the Christmas market," Casey said. As she met Finnick's eyes, her smile was almost shy. A delicate pink glow rose to her cheeks. Had she realized just how close he'd come to kissing her? Then she broke his gaze and crouched down on the floor in front of the play mat, beside Nippy. "Thanks again for your help chopping the tree down. I think it was the reboot my brain needed. Everything's just been so dark and heavy for a long time. It'll be nice to bring a bit of Christmas joy back inside the house. Besides, you were right, there was something kind of therapeutic about it."

She laughed softly, but her eyes and smile were still fixed on the small child lying on the play mat in front of her.

"You don't mind if I leave you to take Nippy for a walk,

do you?" Finnick asked. "I'm going to go later tonight when you and Joey are asleep. I mean, I've been walking him during the day, but I just wanted to double-check before I took him out at night."

"Oh, absolutely," Casey said. She was still looking at Joey. "I keep the doors locked now, and you definitely don't need to babysit me. After all, it's not like you'll be here keeping an eye on me forever." She laughed again, but something almost sad lingered at the edges of her voice. "Not that Joey has any concept on the difference between night and day yet. He was up screaming like a warrior at three in the morning. If I'd been able to get my van out of the garage last night, I'd have taken him for a drive up and down the road to settle him."

Okay then, that was settled.

The rest of the day passed in an easy and gentle kind of calm. Finnick helped Casey move the armchair away from the window and set the tree up in its place. Casey took care of Joey and searched the house and garage to dig out dusty boxes of Christmas decorations that clearly hadn't been opened in over a decade. And in between answering emails and phone calls, Finnick gave her a hand.

He spent most of the day on his laptop, coordinating with the team about how their investigations were going and confirming the final details about the building on the outskirts of Toronto, which the team would be moving into in early January when the task force formally launched. It was close enough to the highway to be able to pop downtown for meetings with other law enforcement entities or easily hit the road to Ontario's wild forests, dazzling lakes and hundreds of small towns. The two-story building had been a house once before being converted into offices. The old paint and carpets had left it feeling a bit shabby and rundown, but the bones were good.

There was a special kind of joy he felt, deep inside, seeing the final plans for the task force come together. He'd never been the type to have strong feelings one way or the other about paperwork. But as he scanned over the final sales agreement for the new headquarters, what the official parameters and scope of the task force would be and the official contracts for those joining his team, Finnick felt an incredible happiness filling his core.

This was what he'd prayed for and hoped for, ever since he'd been a rookie cop and working his first case. Now, in his late forties, just a few years away from when he could've taken early retirement, the door had finally opened for him to lead this team.

Lord, all my life You've been leading and guiding me to this moment. I can see Your hand in every step and I've never doubted the path You've laid out for me.

But then how did the gentle way his heart kept tugging him toward the woman and child now playing on the floor beside him fit into all that?

Dinner was a simple and cheerful meal of leftover bread from lunch and the meat pie that Casey had bought in town. The tree was half-decorated and Christmas garlands lay strewn across the couch and chairs, when Casey went to put Joey to bed just after eight.

"Feel free to keep decorating without me," she said with a tired smile before heading to the spare room. "It would be nice to have everything up for when the social worker comes tomorrow. I'll come join you when Joey falls asleep."

But Casey didn't come back into the living room. So, after half an hour, Finnick went to check on her and found her asleep on the floor beside the sleeping baby's crib again. Her hands were curled up underneath her head like a pillow. Her hair fell softly over the beautiful lines of her face.

His heart ached. That was twice now she'd fallen asleep on the floor watching Joey, her eyes almost level with his, as if she was afraid to let him out of her sight.

He crouched down beside her.

"Hey," Finnick whispered, feeling the simple word somehow catch in his throat.

"Ethan Finnick."

His name slipped her lips like a sigh, but her eyes didn't open. The knot in his throat grew.

"You fell asleep on the floor again," he said, softly. "You should really get a mattress for the floor if you're going to keep lying beside him. Do you want me to help you up?"

"Mmm-hmm, please."

Still her eyes didn't open. Was she even awake? Or was she talking in her sleep? He couldn't tell. He reached out to help her to her feet, but instead, she slipped her arms around his neck, suddenly dropping her weight into his arms. For a moment, his legs felt unstable beneath him. Then he lifted her up against his chest. Her head fell against his shoulder, her hair brushed his jaw and, once again, the scent of her filled his senses. And his lungs seemed to tighten in his chest. Finnick carried her down the hall into the living room, laid her down on the couch, draped a blanket over her and slid a pillow under her head. He double-checked that all the doors and windows were locked, called Nippy to his side and slipped back to his cot in the barn loft.

Finnick's plan was to set an alarm, sleep for a bit and then take Nippy out for a walk when Juniper Cove had fallen asleep. But despite the fact his faithful K-9 companion was quick to stretch out and start snoring, Finnick found himself lying awake on the cot for hours, staring at the wooden ceiling beams, unable to get the image of Casey curled up asleep on the floor, her face just feet away from Joey's.

There was something so strong and tough, and yet so fragile and tender, in the way Casey looked at the little boy. It was altogether beautiful.

He sighed. Were all the cold cases his task force investigated going to be this heart-wrenching? Or was there just something about this one case—this one woman—that got to him?

Lord, my heart aches for her, but I know that the wound inside her is something only You can heal. She got married and moved to this farm, planning on spending the rest of her life here raising a family. I have to have faith that You have a plan for her life, even in the face of disaster. Please, Lord, bring her peace. Bring her joy.

The world outside his window was empty and quiet by eleven, but still Finnick waited until almost one in the morning before carrying Nippy back down the stairs, putting his leash on and setting out into the night.

"Nippy." Finnick's voice was quiet and firm. "Search!"

The dog woofed softly in agreement and began to sniff the air. A bright white moon shone high above the winter's night, casting the snow around them in dazzling shades of silver and blue. They started walking down the street, the crunch of their footsteps seeming to echo in the silence of the night around them. Christmas lights flickered on and off from houses they passed, casting the shadows in red, green and gold. Slowly, they made their way down the street and through the residential neighborhoods of Juniper Cove. They passed the family homes Casey had pointed out earlier today, like the home of Drew and Jessica and their three daughters. A few doors down, they went by the much smaller bungalow where Patrick lived with his son, Tristan. As they reached Eileen and David's house, they saw a light was on in the apartment above the detached garage. Finnick and Nippy paused at the end of the driveway, and Finnick watched as Cameron's silhouette moved past the window. Apparently, Finnick wasn't the only one who couldn't sleep.

But no matter how keenly Nippy sniffed the ground and smelled the air, the K-9 didn't detect the scent of death hanging on any of the homes or vehicles. Which Finnick knew he should thank God for, despite the fact that they were no closer to finding how Ally had gotten to Casey's shed. Eventually, they'd reached the end of Juniper Cove's homes and apartments, and finally looped around and began to walk through the shops and businesses on their way back to Casey's place.

The town had left its lights and displays on overnight, so that every corner still sparkled with holiday cheer, with no actual people there to celebrate it. All the trappings of Christmas, with no sign of life. The emptiness was eerie and reminded Finnick of when he'd wandered into an old-fashioned town inside the Chicago science center as a kid and wondered why all the people had vanished. And he found himself praying again.

Lord, for years I celebrated Christmas by working a double shift to make sure as many colleagues as possible could be home with their families. And every year it felt like the greatest gift I could give and my way of celebrating You. Lord, I don't know if it's Your will for Juniper Cove to win this competition or not. I just pray they won't lose sight of loving each other and You.

"Woof!" Nippy barked sharply, his voice suddenly piercing the stillness. Finnick looked down at his partner. The hackles rose at the back of Nippy's neck. His paws danced urgently on the ground and the dog barked again.

Nippy had found something.

"Show me," Finnick said.

Nippy woofed loudly and started running down the middle of snow-covered Main Street, kicking up fresh powder under his paws. Finnick ran one step behind. Nippy led him down a narrow lane between two buildings. It was slushy with old tire tracks and barely wide enough for a vehicle to pass one direction without clipping its mirrors. A metal chain-link fence, about eight feet tall, with a padlocked gate lay ahead of them. Nippy ran straight for it. Motion sensor lights flickered on overhead. A plain white no-entry sign hung on the fence, telling Finnick it was the private property of Craft and Son Construction and that the main entrance was around the front of the building. The sole security camera was too covered from the recent downpour of snow and ice to catch anything, and it looked like it had been unplugged long ago.

Nippy leaped up at the fence, pawed the chain link and barked.

"I got it," Finnick said. "What you want me to see is on the other side of the fence. Good job."

He ran his hand over the back of Nippy's head and told him to sit. On the other side of the fence sat an empty lot that backed onto the construction building, with a few snow-covered piles of lumber off to the side and a single van about halfway across the parking lot. Judging by the lack of snow on top, it had been parked there recently. Then Finnick scanned the fence itself. The hinges weren't that strong. Probably wouldn't take much to break it open, but Finnick was only here for reconnaissance. That's how it went with undercover work. He'd find the evidence, call Rupert and let the island police move in with the warrant. He glanced behind him and scanned the alley. There was nowhere in the narrow alley that he could instruct Nippy to take cover, so he just instructed him to keep sitting.

Then Finnick leaped up, climbed the fence in four quick steps and dropped down the other side, feeling every muscle in his legs ache from the exertion. He stretched and felt his back crack.

"We never should've gotten old, bud," he told Nippy softly, who woofed softly in response.

Slowly, Finnick started across the snow and slush toward the van, careful not to disrupt any of the tire tracks and footprints, not that he expected they'd be able to pull anything usable from them. He reached the van and shone his flashlight inside. There were red stains on the floor in the back.

Finnick blew out a breath. He couldn't tell if it was blood, but it was definitely enough to call Rupert and get a crime scene investigator out here. He turned and strode back across the empty lot toward the fence and Nippy. The dog's tail wagged in greeting. Finnick reached for his phone, then stopped. He'd hop the fence, get reunited with his K-9 partner and then make the call on their walk back to Casey's. He'd already felt like he'd been away from her and Joey too long.

The fence loomed ahead of him. Finnick leaped up, climbed to the top and swung his leg over the other side. Suddenly a van honked behind him and headlights shot to life, filling the path ahead of him with light. Finnick looked back. They were no longer alone. Someone had activated the van's remote starter.

A figure in robes and a rubber mask stood like a long, tall shadow in the beam.

The Creepy Shepherd.

"Nippy!" Finnick shouted. "Run!"

The dog raced down the narrow alley, even as Finnick felt the instinct to jump down and charge at the man surge through his body. But before he even moved the figure raised a handgun and aimed it between Finnick's eyes.

He had a silencer on the weapon and the closest house was over a mile away. Finnick was alone. No backup. No team. The Creepy Shepherd could shoot Finnick dead right here and no one would ever know.

Lord, please save my life.

"Stop right there!" the Creepy Shepherd shouted. "I don't know who you think you are, poking your nose into my business, but you don't belong here. You leave this island and my family alone!"

Did he mean his literal business of Craft and Son? Did he mean Tristan?

Or was this somebody else? And if so, who was his family? Casey? Joey?

Both?

"I can't do that," Finnick called back. "People have been

hurt and all I'm trying to do is protect them. Why don't you put the gun down and we can talk—"

But before the word had barely left Finnick's mouth, the Creepy Shepherd set him in his sights and fired.

Chapter Seven

Finnick threw himself over the edge of the fence and plummeted down onto the ground below as the gunshot sounded through the air mere inches away from his head. Finnick's body smacked hard against the slushy ground. A second gunshot fired behind him, clanging off the metal chain-link fence and ricocheting into the darkness. The Creepy Shepherd swore and shouted threats. Between the cold, the darkness and the chain-link fence, it would be hard to get a direct shot. But his last two had been dangerously close. A third one might be fatal.

All Finnick could do was run.

He sprang to his feet and pelted down the alley, back toward Main Street, just in time to see Nippy disappear around the corner to safety. But just as he was breathing a prayer of thanksgiving that his partner was safe, he heard a van door slam and then an engine roar toward him. Finnick glanced back. The Creepy Shepherd had given up on the gun for now and had gone for the larger and blunter weapon—one he could be certain wouldn't miss.

He was going to run Finnick over.

Help me, Lord, I need You now!

Finnick pressed his legs to go faster. Behind him he heard

the squeal of metal and a crashing noise as the van drove into the fence. Then came the sound of the vehicle backing up and driving forward again for a second blow. This time, he heard the gate fly off its hinges. The end of the alley loomed ahead. Only a few steps more and he'd be back on Main Street, but he was still blocks away from shelter, and whichever direction he ran the van would still be able to catch him. He heard the van drive over the fallen gate. The Creepy Shepherd was coming toward him.

Finnick burst out onto Main Street.

"Nippy!" he shouted.

The dog was nowhere to be seen and he could only pray Nippy found shelter.

Then a second pair of headlights pierced the darkness, racing down the road to his left and blinding him. He heard the screech of tires breaking on the snow and the most beautiful voice he'd ever heard calling his name.

"Finnick!" Casey shouted. "I've got Nippy! Jump in!"

He ran toward the sound of her voice, his eyesight cleared, and he spotted the passenger door of her van hanging open before him. Then he saw Casey with her hands on the wheel and her strong, determined eyes fixed on him. He dove in, scrambled into the seat and slammed the door behind him.

"Go!" he shouted. "Drive!"

Nippy woofed from behind him. Casey hit the gas. Her van peeled down the empty street. Finnick struggled to clip his seat belt on and then glanced back. Nippy lay on the back seat with his head resting on the edge of the car seat where Joey lay fast asleep. Through the back window, he could see the van shoot out of the alley and race toward them.

"You followed me and put Joey and yourself in danger?" Finnick's voice rose.

"No, I didn't!" Casey's eyes cut to the rearview mirror. "But I'm not going to argue with you now. Who's chasing us?"

"The Creepy Shepherd." Fine, they could hash this out later. "He has a gun."

She fixed her eyes through the windshield ahead. The van sped down Main Street.

"And he's driving Patrick's delivery van?"

"Yeah." Finnick glanced back. The vehicle was gaining on them.

"Good," Casey said. He turned to look at her, and to his surprise, he caught the glimmer of a smile move through her voice. "Then, based on what Patrick told you this morning, the Creepy Shepherd's driving without decent snow tires."

Her hands tightened their grip on the steering wheel. They'd reached the edge of town now. Ahead of them lay the park with its dazzling tableau of sparkling lights, stretching from tree to tree in an endless maze of holiday splendor.

Casey steered straight for it. "Hang on," she said.

The ground grew steeper. The van grew closer until the glare of its headlights filled the van. Casey urged the van faster, pushing the accelerator down as far as she could. The other driver matched her speed. The lights of the park grew closer until they were only a few feet from the entrance. The van smacked against the back bumper, jolting them forward.

Casey yanked the steering wheel hard. The van spun on the icy street, and for a moment Finnick was afraid they were going to lose traction and fly off the road just as his van had done the night before. But instead, just as the tires began to slip, Casey righted the vehicle again and raced down the road parallel to the park. Finnick looked back, just in time to see the van careen straight off the road behind them, through the trees, and smash into a light display of dancing penguins.

Casey glanced at the rearview mirror. A long sigh of relief left her lungs and tears leaped to the corner of her eyes. Finnick's heart lurched, and he wanted to reach out to wipe them away before they reached her cheeks, but she swept her hand across her face before he could.

"It'll be easier for him to try to drive through the park than turn around," she said. "I'm not going to risk my life and Joey's chasing him. But I can drop you off at the far side."

"No," Finnick said, surprised to find that lump he'd felt hours before was back in his throat. "Please take me back to your house. I'm going to call Rupert and get the police to handle it. I'm not going to leave you alone again tonight. Nippy and I will sleep in the living room, and I'll ask Rupert to station someone on the road outside the house."

"Okay." She swallowed hard. "Thank you."

Her voice had dropped to a whisper, as if she had used up all her energy outrunning the van and now she was depleted. She glanced at the mirror again. The road lay dark and empty now. The van was gone.

He called Rupert, waking the police chief up, and filled him in on everything that had happened that evening. Rupert confirmed he'd have an officer on the street outside Casey's house the rest of the night. By the time he'd hung up the phone, Casey was pulling back into the farmhouse driveway. She cut the engine, and he realized she was shaking. He reached out his hand and rested it in between their seats, just inches away from hers, but she didn't take it.

"I meant what I said about not following you and not intentionally bringing Joey into danger," Casey said. "He woke up crying and wouldn't settle, so I took him for a drive in the van, down to Main Street and back. But when I reached Main Street, I saw Nippy tearing out of an alley way and heard what sounded like the pop of a gun that had the silencer on. So I got Nippy in the van and then found you." She shrugged and a small smile crossed her lips. "It's that simple."

Simple.

The word ran circles around in his brain later that night, as he lay on the couch in the living room, with Casey and Joey tucked in their beds down the hall. Nippy stretched out in front of the fire snoring, and the silhouette of an unmarked police car remained parked outside on the street.

He'd been in trouble, called out to God for help and Casey just happened to be nearby when he needed her. It sounded so simple. After all, she'd told him that if Joey didn't settle in tonight, she was tempted to take him for a drive, and Juniper Cove was pretty small.

But somehow, deep in his heart, it didn't feel simple at all. It felt downright complicated and confounding. This was hardly the first time somebody had been there in the right place at the right time. After all, he hadn't thought twice about the fact that he'd happened to crash onto Casey's farm the same night she was attacked by the Creepy Shepherd. He just saw that as God guiding his steps, just as God had done so many times before. Finnick had saved the lives of dozens and dozens of people in his life, and in return dozens of officers had saved his. It came with the territory.

And yet...

Lord, thank You for sending Casey to me when I needed her. Even though nothing I feel about her is simple. Despite the fact I've always believed in Your divine guidance, I don't understand why she tumbled into my life, and why I crashed into hers, right here and now. I don't have time to be in a relationship with anyone, and even if I did, her heart is tied to this island, hours away from where I'm founding my team.

But again, I thank You for bringing her into my life, in Your timing.

Whatever Your plan is for me.

Sleeping on the couch turned out to be more comfortable than he expected, despite the wheezy snores of the dog after their action-packed night. The sun was just beginning to rise when Finnick awoke. He checked his messages first and discovered that the bridge was still closed for a few more hours and that, although police had found Patrick's van had crashed through the ice and sunk into the lake, the man who'd been driving it dressed as the Creepy Shepherd was nowhere to be found.

Finnick prayed that, today, they'd finally get some answers. He got up, fed Nippy, checked his messages and started the coffee. Then he set about hanging up some of the garlands and Christmas decorations from Casey's boxes, focusing on the doorway arches, windows and high places she wouldn't be able to reach on her own without standing on something. After a while, he heard Joey's gentle cry coming from down the hall and the familiar sound of Casey scooping him up into her arms and singing to him as she got him dressed and ready to face the world. And somehow, Finnick knew that when tomorrow dawned, he'd miss them.

Moments later, Casey came down the hallway with Joey in her arms.

"Good morning!" she called, cheerfully. The rising sun seemed to dance in her eyes. Joey squealed and waved his arms in hello.

"Good morning." Finnick felt a slow grin cross his face.

"I'm guessing by the fact that you're not dancing around the tree that police didn't manage to catch the Creepy Shepherd last night?" she asked.

Finnick sighed sadly.

"No," he confirmed with a frown. "The van crashed into the lake and he managed to get out before it sunk. I'm guessing to destroy any of the evidence."

"And they probably won't have the equipment to get it out of the lake until the bridge reopens," Casey said as her smile dimmed. But a moment later, it returned as her gaze darted around the room and settled on a thick green garland with white dangling berries that he'd hung over the doorway between the living room and the kitchen. The corner of her mouth quirked. "I see you've been decorating."

He ran his hand over the back of his neck. Had he done something wrong?

"Yeah, I hope it's okay."

Her gaze finally landed back on his face. "It's great," she said. "Thank you."

"Well, I knew you wanted it done by the time the social worker gets here," he said. "Although, last I heard, the bridge still isn't open yet. They're expecting it to reopen later today."

And he'd finally be getting off the island and back to meeting up with his team. He was down to less than two weeks now until when the Cold Case Task Force would officially be launched and introduced to the country. There was still a huge amount of legwork to be done before that happened and there was only so much of it he could do while he was spinning his wheels in Juniper Cove. It would be up to the local police to process the van, although Finnick doubted they'd be able to pull anything from it after it had crashed into the lake.

The red stains he'd seen in the back would be long gone, with no way to know if they were even blood.

Casey slipped Joey into Finnick's arms and moved to the stove to start breakfast. Finnick tucked the small child into the crook of his elbow and Joey brushed his tiny fingers across Finnick's jaw. Finnick swallowed hard.

"I'm going to miss you too, buddy," he whispered.

He sat down at the table, with one hand cradling the child and the other scrolling through messages from his team, as Casey whipped up a skillet of scrambled eggs and popped slices of fresh bread into the toaster.

"Can I give you a hand with any of that?" Finnick asked. "I may not be much of a cook, but I can whip a mean egg."

"No, I'm good," Casey said, and he could hear gratitude in her voice. "But if you could feed Joey, that would be great."

"No problem."

She wheeled around, and in what seemed like one seamless move, she grabbed the bottle from the warmer, doubled-checked the temperature on her wrist, dropped it into Finnick's waiting hand and then turned back to the eggs on the stove.

"Thankfully, I got the last of my Christmas orders off last week," Casey said, "and won't be starting on my spring soaps and candles until January. So, I've got plenty of free time right now to play with this little guy."

Joey took the bottle eagerly, and after trying a few different methods and angles, Finnick finally figured out how to feed Joey with one hand and check email with the other. A deep and sad sigh seemed to move through his core as he read the officers' reports. Lucas, Caleb and Gemma had turned up plenty of evidence that Ally had spent time earlier in the year with a man whose flashed identification bore a name and face that definitely matched Casey's former husband, Tim Thompson. It was always on Friday nights and never more than twice in a month. And while there were no eyewitnesses who'd gotten a good, close look at the man she'd been with, those who had spotted them together couldn't rule out that it was possibly Tim. In fact, the only thing—and it was a very small thing— in Tim's possible defense was that they hadn't managed to pull up any video surveillance providing concrete evidence that the man she was with was in fact him.

Finnick looked down at Joey. The child's big eyes were fixed seriously on his face.

Lord, I know that this is not the answer Casey wanted to hear. But if Tim truly is alive and fathered the tiny boy in my arms, please give me the evidence I need to bring him to justice.

Regardless of the cost.

Joey drained the bottle. The sound of children's voices singing filled the air outside the window. He looked out. Drew, Jessica and their three little girls were caroling outside the front door, in matching Christmas sweaters and hats. Casey leaned over the table and followed his gaze.

An uncomfortable and almost pained look flickered in her eyes, and he was again reminded of how hard it must be for her to see Drew go on with his life, get married and have a perfect family while she'd felt her own life had stopped the day Drew's former fiancée and her former husband had vanished together. But then she blinked the look away, forced a smile and reached for Joey.

"Come on," she said to the infant brightly. "Let's go listen to the carolers."

She danced into the other room with Joey in her arms and opened the door. Nippy trotted after them and wagged his tail at the visitors.

"Merry Christmas Eve!" Casey said, with a cheerful tone that he suspected was directed at the three little girls. "What wonderful sweaters you're wearing!"

"Ooh, can I hold the baby?" The oldest girl's voice floated in through the open door. Her name was Sophie, if he remembered correctly. "I'll be really gentle and I won't drop him."

"She is really responsible," Jessica said. "She's going to be Mary in the nativity play today."

"No, I'm sorry," Casey said. "He's still getting used to strangers. But your singing was really lovely."

Finnick's phone began to ring. It was Gemma. He stepped away from the table, held the phone to his ear and pressed a finger to the other ear to block out the noise.

"Hey, boss," Gemma said. "So, you got the package of information we sent on the investigation?"

"Yeah." Finnick sighed. "I know that Casey's convinced that Tim is dead, but I've issued arrest warrants based on way less evidence than this, and we've probably got more than enough to get a court to approve it." He glanced from the window to the clock. "I'm not going to be able to get this before a judge until after Christmas. So we've got two days, whether we want them or not. Before I leave, I'm going to talk to Casey and see if we can get her to cooperate."

"Will she?"

"I hope so," Finnick said. "But I honestly don't know."

Lord, please prepare Casey's heart for this conversation and my own heart, for whatever her reaction happens to be.

He looked back out the window. The family had started singing again.

"I might be out of cell phone range for a bit on and off today," Gemma said, "Jackson and I are trying to do some last-minute things for Christmas, and you know what the cell signal is like on the rural roads."

"Yeah," Finnick said. He watched out the window as Drew pointed to the white-berried garland he'd hung up and made some kind of joke about it. He hadn't thought his decorating was that bad. "I know it's Christmas Eve and I promised I'd be there for the big team dinner, but even when the road re-opens, I don't know how long it's going to take to get my van fixed and head out of here."

"Well, we're all looking forward to seeing you and Nippy."

"I'm looking forward to seeing you all too."

He ended the call as Casey thanked the carolers and closed the door. He stood in the doorway between the kitchen and living room, and watched as Casey laid Joey down on the play mat. Nippy took up his usual post on the carpet beside him with his nose on his paws.

"They're just going door to door to remind people about the nativity play," she said. Her cheeks were rosy from the cold air, and although a smile crossed her lips when she looked down at Joey, in the depths of her eyes he could see the echo of an old pain battling the current joy she felt as she looked up at him.

And Finnick wished with all his heart that he knew how to take that pain away.

"Did they happen to mention anything about the break-in at Craft and Son Construction?" Finnick asked. "I imagine a construction van smashing through the park's Christmas display and crashing through the ice into the lake must be pretty big island gossip."

"Molly, the youngest one, asked me if I've heard that a thief stole Uncle Patrick's van and crashed through the lights—"

"Uncle Patrick?"

"They're not actually related," Casey explained, "just Drew and Patrick have always been close, and Patrick never moved on after Tristan's mother left. Anyway, Jessica cut her off before she could get to the part about it sinking in the lake and steered the conversation back to how important it is that everybody comes to the nativity play because we all have to do our part if Juniper Cove is going to win the Most Whimsical Christmas Village competition."

"I'd almost forgotten about that," Finnick said. "Okay, so what am I missing about this garland?" He reached up and tugged on it. "First, you made a weird face at it, then I saw Drew pointing at it."

"Oh." Casey laughed. She straightened up and turned to face him. "That's mistletoe."

"Mistletoe?" The word rang a very old bell in the back of his mind, but for a moment he couldn't place why. "It's poisonous, right?"

"Well, maybe in nature, but those berries are plastic." She shook her head and her laughter grew. "There's an old tradition about kissing someone who's standing under the mistletoe."

Heat rose to his face.

"Oh!" Of course, he should've known that. How had that slipped his mind? "I'm sorry. I didn't mean anything by it..."

"It's okay," Casey said, softly. Her hand brushed his arm. "I know you didn't and that's why I found it funny. You're really sweet and I'm so glad you're here."

Then she stood up on her tiptoes, leaned toward him and brushed her lips against his cheek. Finnick startled and instinctively turned toward her. His lips accidentally brushed hers. Her fingers tightened on his arm. His hand reached around her back and pulled her closer.

And suddenly, Finnick found himself kissing her.

* * *

Casey was kissing Finnick.

For over a decade, she'd never imagined a man like Finnick would want to kiss someone like her. Not after her life had been turned inside out and torn apart. But now, years after first holding his hand, and hours after tumbling into his arms while chopping down a tree, Casey was being kissed by the most incredible, intelligent, kind and handsome man she knew.

She was kissing him back. His second hand wrapped around her waist and pulled her closer. Her fingers slid up into his hair.

The phone in the kitchen began to ring, with a loud jangling clatter, shattering the moment. She leaped back; so did Finnick, and for a moment, they just stared at each other, the surprise in his face mirroring the shock in her own heart. Her heart beat so hard in her chest she could barely breathe. What had she been thinking? Why had she kissed him?

Why had he kissed her?

The phone rang again. Casey stumbled another step back and mumbled a string of syllables that she intended to sound like an apology—not that she was exactly sure what she was apologizing for. Then she rushed into the kitchen to answer the phone. As she reached for it, she realized her hand was shaking.

"Hello," Casey said.

"Casey, I'm glad I caught you." It was the social worker. She sounded almost breathless with relief. "I have some really big and unexpected news about baby Joey."

"Oh, really?"

From the living room, Casey could hear Joey beginning to cry.

"It's okay!" Finnick called. "I've got him."

"As you know, a lot of these stories are pretty tragic," the social worker went on, "especially, in this case, after what happened to Joey's mother. It's not often I'm able to call someone with good news like this, but although I have to keep the specific details confidential for now, as the family wants us to wait until they make it public, we've found Joey's family and he's going home."

"Oh." Casey sank down into a chair, feeling like the balloon of joy that had been building in her core when Finnick kissed her, had suddenly popped.

"Are you okay?" Finnick asked, gently from the doorway. Worry filled his eyes.

She nodded. Of course it was wonderful news that Joey was going to be adopted. Usually the process took months, or even years. While Joey finding a permanent home had crushed the tiny flicker of hope—which Casey hadn't even admitted to herself she felt—that one day the little child would be hers, she also knew the adoption waiting list in Canada was so long, it was almost impossible that he'd ever be her son. The child's big eyes fixed on hers.

"I don't understand how you found an adoptive home for him so quickly," Casey said.

"No," the social worker said, "we found his father."

Casey suddenly felt lightheaded.

"You found Joey's father?" Casey echoed. "How?"

She could hear Finnick exhale a hard breath, but she didn't let herself turn and look at him.

"He contacted us," the social worker explained. "Apparently, he already has a family. It had been a brief relationship and Ally hadn't told him about the child. But when he heard about her death, he contacted social services right away. Of course, when the bridge reopens, he'll be coming here to sort some formalities, and he'll have to provide evidence to establish paternity. But we're hoping Joey will be home for Christmas."

Hot tears of relief, joy and sadness mingled together in her eyes, but she refused to let them fall. This was good news and she would thank God for it. The social worker's happy words were still spinning past her ear, when something she'd said finally caught up with Casey's brain.

"Why would Joey's father have to wait until the bridge re-opens to establish paternity?" Casey asked. She watched as Finnick's eyes widened.

"Oh," the social worker said, "Joey's father lives on the is-land. He said he's hoping to make it to the Christmas event in Juniper Cove today, and if so, he's going to try to meet you and Joey. But again, that's up to him. I can't tell you anything about him or his family until everything's confirmed."

Casey nodded. "I understand."

"And of course, I'll head your way an hour or two after the bridge reopens and the traffic clears," the social worker added. "Apparently, people have camped out overnight to be first to cross over."

No doubt in a hurry to get home and see loved ones.

"Well, thank you so much for letting me know," Casey said. "I look forward to seeing you in a bit."

The call ended soon afterward, Casey hung up the phone and sat there for a long moment, staring at it, like it was a gre-nade about to go off.

"What was that about?" Finnick's voice sounded behind her.

"Joey's father has contacted social services to claim him," Casey said. She stood and turned toward him. Finnick's face was awash with compassion, maybe even worry.

"Are you okay?" Finnick asked.

He slid Joey into the crook of one arm and extended the other hand to her, in the silent offer of a hug. But if she let herself fall into his arms now, she was probably going to start crying and not even know why. So instead, she crossed her arms and he pulled his hand back.

"I'm fine," Casey said. She tried to force a smile and failed. "I'm just a bit surprised and overwhelmed. Apparently, Joey and his family live here on the island."

"Here?" Finnick repeated.

"Apparently," Casey repeated. "But it's good news, all around. Once social services get the details sorted out, Joey will be going home. And since he'll be here on this island, I might be able to get to know his family and watch him grow up. I don't know his father's name, but I'm sure you'll be able to get it once he meets with social services, and then your team will finally have a very solid lead they can chase to find out how Ally was killed. Maybe he even knows who could've killed the mother of his child and who's been dressing up as the Creepy Shepherd."

She gasped a deep breath, not sure why the center of her chest was aching. Finnick didn't answer and the silence that had always seemed so comfortable before now felt painful.

"I mean, I suppose it's possible Joey's father is the Creepy Shepherd," she added after a long moment. "But that doesn't make any sense. Why hide your face, run around trying to snatch Joey away from us, and then walk into social services and admit you're Joey's dad? It doesn't make sense."

"I don't know," Finnick admitted. Something seemed to catch in his throat and he swallowed hard to clear it. "But once I know his name, I'll look into him and do everything I can to make sure he's a good dad for Joey. I promise, I'll do my best to keep him safe."

Casey swallowed too. "I know."

The next few hours passed much the same way as their lazy hours together had the day before. She played with Joey, fed him, put him down for a nap and got him back up again.

Finnick spent hours typing away on his computer, as well as talking to Rupert and trying to call members of his team, who were apparently traveling and out of service range. Unfortunately, there'd been no DNA found in the van once it was pulled from the river and Rupert's interview with Patrick had yielded no useful information.

Casey and Finnick shared a simple and cozy lunch together, which had been cobbled together with things she'd bought at the Christmas market. She hung the last few Christmas decorations, careful not to let her eyes wander to the mistletoe still hanging above the kitchen doorway, or her mind to the memory of the confusing and unwise kiss that still lingered on her lips. But even as they went through all the motions, the hours stretched out like a hollow echo of the time they'd spent together in the same farmhouse the day before, as the constant ticking of the clock reminded her that each bottle she fed Joey, each scratch she gave Nippy behind the ears and each unexpected glance she shared with Finnick brought her closer to her last.

Shortly after lunch, Casey was down on the carpet playing with Joey when the faint sound of church bells filled the frosty air outside her windows. She looked up to where Finnick sat at the kitchen table.

"It's time for the nativity pageant," she said.

He closed his laptop. "You want to go?"

No, she didn't. But did that matter?

"Eileen will be pretty disappointed if I don't." Casey got up slowly and stretched. "Plus, it might be your best opportunity to find out who Joey's biological father is, if he happens to be there."

At least if another man stepped forward and proved that he was Joey's father, it would also prove that it wasn't Tim.

Not that it would prove Tim wasn't alive, and that he hadn't killed Stella or Ally.

She looked out the window, and to her surprise saw just as many cars driving away from Juniper Cove as there were driving toward it. Eileen wasn't going to like that. She was counting on a full house for the nativity play and had messaged Casey three times that morning to double-check she was coming.

Casey glanced back. "Has the bridge reopened? People are driving out of town."

Finnick checked his phone.

"It's almost open," he said. "I guess they're going to join the line. The van is cleared, the repairs are done and they're just doing a safety inspection now. They expect traffic will be able to leave the island in less than two hours, and then once that backlog is cleared, the bridge will open the other direction for people to cross onto the island." A small smile crossed his lips. "It's almost over."

She smiled back weakly. They drove to Juniper Cove Community Church in Casey's van, each in the same position they'd been in the night before during their terrifying vehicle chase, with Casey at the wheel, Finnick in the passenger seat and Nippy curled up in the back with a watchful eye over Joey in the car seat.

She'd been expecting to see yellow police tape up in front of the park where the van had crashed. But to her surprise, any tape that had been strung up had been taken down and the dancing penguins were back up, with only the mess of tire tracks and broken branches as evidence of the van that crashed through the area last night.

"I'd no idea police could clean up a scene this fast," Casey said.

"Well, I got the impression from Rupert that your sister put a lot of pressure on them to get the lights back up," Finnick said. His eyes scanned the whimsical holiday world outside his window. "The competition closes tomorrow morning and she thought it was important Juniper Cove put its best foot forward."

Then he sighed.

"What's up?" Casey asked, as she eased the car into a parallel parking spot on the busy street.

"Last night," he said, "as I was walking through town, before Nippy alerted to the van and everything kicked off, I was thinking about the fact that for years I never really attended Christmas events like this. Because each year I made a point of volunteering for the skeleton crew who worked over the holidays so that other officers could be home with their families. Most years I didn't even have a tree, besides the little six-inch one I put on my table at home and the big one I authorized for the whole K-9 department. Usually the only gift I bought and wrapped was for Nippy. Besides that, I just made a personal donation to charity on behalf of my coworkers and gave out some gift cards to the cleaning and cafeteria staff who were stuck working the holiday with me."

She cut the engine but didn't reach for the door handle. Instead, she turned and looked at Finnick.

"But I never once felt like I was missing out on Christmas," he went on, "even those years that Nippy and I spent at crime scenes, and I was too run off my feet to even eat one of the gingerbread doughnuts in the cafeteria. The knowledge that an all-powerful, loving God had decided to come down to Earth felt closer to me when we were tracking a scent through frozen swamps in sludge up to my knees than it does here, surrounded by all this Christmassy stuff."

Finnick waved his arms in both directions, gesturing at the lights and decorations around them. Then he sighed and ran one hand through his graying hair.

"All of this is really incredible and lovely," he went on, and Casey realized it was probably the most she'd ever heard him talk. "I don't mean to imply I think there's anything wrong with it. It gives people joy and brings the community together. And it's clear people put a lot of hard work into it. I just hope that at the same time, people remember there is more to Christmas than all this, even if they find it in a very different way than I do."

Again, his hand floated in the empty space between them, and again, she was tempted to take it but didn't.

"I hope so too," she said.

Finnick instructed Nippy to stay in the car and left the back window cracked wide enough that the old fellow could get out if he needed to. Then Finnick and Casey headed inside, with Joey in Casey's arms. The church was packed with extra folding chairs, squeezed in at the edges of the pews. Despite the traffic she'd seen heading toward the bridge earlier, it looked like people had come from across the island to watch the nativity play.

There were maybe three hundred people in the room, she guessed, more than five times the usual number they had at a Sunday service. Presumably at least one of the people there was an undercover judge who'd come to judge the competition as well, assuming they'd made it to the island before the bridge was closed. It was funny to think the whole competition could be going on with nobody there to actually judge it.

Casey scanned the crowd. Over a third of the attendees were men—young men, family men and newlyweds. Was Joey's father in the room somewhere? If so, would he come up and introduce himself?

They found two seats near the back, on the aisle, squeezed in and watched as Eileen ran around the stage, organizing kids in long robes and animal costumes, while Pastor David coordinated the choir. Cameron moved silently, like a shadow, at the edge of the room, taking candid pictures. A large stack of song sheets were passed from person to person, down the rows. Pastor David asked everyone to kindly put their cell phones away for now, and that he'd let them know when they were free to get their cameras back out and take pictures during the final carol. Then finally, when Eileen had ushered a final child back behind a curtain, and Cameron had disappeared along with them, Pastor David gestured everyone to their feet, the choir started and everyone began to sing.

Casey bounced the baby in her arms and Finnick held one song sheet between them so they could share it. His shoulder brushed against hers. Music swelled, filling the room and surrounding them on all sides, and despite the pain and uncertainty, she felt an unexpected burst of joy spreading through her heart. Her whole life, she'd never seen this many people from across the island for a Christmas play and if a competition was what it took to bring people together, then she was thankful for it. She scanned the room, then her gaze drifted to the beautiful snow outside the window.

And she gasped.

A man in the Creepy Shepherd mask and robes was watching them through the glass.

Chapter Eight

Finnick heard Casey inhale sharply and felt her hand grasp his arm.

"What?" He leaned toward her, so they could speak in the room filled with music, until their faces were so close they almost touched. As her eyes met his, fear filled their depths.

"The Creepy Shepherd is outside," she said, "watching through the window."

Finnick turned and looked behind him, past the throngs of carolers singing to the window where she was gesturing. For a moment, all he saw was the snowy landscape and bright blue sky. If it had been any civilian other than Casey, he might have questioned if she was seeing something. After all, why would the Creepy Shepherd take the risk of looking into a public space in broad daylight? It didn't make sense. But he'd worry about that later. All that mattered now was stopping him.

He strained his eyes, searching the endless white outside and prayed.

Lord, guide my vision and help me see.

Then, out of the corner of his eye, he saw a flash of green disappear over a snowbank to their right and vanish out of sight. He took Casey's hand and squeezed it.

"I'm going after him," Finnick said. "Stay here, surrounded by people. Don't go anywhere alone or leave until I come back for you. Got it?"

Casey nodded. "Got it."

He allowed himself one more look at her face, wishing he didn't have to leave her and praying today was the day he finally brought the criminal who'd been terrorizing her to justice. Then he set his jaw in determination. "I won't let him get away this time."

Finnick slid past her into the aisle and made his way to the back of the church as quickly as he could without actually breaking into a run. That would wait until he was outside. He reached the front steps and sprinted for Casey's van.

"Nippy!" he called as he ran toward his partner. The K-9 woofed loudly, leaped through the window, hit the frozen ground and bounded down the sidewalk toward Finnick. Within a heartbeat, Nippy was by his side. Together as one, Finnick and his partner turned and dashed down a narrow alley between two buildings and came out in a large, snowy field behind the church. The Creepy Shepherd was nowhere to be seen, but a trail of footprints on the ground led over a hill down into the park.

Finnick and Nippy raced ahead, chasing the trail of footprints through the snow. The park spread out before them in a maze of trees, benches, children's playground equipment and light displays, set in a natural valley with hills on three sides. The figure in the green robe weaved his way through the trees.

"Stop!" Finnick shouted. His hand flexed toward the badge on his waist, but once again, he didn't pull it. The man wouldn't even be able to see it from this distance. Even if he did, Finnick had no reason to believe he'd halt, and he'd just have given up the element of surprise.

The Creepy Shepherd glanced back but didn't stop. Finnick pressed his legs faster than he'd even dared when he was a young man. The old dog beside him matched him pace for pace. The Creepy Shepherd had a pretty good head start. But Finnick had the high ground and he wasn't in a ridiculous disguise.

But did the criminal still have a gun? And if so, would he shoot to kill a dog? Finnick swallowed hard and glanced at his faithful partner running beside him. He hated to put Nippy in danger. But it was what the dog had trained for in the line of duty and the retriever was still a cop, through and through.

Lord, please give me wisdom and keep Nippy safe.

Finnick took a breath and made the call.

"Chase him!" he ordered, pointing at the figure in the Creepy Shepherd robes. "Go!"

Nippy barked like a warrior and ran straight down the slope toward the figure. Finnick darted sharply upward and ran along the top of the hill to his left, weaving behind trees and hoping with each step that the Creepy Shepherd would be too focused on the loud dog charging behind him to even notice Finnick gaining on him.

The shepherd seemed leaner than he'd been the night before. Was that the trick of the light? Or someone new beneath the mask? The shepherd glanced back again and almost stumbled as he saw the dog charging down the hill after him. Then he reached into his robes. Something reflective flashed in his hand.

It was now or never.

Finnick leaped, throwing himself down the embankment like a linebacker, tackling the Creepy Shepherd around the shoulders and throwing him down onto the ground. The assailant shouted in surprise, but his words were muffled as he fell. The object flew from the Shepherd's hand and landed in the snow. It wasn't a gun. It was a cell phone and according to the screen notification a message had just been sent.

"Stay down!" Finnick pinned the guy face down in the snow. "Hands where I can see them and don't try anything."

Nippy leaped to his side. The dog was still barking fiercely, but Finnick signaled the dog to stop. Then he flipped the man over and yanked the mask up, and saw the young, terrified face of Patrick's twelve-year-old-son.

This was no criminal killer. This was a very young man, barely out of childhood.

"Tristan?" Finnick leaped up off the kid, feeling his own head jerk back in surprise. "I'm sorry, I didn't mean to scare you. What are you doing running around in that costume? Who gave it to you and made you do this? Was it your dad?"

The kid's mouth opened and then shut again, like a caught fish gasping for air. Finnick reached down to help Tristan to his feet. But instead of taking his hand, Tristan's eyes darted over Finnick's shoulder and Finnick heard the sound of someone churning up the snow as they ran toward him.

"Leave my son alone!" a voice bellowed.

Finnick spun back. Patrick was charging down the hill toward him. The father's face was flushed with anger. The contractor was a good decade and a half younger than Finnick, a couple inches taller and fueled by the indignant rage of seeing someone lay a hand on his child.

And even though Finnick was certain he'd be able to hold his own against him in a fight, and eventually wrestle him down, he'd probably take a few painful blows in the process—and more importantly lose any hope of getting a real answer out of him. Patrick's fist was clenched in rage. It rose, ready to strike.

Well, if it had to come to blows, Finnick wasn't going to throw down first.

Even if it turned out that Tristan had gotten the Creepy Shepherd costume from his own father, and that Patrick himself was somehow behind all this, Finnick was going to try his best to resolve it calmly, without fighting the man in front of his son.

"Hey, it's okay," Finnick said. He raised his right hand, palm open to show that he was unarmed, and with the left hand, he flashed his badge inside his jacket, making a point to hide it from Tristan's view. "Your son is fine and I don't want trouble. I just need his help and yours."

Tristan scrambled to his feet, yanked off the mask and threw it in the snow. Patrick stopped just a few feet away from Finnick and close enough to strike. His arms didn't drop. Patrick's eyes darted rapid fire from the badge, to his son, to Finnick's face and then back to Tristan's face again. Nippy stepped to Finnick's side.

"Tristan," Patrick called to his son. His voice was protective, but serious too. "Are you okay?"

Tristan nodded. "Yeah, yeah."

"Son, just tell me the truth," Patrick said, "and it's going to be okay."

"I was running," Tristan began, and then his words poured out in one nonstop thought, "and he ran after me, and he yelled at me to stop, and I didn't because I knew I'd be in trouble for taking this costume, and then he tackled me and I fell down, and I'm okay because it's my fault."

"No, it's my fault, Tristan," Finnick said, quickly. "I thought you were someone else. A very dangerous man, who attacked a friend of mine while wearing that costume. If I'd known it was you, I wouldn't have chased you like that. I'd have gone and found your dad."

Patrick hesitated a moment, as if weighing Finnick's words and trying to decide whether he believed them. Then he blew out a loud breath and ran both hands over his head.

"Take it off, Tristan," Patrick said. "Where did you get it?"

"It was in the church storage room with the nativity costumes." Tristan wriggled out of the robe and held it out to his father. But when Patrick didn't take it, he turned to Finnick.

"You can put it in the snow with the mask. That's fine," Finnick said.

"None of the older kids wanted to be in the pageant," Tristan said. The boy folded the robe awkwardly and then dropped it on top of the mask. "But Mrs. Wilks was saying we all have to. Then, when we were getting ready, we found this and everyone said it would be funny if somebody put it on and ran around. And so I did."

The kid squirmed. Nippy walked over to Tristan, with his ears low and tail wagging, and butted his head against the boy's leg. Tristan glanced to his dad as if for permission.

"Nippy's a good dog," Finnick said. "He's really good with kids."

Patrick nodded to Tristan. The boy ran his hand over the dog's head.

"Do you know whose idea it first was that somebody run around in the costume?" Finnick asked.

Tristan shook his head.

"Do you know how the mask and robe got into the storage room?" Finnick added.

Tristan shook his head again. Finnick took in a long breath and let it out.

"Okay, how about you and Nippy go sit on that bench over there—" Finnick pointed to a snow-covered bench a few yards away "—while I have a talk with your dad."

Once again, Tristan looked to his dad for agreement.

"Yeah," Patrick agreed, "and put your headphones on okay? Because Mr. Ethan and I might have some things to talk about, which I don't want you to have to worry about."

Patrick reached out a gloved hand to his son, and Tristan gave him a fist-bump. Finnick signaled to Nippy to go with the boy, and Tristan and Nippy headed over to the bench. Finnick waved Patrick to a different seat, where they sat side by side. The boy and dog began to play in the snow, despite Tristan having just been told to sit on the bench.

Patrick shook his head at his son and grinned.

"You've got a really great kid," Finnick said.

"I know." Patrick sighed. He sounded both tired and frustrated. "Though I don't know what I ever did to deserve a son that great. Is that a police dog?"

"Yeah," Finnick said. "Although, he's technically retired."

"What's his specialty?"

"Cadaver."

"Wow." Patrick blew out another breath and dropped his head into his hands. "Look, I know why you're here and I've got nothing new to tell you. I didn't kill Stella or Tim. I didn't touch that other girl. And I've got plenty of home security footage proving I didn't leave my house last night, let alone break into my own construction yard and run over my own gate. But I know you guys have already made your mind up about me. So just tell me what I need to do to get you to stop harassing me."

"Well, I'm not here to harass you," Finnick said, "I just got here, and I can promise you, I definitely haven't made my mind up about you." Patrick pulled his hands away from his face and looked at him. Finnick stuck out his hand as if to shake his. "I'm Inspector Ethan Finnick, formerly head of the Ontario RCMP's K-9 Unit, soon to be head of the newly formed Cold Case Task Force."

Patrick looked at his hand and didn't take it. But something seemed to soften in his eyes. "So, you're here about Stella and Tim?"

"Yup," Finnick said, "and I'm also trying to figure out why a man in a shepherd costume broke into your lot, attacked Casey, tried to steal the infant who was left in her nativity manger and used one of your old vehicles to potentially kidnap a woman named Ally Neilson, kill her and dispose of her body."

"Well, it wasn't me," Patrick said.

"I do imagine that if you were going to use one of your vans to commit a crime you'd probably choose one with decent snow tires," Finnick said.

Patrick snorted, and for the first time since he'd come running across the snow, the man actually managed a smile. "I'm sure Casey thinks I have something to do with what happened to Tim and Stella."

She does, Finnick thought. But that didn't mean she was right.

"Why do you say that?" Finnick asked.

"Because everybody blamed me for what happened," Patrick said, "because I apparently saw them last. Even though I heard that someone saw them in Sudbury weeks later."

"Do you know who started that rumor that they were seen in Sudbury?" Finnick asked. "Or who supposedly saw them there?"

"No." Patrick shook his head, but Finnick wasn't so sure he didn't at least have some idea, even if it was just a guess. "I was brought in for questioning and declared a 'person of interest.' But I have never officially been cleared."

"Because the case was never closed."

"Right," Patrick said, "and people don't care about the difference between a suspect and a person of interest. I already had a reputation because of Tristan and his mom."

His voice dropped, as if worrying Tristan might overhear him.

"The only thing I'm guilty of is having a kid with a chick who didn't want to marry me, when I was too young to be having a family," Patrick went on. "When Tristan was born, I dropped out of college, started working for my dad full time, and made being Tristan's dad my highest priority. But his mom only wanted to go out, drink and party. She didn't want to settle down and was dating other guys behind my back. Eventually, she left us and we haven't heard from her in years. But, of course, people assumed it was my fault and that I'd done something wrong."

"And you never tried to move on?" Finnick asked.

"It's kind of hard to move on when any woman who researches me online for more than five minutes discovers I'm a person of interest in what looks like a double homicide." Patrick didn't even try to hide the resentment in his voice. But again something softened in his eyes when he glanced at his son, who was now wrestling with Nippy in the snow. "Tristan's an amazing kid and I'm really blessed that I get to be his dad. So what if no one on this island believes me when I say I've never so much as touched a drink in my life, and that I really wanted to marry Tristan's mom? But, I had a child out of wedlock. That was all the reason people needed to think badly of me. And so people are going to believe what they're going to believe, whether it's true or not."

"Not if I can help it," Finnick said.

But Patrick went on as if he hadn't heard him. "And everyone seems to think I might be guilty of something."

Casey had said everyone thought Tim was guilty of something. Rupert had said the same about Stella. And now Patrick was saying the same about himself. It seemed there was more than enough finger pointing and blame throwing to go around.

So, all three of them had been blamed. Did that mean none of them were guilty?

He glanced back at the church where he'd left Casey and Joey. The faint sound of singing still echoed in the air.

Lord, give me clarity. It feels like no one is telling me the whole truth about anything to do with this case—maybe because none of them know it.

Give me eyes to see the truth.

No matter where it leads.

Casey bounced Joey on her lap and watched as Sophie shuffled slowly down the aisle, enveloped in a beautiful pale blue robe with a white-lined blue scarf over her head. She walked between a Joseph with a full false beard and wooden staff on one side and a child dressed as a soft gray donkey on the other.

Up onstage almost two dozen children from Juniper Cove and around the island posed in a tableau of angels, shepherds, wise men and sheep. Every craftsperson in town who'd been able to wield a sewing needle, glue gun, hammer or paint brush had donated their time to work on the costumes and sets. The final impact of it all coming together was spectacular, and despite the constant thrum of worry in Casey's heart as she kept scanning the windows and entrance for Finnick, she was also incredibly happy for her sister and what she'd managed to create.

Eileen had not only put together something truly spectacular, she'd managed to bring the whole town, and even the island, together in a way it never had before.

Lord, thank You for my sister's gifts and determination, for what she's been able to put together for our town. Whether we win this competition or not, please use this Christmas to strengthen our community and bring people closer to each other and to You.

And please, bring Finnick back soon and keep him and Nippy safe.

Mary, Joseph and the donkey reached the stage. Pastor David invited everyone to stand and sing "Silent Night," and announced that those with children, grandchildren and loved ones up onstage were welcome to get their cameras out again and start taking pictures. Cameron stepped in the center aisle and knelt down to take pictures of the pageant.

Joey began to fuss and complain that he was ready for a fresh bottle and a nap, when suddenly Casey realized that something was going wrong onstage, in the center of the nativity scene. Sophie was searching around the manger as if looking for something she couldn't find. Soon, Joseph, a couple of shepherds and the angel Gabriel were helping her, looking under hay bales and glancing to their parents with increasingly distressed looks on their faces. A young angel said something to Eileen in a voice too low for Casey to catch, and from the way her sister's smile tightened, Casey knew immediately that something was wrong.

The children seemed to be getting more confused and frazzled.

But it wasn't until the song came to an end that Sophie's voice finally reached Casey's ears.

"I've looked everywhere and can't find it!" The frustrated girl's voice rose. "Baby Jesus is gone!"

A buzz spread through the crowd, and suddenly the beautiful harmony that had filled the room just moments before had been replaced with whispers, murmurs and even a few snickers. A few parents left their seats to help look for the doll. Smaller children started to wander around the stage. A couple of the more enthusiastic ones began to search more aggressively. And a few of the older teenagers in the audience switched their camera to video mode and started to crack jokes about the final act of the pageant unraveling in front of them.

Some people enjoyed watching other people's tragedies.

There in the middle of the hurricane was her sister Eileen, trying to do everything at once, shooing children back to their places and waving the parents to stay in their seats, while also searching every possible onstage hiding place for the missing doll.

Then through the crowd, Casey felt Drew's eyes on her. As she watched, he leaned over to Jessica and murmured something to her. Jessica slipped quietly to the center of the chaos and whispered to Eileen. Eileen turned and looked straight at Casey, and the baby in her arms.

And Casey felt the tiniest bit of dread begin to drip down inside her core.

Eileen went to the podium, picked up a portable microphone, turned to the congregation and smiled.

"Everybody back in your seats, please," she said. "Kids, let's all get back in position. It's picture time."

People began to settle, kids returned to formation, and even the teenagers who'd been on their phones lowered them and stopped talking.

"I know we are all a little bit surprised by the fact that the baby Jesus doll we practiced with has gone missing," Eileen started, in her best Sunday-school voice, smiling at the kids and the congregation. "Sometimes, things happen that we don't expect, especially at Christmas. My little sister, Casey, got a huge Christmas surprise this week, when a little tiny baby boy showed up in the manger outside her house, needing a place to stay. Thankfully, Casey took him in and kept him safe."

People were turning to face Casey now as Eileen walked down the aisle toward her. A couple of people actually snapped a picture of her and Joey, and Casey couldn't remember ever seeing that many people smiling at her at once.

Casey's breath tightened in her chest and she instinctively hugged Joey closer to her. He nestled into her chest and whimpered softly.

She never wanted to let her sister down. She never wanted to let anybody down.

Let alone while her sister was putting her on the spot, in front of everyone.

Casey's words to Finnick the day before echoed in her mind.

She's impossible to say no to, which is why I never do.

Well, I'll be the one saying no to her, not you.

Casey glanced at the doorway.

Where was Finnick?

Lord, please don't let Eileen ask me something I have to say no to.

"Now, Joey is a very little and very special baby," Eileen said, still holding the mic, "and it's important that we take care of him. But we're going to have a real live baby in the manger this year, not just a doll. Because Casey has agreed that if Sophie is very careful, she can hold Joey for a few quick pictures, to welcome him as a part of the Juniper Cove family Christmas."

There was a smattering of applause. Eileen leaned toward Casey and stretched out her hands. Casey took a painful breath.

"No," she said. Eileen's eyes widened as if Casey had physically pushed her. "I'm sorry. But Joey can't be in the nativity scene."

"But I was told you talked to Sophie earlier, and said you were okay with it."

The microphone was still amplifying her voice.

"Well, I'm sorry," Casey said, again. "But she must've misunderstood. Joey's too little and I'm only his temporary guardian. His father has already contacted social services and is hoping to take him home by Christmas, and he might not want him appearing in pictures for a holiday competition."

Was his father even there? Or any members of his family? If so, why didn't they step in?

Or was he watching her for some reason? And if so, what was he watching her for?

Something sharp flickered in her sister's eyes.

Anger? Pain?

Humiliation?

Then she saw Cameron step up behind his mother. His worried eyes met Casey's and he shook his head.

"Stop it," Eileen hissed. "You're making a scene and embarrassing both of us. This nativity pageant is a really important part of the contest and we can't have nativity pictures with no baby Jesus. It's only going to be for a couple of minutes and then you can have him back."

Joey began to cry, for no other reason, Casey suspected, than he was getting more tired and hungry. But Eileen's lips pursed.

"Look, now you're upsetting him, Casey," she said. "Just let me hold him and I promise we'll just get some pictures and then it'll all be done."

"She said no, Mom," Cameron said. He placed his hand gently on his mother's arm. "It was a good idea, but Casey's got a point. Just let it go and we'll wrap up a towel or something for the pictures."

"Cameron, stop." Eileen turned to her son. "It's fine. I've got it. Stay out of it."

"Mom, he's a kid," Cameron said. "Not a prop for your show."

Casey wasn't sure what drew her eyes past her sister and nephew to the doorway. Was it a sound? A motion? But whatever it was, Finnick was now there. His eyes met hers and he smiled. Her heart leaped.

"I'm so sorry," she said loudly to no one in particular. She slid past Eileen. "He needs me to change him and give him a bottle."

Voices and faces swam around her. She blocked them out, focusing her attention on Finnick. As she drew near, he reached out his hand for her, like she was drowning and he was offering to pull her to shore. She took it and together they hurried down the aisle and out the door.

"Are you okay?" Finnick asked her, softly.

"Yes," she said. "Maybe. I don't know. I might've just wrecked my sister's attempt to win the Christmas competition."

"I'm sure you didn't," Finnick said.

Nippy was waiting for them on the front step. His tail thumped hello.

"Are you okay?" she asked. "Where's the Creepy Shepherd?"

"It wasn't him," Finnick said. "It was Tristan. He said the kids found the costume in the storage room, and he decided to run around in it. I thought Patrick was going to deck me when he realized I'd tackled his kid. But we ended up having a pretty decent talk."

"Oh?" She jostled Joey in her arms but his cries didn't settle.

"I'll explain more when we're in the van."

They hurried down the sidewalk together, and that was when she realized that she still hadn't let go of his hand and he hadn't let go of hers either.

When they reached the van, Joey's fussing had turned to full-out wails.

"Is he okay?" Finnick had to raise his voice just to be heard over him.

"He's just hungry, tired and determined to let us know."

Finnick smiled slightly. "Good for you, kid."

She got in the back with Joey and let Finnick drive, with Nippy in the passenger seat. There was so much she wanted to talk to Finnick about, but Joey seemed to be trying out his lungs at full volume, and they were unable to get a word in edgewise.

When they got home, she was immediately swept up in a flurry of activity taking care of the baby. She changed him, fed him, bounced him and changed him again, while Finnick took phone calls and checked things on his laptop.

She'd been home for over an hour before she finally managed to settle Joey again and he fell asleep peacefully in his crib. She stood there by his side, looking down at the dozing baby, feeling happier and more exhausted than she'd ever remembered feeling before.

"I don't know how somebody so little and cute could make so much noise and trouble," she whispered softly, running a hand down his cheek. "But you're the most incredible kid and even though you're going to be leaving me soon, I'm going to think about you and pray for you every day of my life."

She blinked away tears and refused to let them fall. When Casey slipped out of the room, she could hear Finnick's voice floating down the hall. He was clearly on the phone with someone, probably Rupert. So instead she slipped into her bedroom, plugged her cell phone into the charger beside the bed, lay down on top of the blankets and stared at the wall of Thompson-family pictures facing the bed. The room had never really felt like hers. Instead, it was a memory capsule of all the families who'd lived on the Thompson farm before. There were pictures of Tim's great-grandparents and grandparents, great uncles and aunts, his parents, and Tim as a child. And there was an empty space where her and Tim's picture was supposed to go once they finally had kids of their own.

She closed her eyes, and finally, the tears she'd managed to fight before began to slip out from under her lids and slide down her cheeks. For a moment, she lay there and cried, without even understanding why, just knowing she had to take it to God.

"Lord," she whispered, "I don't know if I've been wrong all this time in thinking Tim did nothing wrong and he was dead. Or if Tim really is alive and was having a relationship with Ally, or how that fits in with the fact that Joey's father has contacted social services. I feel... I feel like I don't really know anything right now. Am I wrong for hoping You want me to be a mother and have a family of my own? Was I wrong to get Tim declared legally dead so I could use his insurance money to save his family farm? It meant so much to him and I felt like I'd betray him if I lost the farm to strangers outside of his family. Should I help Finnick and his team get Tim's death overturned? And if I do, what happens then?"

She took a shuddering breath and suddenly she realized her palms were aching. She'd hadn't even realized her hands were clenched. But now she was aware of how tightly she was squeezing her fingers closed and pressing her fingernails into her skin.

Slowly, she released her hand. Then she stretched her palms up toward the sky, feeling the tension ease from her aching shoulders as she did so, and she wondered how long she'd hunched them.

"Well, I'm lost right now, Lord," she said, "and so all I can do is be open to You. Show me what comes next. And I'll follow."

The sound of Finnick's voice on the phone was still floating down the hall and the tears had dried on Casey's cheeks. So she curled up in a ball on top of the bed and let herself doze.

Sleep came easily and peacefully, enveloping her gently and draining the tension from her limbs. Until suddenly she awoke to the sound of her cell phone ringing. She glanced at the screen. It was just before five, but already the sky was dark outside.

"Hello?"

"Aunt Casey?" Cameron's voice was breathless and panicked. "I need your help."

She bolted upright, swung her legs over the side of the bed and started for the door. A crash sounded down the line.

"Where are you?" she asked. "Are you okay?"

No answer. Just another crash. She flung the bedroom door open and ran down the hall. Finnick was sitting on the couch, but when he heard her coming, he leaped to his feet and started toward her.

"Cameron!" Her voice rose as she spoke into the phone again. "Where are you? What's happening?"

"I'm at home in the darkroom—" his voice dropped to a terrified whisper "—hiding from someone. One second."

The call went silent without ending, like he'd put it on mute. Finnick reached for her hand and pulled her to his side. She held the phone between them so he could listen in too. A cheerful gurgle suddenly broke through the silence. She looked down to see Joey smiling and waving at her from his play mat, and she realized Finnick must've gotten him up from his nap while she was sleeping. Nippy lay in his usual spot beside him. The dog's dark eyes were fixed on her, with his ears down, as if silently asking her what was wrong.

"He's wearing a black mask, clothes and gloves." Cameron's panicked voice was back. "He just broke in and started looking through drawers. I think he's searching for something I took."

"Like a picture?" she asked.

Had her nephew managed to snap a photograph of the Creepy Shepherd? Or who had left his costume in the church?

But any answer Cameron would've given was lost with the

sound of a man shouting profanity and threatening to kill her nephew. Whatever the attacker was looking for, he sounded willing to trash Eileen and David's garage to find it.

"Cameron?" Casey called. "What did you take? Who does it belong to?"

"I'm sorry," Cameron said. "I should've told you before. Ally—"

Then the heart-wrenching sound of her nephew screaming filled the line.

And the phone went dead.

Chapter Nine

Finnick watched the color drain from Casey's face.

"Cameron!" she shouted again. "Are you okay?"

But there was no answer. Casey called back and the phone just rang, but Finnick was already throwing on his jacket and grabbing his boots.

"I'm on my way," Finnick said. "You coming or staying?"

While he hated the idea of letting Casey go into a dangerous situation, he also knew that if one of his loved ones was in trouble, he'd be beating down the door to help them. He also didn't like the idea of leaving her, in case this was some kind of a diversion to get Finnick to race over there and leave Casey home alone with Joey.

"I'm coming," Casey said. She gasped a breath. Her limbs were shaking. "But you'd better drive."

"Hey, it's going to be okay." Finnick touched her shoulders gently with both hands. "We're going to go save him."

She bundled herself and Joey up in winter clothes, and the four of them ran for the van. Finnick opened the back door for her, then once she and Joey were securely inside, he and Nippy leaped in the front and they set off. Finnick called the island police using the van's hand's-free system and they assured him that the police and ambulance were on their way but would be a good twenty minutes out. The sun was already setting and the sky was growing dark. Finnick navigated her van down the icy roads, driving as quickly as he dared.

Minutes ticked past agonizingly slowly. Casey kept dialing Cameron and got no response. No answer from her sister either, which wasn't a surprise as she'd be at the skating event.

Then Eileen and David's house came into view. The lights were off and the driveway was empty, but a two-foot gap of light shone under the partially opened garage door.

"You're going to stay in the van with Joey, okay?" Finnick said. "And at the first sign of trouble, I want you and Joey to get out of here. Don't worry about me."

"Okay."

He reached over the back seat to hand her the keys and their fingertips brushed. Casey closed her eyes and whispered, "Lord, please help."

"Amen," Finnick said.

Then he exited the van, signaled Nippy to his side and ran for the garage. Silence fell from within.

"Hello?" he called. "Is anybody there?"

No answer. Finnick grabbed the garage door, rolled it up and froze.

Cameron's lifeless body was hanging by a noose from a garage support beam.

Casey's nephew was dead.

Sadness crashed into Finnick's chest like a wave as he walked over and touched the man's wrist. No pulse. A van door clicked open behind him. Finnick spun back, about to remind her to stay in the van, but the words froze on his tongue when he saw the sorrow flooding her eyes. She'd opened the back door, stepped just one foot out, with her other foot still in the car.

"Casey, I'm so sorry. Please stay there. I'm going to cut him down—"

But before the words could finish leaving his mouth, he heard Nippy bark and felt the dog butt his head against his leg. He looked down. Nippy's worried eyes were on his face. But the dog wasn't alerting.

"Casey!" Finnick shouted. "Help!" He sprinted into the garage, grabbed Cameron's legs and hoisted him up. "Cameron's still alive!"

She leaped from the van, slammed the door shut behind her and ran to help him.

"I'll hold him," Finnick said. "Find something you can use to climb up and cut him down. Nippy, go sit by the van and guard Joey."

The dog woofed and ran to the vehicle. Desperate prayers poured from Casey's lips. She grabbed a knife from the tool bench. Then ran for a stepladder that had fallen over a few feet away. Casey set the ladder beside Finnick and climbed up.

"You got it?" he asked.

"Yeah." She gritted her teeth. "Just be prepared to catch him."

She made quick work of the rope, and Cameron's full weight fell into Finnick's arms. He eased the young man onto the ground and reached for the knife. Wordlessly, Casey jumped down and handed it to him. Finnick cut the rope free from Cameron's neck, then pulled off his gloves and slid his bare fingers over the young man's red and raw skin, and felt for a pulse again. He didn't seem to be breathing.

Please, Lord, may Nippy be right. May there still be hope.

Casey knelt on the floor beside him and began to pray. At first, Finnick felt nothing, and then, he felt the tiniest flicker of a beat under his fingertips.

"He has a pulse!" Finnick sat back. "It's very slow and weak, but it's there. Can you do chest compressions? I'm going to attempt CPR."

"Thank You, God." Casey's eyes snapped open.

He eased Cameron's mouth open and stopped. There were

remnants of a white powder around his lips, in his mouth and a little on the collar of his shirt.

"I think whoever did this to him drugged him so he wouldn't fight back," Finnick said. "It would explain why I couldn't find a pulse."

Suddenly lights and sirens filled the air. Joey began to wail in complaint at the sudden burst of noise. Police and paramedics suddenly flooded the area.

"We need a paramedic!" Finnick shouted, as uniformed law enforcement ran toward him. "He's alive but unconscious, and he seems to have been drugged with something that sedated him."

He stepped away from Cameron and let medical staff rush past him and do their job. Casey ran back to the van and climbed in to comfort Joey. Rupert strode up to Finnick. Judging by the older man's Christmas-patterned pajama pants, he hadn't even stopped to change.

"Was this a suicide attempt?" the chief of the island police asked, glancing at the rope.

"No." Finnick shook his head. "But somebody went to an awful lot of trouble to make it look like one."

But why?

Finnick walked back to the van, opened the back door and reached for Casey's hand. She took it and squeezed it tightly. And for a long moment, he stood there, holding her left hand while her right hand rested on Joey, praying silently as they watched the paramedics work.

"He stood up to his mom for me," Casey said, softly.

Finnick opened his eyes. "When?"

"At the nativity service." Her eyes were fixed on the cluster of people gathered around her nephew in the garage. He watched as the flashing lights sent colorful shadows dancing down the lines of her face. "The whole thing was going perfectly, until nobody could find the baby Jesus doll. Then Eileen announced to everyone that we were going to have a real live baby in the manger because I was going to let Sophie hold Joey just for the pictures. I think Jessica put her up to it. Maybe in their attempt to get the next perfect picture for their family Christmas card. I don't know. The whole thing felt really manipulative. Eileen put me on the spot in front of everyone."

"And you said no?" Finnick asked.

"I did," Casey said. "Eileen didn't want to take no for an answer, and then Cameron stepped in and defended me. He basically told his mother off. It was a big scene and there's nothing Eileen hates more than a scene. I tried calling her and David when you were talking to law enforcement but couldn't get through."

"And the whole town saw it," Finnick said.

"Pretty much."

If Cameron had been found hanging dead in his garage, would everyone assume that was why? His gaze turned to the house. Paramedics were lifting Cameron onto a stretcher. Rupert hurried down the driveway toward them.

"Good news is that our boy is conscious." He ran one hand over his white beard. And Casey thanked God softly under her breath. "But you were right—he's got some kind of sedative in his system and his windpipe is pretty badly bruised. He tried to talk, but between the windpipe and drugs, he couldn't get much out. We're taking him to the medical center now, but the paramedics are confident he'll bounce back just fine. I'm thankful you guys got here when you did."

"Amen to that," Finnick said.

Rupert leaned in the window toward Casey. "Have you been able to get through to Eileen or David? Because we've tried and haven't gotten any answer."

"They're probably at the ice-skating event," Casey said. "We'll go. I think she should hear this from me."

Rupert nodded. "Tell them to meet us at the medical center."

"Will do."

* * *

Casey switched back into the driver's seat for the trip to the skating event. The outdoor rink had been constructed by the volunteer firefighters. Wooden boards squared off a circle of frozen lake just off the shore. Strings of dazzling lights criss-crossed over the skaters as they laughed and swirled, while on the beach, people gathered around the bonfire, sipping hot chocolate. In a dim patch of light, a little ways down from the skating, she could see a handful of people ice fishing. Casey pulled her van to a stop between two vehicles at the edge of the cliff, overlooking the festivities below.

"There's a closer parking lot below," she said. "But it'll be crammed and it's faster to just run. Hang on. I'll be right back."

She got out and slammed the door. Finnick sat in the van and waited as she disappeared down a narrow path. From the back seat, he could hear Nippy grumbling under his breath and sniffing the air as if the dog was bothered by something.

"You okay, buddy?" Finnick asked. "I'll take you for a run when we get back home, okay?"

Home.

He'd been referring to Casey's farmhouse—almost a six-hour drive from where he was going to set up his team—and he'd just called it home.

Within moments, Casey was back with a panicked-looking Eileen and David. He watched as Casey hugged them both in turn. Then her sister and brother-in-law hopped in their car, which was thankfully parked nearby, and disappeared down the road. Casey got back in the van.

"Do you want to go with them?" Finnick asked.

"No," Casey said. "I think they need some time alone with their son. Besides, do you see that little line of lights over there? Those are cars crossing the bridge onto the island." She pointed and he followed her gaze to where a slow trickle of tiny lights were moving west. "The social worker might be at the house soon. I need to get Joey fed and packed before then." She frowned as if an unsettling thought had crossed her mind. "You said the Creepy Shepherd sighting from before turned out to be Tristan. Did you and Patrick talk about what happened to Stella and Tim?" Casey asked.

"Yeah," Finnick said. "His version of the story is that everybody thought it was him because he was declared a person of interest, and he's felt like the cloud of suspicion has stopped him from ever being able to move on with his life."

"I know how he feels." Casey sighed. For a moment, her eyes seemed lost in the darkness. Then she turned to face him. "There's something I need to tell you. My mind hasn't changed on Tim, even with everything your team has found. But—" the word hung on her tongue for a moment, as she pulled in a deep breath and let it out again "—but I'm going to give you whatever you need to petition the court to have his death overturned."

Then, to his surprise, she reached for his hand and grabbed it. He enveloped it in both of his and held it tightly.

"Are you sure?" he asked.

"Yes." She nodded. He could barely see her features in the darkness, and yet, he knew every line of her face just by memory alone. "Not because I believe he's alive or has done anything wrong," she added. "But because I trust you and your team to find the truth, once and for all, and I'm not going to stand in the way of that."

"I promise you can trust me."

"I know." Casey leaned toward him and her forehead touched his. "I don't feel like I know very much about anything right now. But I know who you are, Ethan Finnick. You are the kindest, strongest, bravest man I've ever met and I trust you with my life."

Something choked in his throat. Her hand slid from his fingers up to his neck. He reached for her and cupped her face in his palms. Slowly and gently, their lips drifted closer.

Nippy barked sharply. They leaped apart.

"What's up?" Finnick turned around and looked at his partner.

Nippy sniffed and shook his head in frustration. His snout snapped the air as if trying to taste it.

"What's going on?" Casey asked.

"He thinks he smells something…but he's not sure."

Casey looked out over the festive scene below.

"What do you mean, he thinks he smells something but isn't sure?" she asked. "You mean there might a body here?"

Finnick was already taking his seat belt off and climbing out of the van.

"Well-trained dogs like Nippy can smell things a mile away and forty feet underground," he said, "from moments after death to up to thirty years later. But sometimes a scent is too faint for them to detect or it gets mixed up with another odor." Nippy leaped out of the van. Finnick ran his hand over the back of the dog's head. "Not to mention, Nippy's getting old and it could just be a dead fish. Not that I've ever known him to get it wrong."

He signaled Nippy to sit and then clipped his leash on.

"Show me," Finnick said. Nippy barked loudly and ran toward the top of the path that led down to the lake, only to stop when he reached the end of his leash. The K-9 barked again. Finnick blew out a long breath. "He definitely thinks he detects something."

"Hang on," Casey said, "I'm coming with you."

Cold wind whipped their faces as they made their way down the path to the ice-skating rink, and she was thankful she'd decided to take the extra moment to zip Joey up in his chest carrier inside her jacket, where he could shelter from the cold.

They moved slowly. Nippy seemed far less confident than he'd been when they'd tracked Ally to the shed. He sniffed both sides of the path, checking out the snow-covered rocks and trees, and often came to a dead stop to snap at the air, as if trying to bite at the scent. As they reached the bottom of the hill, Nippy led them away from the warmth and lights of the skaters, along a darker and narrower path at the base of the cliff. They walked single file. Pools of ice from the lake mingled with the sharp rocks beneath their feet. After a few minutes, lights from the ice fishing huts shone to their left.

"Hey! Stop!" A voice rose from out on the lake. "You can't go that way!"

They looked to see a tall man in a red Canadian-flag ski mask coming over to them. A volunteer firefighter's badge flashed in his hand. He pulled up his mask as he reached them. It was Patrick.

"Hey!" Finnick raised a hand in greeting. "Where's Tristan?"

"Skating with his friends from youth group," Patrick said. "I figured I'd give him an evening off from having to hang with his dad. I'm sorry, but I can't let you walk along the coast. It's not safe."

"The dog thinks he detects something that way," Finnick said, with a shrug. "Do you happen to have any shipwrecks off these cliffs?"

Patrick shook his head. "We don't let boats go that way. It's completely blocked off from the public because the rocks are sharp and the current is nasty. We don't even let people hike in the area above it because there are way too many places to find yourself falling off a cliff and drowning."

Nippy woofed at Finnick impatiently.

Finnick pointed at his partner. "Well, the dog says there's a crime that way."

"Yeah, I heard him." Patrick ran his hand over his face. "Okay, I can load you up on my snowmobile and take you over. I know how to travel it safely and keep you from falling through the ice. But I think we should take Casey and the baby back. It's really treacherous and the wind's not helping."

Finnick turned to Casey.

"It's okay," she told him quickly, before he'd ever opened his mouth. "I've got to go feed Joey and it is getting colder.

Plus, the social worker is coming. You guys stay safe and I'll see you back at the house."

Finnick paused a long moment as if debating what she was saying. But she was right, and he knew it. Still, to Nippy's frustration, Finnick insisted that they all walk her back to the van together. She slid Joey into the car seat and prepared to climb back into the driver's seat.

Then she turned to face Finnick.

"Promise that if you find anything you'll call or text me immediately," Casey said. "Even if it's bad. Even if it's about Tim."

Finnick sighed. "I get what you're saying, but in my experience it's usually easier on people to get bad news in person and when they're not alone."

"Maybe," Casey cut him off. "I don't know. But right now I can't think of anything worse than worrying and waiting. For over a decade, the emotional pain of not knowing has been the hardest part. And I don't want to feel the pain of not knowing the truth for a single second longer than I have to. Please."

She watched as Finnick swallowed hard. His arms slid open like he was about to hug her. Instead, he crossed them.

"Okay," he said. "I will. I promise."

Then she got in and drove down the narrow, winding highway back toward her home. Indistinct shadows of trees, snowbanks and farmhouses moved past her windows in a blur of grays. Joey began to fuss for a bottle. For a long moment, worries swirled around her mind—from Cameron, to Ally, to Tim and Stella, to whoever's scent Finnick and Nippy were now tracking. But after a few minutes, they all had to take a back seat to a sudden and more pressing problem. Her gas level was dropping quickly. She'd still had over two-thirds of a tank when she left the house that morning, having been sure to fill up just before the snowstorm hit. But now the needle had sunk well into the danger zone, as if her gas tank had sprung a leak and had been draining as she drove. As she started to pray that the van would make it back to town, her vehicle coasted to a stop and died on the side of the road.

Her heart sank. Casey climbed out and scanned the road in each direction. Towering rocks and trees surrounded her on all sides. It was hard to tell exactly where she was in the darkness, but if she had to guess, she was still several miles from town. She pulled out her phone. And couldn't get a signal.

Help me, Lord! Her eyes rose to the dark sky above as worry, frustration and fear all battled for dominion over her heart. *Help me get Joey home!*

Then she saw headlights piercing the darkness. And a green van was pulling up alongside her. Sophie, Lily and Molly, their cheeks still flushed and rosy from ice-skating, waved to her from the back seat.

Jessica stopped the vehicle, then leaned over the empty front seat and pushed the passenger door open.

"You okay?" she asked. "Do you need a ride?"

Casey scanned the four smiling blondes in the van and then felt silly for feeling suspicious.

"Yeah, we ran out of gas," Casey said, leaving out the bit about the fact she might have been sabotaged, "and I've gotta get Joey home for a bottle. Would you mind dropping us off at my house on the way into town?"

Jessica patted the passenger seat. "No problem, I'd be happy to."

They buckled Joey's car seat into the middle seat behind Jessica, and the three girls gathered around him, jiggling his toys and cooing as they drove down the narrow highway back to town.

As they reached Juniper Cove's first stop sign, Jessica angled the rearview mirror to glance at them before she started driving again.

"I'm actually really glad I ran into you," Jessica said. She swiped one hand up and down her arm self-consciously, and then snapped it back to the wheel. "I just really wanted to apologize to you for that whole mix-up back at the pageant earlier. I don't know how I got it in my head that you'd said it was okay for Sophie to hold Joey for a few pictures, but I didn't mean to put anybody on the spot."

"It's no problem," Casey said. "I'm sure next year everyone will have a completely new Christmas pageant—related catastrophe to gossip about."

Jessica laughed subconsciously and adjusted her sleeves.

"Well, I'm really glad that everything is okay between us." She pulled the van to a stop. "I'd hate if there were any bad feelings between us."

"Don't worry. It's all good," Casey said.

She looked up and realized that Jessica had stopped in front of her own house first, instead of taking Casey and Joey home. The lights were on and Drew's van was in the driveway. At least Casey now had a phone signal. She sent Finnick a quick text, telling him where she was.

Jessica leaned over and slid open the back door. "Come on, girls! Daddy is waiting for you and has got the living room all set up!"

The girls gave Joey sweet hugs and kisses goodbye, then they ran off squealing into the house. Jessica closed the back door again.

"Drew is doing a special movie night for the girls tonight," Jessica said, and again that self-conscious twinge was back in her voice. "He's got a sheet set up for a screen, and he's going to play a movie off his laptop onto the digital projector. He created a whole fort of blankets and pillows on the floor so they can curl up and sleep there tonight. And he's made them hot chocolate and popcorn and everything."

Casey nodded, not quite sure why the other woman was telling her all this. It sounded like she was trying very hard to convince Casey that Drew was a good father. And the longer she talked, the more she fidgeted with her clothes.

"It sounds lovely," Casey said.

"Do you want to come in for a tea or something before you go?" Jessica asked.

"No, I'm sorry," Casey said. "Another time, please. I have to take Joey home and feed him his bottle."

"Oh, we have bottles for him," Jessica said, quickly, "clothes, formula and everything. Even a brand new crib."

Casey blinked. "I didn't know you guys were expecting a baby."

She smiled at the younger woman. But Jessica didn't smile back. Instead, worry filled her eyes.

"Look, I'm not supposed to tell anybody about this yet..." Jessica said. "But Drew has almost sorted everything out with social services, and you know what gossip is like on this island. So I wanted to make sure that you heard it from me first."

"Heard what?"

"We're adopting Joey," Jessica said. "Drew's talked to social services and it's all taken care of. We're going to be Joey's new family."

Chapter Ten

Finnick's phone pinged in his pocket.

He was sitting on the back seat of Patrick's snowmobile, with a large pile of ice-fishing equipment on the rack behind him, and Nippy trotting alongside, still on his leash, as the snowmobile matched the dog's slow pace.

Finnick braced against the wind, pulled his cell out and glanced at the screen. It was Casey. Telling him she'd run out of gas at the side of the road and was now at Drew and Jessica's house. He texted her back to keep him posted.

"Hang on!" Patrick called. "There's a very sharp turn up ahead. I can't remember the official name for it, but there's a channel between two cliffs. The local kids used to call it Daredevil Point and we'd egg each other on to jump off it into the lake."

"How many times did you do it?" Finnick called back.

Patrick laughed.

"Only once," he returned. "When I was twelve. One of the friends that Drew and I were with landed badly and broke his leg in three places. After that, there was still a lot of talk but kids moved their stupid stunts to a slightly safer place." They rounded the corner. The channel was about the width of an ice hockey rink. Sheer rock faces towered high on every side. Patrick shook his head. "Can I tell you a secret? Drew never jumped off the cliff that day but still ran around telling everyone he did."

Nippy barked sharply and tugged on the leash.

"I think we're there," Finnick called.

Patrick pulled the snowmobile to a stop near the cliff. Finnick hopped off and ran his hand over Nippy's head.

"Good job," he said. "Show me what you've found."

Nippy barked, ran over to a patch of the ice in the center of the channel and started to dig. His paws slipped uselessly on the ice.

"I've got something that can cut through that if you want," Patrick called.

"Sure, thanks."

Finnick called Nippy to heel and ran another grateful hand over the dog's head. "Whatever was buried out here under the ice," he told Nippy, "I think you're the only one who could've found it."

Patrick pulled an auger from his gear on the back of the snowmobile and jammed it into the ice where Nippy had been scratching. The drill was long, thin and the size of a pogo stick. The screeching sound of ice-cutting filled the air as Patrick drilled down into the frozen surface a couple of feet until he reached water and then he stepped back. Finnick grabbed a giant flashlight off the snowmobile and shone it down into the water below. The light hit on something red and metallic under the water. The ice was even thicker here than where Patrick had been icefishing.

"What is that?" Patrick asked.

"I'm not sure yet," Finnick said. But an unsettling picture was beginning to form in his mind as to what the red object could be. And judging by the worry lines that creased Patrick's forehead, he suspected the same thought had crossed the other man's mind too.

An odd and heavy silence began to fall between them as Patrick continued to dig, punching a hole after hole in the ice, breaking it up into giant blocks that Finnick could then, with the help of ice hooks, wrench out.

Now it was crystal clear what Nippy had found buried under the ice, and neither man needed the other one to say it.

It was Tim's car, slipped on its side and submerged under water, with the remains of two people in the front seat, still buckled in their seat belts.

Finnick stepped back from the wreck, pulled out his phone and checked the screen. Casey still hadn't texted. Nippy leaned against his leg. Finnick reached down his free hand and ran his fingers through the comforting fur of the amazing partner who'd been by his side for the past twelve years. "I hope you know how incredibly proud of you I am," he said softly.

Then he pulled his phone from his pocket and placed a call to the Ontario police commissioner Isaac Cannon. Despite the fact it was after work hours on Christmas Eve, Commissioner Cannon answered on the first ring.

"Sir, we've located Tim Thompson's car with two bodies inside," Finnick said. "I think we finally discovered them."

His work here was done, Finnick thought, when he'd finished relaying the pertinent details to the commissioner and ended the call. It was all in the hands of the RCMP now. They'd coordinate with island police, send an expert team to cordon off the area, extract the car, retrieve the bodies inside and officially confirm what a still, small voice inside Finnick's heart already knew—Tim and Stella had finally been found.

He tried to call Casey and when he couldn't get through, he texted her, knowing that she would want to know as soon as possible to put her mind at rest immediately.

I think Nippy found them.

He heard the sound of Patrick's auger drill clattering against the ice and turned back. The man's hands had clenched into fists and he looked angry enough to punch a hole straight through the cliff's side. Patrick turned to the sky and a roar of anger and pain ripped through his lips. Then his shoulders slumped like a man defeated and he faced Finnick.

"This is all my fault," Patrick said.

"I'm sure it isn't," Finnick said. "After all, you brought me here."

"But I should've known." Patrick ran both hands over his head. "The day before Stella vanished she came into work and asked me for help. She showed me these bruises on her arms, the size of fingerprints, and told me that Drew was hurting her. She asked me to take her to the mainland so she could go to a police station that wasn't on the island and get help. And so help me, I didn't believe her." He groaned. "Drew told me that she was lying," Patrick said, "and I believed him. He was my best friend and he'd convinced me that Stella had a habit of exaggerating and making things up. I also believed him when he told me he'd heard somebody say Stella and Tim had been spotted in Tim's car in Sudbury."

"So, Drew was the one who started that rumor?" Finnick asked.

"I think so," Patrick said. "Maybe. When he married Jessica, she seemed so happy. I couldn't believe he'd ever hurt her. But what Stella had said never totally left me. I stayed close to the family and kept an eye on them all these years. Just for any signs of trouble. But the little girls seemed so happy and I just couldn't imagine he'd hurt anyone. But what if Drew killed Tim and Stela, and then hurt Jessica, and it's my fault he never got caught?"

Fear washed over Finnick like a wave. "Casey and Joey are at Drew and Jessica's house now."

Patrick turned and ran back toward the snowmobile, with Finnick and Nippy just one step behind.

"And it's not your fault," Finnick added. "Predators are really good at hiding who they are. If Drew did hide a nasty side of himself from you, it's probably because he knew that you'd try to stop him."

He just prayed it wasn't too late to stop him now.

Three mini marshmallows danced in the mug of hot chocolate sitting in front of Casey on the Thatcher family's kitchen table. Joey sat in a soft baby-lounger chair on the floor, stubbornly refusing his bottle. Finnick's last text burned like a fire in Casey's mind.

Lord, have they really found Tim's and Stella's bodies? Is this nightmare finally over?

Joy and hope filled her heart and she thanked God for Finnick's text. Everything inside her wanted to text him back. No, wanted to run out the door, all the way to where Finnick was, throw her arms around him in joy and relief. Instead, here she was stuck at the Thatcher's kitchen table waiting for Jessica to give her and Joey a ride back to her farmhouse. Casey's vehicle was still stranded without gas at the side of the road. The island didn't have a taxi service and it would be a long walk home in the cold with the baby. She still hadn't seen Drew—or the kids again—since they'd come home. But Jessica had told her that he had made both the hot chocolate and Joey's bottle especially for them.

More importantly, she still didn't know why Jessica and Drew thought they were going to adopt Joey. An eerie feeling began to climb up her spine. *The social worker had told her that Joey was going to be with his father...*

Jessica walked in, sat and downed her drink.

"Is everything okay with your hot chocolate?" Jessica asked, anxiously.

"Yeah." Casey took a sip. "It's wonderful. I'm just not really into sweet things, due to all the sweet-smelling stuff I'm surrounded by in my workshop every day. Chocolate peppermint was my bestselling soap this year. And for Easter, I'm going to make soaps that look like marshmallow bunnies."

She gave up trying to offer the bottle to Joey and shook it. There was sediment in the bottom, like it hadn't been mixed very well. She dropped it into Joey's diaper bag.

Jessica ran her hands over her eyes and yawned. She looked ready to pass out at the table and Casey wondered how many sleepless nights she'd had. She couldn't imagine what Jessica was going through and compassion flooded her heart.

"Hey, it's okay." Casey reached across the table and took her hands. "I'm sure this whole situation with Joey must be really overwhelming. But when the social worker told me that Joey's father had come forward and that his family was going to raise him—"

"Drew's not Joey's father," Jessica said sharply. She pulled her hands away. "He just told CPS that he was. But only because he had to. But…but they know he's lying, because he'd never do anything like that."

"What?" Casey shook her head like there was water in her ears.

"See, the real father is a young man who Drew was, um… mentoring on his business trips." Jessica sounded like she was dutifully repeating a script that she didn't believe a word of. "And…and the guy can't raise a baby. So Drew agreed to pretend to be Joey's dad."

"The adoption system doesn't work that way," Casey said, softly. "He has to go through a whole bunch of steps to prove that—"

"Well, it *has* to work that way," Jessica cut her off. "Because Drew always says he has the perfect family and he would never do anything to jeopardize that."

Before Casey could say another word, Jessica dropped her head onto her arms and began to cry.

Lord, please comfort her and be her rescue.

Casey leaped from her seat, ran around the table and laid a

comforting hand on Jessica's back. "Hey, it's going to be okay. You're really strong, this community loves you and God can do incredible things. But right now, I've got to get back home."

And talk to Finnick about all of this.

Fear crawled up her spine. She didn't know why Drew was lying, she just knew she had to get herself and Joey out of this house.

Jessica's tears turned to soft whimpers and then stopped. But her head didn't rise. Casey stepped back. Jessica's eyes had closed. Casey reached for her shoulder and Jessica's head lolled over to the side. She'd passed out at the table. A warning bell sounded in Casey's head.

"Hey...you okay?" she asked, giving the woman a gentle shake. "You've fallen asleep at the table."

No answer. She reached for the woman's wrist and it flopped limply in her hand.

Now the warning in her head had gone to a full-fledged siren, clanging along with her pounding heart. She threw the diaper bag over her shoulder, scooped Joey up into her arms and ran through the room and into the hall. The movie still danced on a sheet in the living room. But all three girls had fallen asleep, curled up on the blankets and pillows Drew had laid out for them. Casey picked up a fallen mug from the floor. There was some kind of powdered sediment in the bottom.

Was it spiked with something? Thankfully Casey had only had one sip of her drink and Joey had refused to touch his.

"Come on, Joey." She ran for the door. "We're going to get out of here and go get help."

She opened the door and felt the cold wind hit her face. Darkness and snow filled her eyes. She fumbled for her phone and texted Finnick, praying that he'd receive her messages and would send help.

The floorboards creaked behind her. Something sharp pressed deep into the small of her back.

"Going somewhere, sweet pea?" A dark and gritty voice

that she'd remember from her nightmares filled her ear. He snatched the phone from her hand and threw it to the floor. Joey cried softly and Casey hugged him closer to her.

Drew spun her around and she stared into a smile as wide and lifeless as the mask he'd worn over the past few days.

"So, you're the one who's been dressing up as the Creepy Shepherd all this time?" Casey asked. Drew smirked and nodded. "Why would you do that?"

"Thought it was funny," Drew said with a self-satisfied shrug. "I couldn't find Ally and the baby. I needed to see if they were with you. I needed a disguise and there it was."

"So, you killed Ally?" she pressed. "Why?"

She was stalling him now, trying to buy time for Finnick to reach her and hoping that a man who was grandiose enough to try to take people's lives while dressed as a shepherd, could be lured into bragging about his crimes. Her phone began to ring. Drew stomped on it hard and it fell silent. That's when it hit her—he was dressed to go outside.

"Ally was a nobody and a nothing," Drew snarled. "She never even knew my real name."

"Because you told her that you were my long-lost Tim," Casey said, "and she believed you."

He chuckled. "That was clever, wasn't it? Making fake IDs in Tim's name, letting people think he was out in the world getting into trouble."

"No, that was just gross." Casey cradled Joey closer, as for a moment, disgust at his crimes overcame her fear. "So you killed Ally because you didn't want anyone to find out about the sick little game you were playing those two weekends a month you went away 'on business.'"

Drew scowled. "She tried to blackmail me for money, and said if I didn't give it to her she'd tell everyone that Tim Thompson was Joey's father."

"Which meant people might find out it was really you," Casey said. "She threatened me too, but I didn't kill her."

"Instead you took my baby!" Drew's voice rose.

"I protected him!" Casey's voice rose too. "From you! A man who wanted to kill him! And then, what? You set out to kill me and Finnick for protecting him? And my nephew, why?"

"She sent an email to Cameron the night she died and then deleted it from her phone."

Ally...

Cameron's last word to her before Drew had attacked him filled her mind. What had Cameron been trying to tell her?

"Why?"

"I don't know!" Drew shook his head as if he was angry that she didn't understand and appreciate how clever he was and the corner he'd felt backed into. But it wasn't that she didn't understand. It's that she didn't care. "As I told your friend, I'm not about to let anyone mess with my perfect family."

"You drugged your family!"

"And they fell asleep, peacefully and happily!" Drew shouted. "And now they're never going to wake up and know that Ally was trying to blackmail me for money for the kid. Or that if anyone ever did a DNA test on Joey they'd find out he was mine. I tried to get my hands on Joey and kill him along with his mother. But now, you've left me with no choice but to wipe the slate clean and start a new life on this island. But I'll be fine. I got so much love and sympathy from people on this island when they thought Stella left me. I know I'll be okay. Which is more than I can say for you. You're going to wish you drank that hot chocolate because you're going to wish you were sleeping through what happens next."

Before she could even think about how to fight him off, he grabbed her by the neck, shoved her hard across the floor and threw her into the closet. She tumbled inside, sheltering Joey in her arms.

The door slammed and a lock clicked shut. Minutes ticked past and for a long time Casey couldn't hear anything but the sound of her own fist banging on the wood and her own voice calling for help.

Then she smelled smoke.

Chapter Eleven

"Friends of yours?" Patrick asked. His hands tightened on the steering wheel of his van as his eyes darted up to the rearview mirror. "Don't look now, but I think we're being followed. We picked them up after we passed the turn off to Casey's farmhouse."

Finnick glanced over his shoulder, past where Nippy now sat at attention on the back seat of Patrick's van. Sure enough, not one but two sets of headlights seemed to be following them at every turn.

Either that or they were in a big hurry to get to Drew and Jessica's too.

"I don't know," Finnick said, "but there are two of them."

He, Nippy and Patrick had raced back to Patrick's van on the snowmobile, this time with Nippy cradled awkwardly on Finnick's lap. They'd peeled off in Patrick's van soon after, as the younger man pressed his vehicle through faster speeds and sharper turns than Finnick would have dared. And now the two mystery vehicles on their tail were matching their every move.

Finnick tried Casey's number over and over again, fear rising higher in his throat each time it went through to voicemail. His logical brain tried to tell him that the thirtieth call would be no different from the twenty-ninth, and that she'd pick up if she could. But something inside his heart wouldn't let him stop.

Lord, I need Casey to be alive. I don't want to envision a life without her.

Patrick had rolled his window down a crack, sending a stream of wintery air whipping through the cab, producing a similar effect to a cold slap in the face. But as they neared Drew and Jessica's house, something even more troubling slipped in through the gap—the smell of something burning.

Finnick watched as Patrick's face went white and somehow the volunteer fire chief managed to push the van even faster.

Small pellets of ice and rocks kicked up under his tires as Patrick swerved into the driveway. Smoke billowed out from under the attached garage door. Bright orange flames shot out of the home's windows.

"I installed their smoke-detector system myself!" Patrick yelled, as he slammed on the brakes and jumped out. "Where is everybody—firefighters from across the island should be converging here now!"

He snapped his phone to his ear and began shouting to someone from Dispatch. Finnick leaped out the passenger door. Nippy bounded over the middle console and followed him into the snow.

He steeled a breath and stared up at the house.

Where do I start? Where do I run? What do I do?

Lord, I can't do this alone.

The van and car that had been tailing them pulled into the driveway on either side.

"Hey, boss!" Jackson leaped out of the van, followed by his K-9 German shepherd, Hudson. Gemma got out of the passenger seat. Caleb, Lucas and Lucas's yellow Lab, Michigan, jumped out of the car as well. "How can we help?"

Finnick pulled in a deep breath as a prayer of thanksgiving filled his lungs. "How did you find me?"

"That's all Michigan," Lucas ran one hand down his arson-detecting K-9's side. "We'd just arrived at Casey's house and she started barking up a storm. So, we left Amy and Skye there, and went to see what he was making such a fuss about."

Patrick was still on the phone with Dispatch to get every able-bodied person on the island to the Thatcher house.

"Jackson, I need you and Hudson to track the criminal who I think set this fire," Finnick ordered. "Something tells me we won't find him here. You should be able to get a scent from something in that van. Gemma, stay out here and coordinate with civilians as they arrive. We might need some really good crowd control. Caleb, Lucas and Michigan, you're with me."

Together the three men and the arson K-9 ran for the front door. The fire seemed to have been started in the garage and was moving to the main part of the house. The front door was locked, but even as Caleb was preparing to throw his shoulder into it, Patrick rushed up, wielding a fire axe.

They smashed the door open. Thick, acrid smoke filled Finnick's lungs and stung his eyes.

"We've got three children on the floor!" Lucas shouted, making a beeline for the girls. "They're breathing but unconscious. Help me get them all outside."

Lucas, Caleb and Patrick scooped the three girls up into their arms and carried them out of the building into the snow, where Gemma was waiting.

"Casey!" Finnick shouted. "Casey, where are you?"

For a moment, all he heard was the sizzle, cracking and popping sound of the fire moving closer and closer across the house toward him.

Then he heard a faint voice calling his name.

"Finnick! Joey and I are in here!"

"I'm coming!" He ran for the closet nearby. The door seemed to be locked, but when he leveled a good hard kick at the frame, it cracked and came free. He yanked the door open.

There was Casey, down on the ground, sheltering Joey in her arms. He knelt beside her.

"Finnick?" Her voice was weak. She coughed. "Is it really you?"

"Yeah, it's me." His voice grew husky in his throat. "Come on, let's get you out of here."

Suddenly he felt Patrick by his side, gently scooping Joey up out of Casey's arms and carrying the precious cargo outdoors at a run. Finnick slid his arms under Casey's back and legs. She wrapped her arms around him and cradled herself to his chest, and he hustled her out of the fire and into the snow, just in time to see Lucas carrying Jessica out and over to her girls.

"Tell the paramedics that the children and Jessica were drugged," Casey called faintly to Patrick.

"Got it!" Patrick shouted.

He disappeared into the crowd with Joey. Suddenly it was like the entire town of Juniper Cove and a quarter of the rest of the island descended on the house at once, setting up bucket chains and hoses pouring bucket after bucket of water on the burning house, as they worked together to save it. Paramedics and friends gathered around Jessica and the three girls, keeping them warm and safe as they slowly regained consciousness and woke up, no doubt overwhelmed by the chaos around them.

And Finnick walked through it all with Casey tucked safely in his arms.

"Did you really find Tim and Stella?" she asked.

"Yeah," he said. "Their remains still need to be officially identified, but my heart tells me it's them."

"Where were they?"

"Under the water at Daredevil Point."

She sighed and nestled deeper into his neck. He carried her over to where an empty bench lay, at the edge of the action.

"Drew was the Creepy Shepherd," she said. "He drugged his family and there should be evidence of what he used in Joey's baby bottle in my diaper bag. He's been using Tim's identity to cheat on his wife, and was willing to kill Ally, Joey, you, me and his entire family to maintain that perfect image."

She shuddered.

"He won't get away with it, I promise," Finnick said.

He sat down on the bench, expecting her to slide off onto the seat beside him. Instead, she stayed curled up against him, with her arms gently around his shoulders and his around her body. Nippy galloped over to them and sat by their feet.

"Thank you for finding me, Finnick," Casey whispered.

"I had a lot of help," he said. "From Patrick and my team. The woman with short dark hair currently hugging Jessica is my civilian coordinator and private detective, Gemma Locke. The man with dark hair at the front of the bucket brigade is Lucas. His golden Lab, Michigan, is the one who alerted them to the fire. And the blond, unhandsome man talking to Rupert is Caleb."

She laughed.

"I recognize them from the video call," Casey said. "What are they doing here?"

"I think they're here to surprise me for Christmas," Finnick said. "I promised them I'd have dinner with them tonight. I guess they decided to bring dinner to me."

"Hey, boss!" Jackson's voice called from behind them. "Is this the guy you are looking for?"

Casey slid off Finnick's lap, and they both stood to see Jackson and Hudson emerge from the trees with a very angry and muddy-looking Drew handcuffed between them.

"Yup, that's him," Finnick said.

Hudson woofed triumphantly.

"We found him wandering down the road with the most fantastical story to tell," Jackson said, with a laugh. "Apparently, his house caught fire, and although he valiantly tried to save his beloved wife and daughters, the fire was just too strong and he had no choice but to flee and try to find help!"

Finnick snorted. "Take him over to the man with the big white beard talking to Caleb and tell him Christmas has come early."

"Right on!" Jackson escorted his prisoner over to Rupert. Finnick turned to Casey.

"Can you hang tight here for a moment?" he asked. "I need to go coordinate things with my team. Knowing Gemma, I suspect she's already gotten Jessica to agree to cooperate. But even if not, we should have enough to go on to get Drew Thatcher put away for the rest of his life. And that's even before we're able to talk to Cameron and find out what he'd wanted to tell you about Ally before he was attacked."

As he said the words, he saw two women in jeans, jackets and large laminated badges on lanyards coming toward them.

"That's my social worker and I'm guessing Joey's caseworker," she said. "I need to go talk to them and say goodbye to Joey."

Finnick felt his eyes widen. "Why would you have to say goodbye to Joey?" Everything inside him balked at the thought. "There's no way they're going to let Drew take custody of him after what he tried to do..."

"I know," Casey said. "But it may be months, or even years, before the court manages to revoke his parental rights. Until then, he'll probably be placed with a relative of Drew's or Ally's, if they can find one to take him. There's a big, long process here, and the fact he was placed in my manger doesn't mean I get to keep him."

Finnick scanned the crowd for Joey but couldn't manage to find the little boy.

"Hey, it's okay." Casey slid her hand to Finnick's face and turned him toward her. He saw the sadness in his own heart echoed in her eyes. "I always knew I was only a temporary, emergency caregiver. There are thousands of families wanting to adopt and only a few hundred infants ever come up for adoption a year. But have faith that God will guide Joey's life from here and place him into the arms of the right family who will love him forever. Meanwhile, I'll try to open my heart to whatever adventure and child God brings me next."

But, you and Joey belong together! The words burst through his heart, but he didn't let them pass his lips.

"Hey, not all happy endings are instant," Casey said, apparently reading the hesitation on his face. "Some of them take a really, really, *really* long time, especially with adoption and fostering. I promise, it's going to be okay, in God's time."

Before he could even try to find words to say, she reached up and kissed him on the temple, then turned away. She made her way through the crowd, leaving him standing there watching her go.

Lord, all this time I thought I was rescuing Casey. But now I see that in some ways she's stronger than I feel like I could be.

"You okay, boss?" Gemma walked toward him. There was a curious look on the private eye's face, as if she was seeing more than he was intending to show.

"We've solved the crime and caught the criminal," Finnick said, "and I can't believe you're all here to be a part of it."

"To be fair, our plan was just to surprise you for Christmas Eve dinner while Lucas repaired your windshield," she said.

"Well, sometimes everything just comes together perfectly," Finnick said.

And sometimes exactly the opposite was true.

Gemma stood beside him and watched as Casey disappeared into the crowd.

"I wish I could say that we'll all be fine without you," Gemma said, as if she'd read something deeper in his eyes than he'd even figured out yet how to put into words. "But that wouldn't be true. Our task force only exists because of all your hard work to make it happen, and if you walk away from it now, I don't know how long it will take for someone or something else to step up and take its place. If anything or anyone ever does."

The private detective had always been so incredibly perceptive.

Finnick turned to face her. "Why are you telling me all this?"

"Because I want you to know that I mean it when I say that

as much as every single one of us loves this work and can't wait to get started," Gemma said, "we'll understand if you decide to let the task force go."

Bright Christmas morning sunshine beamed upon Casey's face and dazzled the snow around her as she walked down the narrow path that Finnick had dug between her house and the road. Behind her, the farmhouse was full of more people, joy and activity than she'd ever seen before. Caleb, Lucas and Jackson—along with Hudson and Michigan—had bunked out in the garage with Finnick and Nippy overnight, while Gemma, Amy and her baby, Skye, had stayed with Casey in the house.

Now they were all crowded in her living room and kitchen, coordinating a breakfast out of the remains of what she'd bought at the market and the bags full of groceries the team had had the foresight to bring. And she'd stepped outside to pray.

She took a deep breath and felt the winter air fill her lungs.

How many times have I prayed that You fill this house with people, laughter and joy? And today You have answered my prayers in ways that I never imagined.

A door creaked open and then shut behind her. Footsteps crunched on the snow.

"May I join you?" Finnick asked.

She reached out her hand for him without turning back. He took it. And together they looked out at the morning sky.

"I heard Cameron has already been released from the hospital and will make a full recovery," Finnick said.

"He has," Casey said. "Eileen called me late last night and said they'd see me today."

"Gemma has already managed to get Drew's picture in front of multiple people who are willing to testify that he was the 'Tim' who was dating Ally," Finnick said. "They got the car out of the water last night and fast-tracked the dental record identification overnight. Now, the bodies in the water have been positively identified as Tim and Stella, thanks to their dental records. Patrick has already given a full statement to police."

"Your team is absolutely incredible," she said.

"I know." Finnick said, "which is why I can't leave them. No matter how much something in my heart desperately wishes I could stay here with you—"

"Finnick." She turned toward him. "*I'm* not staying here. I don't know where I'm going to move to, but it's time for me to sell this place and move off the island. All this time, I've been holding on to Tim's dream of raising a family here and trying to make it a reality. But it's time for me to go and find my own dream." Slowly, she pulled her hand from his and wrapped her arm around his waist. "I'm not going to be Casey Thompson anymore."

His hands slid along the small of her back and pulled her closer.

"Do you think, one day, you'd be willing to become Casey Finnick?" he asked, softly.

She nodded, feeling happy tears rush to the corners of her eyes. "Yes, I think I'd like that very much."

A long and happy sigh slid from Finnick's lungs. He leaned toward her and his forehead rested against hers. "You are the only home I ever want," he said. "I love you, Casey."

"I love you too."

Slowly, their lips met in a gentle kiss that grew stronger with every passing heartbeat as he pulled her closer to him and lifted her off her feet.

Then she heard the sound of a car pulling up in front of her house, and her sister, Eileen, called her name. Casey slid slowly out of Finnick's arms and turned around.

Eileen was practically running down the path toward her, tears streaming from her sister's eyes. Casey ran for her and caught her in a hug.

"Eileen?" Casey said. "Are you okay? How's Cameron?"

"He's here," Eileen said. Casey looked over her shoulder. Cameron had stepped out of the car and seemed to be getting something bulky from the back seat. "I'm sorry. It's my fault you never got a foster child."

Casey stepped back as if someone had slapped her. "What? It was your fault?"

"Forgive me, please," Eileen said. "Whenever I got called for a reference, I said I didn't think you were ready. But I was wrong. And either way, it wasn't my place to try to interfere like that."

Then, suddenly, a happy baby's squeal filled the air.

"Joey?"

To Casey's amazement, she turned to see Cameron carefully carrying Joey across the snow toward them. She ran for him, but Finnick reached him first. Cameron slid the little boy into Finnick's strong arms and Casey threw her arms around Finnick and Joey all at once. She brushed a kiss over Joey's face. The baby laughed and pinched her cheek.

She turned to Cameron and Eileen. "I don't understand."

"Joey is my son," Cameron said, his words halting and nervous but shining with truth. "I had a relationship with Ally. But we cut it off when she got pregnant because I was a coward… I was afraid my parents would cut me off and disown me." Eileen sniffed loudly and reached out to grab her son's shoulder. Cameron continued, "So, she lied and told Drew that he was the father, thinking he'd support her financially. That's why I was here outside your house the night you found Joey and ran when you saw me. I knew she was coming here and I wanted to stop her. That's what I was trying to tell you about Ally when Drew attacked me. He suspected that Ally had told me about their relationship."

"Looked like he was trying to tie up all the loose ends," Finnick said.

"That you're Joey's father?" Casey asked, softly.

"Yes, and I have the DNA test to prove it," Cameron said.

She looked to the tiny child in Finnick's arms. "So I'm his great aunt."

"Yes." Cameron stepped away from his mother and grabbed her hand. "But I want him to live here with you. I want you to adopt him and be his mother. And if you want to leave here and go be with Ethan in Toronto, that's good by me too. It's close to my college and I can visit him all the time." For the first time in a long time, she saw a huge and genuine smile cross Cameron's face. "I love you, Aunt Casey, and you're the best possible mother for Joey. I've talked to my parents, and I know they feel that way too."

Casey glanced to her big sister. Happy tears filled Eileen's eyes. Then Casey threw her arms around her nephew and pulled Eileen and Finnick into the hug, and for a long moment, they held each other in the snow. When they finally pulled apart, Eileen said that she and Cameron had to go get ready for the Christmas service. But they would be back later with David and a mountain of food to join in Christmas dinner with Finnick's team.

Then Finnick, Casey and Joey stood together in the snow and watched as they drove away.

She turned to look at Finnick. A tear glistened in the corner of his eye, as he cradled Joey to him.

"Are you all right, Finnick?" she asked.

"Better than I've ever been." He turned to face her and love filled his gaze. "Please promise me that you'll marry me, and I'll never have to go a single day—Christmas or otherwise—without you and Joey in my life."

"I promise. I love you, Finnick."

She stood on her tiptoes and kissed him. He kissed her back. Then they turned toward the farmhouse.

"Don't pretend you're all not watching!" he yelled. "Let Nippy out and come join us!"

Casey laughed, as her farmhouse door opened and Nippy

raced out across the snow toward them, followed by the grinning and clapping members of the Cold Case Task Force.

She felt Finnick's hand take hers and hold it tightly. And she knew with complete certainty in her heart that she'd found a life and a love that was deeper, stronger and more glorious than she'd ever imagined.

* * * * *

Taken At Christmas
Jodie Bailey

MILLS & BOON

Jodie Bailey writes novels about freedom and the heroes who fight for it. Her novel *Crossfire* won a 2015 RT Reviewers' Choice Best Book Award. She is convinced a camping trip to the beach with her family, a good cup of coffee and a great book can cure all ills. Jodie lives in North Carolina with her husband, her daughter and two dogs.

Books by Jodie Bailey

Love Inspired Suspense

Fatal Identity
Under Surveillance
Captured at Christmas
Witness in Peril
Blown Cover
Deadly Vengeance
Undercover Colorado Conspiracy
Hidden in the Canyon

Rocky Mountain K-9 Unit

Defending from Danger

Pacific Northwest K-9 Unit

Olympic Mountain Pursuit

Mountain Country K-9 Unit

Montana Abduction Rescue

Trinity Investigative Team

Taken at Christmas

Visit the Author Profile page at millsandboon.com.au for more titles.

Thine eyes did see my substance, yet being unperfect; and in thy book all my members were written, which in continuance were fashioned, when as yet there was none of them.
—*Psalm* 139:16

To Kay King

You once told me I could be anything I wanted to be...

And I believed you.

Thank you.

Chapter One

Why is that woman carrying a backpack?

Mia Galloway set aside her phone, which displayed the Are you okay? text she'd typed to her daughter's birth mother, Paige Crosby, and tried to breathe normally. The conversations in the crowded café seemed to soak into the dark wood walls, retreating into a dull roar as Mia's anxiety rose. The fact that Paige had asked to meet and was now nearly half an hour late only heightened her tension.

The woman, in her late twenties with a small scar on her temple and tousled blond hair that made it appear she'd just crawled out of bed, wound slowly between the tables, her gaze darting nervously. Something about her was familiar, but the full memory wouldn't form.

What was in the blue backpack held over her shoulder in a white-knuckled grip? Why was she so skittish? Mia's stint in the army had taught her that out-of-place backpacks and nervous strangers meant danger.

And after she became a deputy, a dark November night, lit by flashing red and blue lights, had taught her that not even the home front was safe.

The woman stopped in the center of the room, one hand nervously tapping the backpack's strap.

She was up to no good.

Mia's heart pounded. Sweat sheened her skin. Dark dots swam in her vision. She should sound the alarm before something terrible happened. If she didn't—

The woman's blue eyes locked on to Mia's and narrowed. After a silent stare down, she seemed to almost smile, then turned and darted out, disappearing into the lobby.

Mia gripped the sides of her chair. Had that woman been looking for her? For Paige? Where had she gone?

Outside the plate glass windows that fronted Harvest Café, shoppers strode along the riverwalk, arms laden with bags as they enjoyed the sights and sounds of Christmas in the historic town. The unusually cold weather hadn't kept revelers from clogging Wincombe's downtown.

There was no sign of the woman.

Around her, other diners chatted and laughed as the longing strains of "I'll Be Home for Christmas" drifted down from the speakers. They behaved as though nothing bad could happen here.

But it could.

Mia dug her fingers into the wooden chair. That song brought to mind movies that featured scenes of a soldier fighting a horrific battle intercut with images of a family celebrating joyfully around a tree, smiling unaware as their loved one died a terrible death.

She shuddered. There had been Christmas music pouring through the speakers of the Double R Convenience Store on that November night when—

Shaking off the memory, Mia scanned the room, her emotions screaming for flight while her mind reasoned that it would be foolish to rush out of the restaurant when she had no idea if the danger was real.

She couldn't stay here, though. There were too many people. Too much noise. Too many colors.

Hands shaking, Mia pocketed her phone, tossed a twenty onto the table and bolted for the door, desperate for fresh air. She'd text Paige to meet her at home. What had her daughter's birth mother been thinking when she suggested they meet downtown on the busiest tourist day of the year? She knew how Mia reacted to crowds.

"Ma'am? Are you—"

Mia ignored the hostess's concern and burst onto the sidewalk, letting the door slam behind her as she looked left and right for a place void of the Christmas crowd.

There. An empty bench on the riverwalk offered an oasis amid the people clogging River Street, which had been closed for the upcoming Christmas parade. Hurling herself across the uneven cobblestones, Mia dropped onto the bench and braced her hands on her knees, gulping damp December air until the vise around her chest eased and her thoughts settled.

Shame chased the panic, searing her skin and heart with an entirely different sort of burn.

She was a grown woman. A mother. A former soldier and deputy sheriff. And yet...

She ran from shadows and fled nonexistent threats. That woman had probably reacted to Mia's frightened stare, nothing more.

Turning her face to the sky, she dug her thumbs into her knees. *Come on, God. It doesn't have to be this way. You could make this better. You could take away this fear.*

There was only silence.

Mia sat back and drew another deep breath, desperate not to call attention to herself. Her display in the café had done a fine job of that already. The last thing she needed was for law enforcement to respond to a call about a woman falling apart in the middle of the Christmas cheer.

The festive music and decorations had her emotions spun

up more than usual. That was all. She'd known better than to come to River Street on the Saturday before Christmas. Tourists flocked to the small town of Wincombe on the Inner Banks of North Carolina to shop on the historic streets that reflected the town's colonial village roots, to watch the street parade in the morning and the boat parade on the river after dark. The normally quiet town was nearly burst with people celebrating the season.

She'd hesitated to meet in town, but Paige had been insistent about getting together as soon as possible in a public place and without Ruthie. It was an odd request. Her daughter's birth mother had never been shy about coming by the house, even spending weekends with Ruthie and Mia on occasion. Mia considered Paige to be like a sister, but today Paige had seemed hesitant to speak and had refused an invitation to the house.

Then she'd been a no-show. Mia's concern had already been heightened by Paige's unanswered calls and unread texts when she'd spotted the woman with the backpack. It was a perfect storm of panic, given that Paige was thirty minutes late and the café had grown more crowded as lunchtime neared.

Inhaling another fortifying breath, Mia pulled her cell from her pocket and flicked the screen, sending the Are you okay? text she'd already typed.

Like the four before it, the message went unread.

This wasn't like Paige. A student at East Carolina University, Paige was conscientious and kind, driven to succeed but compassionate at the same time. She would make an amazing social worker after she graduated with her master's degree in the spring, and Mia would be her biggest cheerleader. After all, she owed Paige for one of the greatest gifts in her life.

When Paige had learned she was pregnant as a college freshman, she'd reached out to Mia and her husband, Keith, at their small church, where they had been requesting prayer during their infertility journey. Paige had been bold in asking if they wanted to adopt her unborn child and, after weeks of prayer, they'd agreed.

Although adoption hadn't been on their original agenda, it had turned out to be the exact right plan. Ruthie was now a perfect little four-year-old girl.

But becoming a widow four months after Ruthie's birth hadn't been something Mia had ever imagined.

She'd also never imagined PTSD so severe that it would rip away her career as a Tyrrell County sheriff's deputy.

Mia shuddered and reflexively flicked her finger over the screen to call Paige. Four rings then voicemail. Where was she?

Adrenaline waning, Mia tapped her finger against the screen, calling the one person who would listen to her fears without judgment.

Hayden McGrath answered on the first ring. "What's up?"

Relaxing into the sound of his familiar voice, Mia stared across the Scuppernong River toward where it emptied into the Albemarle Sound. "Paige hasn't shown, and I nearly accused a woman of being a suicide bomber. I'm having a fabulous day. How's my daughter?"

Hayden was Ruthie's godfather and Mia's closest friend. He had been beside her the night her world shattered. He'd been Keith's best friend and her colleague. Hayden and his now former fiancée, Beth, had walked Mia through her darkest days.

"Your daughter conned me out of half of the books in the kids' section at Booker's, then managed to wrangle ice cream out of me at Tastee Cone."

The lighthearted rundown of her daughter's morning eased Mia's tension. "It's barely lunchtime, and she's having cake at Ashley's birthday party later. If she's sick half the night, I'm calling you."

"She's a kid. She'll be fine. I've pumped her up with more sugar than that when you weren't looking."

"You did what?"

Hayden continued like she hadn't spoken. "And she keeps reciting her line for the Christmas play over and over again."

Mia chuckled. "Yeah, she's excited." That was the understatement of the year. The play tomorrow night could not come quickly enough.

"I just dropped her off at Javi's for Ashley's party, and I'm actually headed your way to see if I can find some lunch. What are your plans since Paige hasn't shown?"

"Not going back into Harvest Café, that's for sure." Everyone would eye her with pity or suspicion. She ran her finger along the seam of her jeans. Now that she was in fresh air, the whole incident seemed silly. "I just want out of the crowds." She'd have to head directly through them to get to a quieter, safer place, so she really couldn't win.

"Hey, no putting yourself down. You've been through a lot. From a literal war zone when you were in the army to… Well, it's been a lot, and you're doing great." A stretch of silence let road noise filter through his truck's Bluetooth. "As for Paige, maybe she slept in. Want me to drive by her parents' house and see if she's there? She's home for winter break, right?"

Mia twisted her lip and stood, turning to scan faces as she leaned against the metal railing about ten feet above the river. "Maybe she put her phone on silent and she's just running late. It's nuts down here." The crowd was getting thicker, and it spilled from the street onto the riverwalk. A man's shoulder brushed hers as he passed. Turning toward the river in an effort to ignore the growing mass of humanity, Mia stared into the water, trying to ignore the people clogging the sidewalk. "Don't check up on her like she's a child." Another shopper bumped her back, shoving her against the rail.

"I understand. Hey, when Ruthie and I were in Booker's, I saw their special in the café today is a French dip, your favorite. You're only a couple of blocks away, and they weren't busy. The crowds seem to be concentrated on River Street. Why don't you text Paige that you're headed there, then we can grab a bite while you wait for her. I'll meet you at the end of Watchman's Alley."

Smart. The narrow alley curved between two buildings and was covered by an arched brick roof. It would be quiet, as most people chose the wider sidewalks along Water Street to get to the riverfront.

Mia dashed across the cobblestone street, and her shoulders relaxed as she stepped into the quiet alley. "Hang on." She pulled the phone from her ear, grateful that Hayden understood the PTSD that shadowed her life. Her thumbs tapped the screen. Heading over to Book—

Footsteps pounded into the alley behind her, echoing off the ceiling.

Before she could turn, a force shoved into her back, driving her to the brick floor. Her phone flew from her fingers and skittered along the ground. A palm pressed against her head, grinding her cheek against the gritty bricks.

Mia tried to scream, but the oxygen had been driven from her lungs. Her muscles seized. She couldn't move. Couldn't breathe. Couldn't fight. Reality vanished, and all she could see was Keith in a pool of blood, ripped violently from her life.

Now she was the victim. It was her worst nightmare.

Fight. Fight for Ruthie. Her mind screamed. Her body refused to respond. She had to do something. She couldn't leave her daughter as an orphan. She couldn't—

The weight shifted, and hot breath hit her ear with a deep hiss. "Your daughter deserves better than you."

"Mia?" Hayden McGrath's voice pitched up, echoing off the arched brick roof of Watchman's Alley. What had happened?

He dashed into the dim space and rounded the bend, his heart racing to a frantic beat.

A figure in baggy jeans and an oversize purple East Carolina hoodie pinned Mia face down, a brick raised to smash into her skull.

Hayden's feet stumbled on the uneven brick. "Stop!"

At Hayden's shout, Mia's assailant jerked back. The person pulled the brick higher over their head, increasing the chances a blow would be fatal. Sunglasses covered their eyes. A mask obscured the lower half of their face.

With her attacker off balance, Mia clearly saw a chance to save herself. As Hayden ran closer, Mia bucked, throwing her attacker to the side.

The brick flew, bouncing off the wall before it clattered to the ground.

The person rolled, scrambled up and raced toward River Street.

As Mia leaped to her feet, Hayden dashed past, bursting into the cold sunlight at the end of the alley. He looked left and right along the crowded street.

The mass of people was too thick to spot his target. Multiple tourists sported the iconic purple of East Carolina University, which was only an hour away. No one seemed to be disturbed and nothing seemed out of place, so Mia's attacker had probably slowed when entering the crowd, lowering their hoodie in order to blend in.

Hayden's shoulders slumped. There was nothing he could do. Sure, he would have Mia file a report, open an investigation and wait for the sheriff's department to pull camera footage from the businesses closest to Watchman's Alley, but that would take time.

But in the moment, he'd failed.

"He got away?" Mia appeared beside him, eyeing the crowds she'd been so frantic to escape only moments before. Little had either of them known the multitudes she'd feared had offered her protection.

When Hayden faced her, he winced. A dark red mark marred her cheek, small scratches from the grit on the brick leaving thin red streaks in what would likely be a bruise by morning. He let his hand hover near her face. "Are you hurt?"

Mia jerked back. Her breaths sped up, and she backed into the alley, her eyes on Hayden. "I'm fine. I'm—" But her head swung back and forth as though her body wouldn't allow her to continue the lie.

She was definitely not *fine*. Not when she'd just lived through something very close to both of their worst nightmares.

As though her knees refused to hold her anymore, Mia sank onto a bench halfway up the alley and bent forward, her elbows on her knees. "What just... How did... Hayden?"

He hadn't heard that kind of desperate, helpless plea in her voice since the night Keith was murdered.

There was no way they were going to find her assailant today, and Mia needed him more than he needed to rush into the street to search for witnesses. He went to her, praying no one else would venture into the alley, and knelt in front of her. Resting his hands on top of hers, he bent to look into her eyes.

The fear in her expression nearly undid him.

"Mia, I am so sorry I wasn't here sooner." He should have told her to stay by the river until he reached her. He should have suggested she keep to the crowds instead of venturing into the deserted alley. He should have—

"No." Mia sniffed and raised her head, trying to put on a brave front although her fingers shook beneath his palms. Her skin was so pale that the red bruise and scratches seemed to glow in the semidarkness. "Not your fault." The words trembled. She swallowed hard and sat taller. "I'll be fine."

He knew better than to let her retreat into herself. Over the past four years, she'd become the queen of stuffing things inside to deal with at a later time that never seemed to come. It was the coping mechanism she used to hold panic attacks at bay. Since Keith's murder, she'd lived in a state of extreme fear and mild paranoia. She knew every route to every exit, and she lived in the small spaces that she could control. Crowds were her kryptonite.

Mia also played the guilt game like a champion. Hayden did as well. They'd both been on duty the night the call had come about an armed robbery in progress at the Double R Convenience Store on Highway 64. They'd both responded. If either of them had arrived even one minute earlier, then Keith might be alive today.

Fear and guilt had been unleashed on that night, and they hovered over Mia's life as well as his own.

But this wasn't paranoia. It was real, and Mia needed to face reality if she wanted to get through this, no matter how hard it was.

"Mia, I let you fall into the hands of an opportunist who was waiting for—"

"No." Mia's face collapsed. As if someone had thrown her into a deep freeze, she trembled from head to toe. "No. I messed up. I—" The words rattled and quaked.

Hayden was on the bench beside her in an instant. He wrapped his arms around her and pulled her close to his side. She shuddered as though someone had grabbed her shoulders and was shaking them.

He'd walked her through a panic attack before, but this one felt different.

No, this wasn't a panic attack. When she was in the throes of fear, Mia didn't want to be touched. She preferred to be left alone while she fought the darkness until she regained control. Right now, she seemed to seek safety as she clung to him.

Mia breathed in through her nose and out through her mouth, trying to center herself. The breaths were stuttered, but at least she wasn't hyperventilating.

Hayden waited, his grip on her shoulder tightening. Someone had hurt her, and he wanted to race out into the street to search for the perpetrator and mete out justice. To ask them why anyone would want to take down a seemingly defenseless woman who had already been through more than enough in her lifetime.

With a deep breath that caught in her throat, Mia shook her head. "I froze. I froze and then—"

"It's understandable." He couldn't let her condemn herself over her reaction to a traumatic event, one that was doubly horrible for someone whose life had already been shredded by horrific violence.

"No." Mia jerked free and rocketed to her feet. She whirled on Hayden. "I froze. I couldn't protect myself, not even for Ruthie." Her words echoed off the bricks. "I kept thinking I had to. She could have been an orphan, Hayden. She could have...have lost me today and..." Her eyes widened, and she stepped back as though someone had pushed her. Her face paled as her hands flew to her mouth. "Hayden."

"What?" He stood and reached for her as she swayed, grabbing her upper arms to steady her. "You remembered something."

"That person said..." She lowered her hands, her gaze locked on to his. "Said my daughter deserves better than me."

Hayden's own knees reacted to her words. For a second, it was tough to tell if he was holding Mia up or if she was supporting him. "This was targeted."

"By someone who knows me. Or at least knows about me." She lifted her gaze to the arched brick ceiling. "I have to get to Ruthie." She pulled away from Hayden. "If someone came after me, they might make a run at her, and I can't... If I lose..."

There was nothing more to say. Hayden was right there with her. He'd protect his goddaughter with his life.

Reaching for Mia's hand, he tugged her into a run toward his truck, which was in the parking lot at Booker's. "I'll drive." They made it to the truck and buckled up in record time. He looked both ways before pulling onto Fifth Street. "Call Javi." Ashley's father, who was throwing the birthday party Ruthie was attending, was a deputy who'd worked with both of them. He'd protect Ruthie until they arrived. "Tell him what's happened but caution him to be careful not to alarm the kids. Let him know that no one is to pick Ruthie up except us, no matter who they are or what they say." Javi was a good father and friend who would handle this with care and discretion. "Have him contact the sheriff as well." Everything had happened so fast that he hadn't even considered calling law enforcement. Someone needed to retrieve that brick in case it held evidence that could lead to Mia's attacker.

With trembling fingers and words, Mia made the call, then rested her phone on her knee. "Hay?"

He didn't take his eyes off the road. The uncertainty in her voice spoke the question without her having to ask it out loud. "I don't know if Paige is involved in this, but I hope not." On their run for the truck, the horrible thought had formed. Paige had been a no-show for a lunch with Mia that she'd requested. She was the reason Mia had been downtown.

"She knows I don't do crowds, but she asked to meet me on River Street. I mean—"

"But the woman in the café. How would she know about that? It seems like she might have been a random person."

"But what if she wasn't? What if someone sent her to spook me so I'd run? If someone knows me, they'd know what would push me over the edge. They'd get me to flee, and they'd know I'd take a path out of the crowd. All they'd have to do is follow me."

It seemed like a big risk that depended on a lot of uncontrollable variables. Unless she was right and someone had been watching the whole time, just waiting for a chance. Still… "What would the motive be? Why would Paige set up something like this? You guys have had a great relationship since long before Ruthie was born. She approached you about adopting. She's practically your sister. If she was feeling some kind of way, she'd have told you."

"Maybe." Her voice was uncertain as she dragged her thumb

down the side of her phone. "But if it wasn't Paige, then where is she?"

He wished he knew the answer to that question, because either Paige was behind the attack or she was also in danger.

Chapter Two

For a small town, Wincombe suddenly seemed very large.

Mia wrapped her fingers under her thighs and dug into her jeans. The handful of miles to Javi's house felt like a cross-country road trip. While Hayden pushed the speed limit, he didn't roar over it. The streets were too narrow and often filled with people walking or pushing children in strollers, even during this unusual cold snap.

Still, he could go a little faster. Leaning toward the windshield of Hayden's blue pickup made her feel like she was closer to Ruthie, even though that was foolishness.

"Hey." Hayden's voice was irritatingly calm. "Everything will be fine. Javi won't let anything happen to Ruthie, and I won't let anything happen to you."

It was a nice thought, but Mia didn't relax. She wouldn't be at ease until she had her little girl in her arms.

Maybe not even then.

"So…" The tone in Hayden's voice was familiar. He was shifting into investigator mode. He'd left the sheriff's department not long after she'd stepped away, bruised by Keith's murder but not broken as she had been. For the past three years, he'd been living an hour away in Elizabeth City, working for

Trinity Investigations. The organization worked closely with attorneys and other law enforcement agencies to reinvestigate complicated cases from the beginning, ensuring that no evidence of guilt or innocence had been overlooked before trial. Occasionally, they assisted during complicated investigations, offering additional eyes and minds.

She looked over at Hayden, whose white knuckles betrayed his anxiety. Talking often kept him mentally focused and out of his emotions, so she might as well humor him. Conversation might help her as well. "Ask whatever is on your mind."

He navigated a turn off of Highway 64 onto Raleigh Street, headed toward the river through an older neighborhood. "Can you talk about what happened in the alley? Get the details out before they fade?"

The last thing she wanted to do was relive those awful moments, but he was right. The more she spoke while the memories were fresh, the more she'd be able to offer investigators later. Mia closed her eyes, trying to envision every detail. She walked Hayden through the moments leading up to the attack, forcing herself to look at the scene through an emotionless lens. If she allowed the terror of the moment to invade, it would overwhelm her and shut down her system. "Whoever it was had me pinned. He…" Her hand went to her cheek, the sting at her light touch indicating that a bruise was forming. "Well, you saw. You came in right after he took me to the ground."

"And he said…?" The words were gentle, but steel wound through them. Hayden was angry, but was it at the perpetrator? Or was he upset that he hadn't arrived sooner? He viewed himself as her protector as well as Ruthie's, and he stumbled under the weight of guilt when he believed he'd fallen short.

"It's not your fault." She tried to force the truth across the space between them. He carried so much guilt from the night Keith died. They'd both responded to the call, not realizing that the armed robbery in progress was about to change their lives. Hayden had been the first on the scene, and Mia had pulled into the parking lot less than a minute behind him. All of the reports said Keith was dead before they arrived, but she'd lain awake too many nights wondering what would have happened if she'd driven faster.

How often had she heard Hayden say the same about himself? She couldn't let him carry the burden of today's attack as well.

Hayden spoke before she could. "I asked what the guy said, not who's at fault."

Mia winced at the sharp retort, then bit the tip of her tongue. Neither of them needed to spiral into their emotions. They were raw from the events of the day and from the events of four years ago. "Like I told you, he said, 'Your daughter deserves better than you.'" Her stomach shuddered despite her best efforts to maintain emotional distance. *Why?* Because of the PTSD? Because of the sleepless nights she paced the house? Because she tended to shelter her daughter instead of letting her explore the world around her? Because—

"Mia, listen. No matter what some lowlife says, you're the most amazing mom I know. Don't beat yourself up over some creep's threat." He slowed and turned onto Columbia Drive. "We keep saying *he*. Are you certain it was a man?"

"It wasn't Paige." There was no way. Despite their earlier suspicions, everything about the attack went against Paige's nature.

"I didn't say it was, but I couldn't tell if it was a man or a woman. The oversize sweatshirt, the baggy jeans, the hood, the mask, the sunglasses… Everything happened so fast, it was impossible to tell anything unique about the person. You were the closest, and you keep saying it was a male. I just want you to be sure when you talk to the sheriff."

No matter how hard she tried to remember, there was no way to say for certain. "Given that assaults like this are typically perpetrated by men, I assume it was a male. The words were hissed, so I couldn't describe their voice. They were solid. They were strong, but I can't say with certainty. I can only tell you what my gut says."

As they pulled into Javi's driveway, Hayden scanned the area, searching for threats Mia didn't want to consider. "Go inside and see Ruthie. I'll call Sheriff Davidson and arrange for him to meet us at your house to take your statement." Wincombe was too small for a dedicated police department and relied on the sheriff for law enforcement.

"Okay." As soon as Hayden stopped behind Javi's Bronco, Mia turned for the door.

Hayden's hand on her shoulder stopped her. "I know that I'm not a parent and that you're Ruthie's mom, but you're understandably spun up right now." His grip tightened, though it remained gentle. "Don't frighten her by drowning her with your fear."

If anyone else said such a thing, she'd rage in anger, but Hayden was right. Ruthie had no idea what her mother had endured, either today or on the night her father died. She was simply a four-year-old enjoying a friend's birthday party. The last thing she needed was for her mother to snatch her away from the fun. At her age, being hastily pulled out of a much-anticipated party would be a major event.

Mia needed to slow down and settle for watching her daughter play with the other kids if she wanted to maintain Ruthie's innocence.

She took a deep breath and squared her shoulders. No matter how much she wanted to rush in and pull her child close, she was the mommy. Her daughter would take cues from her. With great effort, Mia shoved her emotions into the dark place where they couldn't touch her and locked them away.

It was the opposite of what her therapist told her to do. Cramming away the emotions made her numb and took her out of the moment, but it was the only way she could get through this without subjecting Ruthie to the trauma of watching her mother fall to pieces.

When she got out of the car, Hayden was already calling the sheriff. They'd find the person who did this to her, and hopefully the ordeal would be over by nightfall.

As soon as Mia's shoes hit the sidewalk, Javi stepped onto the porch, shutting the door behind him. At just over six feet and a regular at the gym, Javi was an intimidating force when he was in uniform. Given that she'd been friends with him and his wife, Celia, for years, he looked more like a big ol' teddy bear to her, especially now, when he was wearing a very ugly Grinch Christmas sweater.

It was almost enough to make her smile.

Javi caught her expression and looked down at his chest. "Yeah, we'll do anything to make our kids laugh, right? Ashley picked this thing out and wanted me to wear it for her fifth birthday." The amusement in his dark eyes disappeared as quickly as it flared. "Ruthie is fine. They're in the den watching Jim Carrey do his Grinch thing since it was too cold for them to play outside. You want to talk about what's going on or go in and see her?"

That was code for *Are you going to freak out the kids, or do you need a minute to pull yourself together?*

"I'm fine. I know Ruthie is safe, and it's enough to be close to her." It would be a different story tonight, when she tried to sleep. The terror would rush in once her house was dark.

But that was a problem for later. "Hayden is with me. He's on the phone with Sheriff Davidson." She gave Javi a quick, bare-facts rundown of the situation.

Javi crossed his arms over his chest, nodding soberly. "I don't blame you for rushing over here. I'd want to get to my kid quick if someone said something like that to me. And no sign of Paige?"

Paige had been a fixture at church and had volunteered often with the children's department. Everyone knew her well, particularly the parents. "I don't think—"

Javi held up his hand. "I didn't say she was involved, but I'm concerned about her. She covered the nursery when Ashley was a baby and worked in the toddler class on Sundays when she was older. Paige is a solid kid. I'm more concerned about—"

"Someone coming after her, too?" It was chilling that Javi's thoughts ran along the same tracks as her own. With Paige not answering her phone and someone directly attacking Mia as a parent, it made sense that Ruthie's birth mother might be in the crosshairs as well, although motive was a sticky question. "I'm not sure what's happening, but—"

A slamming truck door stopped her. "Mia. Javi." Hayden's tone was urgent. Gravel crunched under his feet as he jogged up the driveway. He stopped beside Mia, angling so he could see both her and Javi at the same time.

Something dark furrowed his brow. He wasn't the type to overreact, so whatever the sheriff had said must be bad.

Mia grabbed his elbow. "Is it Paige?"

"Deputy Angeles called the house and talked to her mother. Paige left over an hour ago to meet you." He flicked a glance at Javi, carrying on an unspoken conversation.

"What are you not saying?" Mia's grip on Hayden's elbow tightened. "I'm a big girl, Hay. I used to be a deputy, too, in case you forgot. Don't treat me like a child just because I'm going through some things."

"Some things?" Hayden clamped his mouth shut, seeming to realize the terse comment might have gone too far. "I'm sorry." He pulled his elbow from her grasp and stepped closer as though she might need support. "Deputy Angeles traced the route from her house to River Street, and when he got into town…" He exhaled loudly.

Mia's ears roared. She'd seen Hayden's expression before, and it only came when he was delivering bad news. "What?"

"Angeles found Paige's car in the lot at the end of River

Street. There are signs of a struggle. Her phone and purse are in the back seat. Mia, I'm sorry. It looks like Paige may have been kidnapped."

"I'm really not sure what's happening, Elliott, but I don't think I need you to send in some kind of geared-up quasi SWAT team." Pressing the phone tighter to his ear, Hayden stepped farther into Mia's backyard, away from the stairs that led to the covered wooden deck. Although Mia was inside the house, the last thing he needed was for her to come outside and overhear this conversation with his boss. They'd come here to await the sheriff after letting Ruthie enjoy the remainder of the party.

He walked farther onto the wide lawn that ran to the river. Although the water view was obscured by a privacy fence, the soft sound of the Scuppernong making its lazy way to the Albemarle Sound whispered in his ears.

Normally, the melody of the water was relaxing, but not today. After all that had happened over the past few hours, it only served to grate his nerves.

Over the phone, Elliott Weiss, founder of Trinity Investigations, chuckled. Somehow, every time he did that, it sounded slightly sarcastic. The former Special Forces soldier carried a healthy dose of cynicism, and it bled into most of his interactions so that even his humor seemed laced with it. Still, he was a good boss and a better friend, one of the few people in the world whom Hayden trusted completely.

"Nothing's funny, man." Hayden wasn't in the mood for humor or sarcasm.

"So the comment that implied I was going to go full battle rattle and come fast-roping out of a Chinook onto the roof of Mia's house wasn't supposed to be funny?"

"Not really. It was more of a—"

"Warning?" Elliott's deep voice held a thin thread of amusement. "I get it, McGrath. We all know I can be a little too full-steam-ahead sometimes. I freely admit it." His tone turned serious. "You can tell me what's going on, but I reserve any promises about how I'll respond until the end."

It was tough to tell if Elliott would be hands-off, but Hayden needed to talk to someone who wasn't involved. He'd never get his head cleared otherwise.

Walking to the fence, he flicked the padlock on the gate, then leaned against the wood slats, facing the house so that he would see Mia if she stepped outside. She was already keyed up waiting for someone to come and take her statement about the attack. She refused to stop cleaning the downstairs while Ruthie napped.

Overhearing the full details surrounding Paige's disappearance would only make things worse.

Hayden ran down a quick summary of the attack on Mia and their race to Javi's. After a peek at Ruthie so she could see for herself that her daughter was safe, Mia had stayed at the party while Hayden went to speak with Sheriff Davidson and Deputy Angeles, whom he'd worked with in the sheriff's department. What they'd told him and what he'd seen...

He dragged his hand down his face, wishing he could erase the images.

"So you're certain this thing with Mia was targeted?" A soft scratching in the background indicated that Elliott had pulled his trademark yellow legal pad from his desk drawer and was making notes with a sharpened number two pencil. The man might only be in his late thirties, but he was old-school through and through.

"It had to be. Mia was alone, yet her attacker specifically mentioned her daughter. If nothing else, they've seen the two of them together before. Whoever it was, they would have cracked her skull open with that brick if I hadn't gotten there when I did. That seems personal." Hayden leaned forward, trying to relieve the slight nausea that plagued him. He'd been too late to save Keith, and he'd nearly been too late to save Mia, but he couldn't think about that now. There was too much at stake to risk losing focus. "It gets a lot worse."

"Go on." Elliott was still writing.

Hayden waited for him to finish, hunching his shoulders against a stiff breeze that blew between the fence slats. He should have grabbed his coat. "I left Mia at Javi's and was on-site at a distance while they processed Paige's car." He almost wished he'd stayed away. "It's not just that they found her phone and her purse. There was blood. Lots of blood." Almost as much as the night Keith had been shot.

Elliott's sigh was heavy. "Too much?"

"Hard to tell. I wasn't allowed to get too close, and you know how a little can look like a lot, but... It was enough to concern me. Obviously, we won't know whose blood it is until lab results come back, but the facts point to it being Paige's. If it is, she may not have survived whatever happened to her."

"Let's operate on the assumption that it's hers. Given what we know, that's the most likely scenario. Was it in the passenger's seat or driver's seat?"

"Passenger's."

"So if it's Paige's blood, she wasn't driving the car."

"No. And here's what I don't understand... How did someone get to her when she was parked in the lot at the end of River Street? How did no one see anything? The lot was swarming with people. If someone wanted to hurt her or take her, they'd have done it somewhere secluded. Her house is surrounded by trees and set back from the road. She drives up an isolated strip of two-lane road with woods on both sides in order to get to downtown."

"You're too close to this. Take a step back and get your emotions out of the way."

When Hayden had resigned from the sheriff's department after Keith's murder, questioning his abilities and instincts, he'd reached out to a buddy from his army days, seeking guidance. Elliott had just started Trinity Investigations, and he'd been happy to bring an old friend into the fold. He'd funded Hayden's training as an investigator, putting him through classes and working with him on cases. Technically, Hayden was the junior investigator on the team of seven, and Elliott was always working on ways to hone their skills.

Hayden exhaled and closed his eyes. He tried to treat the scene as though he'd seen it in a textbook, as though it was a puzzle to be solved, not as the place where Ruthie's birth mother had likely been in danger...or worse.

He'd been standing about twenty feet away, so the details were fuzzy, but it wasn't always the details that mattered. The important thing to look at here was the actions of the criminal.

He replayed his conversation with one of the deputies, who'd pointed out that the area where the car was parked was beneath a tree in a blind spot to the cameras at either end of the lot. While there might be a shot of the car pulling into the lot, it was likely the cameras wouldn't have been able to pick up the car after it parked.

A shot of the car pulling in...

Hayden's eyes flew open. "Paige probably wasn't attacked in the parking lot. She was probably never even near it. She was attacked somewhere else, then someone moved her car because they wanted to throw us off."

"Those are my thoughts as well." The background was silent. Elliott had stopped writing.

Hayden could practically see him studying his notes. While the man had been a more than capable SF operator, his mind had always been one that noticed details and put together puzzles. "There's another angle to consider. It's possible that Paige's disappearance isn't about her at all. It's possible it's meant to serve as a threat to Mia or Ruthie."

"But why?" Hayden slumped against the fence. "Wait a second..." Was this more about Ruthie than Mia? "Ruthie's birth father is a guy named Blake Darby. He and Paige dated for several years, and he fully supported the adoption, but what if he's having second thoughts?" Bile nearly gagged him. "What if he wants to take her for himself?"

"I'd say that's a stretch if he's never expressed regret, but it's not out of the realm of possibility. I'm sure he's already on the sheriff's radar, given that he was the boyfriend. He's the first one they'll look at in Paige's disappearance, even though he has no history of violence. I will say it's a good thing you're in town, though. Sounds to me like Ruthie and Mia are going to need you now more than they ever have." Elliott cleared his throat. "Speaking of that…have you told Mia why you're really there?"

"Not yet. I told her I came home early for Christmas." Although he'd received his assignment several weeks ago, every time he'd tried to tell Mia about it, the words had choked him. He'd arrived at his parents' house the night before and had told Mia he'd take Ruthie for the morning so she could meet Paige, but he'd said little else. "I was planning to sit down with her after I brought Ruthie back home this afternoon, but now…" He dragged his hand across his face, his palm scrubbing against stubble. "It might be too much for her to hear right now."

"Time won't make it easier."

The sound of tires crunching gravel pulled Hayden's attention toward the front of the house, where the lights atop a sheriff's department SUV were just visible over the front privacy fence. He should go inside to give his statement and to support Mia as she gave hers.

Then he'd have to find a way to tell her that Trinity Investigations had sent him to Wincombe on an assignment that might just tilt her world and catapult them both straight into darkness.

Chapter Three

Mia shut the door behind Sheriff Davidson as he left and leaned her forehead against the cool painted steel. She'd rehashed the morning so many times that the telling had become rote. Far from being overwrought, she was drained. Between the attack and Paige's disappearance, her emotional capacity was drained. She couldn't *feel* any more.

She was simply exhausted. Although it was only five in the evening, she was ready for bed.

Except she wasn't. Once she shut off the lights and pulled the blankets to her chin later this evening, the day's images would hunt her in the darkness, chased by wild conjectures of what might be happening to Paige. The night hours would drag on for sleepless years.

Footsteps rushed in thuds across the hardwood entry, and tiny arms wrapped around her thighs. "Mommy!"

Despite everything, Mia smiled. Lately, she heard *Mommy* shouted more than spoken. She leaned down to pull her daughter's head against her stomach and wrapped her arms around precious little shoulders. No matter how tumultuous life was, she needed to paste on a brave face for her daughter.

"Ruthie!" Mia yelled in return, then planted a kiss on Ruthie's sandy-blond hair. "How about you find your inside voice and drag it out from wherever it's hiding?"

Ruthie giggled and whispered loudly, "Is this better?"

"Very nice. Now, what do you need?"

Wriggling away, Ruthie planted her hands on her hips and looked up with a very serious expression. "Can we have hamburgers for dinner?"

Mia mimicked her posture. "Is that a Ruthie request or an Uncle Hayden request?" Left to her own devices, Ruthie would eat fish sticks with mac and cheese for every meal, every day. Hayden, on the other hand, referred to himself as a "meat-at-arian." All red meat, all the time.

Ruthie's head tilted, and she pursed her lips. It was a look that said *Do I tell the truth or do I make up a wild story?*

That child had a tell that gave her away every time. Mia smiled. "The truth, little ma'am."

Ruthie wrinkled her nose. "An Uncle Hayden request, but he said he'd make them on the stove like Noni does."

"Well, since he wants to do the cooking, how can I refuse?" If he was going to fry burgers like her grandmother did, then she was all in. Noni soaked bread in milk, chopped up onions, then mixed it all together with ground beef. She fried the patties until crispy edges—

Her mouth watered at the thought of her favorite comfort food, and she smiled at the thought of Noni, who'd arrive on Christmas Eve. Although her parents were out of town on a Christmas cruise, they'd celebrate quietly with her grandmother.

"Yay!" Clapping her hands, Ruthie bounced on her tiptoes, then bolted up the hallway into the kitchen, screaming Hayden's name.

Mia shook her head. Anyone would think the idea had been Ruthie's. That girl would do just about anything for "Uncle Hayden." Since he'd moved to Elizabeth City to work for Trinity, they saw him less often, which meant his visits were more of a reason for Ruthie to get spun up.

Having Hayden in town for a few days allowed Mia to breathe easier, even after the drama of her morning and her concern for Paige. Hayden staying close by at his mom's house on Eighth Street always tended to make her feel a little more secure.

That was a phenomenon she didn't want to read too much into.

After double-checking that she'd turned the dead bolt, Mia wandered through the house, closing the plantation blinds. Detouring through the living room, she plugged in the Christmas tree, and the white lights glowed against the soft white walls, dark hardwoods and denim-blue furniture.

If she had her way, she'd avoid decorating for the holiday, but Ruthie deserved to celebrate like other little girls who hadn't violently lost their fathers two days after Thanksgiving. So for a few weeks a year, she managed to grin and bear it as her refuge became a reminder.

After Keith's murder, PTSD had driven Mia inside with uncontrolled agoraphobia. She had taken out her excess emotions on the remodel she and Keith had planned but had never found time to complete. She'd worked with her father to polish the dark hardwoods. They'd painted the walls a cheerful white, and she'd scoured the internet for deals on decor that gave the home an airy waterfront vibe.

When a colony of bees had settled behind the siding, she'd opted to have the entire exterior of the house redone as well. While it had been a circumstance she hadn't foreseen and an interesting journey, it had afforded her the opportunity to create a "new" home from her "old" one. It was truly her safe space.

Although she was now able to venture out, life was anything but "normal." She maintained careful control, knew all of the exits and was always on edge, waiting for the next panic attack to stop her in her tracks. Her home remained the one place she felt truly safe.

Keith's life insurance had provided enough to care for herself and Ruthie, but she ached to work again, to move forward into the detective position she'd always longed for.

Given the certainty of diving into violent crimes like the one that had stolen her husband, a return to her career was impossible. She envied Hayden's job, although he sometimes dealt with cases she'd never be able to handle.

When she made her way to the kitchen, Hayden was alone at the large island. He looked at home amid the dark hardwoods and white cabinets. He looked kind of handsome in his green Henley.

Not that she'd ever tell him that.

Mia slid onto the bench in the U-shaped breakfast nook by the bay window, where Hayden had already closed the blinds. "Where's Ruthie?"

He looked up from slicing an onion. "Upstairs. She stole my phone and started a video call with Noni." As assortment of veggies from her fridge were scattered across the deep blue granite counter. "Apparently, she doesn't trust that I know what I'm doing in the kitchen and needs confirmation. Also, that kid works my phone better than I do. It's embarrassing."

"Which is weird, because I never let her play with my phone. Could it be that somebody else in this kitchen has handed theirs over too many times when the chattering from the back seat got out of control?"

Hayden scanned the ceiling with exaggerated innocence, then looked at her. "I called my mom. She's running by the store to pick up the stuff for burgers and bringing my things over from her house. I'm bunking on your couch tonight. You and Ruthie shouldn't be alone."

Mia didn't protest. As much as she wanted to argue that she could take care of herself, there was no denying that danger lurked closer than she cared to admit. She and Ruthie would be safer with Hayden here. She'd also sleep better with him in shouting distance.

It wouldn't be the first time he'd camped on her couch. It had happened so often when he lived in town that she'd purposely bought an extra-deep sofa so he could be relatively comfortable.

Mia fingered the fringe of a blue-and-white-striped place mat. Hayden was a better friend than she deserved. He certainly sacrificed more for her and Ruthie than she could ever repay.

Hayden cleared his throat. "I need to talk to you about something."

The shift in his tone lifted her head. Was he finally going to tell her everything he'd learned about Paige's disappearance? It was obvious he was holding back details.

Hayden slid the onions onto the plate, then grabbed a tomato, intently creating perfectly even slices. "There's a reason I'm in town, and it's not because of Christmas."

Mia's fingers froze, his words not remotely close to what she'd expected. Given that the multiple shocks of the day had shorted out her ability to react, his tone pooled dread in her stomach rather than inciting panic. Was something wrong with his parents? With him?

What would happen if she lost her closest friend? She wasn't sure she could survive another bout with grief.

Hayden glanced up, then returned his focus to the tomato. "Trinity caught an assignment from the State Bureau of Investigation. The SBI is putting together a case against an organized crime ring, and they want an outside party to reinvestigate a handful of crimes that may be tied to the ring."

She wasn't sure where he was headed with this conversation. Hayden had worked several investigations for Trinity, looking back through cases as though they were brand-new so that law enforcement or attorneys could be certain no details had been missed. There was no need for him to be so concerned, unless—

Her hand went to her mouth. "Keith." Her late husband's name breathed between her fingers.

Laying the knife aside, Hayden braced his hands wide on the counter. "The SBI has tied together a string of armed robberies and have linked them to a drug ring. They aren't certain if the robbery on the night of Keith's death is connected. Since it's unsolved, they want everything looked at again to see if they're onto something or if they're tilting at windmills. Since I was on scene that night, Elliott asked if I could take point."

Curling her lips between her teeth, Mia stared at the shuttered windows. Though she'd thought her feelings were squashed by the overwhelming stress of the day, the pain that washed over her was sharp, drawing tears. "So they might finally know who killed him?"

Hayden was quiet so long, she looked over at him. He hadn't moved, but he watched her intently. "I can't comment on an investigation other than to tell you that it's happening."

After four years, there might be a lead in the shooting death of her husband. Numb, Mia slipped off the bench and mechanically made her way upstairs, pausing outside Ruthie's door.

Her daughter chattered away to her great-grandmother, who lived on the other side of the state in Flat Rock.

The pain ebbed and flowed, a sickening cycle of grief and numbness as suffering tried to break through her spent emotions.

She shut the door to her room and sank to the chair in the corner. Bracing her elbows on her knees, she buried her face in her hands.

Downstairs, the doorbell rang.

She ignored it. Hayden would let his mother in. She wasn't up to polite conversation.

Hayden's words had unlocked the memories she typically held at bay. On the night Keith was murdered, Hayden had just come on duty and she had been about to call it a night. Thanks to a rash of holiday-partying-impaired drivers, she'd worked overtime.

Keith had left the house around eleven to pick up the diapers she should have brought home. He'd assured her he was fine, but mom guilt was real. She'd only been back on shift for a couple of weeks after taking time off for Ruthie's birth, and it had been tough being away.

When the call came about a silent alarm at the Double R Convenience Store on Highway 64, she'd sped toward the scene and had arrived right after Hayden. The store had gas pumps and entrances on two sides, with the cash register situated in the center of the convenience store. Through the front windows, a masked gunman paced in front of the cashier, waving a pistol, his shouts muffled by the glass.

They'd thought no one else was in the store until Hayden had moved to the street side of the building while Mia circled around to the second entry on the back side, keeping to the shadows at the edges of the lot.

She'd frozen when she saw Keith's Ford Explorer parked near the second entrance.

On the other side of the glass door, her husband lay near the register, blood pooling beneath him and Ruthie's baby carrier beside him.

She had few memories past that point.

Hayden had found her on her knees, frozen in shock, after backup roared onto the scene.

The shooter had disappeared on foot.

Mia rocketed to her feet, fighting nausea. She hadn't rushed forward to help her husband or her baby. She hadn't been strong enough to rescue them.

No, she'd collapsed.

And because she'd failed, Keith's killer had escaped.

Her husband was dead…

Because of her.

* * *

After a relatively quiet dinner and an evening fueled by Ruthie's emotional overload, the house was finally quiet. Hayden opened the wide plantation blinds that covered the French doors. The living room was lit only by a soft night-light that glowed through the arched opening to the kitchen, so the night outside was clearly visible. With the house elevated nearly one story to protect from potential river flooding, he could see the moonlight sparkling on the river, though the low bank was obscured by the privacy fence.

He skirted the coffee table and dropped onto the sofa that faced the doors. Sitting back against the cushions, he stared out at the water and the stars above it. He was avoiding his closed laptop, which rested in the center of the square white barnwood coffee table.

At least with the blinds open, the house didn't feel so much like a walled-off prison.

In fact, with the inside lights off, the moonlight outside shone brighter, revealing a night that was clear and calm and beautiful.

If only the home's interior had been that peaceful.

Ruthie had been so keyed up after dinner that it had taken Mia over an hour to get her ready for bed. It was likely the little girl had picked up on the tension in the adults without being able to articulate what she was feeling. For nearly an hour, she'd repeatedly shouted her lines for the upcoming church Christmas play, insisting they listen. When Mia put her in time-out, she continued to recite. After a splashing bath that Hayden had cleaned up while Mia handled her daughter's screaming hissy fit, Ruthie had finally dropped off sometime after ten.

About fifteen minutes ago, shortly before one, the floors in Mia's room had stopped creaking. The sounds from above his head said she'd paced for a long time before settling. Hopefully, she'd fallen asleep, though he wasn't sure how likely that was. Today had been horrific for her, starting with the attack and Paige's disappearance, then ending with his news about a possible lead on Keith's killer.

He should have waited to drop that bomb, but he felt guilty keeping it from her. She deserved to know he would be digging into the night that had derailed her life and had shifted his onto an entirely different track.

Dragging his hands down his face, Hayden stared into the night.

Although search teams were out in force, there was no news about Paige. Javi had texted shortly after midnight to pass along what little he'd learned. A team had spent the afternoon investigating the two-lane back road that Paige had traveled from her house, as it was the likeliest scene of an attack, but there was no intel yet.

Cameras near the downtown parking lot had picked up Paige's car entering with only a driver, but glare prevented them from seeing details through the windshield. Only the steering wheel had been clear, and the person wore gloves. They'd idled at a partial blind spot in the lot until a space opened under the trees where the camera's view was obstructed. After that, they'd apparently slipped away through backyards and alongside streets, because they were never caught on camera again. The sheriff's department was seeking doorbell camera videos from along the street, though they weren't hopeful. Clearly, whoever had ditched the car knew enough to avoid video detection, so they were familiar with the area or had studied it beforehand. This wasn't a random attack. Someone had clearly targeted Paige and possibly Mia.

All of the evidence indicated that Paige's attacker had parked the car and vanished about ten minutes before Mia's assault. That was plenty of time to make it to the alley.

Hayden stretched his neck, mentally walking the route from the parking lot to Watchman's Alley. There were a lot of moving pieces that had to fall into place just right for this to be the work of a single perpetrator. Additionally, he couldn't conceive of a clear motive for a coordinated attack on Mia and Paige. The only connecting link was Ruthie, but no one had come after his goddaughter while she was in his care or Javi's.

Nothing made sense.

Dropping his head to the back of the couch, Hayden stared at the dark ceiling. *Lord, please bring Paige back to her family safely. We need some sort of clue. Something to lead us to where Paige is and to who's behind this.*

He curled his lip. Yeah, that was a familiar prayer. He'd prayed for information so many times over the past four years. He'd argued with God again and again over why Mia and Ruthie had lost Keith, especially so soon after the adoption was finalized.

Maybe investigating Keith's death for Trinity was the answer to that prayer. The county had done a thorough investigation and had come to a dead end, but perhaps fresh eyes would yield something worthwhile.

If he could do this.

Sitting up, Hayden slid to the edge of the couch and pulled his laptop closer, resting his fingers on the top of the case. The files it contained seemed to burn his skin. He hadn't expected the text from Elliott that had come during dinner. The one that said the state had sent security camera footage from the night of the murder.

Footage Hayden had never watched. The pain of losing his best friend had been too sharp.

He'd grown up with Keith Galloway. They'd played together in the nursery at Riverside Christian Church from the moment they were old enough to walk. They'd gone to school together from pre-K all the way to high school graduation. They'd been the closest of friends and had remained tight even when Hayden joined the military and Keith went to ECU to get his degree in cybersecurity.

While Hayden had spent six years defending the country

against the physical worst that her enemies could attack with, Keith had spent those same years defending against the technological worst that her enemies could devise. He'd taken a job with the state of North Carolina, working remotely from home and occasionally traveling to monitor network infrastructure for the Department of Transportation.

Keith and Mia had dated since middle school, parting ways only when he left for college. Mia had been two years younger than Hayden and Keith, though she'd returned from her four years in the military around the same time as Hayden returned from his six. Although Keith and Mia had been apart for several years, they'd picked up where they'd left off, marrying within months of their reunion. Still longing to serve, she'd joined Hayden as a deputy in the Tyrrell County Sheriff's Department.

Maybe if he'd kept his mouth shut about how much he loved being a deputy and how good it might be for her...

Hayden jerked his hands from the computer, then stood and walked to the door. *No.* Those were mental paths he couldn't wander. If Mia hadn't been on duty, then *she* might have been the one on a late-night diaper run when the robbery went down. Or Keith could have died another way. Or any number of a thousand possibilities.

So many verses in the Bible said that God knew what was going to happen in their lives from before they were born. If he believed that was true, then why did he lie awake at night wrestling with why horrible things happened?

With a heavy sigh, Hayden turned his back on the night beyond the glass and stared at his laptop in the near darkness. He'd volunteered to take point on this investigation, needing to see justice for Keith. Needing to find closure. Needing to atone for his failures.

He hadn't considered the emotional toll diving into the past would take on him. While he should have known he'd be given access to the video that documented Keith's final moments, the thought hadn't crossed his mind until Elliott's message dinged into his inbox.

Crossing to the couch, Hayden eased onto the cushion, opened the laptop and keyed in his password. He logged on through a virtual private network, then navigated to his work email and opened Elliott's last message. Sliding the pointer to the video attachment, he let his finger hover over the track pad.

This was what it felt like to teeter on the brink. Once he watched the footage, he'd never be able to unsee it.

He pulled his hand into his lap. That night already dripped evil over his nightmares. Once he pressed Play, the horror of Keith lying face down in his own blood would cease to be a static image. He'd have the sound of the gunshot and the motion of Keith's last breath seared into his brain.

He should call Elliott and tell him he couldn't do this. With immediate danger closing in on the two people he cared most about in the world and with Paige missing, this storm was already bigger than he could handle. He should take a leave of absence and help Mia deal with what was swirling around her in the present.

He should not open an emotional can of worms from the past. They might turn out to be poisonous snakes that could devour all of them.

But nobody else at Trinity had firsthand knowledge of that night. If he wanted to bring Keith's killer to justice and bring closure to Mia and to himself, then he needed to set his emotions aside and face the past.

Tilting his head, he listened to be sure Mia wasn't roaming the house. The last thing either of them needed was her walking into the living room to the sights and sounds of her husband's murder.

With a silent garbled prayer for his stomach to endure what he was about to view, Hayden clicked on the attachment.

The video played automatically though silently. He couldn't bring himself to turn up the laptop's volume. He needed to absorb the scene one sense at a time. He'd play it for as long as he could, then stop until he was ready to start again. The first time through would be the worst.

Hayden leaned forward, elbows braced on his knees and fingers clasped so tightly they ached. His body tensed as the gunman entered the store, his sweatshirt hood pulled over his head and a blue medical mask covering the lower half of his face.

The cashier behind the counter tensed, watching intently as the man wandered the aisles.

What was the gunman waiting for?

Hayden's eyebrows drew together. Was he trying to gather his courage? Waiting for a signal from someone outside? Most armed robbers got in and out as quickly as possible. This guy was either an amateur or he had an agenda.

Given the fact that this case might be linked to organized crime, the "amateur" angle likely wouldn't pan out.

But why was this guy wandering the aisles?

Headlights swept the windows near the side of the convenience store, capturing the cashier's attention.

Hayden's hand shot forward and smacked the space bar, pausing the scene. His breaths came rapidly. His palms dampened with sweat. His heart pounded.

Keith was about to walk into the store holding baby Ruthie's carrier.

He had reached the last moments of his best friend's life, captured forever on video.

Hayden closed his eyes. Maybe he couldn't do this. Maybe—

A distant thump sounded from the backyard.

Hayden jumped up as the laptop screen timed out and went dark. He walked around the coffee table to the door as he strained to hear over the sound of his own heartbeat. Maybe he'd imagined it. Maybe Mia or Ruthie had gotten out of bed. Maybe—

A shadow moved near the rear gate in the privacy fence,

eerie and shapeless in the blue moonlight. Something on their clothing caught the light, then went dark.

Someone was in the yard…

And they were headed for the house.

Chapter Four

The shadow moved slowly and deliberately, keeping close to the tall wooden privacy fence. The person appeared to be carrying something heavy in one hand, leaning with the weight of their burden.

This was a foe and not a friend, and they'd worked hard to gain entry to Mia's backyard. Mia kept heavy-duty padlocks on the front and rear gates of the privacy fence. There was no way someone had managed to unlock the fence from the outside, so that noise he'd heard had probably been an intruder scaling the fence or removing slats in order to slip through.

He clenched his fists and eased closer to the door, keeping to the side to watch the figure's slow approach. A flash of light occasionally bounced off the person's shirt and pants. *Odd.* Anyone sneaking in should want to be invisible, not...reflective? They almost seemed to be wearing the kind of reflective tape that runners used in order to be seen at night. Why?

Hayden forced himself to focus on the bigger problem. He had no way to defend himself. His investigative position with Trinity didn't require carrying a firearm. Although he kept one locked away at his house, he hadn't imagined he'd need to bring it to Wincombe to defend Mia and Ruthie.

All he had was training and the element of surprise. Combatives in the army had taught him some hand-to-hand techniques, but he was definitely rusty.

Hopefully it would be enough.

If he went out the French doors, he risked immediate confrontation, because he'd be visible from the trespasser's position. His only option was the door that led out of the kitchen onto the side deck. If he could slip out quietly, he could stay low as he circled the deck, using the railing to partially camouflage his movements. That should allow him to make it down the stairs to ground level without being spotted.

If he revealed his presence, he lost his only advantage.

With a prayer for safety, he padded across the hardwood in his socks and grabbed his phone from the coffee table. In the kitchen, he texted Javi to come quickly and to run silent. It was quicker to reach out to a buddy on duty than to deal with the emergency call center and dispatch.

Pocketing the phone, he made his way to the door. He should probably wait for help to arrive, but if he hesitated, the fight might make its way into the house. While he should probably alert Mia, he didn't want to pull his attention from the intruder, and he didn't want to traumatize her if he didn't have to. Hopefully, he could handle this and have the bad guy hauled away with minimal fanfare.

Grabbing the spare key off the counter as he passed, Hayden stopped in front of the alarm keypad. Entering the code would cause the keypad to chime. Hopefully, it wouldn't alert Mia. He held his breath as he beeped through the code, then hesitated.

No sound came from above.

Exhaling, he grabbed the key from the drawer and slipped it into the lock. The click of the dead bolt sounded like a gunshot in the silent kitchen, though it was unlikely the sound traveled. He pocketed the key and eased onto the porch, locking the door behind him. Crouching below the level of the deck railing, he crept along until he made his way to the rear of the house.

After several breathless moments, he spotted a quick flash of light in an open space near the house. The intruder had left the shelter of the fence and was making his way quickly across the open side yard. Likely, they were heading for the porch stairs.

They'd be surprised when they realized Mia had installed a shoulder-high locked gate at the foot of the stairs.

As the figure disappeared from view, Hayden moved to the top step and pressed his back to the wall, waiting for the person below to rattle the locked gate.

Silence.

Where was he? Hayden eased down a few steps, listening. There was only a slight rustle near the gate, barely audible in the cold, silent night.

Were they trying to access the garage under the house? Would they scale the fence and try to circle around to enter through the front door? That would be foolish, putting them in view of the street. What was the—

A sloshing sound rose from ground level. Within seconds, a familiar, horrifying odor wafted past.

Gasoline.

Hayden pressed tighter against the wall about halfway down the steps, his heart racing. This guy wasn't trying to come inside.

He was attempting to smoke them out.

If he set fire to the house, it would force Mia and Ruthie out. They'd run outside in a panic without a plan, making them easy targets.

There was no way Hayden would let that happen. This house was Mia's safe place. Not only was it his responsibility to protect her and Ruthie, it was also his duty to protect the one place where she felt secure.

No longer caring if he was heard, Hayden raced down the wooden steps, his footfalls clattering against the wood. He hit the gate at the bottom hard, then stopped to listen. The sloshing had stopped, but he had no idea where the person had gone.

There wasn't time to figure it out.

Flipping the dead bolt, Hayden shoved the heavy wooden gate with all of his strength.

The door collided with something hard.

A muffled grunt and a curse told Hayden he'd struck a blow. He stepped around the door to find a person scrambling to their feet.

Balling his fists, he addressed the figure, who wore what appeared to be baggy pants and a bulky coat. "Get up. Now." Javi would be here soon. All he had to do was keep this guy from lighting a match or getting away.

This ended now.

The person paused, head bent. Rising slowly, they moved their hands to their neck, pulling something up over the lower half of their face. Based on the person's broad-shouldered bulk and stance, he was dealing with a man.

Moonlight glittered off reflective strips on the person's jacket and at his ankles.

Was he wearing…? Hayden squinted. Was he wearing turn-out gear?

Sure enough, when the guy came to his feet, hands out to the sides, the dim light revealed the heavy baggy pants and bulky jacket of a firefighter.

What was happening here?

The two men squared off. Although the other guy had a couple of inches of height advantage, Hayden wasn't worried. The heavy gear would hamper his opponent in a fight.

The man flexed his fists.

"I wouldn't if I were you." Hayden pulled himself to his full height. "The sheriff is already on the way. This is over."

"Not by a long shot." The man growled and lunged at Hayden, driving him backward against one of the thick posts that lofted the porch one story off the ground.

Hayden's head cracked against the heavy wood, and he stumbled forward, shaking his head to get his bearings while stars whirled in his vision.

It was enough to give his attacker the advantage. The man shoved Hayden in the chest, pushing him backward into the plastic trash cans beside the house, the clatter deafening. As Hayden scrambled in the heap of bins, the man ran for the back gate.

Hayden stumbled to his feet and gave chase, but the guy had too much of a head start.

He squeezed through the space where two slats had been removed. Just as Hayden reached the fence, the sound of a small engine reached his ears.

Hayden staggered out onto a narrow river beach, his socks sinking in damp dirt. A small fishing boat with an outboard motor roared across the river, headed for the other side.

Hayden balled his fists and fought the urge to punch the privacy fence. An injured hand wouldn't help Mia. It wouldn't bring that guy back. It wouldn't end this war.

His shoulders slumped with the weight of failure. By the time the sheriff's department got boats on the water, that guy would be long gone.

Hayden trudged toward the house, trying to shake off the blow. He needed to alert Javi, then find Mia's tools and repair the fence.

"Hayden?" Mia's voice rained down from the deck above. "What's happening?"

He couldn't look up. His head spun and his stomach whirled, possibly from the blow against the piling.

But more likely, because he knew what he was.

A failure.

Once again, he'd failed to protect Mia and her family from life-threatening danger.

Mia wrapped her arms around herself as she leaned against the door frame of Ruthie's room, watching her daughter sleep in the soft glow of the dolphin-shaped night-light Hayden had bought on one of their outings.

The heavy sweatshirt she'd pulled on before she rushed onto the deck was too warm to wear inside, but she felt safer in layers, as though the bulk of the fabric provided protection. It was as foolish as tucking her foot under the blankets to keep the "monsters under the bed" at bay, but she wasn't above psychological self warfare if it helped hold her together.

Male voices drifted from downstairs, low and urgent. Hayden was giving a statement to Javi, but she wasn't sure she wanted the answers to what the horrible noise outside had been, why Hayden had been in the backyard in his pajamas or why he'd called Javi.

And worst of all…why the fire department had arrived to deal with a "gasoline spill."

Her brain did a fabulous job of piecing the images together into a picture of terror. Her imagination worked so well that she'd bolted up the stairs to check on Ruthie, who was sleeping peacefully despite the noise.

She wanted to bar the doors and windows so they'd be locked inside this house, the one place where she'd always felt nothing bad could reach them.

Mia hugged her stomach tighter. After tonight, she'd never feel that way again.

If she lost the refuge of her home, what did she have left?

"Hey." Hayden's soft whisper washed over her, warmer than her sweatshirt could ever be.

Easing Ruthie's door closed, she turned toward the stairs.

Hayden stood on the top step, his head tilted to one side. The way his eyebrows drew together and his forehead creased, he almost looked confused.

With a last glance at Ruthie's door, Mia stepped softly toward him, avoiding the third plank from the stairs that tended to squeak.

Why bother? Ruthie had slept through the whirling lights and the shouts of first responders. A noisy floorboard was nothing.

When she reached Hayden, he backed down a step. "How's Ruthie?"

"Knocked out." Hayden's presence brought an inexplicable sense of calm. It wasn't just that there was another person standing by her—it was Hayden himself. She'd said something to her mother about that a couple of months earlier, but Mom hadn't commented. She'd just stared at Mia for a long time before smiling the smile Mia remembered from every Christmas Eve of her childhood, as though she carried a special secret.

Of course, that had nothing to do with what was happening now. "Is Javi still here?" The fire trucks had pulled out about ten minutes earlier, but she hadn't heard tires on the gravel drive since.

She liked her driveway. The popping of rocks under tires alerted her when someone pulled up.

Her stomach dropped. Even how she'd graveled her drive spoke of a way to protect herself. How much did fear control her life?

She reached for the handrail to steady herself, and Hayden backed down another step.

Mia frowned, trying to shake a sense that she was dreaming. "Any word on Paige?"

"No, and Javi's gone. The search teams are still out, and the sheriff is putting boats in the water."

"Why boats? What happened out there?"

Tilting his head toward the first floor, Hayden turned to walk downstairs. "I'll make you some tea and we'll talk."

"I don't want tea." She muttered the words, her heart rate picking up as she followed Hayden. Whatever had happened to bring half of the county's emergency personnel to her house must have been bad.

Hayden must have heard her refusal, because he went into

the den and turned on the lamp by the couch. He walked to the French doors and stared at the closed blinds.

It was odd that they were closed. Mia sank onto the denim-blue couch and watched Hayden. When he bunked in her living room, he opened the blinds after she went to bed so he could look out at the river. He was a nature guy and hated being cooped up.

His laptop was on the coffee table beside a closed file with a case number on the tab. A piece of paper covered all but the first three numbers, indicating the file was from the state. She didn't want to consider that it might be the details of Keith's murder. Her mind couldn't handle the past when the present was out of control. "What's going on, Hay?"

"There's not an easy or gentle way to say this." He didn't turn from the doors. "Someone tried to burn your house down."

The stark words hit like a bomb. The blow was so hard, she dropped against the back of the couch. "What?" She'd heard him wrong. He had to have said something else, something much less frightening. Maybe she was dreaming. Maybe this whole day had been a nightmare. *Please, let me wake up soon.*

But the pulse in her cheek from impact with the rough bricks in Watchman's Alley said otherwise.

Regret softened Hayden's features. He moved in front of the couch and sat on the coffee table, facing Mia. He clasped his fingers between his knees. Instead of looking directly at her, he looked over her shoulder at the front door. "I should have eased you into that."

"It wouldn't have changed anything." Piled onto the horrors of the day, this new terror in the night exploded like a rocket-propelled grenade. The concussion from the blast was brutal, but eerie silence followed.

Her brain couldn't comprehend. Her emotions couldn't process. She was simply numb. Empty. It was as though she'd stepped out of her life to watch it pass on a movie screen.

Disassociation. A hallmark of the anxiety that had plagued her since the night Keith died.

Exhaling through pursed lips, she sat up taller. "Tell me what happened."

Hayden slid until the backs of his knees touched the table. He pressed his palms against the rough wood on either side of his knees and wrapped his fingers around it, gripping so hard that his knuckles turned white. "I had the blinds open, and I saw someone in the yard." He quickly recapped the confrontation with a man who'd poured gasoline around her home's support pillars before fighting with Hayden and escaping in a boat.

It was as though he was telling someone else's story. It didn't compute that this was happening to her...to Ruthie. The *why* eluded her. She tried to piece together facts, but nothing made sense. "That's why the sheriff put boats on the river."

Hayden nodded.

Mia stared at the French doors as though she could see the river on the other side. "It's too late. That man is long gone. He could have tucked into a little cove, could be all the way out to the sound. It's a waste of energy. Sheriff Davidson should let everyone go home and sleep. They're all probably already exhausted from searching for Paige."

"No one would take him up on the offer. You're family, and they're going to do their best to stop someone from doing this to one of their own."

The words brought a lump to her throat. Her next breath was a whimper. Tears stung her eyes. She stared at Hayden's chest, unable to look him in the face. "Well, I don't feel like one of them anymore." Since panic attacks had forced her out of her job four years earlier, she'd felt like a wanderer and an outcast. The deputies visited and offered encouraging words, but those things smacked of pity. Hayden made it sound like they wanted to help, like they still truly cared.

Their concern squeezed her heart. It also made her feel like a giant burden. A bother. An added weight to men and women who were already overextended and had families of their own to care for.

Hayden's exhale almost sounded like defeat. Slowly, as though he was afraid she might reach across the gap and punch him, he laid his hand on hers. "Let them do this for you." His grip tightened. "It makes you feel helpless when you see someone you care about suffering. They need to be on the move for you and Ruthie."

"I'm not good at this." The panic attacks had driven a need for control deep into her soul. She hated asking for help. Hated releasing things to other people. She should be able to take care of everything by herself. To protect her daughter, her home...

Yet she couldn't. Everything was violently *out* of control, spinning like a hurricane, threatening to destroy what was left of her fragile existence.

She sniffed, staring at Hayden's hand covering hers. The unknowns rushed in, crowding her mind while her emotions remained untouched. Still, her brain knew what she *should* be feeling. "Hay, I'm scared."

"I know." His low words calmed her thoughts, allowing rationality to take over.

She pressed her feet against the floor, trying to ground herself. "Somebody's targeting me. They know how to get to me and to Ruthie."

Hayden tensed. After a long moment in which he seemed to hold his breath, he let go of her hand, then moved to sit beside her, resting his shoulder against hers. "I won't let that happen."

The words shuddered through Mia, both comforting and chilling.

Comforting because she wasn't alone. *Chilling* because standing in the gap for her just might get Hayden killed.

Chapter Five

What was he thinking?

As Mia leaned her shoulder against his, Hayden wrestled with dueling urges. Half of him wanted to put his arm around her, shielding her from the world while reassuring himself that she was safe. The other half wanted to pull away and sit on the far side of the room to escape the wave of longing that roared through him at her touch. This was something he'd never felt with her before, and it was *not* what either of them needed. Not now, not ever.

Mia breathed deeply, her shoulder sliding against his. "What now?"

How did he answer that question? *What now* with the threat outside? Or *what now* with this weird feeling? He'd never kept anything from Mia before. She was his closest friend. Although he'd hugged her and comforted her many times, he'd never wanted to hold her close and never let go. Not like this.

No. He shouldn't be feeling like he needed her as much as she needed him. Wasn't he supposed to be the strong one here? And wasn't she Keith's wife?

"Hayden?" She pulled away to see his face, then turned toward him. "Are you hurt? I didn't even ask—"

"I'm fine." The words were gruffer than he'd intended, but it had taken a lot of force to get the sound out without choking. He cleared his throat. "I'm not hurt. The couple of blows he landed weren't bad."

"You're sure? Because you and I are about to have some twin facial bruises." She reached out to touch his cheek, where he'd just realized a pulsing pain had set in.

But if she touched him...

He jumped up and went to the doors, lifting a slat on the blinds and looking into the darkness.

Thankfully, Mia stayed on the couch.

He shoved his hands into the pockets of his flannel pants and balled his fists. She'd asked a question, and he needed to get out of his feelings enough to answer.

If only he *had* an answer. "What comes next? I don't know." When he faced her, he focused on the front door, which she'd painted a deep blue to contrast with the white walls. "I don't think you can stay here, though." She wasn't going to like that. This house was her anchor. Moving her to another location would pile on the trauma for her and likely for Ruthie as well, especially since they were knocking on the door of Christmas.

Mia flinched, the motion obvious even in his peripheral vision. "The tactical part of me won't stop spinning a plan. Pack up. Get out. Find somewhere safe where this guy can't get to Ruthie or me. But the other part of me..."

When her voice faded, Hayden let his gaze slide to her.

She fiddled with the hem of her shirt. "The weak part of me is scared."

The jagged confession shredded his heart. Whatever feelings his mind was inventing due to fear and exhaustion, he needed to set it all aside. She needed him.

With a quick prayer, Hayden locked a lid on his roaring emotions and sat beside her. He wrapped his arm around her shoulder and drew her to his side, the action raising an ache deep in his chest. "This fear isn't weakness. After what's happened to you today, it's normal. Fight or flight. Your body is prepping you for one or the other. Any living, breathing human would be processing this the same way you are."

"Maybe." When she shook her head, the motion brushed her hair against his shoulder. "I don't want fight or flight, though. I want option C. Hide in my house and pretend nothing is happening." She chuckled bitterly. "I'd definitely call that *weak*."

If he could take all of this away, he would. He'd fly them to the moon, hide them behind the stars that dotted the sky.

But that was impossible. The fight was here, and they both knew it. "You are the strongest person I know. No discussion. Stop calling my favorite person *weak*." He squeezed her shoulder. "Right now, you don't have to think about anything. You can let go for a few minutes. I'm right here, and I'm going to make sure nothing else happens." He wasn't alone. A couple of other off duty deputies were hanging out on the fringes of the yard. He'd never tell her that, because she'd fall into a guilt spiral and tell them to go home. "I'm not going anywhere." He'd die first. "I'll figure this out. You rest."

"Thank you." Her whisper was barely audible. Hayden felt it in her breathing more than he heard it with his ears.

Gradually, her breaths fell into a rhythm, and her head rested heavier on his shoulder. In spite of everything, she'd dropped off to sleep.

Hayden didn't dare move. He let his head fall to the back of the couch and stared at the ceiling, trying to unravel the knots in his thinking. The tangles had nothing to do with the danger around Mia and Ruthie.

No, this was much worse.

Mia had been one of his closest friends since she started dating Keith in middle school. She'd never needed a defender. She'd been as strong in body and spirit as any of the guys. She'd also been Keith's girlfriend and therefore Hayden's de facto "little sister," so he'd looked out for her. When they'd both joined the sheriff's department, she'd been his coworker, and they'd have defended one another to the death. In those days, he'd been engaged to Beth, and their group of four had fallen into an easy rhythm as couple friends, "doing life together," as their preacher liked to say.

When Ruthie was born, Hayden had learned what it truly meant to want to protect someone with his life. The honor of being her godfather had been a natural fit, and he'd taken the responsibility seriously. If anything had happened to Keith and Mia, it would have been up to him and Beth to teach Ruthie how to navigate the world and to know God. He'd been "Uncle Hayden" from the moment the little girl could form words.

Of course, Beth had been gone before Ruthie learned to speak. She'd walked away, unable to deal with Hayden's grief over his best friend's violent murder.

Hayden's jaw tightened.

Keith's murder had solidified his protector role in Mia's and Ruthie's lives. The need to shield them from the world and to help in any way he could had driven him since that moment.

But something different had hit him this evening as he'd stood at the top of the stairs watching Mia. Something terrifying. Something he could honestly say he'd never felt before, not even with his fiancée.

He needed Mia. Somehow, she made him whole.

When he'd walked up the stairs, he hadn't expected her to be standing at Ruthie's door. The sight of her had stopped him. She'd wrapped her arms around her stomach, digging her hands into her heavy sweatshirt as though it was armor that could protect her from the world. Her entire being radiated vulnerability.

But that hadn't been the thing that struck him so hard he'd nearly run down the stairs and bolted out into the night.

No, rather than feeling the need to protect her, his own vulnerability had risen up. While he'd wanted to take care of her the way he always had, a deeper need had surged from his stomach into his chest. He *needed* to pull her close and to feel her breathe, to hold her in his arms, not because he wanted to keep her safe, but because he wanted to draw strength from her. To be comforted by her as much as he comforted her.

Mia had become his safe place.

He closed his eyes as the truth assailed him. On days when work was tough or he felt as though he'd failed yet again, he called her. On days when he had something to celebrate, he called her. On days when he was bored or sad or simply had the best burger he'd ever eaten in his life and wanted to share the joy, he called her. Mia knew his best and his worst in ways Beth never had.

At some point, this friendship had shifted. He'd always thought he was the strong one who helped to steer the ship around the shoals and piloted it through storms, but the truth was, Mia anchored him.

This can't be happening, Lord. He fired off a desperate prayer. *Mia is Keith's wife. You didn't give her to me. You gave her to him. You gave me the responsibility of keeping her safe, of helping her out, not...not of feeling things for her. This is wrong. Make it go away. Please.*

The prayer only unsettled him more. It dropped into his stomach and smoldered, burning so hot that it made his abs clinch.

He should pull away, physically and emotionally. Even right now, he should slip his arm from around her and walk away. He shouldn't stay here resting in the feel of Mia in his arms as though it was right and real.

But he couldn't. He was the first line of defense, the *only* line of defense, between Mia and Ruthie and whoever was coming at them. He was a constant in Ruthie's life, and he wouldn't walk away from that little girl. That would make him no better than Beth.

He couldn't walk away from Mia, either. He might as well rip his heart out of his chest and leave it beating on her hard-wood floor.

He groaned, the rumble low in his chest. What he ought to do was—

A low, repetitive buzz sounded to his right. His phone screen lit up where he'd laid it on the couch an arm's length away.

Trying not to jostle Mia, he reached until his fingertips brushed the screen, then dragged the device closer.

The text was from Javi.

Keeping the phone next to his thigh to prevent the light from waking Mia, he flicked the screen and keyed in his passcode.

A message popped up, dousing the burn in his stomach with icy water. Body found in river. Female. ID pending.

Hayden pressed his lips together tightly to hold in an anguished groan. He prayed it wasn't so, but his gut said this was the end none of them wanted.

His gut said Paige was dead.

Mia cradled her coffee cup in her palms and walked across the dark kitchen to the bay window, where she stared at the closed blinds. Blue light filtered around the slats, indicating the softening of darkness just before sunrise.

Darkness was her enemy. Daylight was her friend.

As much as she welcomed the dawn, it was too early to be awake. Mia sipped the black coffee that Hayden had made during the night, then tilted her head from side to side, trying to loosen the tightness in her neck.

She'd awakened around five, muscles stiff and mind fuzzy, her neck awkwardly resting on the couch cushion. Hayden was racked out in the chair across from her, his feet propped on the coffee table. He'd moved at some point during the night, probably to get more comfortable.

He'd be hurting worse than her when he got moving. Maybe it was a good thing she'd invested in the big bottle of ibuprofen from the warehouse store. Aging was no fun for "normal" people. It was a lot worse for someone like her. Although she was only in her early thirties, raging anxiety had forced entirely too much tension into her body.

The hardwood behind her creaked. Her hand jerked, sloshing coffee over her wrist. It took half a second for her mind to remember she wasn't alone. "Did you get decent sleep?"

When she turned, Hayden stood in the entry, hair rumpled and face saggy from sleep. The lines around his eyes were deep with exhaustion. Somehow, he still exuded strength and safety.

And he didn't look half bad, either.

Something deep in Mia's chest tweaked, almost like her heart skipped. She looked at the black coffee still making waves in her mug. Yeah, she probably needed less of that. Or maybe she needed more if her brain had decided to be attracted to Hayden for even one of those extra beats. He was her closest friend.

He was *Keith's* closest friend.

If her weary heart wanted to pound an extra beat at the sight of Hayden McGrath, it could get itself into line. She was never exposing her heart to be shattered again.

Maybe she needed a pacemaker. There was no doubt she was old before her time. The past few years had aged her immeasurably.

The lines around Hayden's eyes deepened.

Mia set her mug on the counter, concerned. "Are you okay?"

"Yeah." He shook his head as though he was shaking off a spiderweb, then scrubbed the top of his head, rumpling his hair even further. "Do I look that bad? You're staring like I've got the cooties Ruthie is always talking about."

Mia snorted. "You look like you slept in a chair. How's your neck?"

"Probably the same as yours. Ibuprofen is still in the cabinet by the sink?" He headed that way before she could respond.

"Yeah, but you might want to eat before you pop one." While she used to down them dry on an empty stomach when she was in the army, age and wisdom had taught her she felt a whole lot better if she gave the meds a cushion to land on.

Hayden looked over his shoulder as he opened the cabinet door. "You getting old, Galloway? Losing your army toughness?" He popped two and swallowed them without breaking eye contact. "*Hooah*, Sergeant."

In spite of the tension, a laugh bubbled up. "It's your gut, soldier." She lifted her mug. "I turned the burner back on, so the coffee's warm. There's cereal and breakfast bars, or I can make eggs." Ruthie was on a cheese omelet kick, so eggs and shredded cheddar were in plentiful supply.

"I'll wait and eat with the kid." He poured a cup of coffee, seeming to be in constant motion. "How'd you sleep?"

"Like a baby." Sarcasm dripped from her words. "Waking up frequently all night long. What time did you pass out?"

"No idea. Probably a couple of hours ago. I wasn't planning on falling asleep, but…" He shrugged, sipped his coffee and then walked toward the living room, making a wide berth around her. "We need to talk about a plan."

Mia's chin dropped to her chest. She left her coffee on the table to prevent her shaking hands from soaking her wrist again. He wasn't telling her anything she didn't already know, but she'd prefer to act like this was a normal Sunday. Like she was going to get Ruthie dressed, then head to church, where they'd sit with Paige and her family before coming home for lunch with friends who understood that she wasn't always a fan of crowded restaurants.

She had two truly safe places. One was this house. The other was her church. Today, both were being ripped away. As much as she wanted to make like an ostrich and stick her head in the sand, she needed to face reality.

Someone wanted to harm her, which meant Ruthie was in danger as well. Even if she lacked the energy to protect herself, mama bear needed to make sure her daughter was safe.

This was harder than she'd expected. Although she spent

time with God every day, church was a boost to her system. Without it, she felt weak and lost.

She also felt trapped. As sunrise pinked the light around the blinds, she longed to open them as she always did. Flooding the house with light would boot out the darkness.

She settled for lifting a slat and peering out into the new day.

Movement near the fence jerked her hand back, the slat rattling into place.

Someone was out there.

Her hands shook. She should alert Hayden, but his name stuck in her throat. She peeked out again to watch the shadowy figure, trying to determine the severity of the threat.

The man walked toward her, his gaze on the fence before he turned his face toward the sky.

A familiar face.

Mia let the blinds fall, then stalked into the living room, where Hayden stood in front of the French doors with one set of blinds open, watching the sky brighten. "Hay, why is Deputy Gallagher in my yard?"

Hayden sipped his coffee as though Drew Gallagher wandered around her yard every morning. "He's keeping an eye on the perimeter to the north and east. Peña is walking the west and south."

Mia sagged, her shoulder braced against the frame of the large opening between the kitchen and living room. "Amelia Peña was on duty yesterday, and I know for a fact she's got a shift today, because last week she told me she wouldn't be at church. She should be home asleep. And the Gallaghers have a three-month-old. His wife needs—"

"Don't you dare go out there and run them off." Hayden's voice held the weight of authority. "They volunteered to stay. We talked about this last night. Be grateful, not guilty."

Mia's jaw dropped, but she forced it closed as she straightened. He had no idea what it was like to be her. No one should sacrifice for her, not when she couldn't offer anything in return.

Amelia needed to take care of herself, to rest between shifts. Drew should be home with Cassidy and their precious baby, not shivering on patrol in her backyard. She was no more special than anyone else who needed help.

Hayden could tell her all day not to feel guilty, but it wasn't going to change anything. "They don't need to do this. Neither do you." She was keeping him from his life. He was here way too often, taking Ruthie on outings or doing things around the house, offering emotional support and carrying some of her burden.

Hayden was a handsome guy, one who turned heads, especially when he'd worn a uniform. While his dark hair now sported a few threads of gray, it only served to make him more attract—

Mia shuddered. *Nope.* That was the second time in ten minutes that she'd headed down that road. *Why?*

She had no idea. The point was... "They have lives. You have a life. You've been stuck ever since Keith died, taking care of me and Ruthie. You should be..." She waved her hand toward somewhere out there. "You should be taking care of your own life. Finding a woman who loves you. Settling into—"

"I'm fine." The words snapped. "My life is exactly what I want it to be." He didn't look directly at her, a habit he seemed to have picked up in the past twelve hours. "And everyone else? They care about you. They care about Ruthie. You wore the uniform with them, and you're still one of them. They feel just as helpless as—" His brow furrowed. "They want to help you. Let them. You've given so much to each of them. You're their family. They're your family. Don't wound them by fussing at them instead of thanking them."

"I haven't given anybody anything." She sank onto a bar stool by the kitchen entrance and threw her hands into the air, ashamed of her impotence. "All I do is take." That was the worst part of the PTSD-induced panic attacks that drove her into a near reclusiveness. She could no longer have anybody's back. All of her energy went to staying alive and raising her daughter. By the time night fell, she was exhausted, but sleep had ceased to be her friend so the cycle never ended.

"Mia." Hayden exhaled her name, then stepped around the couch to stand in front of her. Reaching around her, he settled his coffee on the counter, his chest brushing her nose.

He smelled like coffee and…well, like Hayden. She closed her eyes and breathed him in, not bothering to consider why his presence had a different feel today.

When he backed away, he rested his hands on her shoulders. "You really have no idea, do you?" The words were soft.

Mia stared at the stylized mountain logo on his sweatshirt. Something cautioned her against looking him in the eye. He was standing so close, and it was…different. Comforting but different. Charged. Magnetic.

"People love you because they choose to. They help because they want to. And, Mia?" He hooked his finger under her chin and gently forced her to meet his gaze. "You opened your home to Amelia when she first took this job and was looking for a place to live. You cooked a billion freezer meals for the Gallaghers when the baby was born."

"That was nothing." It hadn't taken much effort to do those things.

His gaze was intense, searching hers. "You don't see your own value, do you?"

What value? She had nothing to give.

But somehow, with Hayden looking at her the way he was right now, with a wonder she'd never seen before, she felt treasured. Special. Like maybe she had something to share… with him?

The realization jolted, and she jerked away from him,

scrambling off the stool and deeper into the kitchen, her mind spinning. "I'll... I could at least make them fresh coffee."

Hayden stayed where he was, seeming to be frozen, until a buzzing sound forced his hand to his pocket. He glanced at his phone, and his jaw hardened.

Something was wrong. "Hayden?"

His eyes were dark. It was clear he wished he could say something different than what he was about to say. "They found Paige."

Chapter Six

"This is the exact last place you should be." Hayden killed the truck's engine and leaned over the steering wheel as he surveyed the front of the two-story white house where Paige had grown up.

The home was situated in the center of a tree-covered lot, isolated from the road. A half dozen cars were parked along the edges of the winding driveway.

Paige was a popular member of their church. The kids all loved her and so did the adults. Her family was well respected in Wincombe. They wouldn't lack for support on this darkest of days.

"Are you listening to me, Mia?"

They were not getting into this conversation in front of her daughter. Mia stared at Hayden until he looked at her, then she cut her eyes toward the back seat of his pickup, where Ruthie played happily with his phone. This was hard enough without Hayden questioning her every three seconds.

It had taken every ounce of her rapidly dwindling reserves to pack bags for her and Ruthie and to hold it together on the short drive to Paige's family home. As soon as they made this stop at the Crosbys', they were headed to Hayden's house about an hour away, near Elizabeth City.

It was a risky move, but Hayden felt they'd be safer out of town.

Right now, nowhere felt safe. Her home was compromised. The routine she depended on was shattered. She wasn't in church. She wasn't making last-minute preparations for Christmas, just a few days away.

Instead she was offering condolences to her daughter's birth family, then fleeing the threat that had likely killed their youngest child.

Anxiety often made her feel like she stared at life from the outside, but this level of surreal was something she hadn't felt since the initial weeks after Keith's murder.

A gray sedan tucked in close to the pickup's bumper. Two of Hayden's Trinity teammates had arrived while Hayden was loading the truck, but they hadn't come into the house. All she knew was that one man and one woman were acting as her bodyguards.

How had this become her life? Wasn't it bad enough that her husband had been murdered? Now Paige was dead, and both she and Ruthie were targets?

Swallowing fear that threatened to choke her, Mia slid her gaze to Hayden. *Focus on the moment.* It was the only way to survive. "I know this is ill-advised." Although protecting herself and Ruthie was top priority, she couldn't leave without seeing Paige's mother. Sue Crosby, her daughter, Eve, and son-in-law, Daniel, were basically family. In the wake of tragedy, she couldn't simply disappear.

She might be living a life that had slipped off its foundation, but she wasn't built to ignore hurting people. Guilt would kill her before fear or an assailant got the chance.

"Ill-advised?" Hayden scoffed. "That's an understatement." He'd been irritable and distant since they'd received word of Paige's death.

Paige. All Hayden had told her was that Ruthie's birth mother had suffered a blow to the head. With the holidays, it would take a while before the coroner made an official report. Even at that, Hayden was keeping something from her. He was rarely this moody. While she understood, she needed him to offer her some stability.

Mia winced. Could she be more selfish? She wasn't the only one grieving. Hayden had to feel pain as well. And Paige's family… "I have to do this." She stared out the window at the pine trees.

Her life had already been marred by violence. She could understand what the Crosbys were enduring. While the idea of stepping into that crowded house without knowing the identity of Paige's killer twisted her stomach into knots, she couldn't stay away.

Hayden's hand wrapped around hers, warm and comforting. "I don't like it, but I understand, and I'm sorry for being snappy. I'll walk you to the door, then take Ruthie around back to the tire swing."

Mia nodded. She'd chosen not to tell Ruthie what had happened until things calmed down. The little girl adored her "Pai-pai," as she'd called Paige from toddlerhood. Although she was too young to understand the true nature of their relationship, the death of her birth mother would devastate Ruthie. Combined with leaving home just a few days before Christmas, this might be more than her daughter could handle.

They'd simply told Ruthie that Pai-pai wasn't home and she could play outside while Mommy talked to the grown-ups. Because she loved the tire swing in the backyard, she'd happily agreed.

"Have Sue text me when you're ready to leave, and I'll meet you on the porch. No more detours after this. Even with an escort, I'm not excited about having you in the open."

Ignoring the hint of danger, Mia walked to the house, her heart pounding. When Hayden left her at the door, it took all she had not to beg him to go inside with her. She needed his support, his presence. She felt exposed as she pressed the doorbell.

The door immediately swung open, and Sue Crosby enveloped her in a hug. "Mia." The older woman broke into sobs as Mia returned the embrace.

As she eased Sue inside and tapped the door closed with her foot, the band around Mia's lungs loosened. The biggest lesson she'd learned about panic attacks was that when she focused on the needs of someone else, the walk became a little easier. Although she was drowning in grief and fear, reaching out to Sue eased those emotions, if only for a moment.

There would be time to fall apart later. Right now, Paige's mother needed her. They stood in the foyer, Sue weeping as Mia comforted her.

No one came upon them there, although indistinct voices drifted from the kitchen at the rear of the house.

When the storm subsided, Sue swiped at her face. "I was hoping you'd come." She sniffed and looked to the side, toward the formal living room. "Who would do this? Are you and Ruthie safe? The sheriff said there was an incident—"

"I don't know." Oh, how she wished she did.

Sue frowned, then fluffed her hair as though she was putting herself back in order. In her midfifties, Sue's brown hair was streaked with silver and, even in her grief, perfectly in place. She was always put together, even in the midst of her world falling apart. After a glance toward the kitchen, she looked at Mia, her expression gentle. "The family is here, along with a few of Paige's friends. Do you want to speak to them or is that too much?"

As a social worker for the school system, Sue understood the psychological battles Mia faced. Sue had been a confidant during their fertility journey and an advocate during Ruthie's adoption. Together they'd built a sort of blended family that benefited Ruthie, particularly in the wake of Keith's death.

They needed one another now more than ever, yet she was packing up Ruthie and running away.

Was it the right thing to do?

What choice did she have? She'd offer comfort while she was here, but then she had to consider Ruthie's safety above all else. She waved her hand for Sue to lead the way up the short hallway. "Is Cade here?"

Cade Crosby was Sue's ex-husband and Paige's father. He'd been the lone voice of dissension during the adoption discussions, wanting Paige and her ex-boyfriend Blake to "own up" to their "mistakes," to drop out of college and raise Ruthie themselves. He lived several hours away near Wilmington and rarely visited. When he did, he radiated disapproval.

Sue stopped in front of the closed kitchen door. "Cade is upstairs in Paige's room. He's not ready to see anyone. He needs time, and I doubt he comes downstairs, but Mia..." She winced. "Blake is here."

Mia turned toward the backyard where Ruthie was playing, though she couldn't see anything from the windowless hallway.

Ruthie hadn't seen her birth father since the day she was born. While Paige was fully involved in Ruthie's life, Blake had made it clear that it was easier for him emotionally to step away. He'd willingly consented to the adoption and had never expressed regret. Although he'd remained friends with Paige after they broke up, he'd maintained a respectful distance from Mia and Ruthie.

Mia rarely saw him, since he lived in Greenville near the college. The few times they'd spoken, it had been awkward. She never knew what to say. The tiniest part of her wondered if he resented their family.

"Should he be here?" As her ex-boyfriend, he'd be among the first the police questioned.

Sue clearly picked up on the real question. "He spoke with the police already. He has an alibi but, Mia, I'd never suspect him. He cared too much about her to harm her."

Mia wanted to believe so, but her nature was to suspect everyone. The world wasn't safe.

This would be easier with Hayden beside her, but there were some things she needed to do alone. With a swift prayer, she followed Sue into the kitchen. She was here to support Paige's family, not to be a burden.

The dozen or so people scattered around the island and the breakfast nook in the large, airy kitchen were somber, talking in low tones. When Mia appeared, the conversation ebbed, but it picked up again when Paige's older sister, Eve, approached with her husband, Daniel.

Eve hugged Mia, then stepped back under her husband's arm. "I'm glad you came. Mom was wondering if you'd—" She leaned more heavily on her husband. "Is Ruthie here?"

"She's outside with Hayden. We're..." Should she say something? "We're going to go somewhere and lay low for a bit."

Daniel nodded, his expression drawn. "That makes sense. This thing is so... I can't believe it all." He offered a tight smile. "I'd been hoping to take Ruthie fishing if the weather warmed up."

"Hopefully we'll be back soon." Ruthie loved fishing with Daniel and had gone several times with him and Hayden.

"If you're going to be here a second, we'll run to the house and get Ruthie's Christmas present. It's this talking globe that you connect to your phone and it does all of these augmented reality things." She smiled up at her husband. "Very tech."

Glad for the distraction, Mia smiled. "I'm not surprised." Daniel worked in IT for the state's Department of Natural Resources. He'd been a college classmate of Keith's and had met Eve through him.

"We'll be quick." Eve grabbed Daniel, and they slipped out of the kitchen.

Why was she taking her daughter away at Christmas? There had to be another way, right?

In her heart, she knew there wasn't.

She scanned the room, searching for Sue, who'd vanished.

Near the sink, Blake leaned against the counter. His expression was dark, and he stared at the far side of the room without seeming to see anything. The grief radiating off him was palpable. Her heart ached for him, and she started to cross over to speak to him, but Sue approached with a couple in their fifties.

Sue, her red eyes the only thing that betrayed her overwhelming grief, drew Mia closer. "This is Amanda Rhinehart. She was Paige's professor in some of her undergraduate classes and has been mentoring her as she's moved through the master's process."

"I've heard your name many times." Mia hugged the woman. "Paige looked up to you."

Amanda offered a watery smile. "This is my husband, Trent. He works for the college as well, in the Office of Student Financial Aid."

The man appeared to be as grief-stricken as his wife. He extended his hand to Mia and shook it warmly. "You adopted Paige's daughter?"

Mia flinched internally. What an odd way to address her. She nodded slowly, unsure how to proceed.

Trent studied her for a moment before he dropped her hand. His eyes drifted over her shoulder, creasing with concern.

Mia turned to follow his gaze.

Blake was watching them, his expression dark and angry. He stared for a long moment, then stalked out of the room, violently shoving through the hallway door.

Sue's face registered sympathy. "I'll check on him." She followed Blake out the still-swinging door.

Amanda watched them go. "I hope everything is okay."

Was it? Because Blake's expression said he could be consumed by more than grief. His expression had spoken of anger...

Anger that had seemed to be directed at her.

* * *

"Spin me again, Uncle Hayden!" Ruthie's feet were straight out from her perch in the old motorcycle tire tied to the high branch of a pine tree. She gripped the tire's sides as she giggled.

Hayden looked up the sloped yard toward the house, where someone occasionally passed the kitchen window, but he was too far away to discern more than figures. Being away from Mia while a threat hung over their heads made him antsy.

Worse, thickening clouds blocked the sun and cast deep shadows among the trees around the house, offering too many dark places to hide. The wind was picking up, and the movement of limbs and branches created the optical illusion that someone was prowling through the woods.

His adrenaline ran high.

Still, it was nothing compared to the seismic shift his emotions had endured earlier that morning, just before the call about Paige had come in. The same emotions that had distracted him ever since and had made him snap at Mia in the truck.

He'd been overwhelmed in her kitchen by something he hadn't felt in years.

Overwhelmed, swamped, wiped out by the urge to wrap his arms around Mia and to kiss her in a way that let her know how much he needed her. That she wasn't a burden to him. That he might just be in—

"Uncle Hayden!" Ruthie's shout pierced his thoughts at the same moment her tiny sneakered foot caught him in the thigh. "Spin me again!"

He winced at the sharp pain. *Wow.* He needed to get his head out of his heart. If he didn't, he was in far more danger than a small bruise from a tiny foot.

Focusing on the physical pain, he drew himself into the moment with his goddaughter. "You have manners, little miss. We say *please*. And we don't kick people."

"Sorry. And *please* spin me again?" Big hazel eyes looked up at him with every ounce of puppy dog expression that Ruthie could muster.

Hayden glanced at his watch. It had been over ten minutes since they'd arrived, and he was anxious to get moving, but he couldn't drag Ruthie into the house. He'd promised Mia he'd keep the little girl away from the grief of Paige's family until they could find a way to explain what had happened.

With a sigh, he pasted on a smile and looked down at his favorite kid. "You feeling okay?" The way she whirled and twirled through life, he doubted she would ever suffer from motion sickness, but he wanted to be sure before he set the tire swing into another wild spin.

"Yes! Again!" Ruthie's shriek could pierce eardrums.

He winced. "Hold on tight." He slowly turned the tire, twisting the rope into mini knots. "Ready?" At Ruthie's enthusiastic nod, he released the tire. It spun wildly as the rope unwound.

Ruthie laughed and shouted with excited delight.

"Hayden?" At the sound of a voice, he looked over his shoulder to find Gavin Mercer approaching. The dark-haired former CID investigator's hand rested on his hip near his side, where he carried a Glock on the rare occasions he was armed. "Everything okay back here? Rebecca and I heard Ruthie scream."

Behind Gavin, Rebecca Campbell appeared at the corner of the house.

Gratitude for his Trinity team washed through Hayden, easing some of his anxiety. Gavin and Rebecca had left home on their day off to come and back him up, offering security and peace of mind as he moved Ruthie and Mia out of town. He was certain they were ready to get going as much as he was.

None of them were trained bodyguards, though they were all prior military and had some experience in pulling security. Their main specialty was investigations, and they'd been well trained to pick up on details other people might not notice. That attention to detail should give them an edge in surveillance, helping them to see things coming that untrained eyes might miss.

"We're fine." He tilted his head toward Ruthie, who giggled loudly as the spinning tire slowed. "Somebody is hopefully going to take a nice nap once we get moving."

Rebecca walked down the hill to join them, her brown ponytail swinging with her steps. "I'm taking notes. My sister's kid is due in a few months."

"And you're planning to be the best aunt ever?" Gavin elbowed her arm.

"You know it. I'll be spoiling that kid rotten." Rebecca grinned, then glanced at her watch and sobered. "How much longer do you think Mia will be?"

"Hopefully not much." Hayden held up a hand to press pause on the questions, then walked over and twisted the tire in the opposite direction. Maybe a reversal would counteract any dizziness and keep Ruthie from falling over when they walked back to the truck. "One last time, Ruthie. Are you ready?"

"Yes!"

As soon as she gave the affirmative, Hayden let go of the tire and stepped back to rejoin Rebecca and Gavin. Ruthie should be sufficiently distracted for at least sixty seconds. "I may go in and get her if she's not out soon, if you guys can keep Ruthie occupied. The longer we stay here, the more time and opportunity we give for someone to make another run at them. I won't feel easy until we're settled in at our destination." He was careful not to say where they were headed. There could be listening ears. While it wouldn't be hard to figure out where he lived, he didn't want to make it easier for someone to find them.

"Copy that." Gavin backed up a few steps toward the house. "I'll go to the car and make sure we're ready to roll."

Hayden nodded and turned to Rebecca. "I'll get Mia if you'll keep an eye on Ruthie."

"On it." She stepped around him to walk closer to Ruthie,

who was kicking her legs as she spun. "And I'll watch out for flying feet."

"They hurt." Hayden chuckled and rubbed his thigh, then followed Gavin up the hill. He stopped a few feet behind his teammate as Gavin slowed at the corner of the house. "If we can get on the road in the next ten minutes, then—"

The words died as Gavin drew his pistol, then turned and motioned Hayden forward, anger reddening his face. Hayden rushed to his teammate's side, fear and helplessness swimming in his stomach. Whatever Gavin saw, it upset him. Worse, Hayden was unarmed, having left his pistol locked up at his house, never dreaming he'd need it in Wincombe.

When he reached Gavin, his teammate didn't turn away from what he was watching. "Text Mia. Tell her to stay inside." His voice was barely a whisper.

"Can't. We left her phone to prevent being tracked." In hindsight, that might have been a bad idea.

Gavin muttered something under his breath. With two fingers, he pointed at the driveway where their vehicles were parked.

Although Hayden's truck largely blocked their view, blue-jeaned legs were visible beneath the truck near the tailgate where a person had crouched on their knees.

Someone was tampering with his truck.

Hayden's blood ran cold. This was a monumental failure on his part. He should have insisted they go straight out of town. Should have told Rebecca and Gavin to stay with the vehicles. Should have done so many things differently.

Gavin leaned forward, trying to get a better line of sight. "How do you want to handle this?"

Regardless of how wrongly he'd played this from the start, the opportunity to catch the person terrorizing Mia and Ruthie now lay before him. Swallowing his self-recrimination, Hayden laid a hand on Gavin's shoulder. "We end this. Now."

Chapter Seven

Hayden stared at the legs of the person behind his truck. While he wanted to charge forward and tackle the suspect, priority number one was getting Ruthie to safety and keeping Mia from stepping outside.

While Gavin kept watch, Hayden fired off a text to Rebecca. Get Ruthie inside. Tell Mia to stay put. Don't alarm anyone. While everyone should shelter in place, the last thing the Crosby family needed was to be alerted that Paige's killer might be on their property.

After all, this could be a huge misunderstanding.

He wasn't sure if he hoped this was a false alarm or if he wanted this to be a full-blown threat so they could stop the madness.

Tapping Gavin on the shoulder, Hayden held up his empty hands to indicate he was unarmed. At Gavin's nod, Hayden pointed to the right, then aimed his finger at himself before swinging it to the left. They had no way of knowing if the person was armed, so as the one with a weapon, Gavin would approach from the front while Hayden operated with the element of surprise and moved in from the rear.

This thrown-together plan had better work.

With a deep breath and a quick prayer, Hayden signaled a silent order for Gavin to proceed.

Gavin stayed below the house's window level as he crept past the porch. While there wasn't a lot of cover, he was at an angle that their target couldn't spot him unless they stood.

Hayden gave his teammate a few seconds' head start, then he crouched and darted from his position to the far side of the nearest vehicle, a full-size SUV. He'd have to move quickly through the gaps between cars, navigating several feet of open space each time where he could easily be spotted.

He rushed from the cover of the large SUV to a smaller crossover, then stopped. He was directly across the wide gravel drive from his pickup, but there was a vehicle-length gap between the crossover and the sedan that was next in line.

Someone had left the house since they'd arrived. How had he not heard a vehicle leave down the gravel drive? Why hadn't Gavin or Rebecca said something? Likely it was innocent, but he should have been aware of it.

He swallowed the burn that tried to rise in his throat. He'd been too distracted with keeping Ruthie occupied, and he'd missed sights and sounds that could have indicated potential danger. He had to do better.

That included honing his focus now.

Hayden eased back along the side of the crossover to the hood and raised his head to look for Gavin. Rather than risk being spotted as he moved between the crossover and the sedan, he'd have to make his move from the side instead of from the rear.

Gavin was hidden, so Hayden couldn't signal the change in plan. Guess they'd have to go with the flow.

At the crossover's rear bumper, Hayden took up a runner's crouch, ready to dart out as soon as he heard Gavin's shout.

Blood raced through his veins. This could be it. This could be—

Gavin's voice broke the stillness. "Got a runner!"

Hayden leaped from his concealed position and dashed into the driveway. Following Gavin, he dove into the woods, dodging tree branches and trying not to trip over roots in the thick vegetation.

Ahead of them, the shadows were deep on the cloud-soaked day, and they danced with the wind. The damp air that promised rain threatened to suffocate him, but he pushed forward, following Gavin and the sounds of someone crashing through the trees ahead of them, though he had no visual on the person they were chasing.

His breath came in heavy gasps. A side stitch threatened to take him down, but he pushed on. This was for Mia. For Ruthie.

For Paige. For Keith.

Gavin stopped so suddenly that Hayden nearly crashed into his back. Holding up his hands, he stopped himself by bracing against Gavin's shoulder blades. "What?"

"Lost him."

Around them, the woods had fallen silent. No footsteps on leaves. No breaking of branches. The only sound was their breathing, and the only movement was the wind tangling the tree branches above them. It was as though the person they were chasing had disappeared. "How?"

Gavin stepped a few feet ahead, scanning left and right, then returned to Hayden's side. "I don't know, but as much as we'd both love to charge forward..."

He didn't need to finish the thought. They had no idea what they were heading into. The suspect could be armed. Could have backup. They could race deeper into the woods, straight into death.

While Hayden had made his peace with breathing his last *someday*, he certainly didn't want to rush into eternity on *this* day. Who would protect Mia and Ruthie if he was gone?

Reluctant to admit defeat, he scanned the thick undergrowth

and tightly packed trees, searching for movement, listening for sound.

Only nature spoke.

Resisting the urge to punch a tree, he looked at Gavin, then turned and trudged toward the house, which was out of sight through the thick wooded area.

They'd walked several steps before Gavin spoke. "It's not your fault, man."

Hayden didn't dignify the comment with a response. Gavin had no idea. Mia and Ruthie were his responsibility, and now, three times, he'd let someone slip past him.

Gavin holstered his sidearm. "I'm the one who lost him. Whoever that was, they clearly know these woods well."

His teammate wasn't the one at fault, but that was a discussion for later. If their runner knew the area, they were likely someone who knew Paige and the Crosbys well.

They could also simply be very comfortable in the outdoors. "Did you get a good look at whoever it was?"

"Jeans. A hoodie. Nothing that stood out. Couldn't even tell you if it was male or female, adult or teen."

No help there. Again. "The person I confronted at the house last night was a man, but the mask and the hood covered too much for me to give a positive ID. I couldn't pick him out of a lineup."

"So basically our suspect pool is—"

"Everyone." They needed more to go on. "I'm not even sure if there's only one attacker or if this is some coordinated effort led by..." He waved his hand to indicate the whole planet.

"Why would there be a coordinated effort against a widow and her kid?" Gavin let the question hang as they neared the house, but he stopped walking when their vehicles came into view. "Hayden, aren't you looking into her husband's murder?"

"Yeah." The last thing he wanted to think about was Keith's death. "Why?"

"I'm just throwing out an angle here, something maybe we

should consider, but if the SBI is looking into an organized crime link with the shooter, could it be that all of this is somehow connected?"

Hayden stopped so quickly he had to grab a nearby tree for balance. His head spun through Gavin's words, trying to make them translate. "Are you suggesting that Keith's murder wasn't the result of a botched robbery? That he was targeted?"

"I'm just throwing it out there as an angle that was never investigated. That's all."

Who would mark Keith for death? And why? It made no sense.

Although it might explain why the gunman had paced the aisles, seeming to wait for something before he pulled his gun.

Hearing the thought expressed out loud was a gut punch. What if someone had intentionally killed Keith, and now they wanted to harm Mia and Ruthie? How did any of this play into the comment in Watchman's Alley about Mia being a bad mother? "I don't—"

"Hayden McGrath? Is that you?" A voice from the driveway jerked him into the present. They were in an active manhunt, and he needed to pay attention. The past could wait.

He looked in the direction of the person speaking. Eve Warner, Paige's older sister, stood at the edge of the driveway. Her husband, Daniel, walked over from a rugged SUV that was parked in the formerly empty space in the line of cars.

Eve stepped closer. "What are you doing running around in the woods?" Worried lines wrinkled her forehead. "Is my family okay?"

"Everyone is fine. They're all inside." With all of the trauma of the past twenty-four hours and the new suspicions Gavin's conjecture had ignited, Hayden's brain refused to come up with a creative reason for their jaunt through the trees.

Gavin leaned around him, offering his hand to Eve. "I'm Gavin Mercer, and I work with Hayden at Trinity Investigations. We were just looking around while Mia is inside to see if we could locate any evidence concerning what happened to your sister." He tipped his head. "I'm so sorry for your loss."

Eve's expression drooped as she shook Gavin's hand. "Thank you."

Laying a hand on his wife's shoulder, Daniel clasped Gavin's offered hand. "Thank you. We're all in shock." He gestured toward the house. "Do you want to come inside? When we stepped out, Mia was talking to some friends of the family."

"You were here and you left?" Gavin's voice was even, but it was his investigator voice, one Hayden knew he'd schooled to hide his emotions.

Eve lifted a red-and-green-striped gift bag. "Mia said she and Ruthie are going out of town for Christmas and... Well, here's Ruthie's gift. If she won't be here, I wanted her to have it with her to open on Christmas morning, so I ran home to grab it."

Hayden's heart thawed slightly. The way Mia had included Paige's family in Ruthie's life was rare and beautiful. "I'll put it in the truck, if you'd like."

"Thanks." Eve passed him the bag. "Do you want to come inside and get some coffee or something?"

"We need to get on the road. We've got a long drive ahead of us." Hopefully, they'd assume Mia was going to her grandmother's house on the other side of the state. Hayden passed the present to Gavin, who settled it on the truck's hood. "If you'd tell Mia and my friend Rebecca that we're ready to go, I'd appreciate it."

The Warners said their goodbyes and disappeared into the house.

Gavin watched them go. "So those two were unaccounted for when someone was tampering with your ride?" He walked around to the rear of the truck.

Hayden followed. "No motive. There's no reason for them to harm Mia or to question her parenting." He scanned the rear of his pickup, noting the disturbed gravel where their mystery person had knelt.

He squatted and ran his hand beneath the bumper, feeling for a tracking device or an explosive, but nothing was out of place. He shifted his attention to the exhaust. Something had rubbed the interior of the pipe, wiping away accumulated dirt and grime. "Gavin." He pointed at the streaks. "Go check your vehicle."

Leaning down, Hayden peered into the tailpipe. Sure enough, a thick rag had been shoved far enough in to avoid easy detection.

Hayden rocked back on his heels as Gavin returned, dangling a torn dirt-streaked beach towel from two fingers. "I assume you found something similar?"

He nodded. The method was crude but effective. Block the car's exhaust and the engine would eventually shut down.

Smart play. Incapacitating them would have dropped them helplessly by the side of the road, where they'd be easy targets. He looked up at Gavin, who was watching him with a grim expression.

For the first time, Hayden was truly afraid.

Mia stared out the kitchen window above Hayden's sink, looking almost directly into the kitchen of the neighbor behind him. While large open spaces made her feel exposed and unprotected, Hayden's relatively new, tightly compacted neighborhood induced a claustrophobia that reminded her of a prison.

Worse, the interior of his house had no warmth. It was artfully designed yet void of personal touches. The builder had painted the walls a beautiful gray set off by white trim, but nothing about the space felt like a home. Hayden had bought furniture from one of those design-your-room-for-you big-box stores. It was all a showroom, made to be looked at but not lived in.

Hayden wasn't image-conscious, but he had no concept of how to decorate, so he'd leaned heavily on the ideas of others. He'd bought the first house he could afford when he took the job with Trinity, putting little thought into anything other than having a place to watch TV and to sleep. Mia had worked hard to keep her mouth shut during the process. It wasn't her business.

The sprawling subdivision featured two-story, four-bedroom homes on quarter-acre lots. There was no view of anything except vinyl siding. While Elizabeth City itself was situated near the mouth of the Pasquotank River where it flowed into the Albemarle Sound, nothing about Hayden's neighborhood spoke of life on the water.

Having been born and raised in Wincombe, living most of her life in view of the Scuppernong River or the Albemarle Sound, Mia had spent her days swimming, paddle boarding and kayaking. Being landlocked wasn't something she was used to. It reminded her of Afghanistan, where there had been no large expanses of water and where danger had lurked around every corner.

Resting her hands on the cool porcelain sink, Mia dropped her chin to her chest. *Lord, I want to go home. I want Ruthie and me to be safe and...* She swallowed icy grief and fear that rushed up her spine. *I want to go back four years to when I felt safe. When I wasn't scared. When I was capable of taking care of my family.*

It felt like centuries had passed. Her life was divided into *before* and *after. Before* felt so bright, so safe, so stable. *After* was dark, dangerous and rocky. She'd been a hollow shell of herself for four years.

Maybe the person in Watchman's Alley was right. Maybe Ruthie did deserve a better mother. Even now, Mia was hiding in the kitchen trying to pull herself into some semblance of sanity while Hayden explored the bonus room with Ruthie, where he'd long ago set up a toy land for her visits.

Hayden had been avoiding her since they arrived at his house. Once again, he was hiding something. Everything had been fine at the Crosbys until suddenly, Rebecca had appeared in the living room with Ruthie, subtly herding everyone away from the windows. Likely no one else noticed, but her actions had ignited memories from Mia's time as a deputy and in the military, when slight movements and suggestions shifted people to safety without alarming them.

When they'd set out for Elizabeth City, Hayden had said nothing about a threat. He'd simply driven as fast as legally possible, his eyes shifting constantly between the mirrors and the road. He'd refused to stop, even when Ruthie had complained of hunger. He'd merely reached into the console, passed her a package of peanut butter crackers and trucked on.

They needed to discuss the difference between *protecting* and *lying*. He'd hidden details about Paige's kidnapping from her until it was too late, was keeping something about the attack at her home secret and was up to something when it came to their flight out of town. She was tired of being kept in the—

"Well, Ruthie is excited because the doll she brought with her fits in the new 'take care of your toy baby' set I found online." Hayden's voice, dripping with forced amusement, came from the kitchen door.

Mia straightened and turned, ready to go to battle about the need to know what was happening in her own life. She crossed her arms over her stomach, eyeing the friend she was supposed to trust. "Cut it out, Hay."

He tilted his head, one eyebrow inching toward his hairline. "I'm sorry?"

"I might be dealing with a lot of things, but I'm not made of glass. I won't break." It was a lot easier to be brave when Hayden was standing in front of her and when Rebecca and Gavin were outside watching the perimeter. Their presence gave her the freedom to let go of the fear of physical threats so her emotions could freely breathe. "I want to know every-thing you aren't telling me."

Hayden stared at her, seeming to gauge how sincere her anger was. Finally, he pulled a stool away from the penin-sula that separated the kitchen from the dining room and sat, lacing his fingers on the granite counter. "Somebody tried to make sure our vehicles dumped us on the side of the road on our way out of town. Gavin and I caught them in the act and chased them through the woods, but they got away."

The blunt admission jolted her. Mia reached behind her and grabbed the granite counter. She'd expected him to stall or to deny her accusations, but he'd simply laid everything on the table. It took a second for the shift from expectation to reality to allow understanding. "Someone knew we were at Paige's and tried to sabotage us?"

He nodded, his expression grim. "Either they followed us or..." His gaze slid away from her toward the refrigerator, but he didn't need to say more.

Or they were already at the house and took advantage of the opportunity.

The implications of the unspoken statement weakened Mia's knees. She walked around the counter and sat beside him. Bracing her elbows on the granite, she buried her face in her hands. "So what you're saying is, either you and your team missed a tail or someone in Paige's family is out to get me or Ruthie."

"I'm not saying anything for certain. I'm simply laying out the possibilities." He rested his warm hand between her shoulder blades.

His touch stopped the world from spinning. Hayden was here. His friends were here. Ruthie was safe and she was safe, for the moment at least. In this quiet space, she needed to think like her old self, not the weak, lost, exhausted woman she'd become. "So to figure this out, we need motive as well as opportunity."

"I'm afraid so." Hayden's voice was a low rumble as his thumb swept back and forth along her shoulder blade. "Can we talk about who might have had both of those things this morning?"

His touch soothed the ragged places deep inside of her.

Something in her heart that had felt disjointed since Keith died slipped back into place. For a moment, she felt...whole.

It was unsettling. Sitting up, she effectively dropped Hayden's hand from her back. She placed her palms flat on the counter and forced herself to think through Hayden's question.

She mentally scanned the faces of the mourners and dismissed each one. "Several opportunities but no motives."

"So let's start with opportunity. Walk me through it. Who was out of your sight at any point?"

"The most obvious is Blake Darby."

"Ruthie's bio-dad."

"He was quiet, almost angry. I mean, that's understandable given Paige's death. They were close friends even though they'd broken things off. But he left in a huff a few minutes before Rebecca brought Ruthie inside." She hated to think the young man would harm them, but... "He *is* Ruthie's biological father. Maybe something snapped in him? Maybe he regrets the adoption?" The words sank in rising bile. The idea of someone trying to take her daughter away by any means necessary was—

"Let's remember he willingly signed away his parental rights. He chose to distance himself from Ruthie. He can't go back now, four years later, and rescind that. Don't let an impossibility hang you up. Ruthie is your daughter. Period. Nothing can change that."

Mia drew in a shaky breath. She knew this, but the reassurance was appreciated.

"So, Blake." Stretching across the counter, Hayden grabbed a pad and a pen and started taking notes. "We'll come back to possible motives later. Focus on opportunity now."

Smart man. Conjecturing about motives would spiral her imagination out of control. Facts would keep her steady. "Okay. Paige's dad was supposedly up in her room, but I never saw him." She picked at a hangnail on her thumb. "He was never happy about the adoption so—"

"No motives. Just opportunity." Hayden wrote *Cade Crosby* on his list. "Who else?"

"I hate to say it, but Sue followed Blake out." There was no way Paige's mother was behind any of this, though.

"We have to consider every angle." Hayden made the note. "Anyone else?" He looked up. "Wait. Daniel and Eve pulled up after we chased the man into the woods. They said they'd run home to grab Ruthie's Christmas present."

Mia nodded. "Yes, but I can't imagine a reason they'd—"

"Every angle."

As long as they were conjecturing, there was one thing that bothered her. "Paige's mentor, Amanda Rhinehart, and her husband, Trent, were there. They didn't leave, but he gave me an odd feeling."

Hayden's pencil paused over the page. "How so?"

"I can't really explain it. It was something about the way—"

"Mommy!" Ruthie burst into the kitchen, a doll strapped into a miniature purple carrier on her chest. "I'm hungry! Can we get nuggets?"

Mia jumped and laid her hand on her chest. "Ruthie. Inside voice. Please."

Skidding to a halt next to Mia, Ruthie planted her fists on her hips and tilted her head. "Penelope and I want nuggets. Please."

At least her voice was a little softer on this go-round. They could work on requests in the form of questions instead of demands later.

Mia looked over her shoulder at Hayden, who mouthed, *Penelope?* He turned the notepad face down on the counter as though Ruthie could read cursive.

Then again, when it came to her daughter, who knew what deeper talents she was hiding. She was a smart one.

Mia took a deep breath, pulled herself into the moment and smiled down into her daughter's hazel eyes as she answered Hayden's question. "*Somebody* has watched a lot of *Wreck-It Ralph*. And *somebody* wanted to be just like Vanellope von Schweetz, but *somebody* had an easier time with their *p*'s than their *v*'s."

"And I like Penelope better." Ruthie bent at the waist to lean closer, her fists still on her hips. "Nuggets, *please*."

It was obvious from the bossiness that Ruthie was pushed to the edge of her four-year-old limits. As much as Mia didn't indulge her daughter's every whim, it was still wise to tread lightly when food and a nap were needed. "Let's do that tomorrow. It's Sunday, and we can't go get the chicken nuggets that are your favorites. I'm sure—"

"It's *Sunday*?" Ruthie's voice screeched to nuclear octaves. She stepped back as though Mia had personally insulted her. "My Christmas play! We can't stay at Uncle Hayden's. We have to go now. It's tonight!" She grabbed Mia's wrist and tugged.

Hayden grabbed the back of Mia's shirt to keep her from toppling to the floor.

The Christmas play. The children's reenactment of the Christmas story was a Sunday-night-before-Christmas tradition. It had been the topic of discussion in their house morning, noon and night for weeks. Anyone listening would think Ruthie's small speaking role had her Tony-Awards bound.

As tears welled in her daughter's eyes, Mia dug her teeth into her lip. How could she explain to a four-year-old that the event she'd looked forward to the most might just get them killed?

Chapter Eight

Hayden's heart broke for his goddaughter. She'd recited her line, "Look at all of the shiny angels," complete with a dramatic flourish toward the sky, at least a hundred times on their outing the morning before. He'd heard it at least a thousand more during her pre-bedtime energy surge the night before.

In their rush to safety, the adults had forgotten the importance of a little girl's Christmas excitement. This would crush Ruthie.

He had to fix it.

Mia tugged her sweater from Hayden's grip, then slipped down to kneel in front of her daughter.

Right. Hayden sat against the stool's back and braced his hands on his thighs. This wasn't his to fix, but he'd do anything to dry the tears already pooling in those precious little eyes.

"Baby, I know this isn't going to make a lot of sense to you, but I need you to listen." Mia laid her hands on her daughter's shoulders. "Sometimes we look forward to things for a really long time. We dream about them, and we plan them, and we look forward to them. They're wonderful and important, and we're really excited about them, just like you've been so excited about the play tonight."

Ruthie tried to pull away, angling for the arched opening that led into the living room. "So we have to go. This is wonderful and important, and we're going to *miss* it."

Hayden wrestled a rush of emotion. He looked down at his hands, running his thumb over a fresh cut on his wrist, probably from his dash through the woods earlier.

Mia's words resonated. Sometimes dreams and plans fell apart. That truth wasn't fair to Ruthie today. It wasn't fair to Mia four years ago. It wasn't fair to him when Beth walked away. *Sometimes, God, life just seems mean.*

Gently, Mia turned her daughter to face her. "Ruthie, I need you to hear me. Can you look in my eyes and listen?"

Ruthie huffed and crossed her arms over her baby doll, eyeing her mother with suspicion.

Mia laid her hand on the baby's head. "You love Penelope, right?"

Like a real mother, Ruthie's expression softened. "Yes." She tucked her chin tightly to her chest and kissed the doll's head.

"And you'd do anything to keep her safe, right?"

"I won't let anything happen to her. I promise."

"I know that, and Penelope knows that. What you need to know is that's how Mommy feels about you. And that's also how God feels about me and you and Uncle Hayden. We all want the people we love to be safe, right?"

Ruthie's eyes narrowed as though she was beginning to understand that there would be no Christmas play.

"Well, sweetie, there are some grown-up things happening right now, so the grown-ups have to keep everybody safe. One of the things we have to do is stay at Uncle Hayden's for a few days."

"Like a sleepover? Like when we went to Noni's during the hurry-cane?"

"Just like that."

Hayden nodded, impressed at Ruthie's understanding. Back in September, Mia had packed up Ruthie, then Hayden had driven them across the state to her grandmother's house as a precaution when Hurricane Jessica threatened to hit the area. The storm had turned eastward at the last second, dampening its effects on the coast, but this was the perfect way for Ruthie to relate to what was happening.

For a moment, it seemed Ruthie accepted the situation, but she suddenly stood taller. "So we're going back for the play. Right now. Because there isn't a hurry-cane."

"Baby, no. This time is different. It's not a—"

"My play!" Ruthie stomped her foot, a full-blown tantrum raining like the hurricane under discussion. "I tell about the angels. Somebody has to tell about the angels. It's important!" Her voice rose to window-rattling levels. "I have to go!"

Mia's posture mimicked her daughter's, spine straight and expression brooking no more discussion. "Ruthie, I'm sorry. I really am. But you can't yell at adults. I know this is making you sad and angry, and I hate that more than anything. Do you need a hug or do you need a few minutes in the playroom by yourself?"

Ruthie's face was stormy. "By myself." She practically shouted her decision, then turned and flounced from the room.

No teenager had ever strutted in such a dismissive manner. Hayden wasn't sure whether to be impressed or terrified as Ruthie thumped up the stairs with the foot-stomping force of an elephant.

Both he and Mia jumped when the door to the bonus room slammed.

With a loud exhale, Mia dropped back onto her heels. Her head bent forward.

Hayden's already broken heart shattered. Ruthie's pain was Mia's pain, and all of it was his pain.

He slid off the stool and sat on the floor, facing her. "I'm sorry."

"It's not your fault." Mia swiped at a tear that ran down her cheek. "It's just not fair."

"No, it's not." He warred between sorrow and anger, his heartache for those he cared about clashing swords with fury at the person who had made this flight necessary. He wanted to hold Mia and Ruthie close and to dry their tears, but, at the same time, he wanted to storm out the door and hunt down the villain behind this.

He'd never felt so torn in his life.

Mia sniffed, cooling some of his ire. At the moment, he couldn't fight the forces outside, but he could do something about the storm raging under his roof.

He watched Mia swipe away another tear. Recent...feelings...said he should be careful about touching her, but he couldn't let her drown in anguish while he simply sat and waited for it all to somehow get better. He'd comforted her many times in the past, so why should now be any different?

It could *not* be any different. He had to maintain their friendship, because if things changed between them...

Shaking off the thought, he rested his hand on her shoulder. "This won't last forever. Nothing ever does."

Mia sniffed. "Good or bad, it all ends, doesn't it?"

She wasn't just talking about Ruthie's tantrum or their present danger.

"What did you just tell Ruthie?" Her words to her daughter worked their way from his head into his heart. "That God loves us and wants us to be safe? He has our best in mind, just like mommies and daddies do for their kids? That applies to you, too."

Her head jerked toward him, and she stared at him through narrowed eyes. It was tough to say if she was angry or thinking. After several heartbeats, she swiped her face and twisted her lips to the side. "Keith and Paige both being murdered is way bigger than a missed Christmas play."

"Not to be disrespectful or to dismiss the severity of what's happened but, in this moment, that Christmas play means the world to Ruthie."

"Four-year-olds don't see the world the same way adults do, especially when they've been sheltered from the truth." Mia shook her head and turned her attention to her fingers, which were knit in her lap. "Thanks for the reminder. You're going to be a great dad someday."

The sentiment drove straight into his heart, skipping the beats out of rhythm. There were a lot of things he could say about that statement, from sappy to serious to way out of line. He chose a fourth option. The moment could use a little levity. "Hey, I'm already the greatest godfather that ever existed."

Mia sniffed and laughed. "You sound like you're about to make me an offer I can't refuse." She quoted one of the most famous lines ever uttered in a movie, tilting her head to meet his gaze with a spark of humor in her eye.

But a different implication to the words zipped through Hayden. What if he offered her his future?

Mia must have seen the shock his own thought rattled through him, because her expression shifted, her smile melting into something Hayden couldn't read. Something that might be surprise or even fear.

He needed to backpedal fast. This thing that had churned up inside of him over the past twenty-four hours was just a side effect of overwrought emotions. It would pass.

He forced a smile. "Actually, I don't have an offer, but I do have an idea to help Ruthie cope with the disappointment." It was risky, but the risks could be mitigated. If it helped the little girl, who had wrapped him around her little finger from the moment she was born, to cope with the chaos swirling around her, then he'd find a way to make it happen.

Tilting her head, Mia regarded him almost as though she knew he was running away from something in his heart. She didn't call him on it, though. She merely stood and brushed off her jeans. "I'm good with anything that will help her. Within reason, of course. This whole situation is so unfair to her."

Hayden scrambled to his feet. "It is. I can't offer her the dream role of Heralding Shepherd in a play, but I can provide a relatively safe substitute."

"Go on."

"There's a farm about twenty minutes from here. They do this huge, multi-acre drive-through Christmas light display. We don't even have to get out of the car to see it. It starts just after sunset and, if we get there when the gates open, we won't have to deal with as many people. I promise she'll be wowed by it." His church small group had volunteered in the prayer tent and had made the drive the previous year, and even the adults had been impressed.

Mia leaned against the counter and stared out the window above the sink, chewing her thumbnail. There was no way she realized she was doing it or she'd have already stopped.

Hayden refrained from reaching over to pull her hand from her mouth, although she'd often told him to do that. It would only distract her from the risk assessment she was running in her head.

She lowered her hand. "Rebecca and Gavin would trail us?"

"I'm thinking they'd love to see the lights themselves, so most definitely." He hoped. He'd certainly call in a ton of favors to get them to do so. And if not them, Kelsie McIlheney and Elliott had offered to step in to add an extra level of security if needed. "I don't think whoever was coming at you realizes we've relocated here. Unless they know you really well and know where I live, I doubt they'll find us." It wasn't totally without risk, but Ruthie needed something, and they couldn't let fear hem them in.

Mia nodded, though the tight lines around her mouth indicated she did so with reservations. "Okay. Hopefully this will help her out."

And hopefully, his soft heart for his goddaughter wasn't about to drive them straight into danger.

* * *

"Mommy! Look!" How Ruthie's squeal hadn't already broken the windshield of Hayden's pickup was beyond Mia's ability to comprehend. Her ears were still ringing from the last eight excited outbursts.

Hayden chuckled, though he kept his attention on the car in front of them. They snaked along in a line of cars that wound through trees and fields filled with too many Christmas lights and displays to count. He had tuned the radio to the instructed station at the beginning of the twenty-minute drive, and the familiar litany of the Grinch's many faults graveled from the speakers. Despite his belief that they'd beat the crowds by coming early, they were far from the first car in line.

Trying to shake out the discomfort in her ears, Mia swallowed the automatic *Inside voice, please* that wanted to rise up. Her daughter needed the freedom to be an awestruck child tonight.

They all needed to be awestruck children tonight.

She looked to where Ruthie was strapped into her booster in the back seat. "What do you want me to see?"

Ruthie waved excitedly toward the windshield. "It's the Grinch and Max! And they're zooming down the mountain!" She swooshed her hand to illustrate their journey.

Hayden tapped Mia's knee and pointed to the left. Sure enough, on a small hill that sloped down to the wide path they were on, a Grinch made entirely out of lights guided his sleigh toward them. His long-suffering dog, Max, galloped in the lead thanks to the magic of multiple flashing lights.

Mia laughed. The Grinch was Ruthie's favorite, and his story was interspersed with the various other displays throughout the show.

As Ruthie giggled, Mia glanced into the side mirror, where the headlights from Rebecca and Gavin's sedan followed close behind.

The song on the radio faded and shifted to the Chipmunks singing about their two front teeth as a lit display of the animals appeared in front of them.

Mia allowed herself to relax and take in the Christmas cheer. For the moment, they were safe. Ensconced in the pickup with the heater blasting and the cheerful music playing, she could almost pretend that the world was as it should be.

Almost. Outside of the relative safety of the winding drive and the hundreds of other cars in front of and behind them, danger lurked.

But what had her therapist said to her so many times? *Be in the moment you're in. Not in the past. Not in the future. Enjoy the now.*

The *now* was pretty close to, well, *normal.*

Ruthie squealed again.

The *now* was also pretty loud.

Pressing her palm to her ear, she looked at Ruthie and laughed as her daughter bounced in her seat. It was a good thing the cup of hot chocolate Hayden had purchased through the window as they'd pulled up to the gates had a lid on it. Otherwise, the interior of Hayden's truck would never be the same.

Ruthie didn't offer an explanation for her excitement this time. She simply looked from right to left, trying to take it all in. The lights reflected in her eyes, filling them with wonder.

For the first time in four years, wrapped in the safety of Hayden's truck, Mia felt fear release, allowing in a peace she'd chased for what felt like an eternity.

As she started to turn back to the front, she caught Hayden's gaze. In the brief moment that their eyes locked, electricity zipped between them, arcing down her spine from the top of her head to the tips of her toes.

What was *that*?

She whipped to the front, pressing her back into the seat and her toes into the floor. An electric tingle chased the zap down her spine until her nervous system finally righted itself.

Gratitude. That's all it was. Hayden was always here, always taking care of her and of Ruthie. He was a constant in their lives, and he sacrificed so much more than she would ever dare to ask of him. It was as simple as that.

"You okay?" Hayden's voice barely drifted over the Chipmunks' song. It was the first time he'd spoken since they'd followed the car in front of them onto the path of Christmas cheer.

"Fine." She'd better get herself back to normal quickly. Hayden was perceptive, and that little *zap* could definitely put the awkward into their friendship if he picked up on it. "I'm just…content. At least for right now." She dared to squeeze his wrist where his hand rested on the gearshift. "Thank you. This was so much more than I thought it would be, and I think I needed it even more than Ruthie did."

When she gathered herself enough to look up, his gaze darted between hers and the slow-moving car in front of them. "I'm glad." He slipped his hand from the gearshift and entwined his fingers with hers, offering a quick squeeze.

Mia squeezed back, but when she tried to pull away, Hayden didn't let go.

The warmth of his touch, the solidness of his presence, the oasis of calm inside the vehicle… It all washed a peace through her that she hadn't experienced in years. A feeling of being in the right place with the right person.

Digging her teeth into her lower lip, Mia gently untangled her fingers from his and pulled her hand into her lap. She was only feeling safe because Hayden was her friend and was a constant in her life. She couldn't sink any deeper into this than friendship. There could never be anything past that. Hayden deserved more than to be shackled to a broken single mother whom he'd have to take care of for the rest of his days.

He deserved someone…normal.

With a sigh, she looked out the side window, desperate for a distraction. "Ruthie, look." She pointed into the woods at the edge of a large field. "There's Snoopy."

Ruthie clapped her hands as the song on the radio changed to the tale of Snoopy and the Red Baron. It was a thing of wonder how technology could so seamlessly line everything up into a precise, dependable experience.

If only life worked that way.

As they wound toward the end of the drive, the music shifted to traditional Christmas hymns, and the lit displays featured the story of Jesus's birth, from Mary on a donkey with Joseph leading the way to a chorus of glowing angels suspended from the trees above a group of gaping shepherds.

"Hey, Mommy!" Ruthie leaned forward as far as she could, pointing to the angels. "Look at all of the shiny angels!" She recited the line she should have been speaking at the church at almost this exact moment, had things been as they should. Rather than disappointment, though, she sounded excited and happy, and she joined in with the radio to sing "Away in a Manger" as they passed the Nativity scene that was the last display on the drive.

Her daughter's joy was thanks to Hayden and his quick thinking.

She started to tell him so, but Ruthie's voice shattered her thoughts. "Mommy! Uncle Hayden! Look!"

Hayden muttered under his breath. In the dim light, he winced and mouthed, *I forgot.*

As Ruthie bounced in her seat, Mia looked out the windshield. Across a large grassy parking lot, a painted plywood Christmas village that included several small stores and a café shone through the darkness. To the right, a large open gazebo featured a live Santa and Mrs. Claus, visiting with children who raced toward them.

Oh, no. Every ounce of cheer drained out of Mia. Ruthie would melt down if they bypassed the scene to follow the exit signs onto the road.

But they didn't dare stop and join the crowds making their way between the shops and the Santa display. There were too many people. It was too risky. The crowds were more than Mia was prepared to handle, and there was no way for Hayden and his friends to ensure they'd be safe if they exited his truck.

Her peace shattered, and the shards sliced into her lungs, making it hard to breathe. Everything she knew about being a mother said her child pitching a hissy fit wasn't the end of the world. Piled onto everything else, though, it felt like more than either of them could handle.

Hayden slowed, increasing the space between his truck and the car in front of them. "Ruthie, let's make a deal."

The excited chatter stopped, followed by a suspicious, "What kind of deal?"

The child was savvy. She knew a *deal* meant she wasn't going to get what she wanted.

Hayden tapped Mia on the knee. When she looked up, he whispered, "Trust me?" His arched eyebrow spoke of uncertainty.

Mia nodded. He knew she did.

With an answering tip of his head, he proceeded in an overly cheerful voice. "The line for Santa is really long. How about instead of freezing our toes and fingers off waiting to see him, we go back to my house and watch the Grinch movie instead."

"But, Santa!" The whine was in full effect.

"I wasn't finished." Hayden upped the cheer another notch.

"Okay." Ruthie's reply was dubious.

"I'll take you through the drive-through at the ice cream place and you can have whatever you want."

"Even sprinkles?"

Mia slumped in her seat. It seemed the crisis was averted. While she wouldn't typically approve of bribing her daughter out of a tantrum, extenuating circumstances ruled the day.

"Triple sprinkles." Hayden agreed to the terms of surrender.

"Yay! Let's go!" Ruthie's cheer was restored, but her voice quickly changed. "Mommy?"

Mia squeezed her eyes shut. She knew that tone. What was

coming would be tough to wriggle out of, especially since they were twenty minutes from any sort of civilization besides the light show. "Yes, baby?"

"I have to go potty."

Air hissed between Hayden's teeth. Yeah, even he knew this was going to be difficult. He followed a path, parking the truck at the end of a long row of vehicles. "Our church worked out here one year, staffing the prayer tent they have by the Santa display. There's a smaller separate set of bathrooms used by volunteers that the public doesn't know about." He looked at her. "There might be a couple of volunteers who come in and out because there are two stalls, but it'll keep you out of the crowds."

She could handle that.

As Rebecca pulled up beside them, Hayden walked around the truck to tell her and Gavin what was going on.

Ruthie started the little dance that let Mia know she wasn't going to make it much longer.

No one was around the small plywood building Hayden had indicated, tucked away several feet from the end of the row of shops. Hayden could see her from where he stood.

Tugging Ruthie's hand, they headed for the restroom, and Mia waited by the sinks for Ruthie to take care of herself. After Ruthie washed her hands, she wandered to the open doorway while Mia washed hers, keeping one eye on her daughter.

Ruthie leaned out the door. "Hello!"

Mia's heart picked up speed. Ruthie had never met a stranger she wouldn't talk to, but now was not the time for her to be making new friends. She quickly shook off her hands as Ruthie stepped closer to the door.

A low voice spoke outside, and Ruthie nodded. "The lights were so pretty, and I saw the Grinch so many times!"

The voice spoke again, and Ruthie took another step toward the door.

Mia practically leaped for her daughter. "Time to go,

Ruthie." She latched on to Ruthie's shoulder as a person kneeling in the shadows to the side of the door stood and backed away.

A familiar person.

Reflexively, Mia jerked Ruthie up into her arms and screamed for Hayden.

Chapter Nine

Hayden sprinted toward the small huts with Mia's scream echoing in his ears. He'd had the restrooms within his sight the entire time. What had happened?

Two car doors slammed. Rebecca and Gavin were right behind him.

Mia was backing into the open door of the bathroom, holding Ruthie tightly against her.

A figure darted into the shadows, running into the space between buildings and disappearing into the darkness behind the row of shops.

Hayden yelled orders over his shoulder. "Rebecca. Gavin. Behind the building!"

"Saw them." Rebecca acknowledged the command, veering in that direction with Gavin at her heels. They were more than capable of handling the threat that was, fortunately, heading away from the holiday revelers in the Christmas village.

It took him what seemed like years to reach Mia and Ruthie. By the time he got to the wooden steps of the small building, his heart was pounding as though he didn't run five miles most mornings.

Mia's face was pale, even in the dim light filtering out from the restrooms.

Ruthie's eyes were wide with shock. Her young mind was likely incapable of processing anything that had happened.

Hayden pulled them close, with Ruthie sandwiched between him and Mia. Mia began to tremble so hard that Hayden could hear her teeth knocking together. "What happened?"

Ruthie wriggled and squirmed until Hayden was forced to back away so Mia could set her down. He looked at Ruthie, who stood in the gap between them, her fists pressed into her hips in a familiar exasperated gesture.

She glared up at Hayden. "I was talking to a nice lady, and Mommy yelled and scared me."

Hayden's gaze rose to Mia's. Had she panicked at the sight of one of the volunteers and frightened an innocent woman into the woods?

No. The fear in Mia's expression was different. This wasn't like the moments when her emotions took over her rational thinking. Her wide eyes were clear and terrified.

She kept her hands firmly planted on her daughter's shoulders. Her lips parted as though she might speak, but then she looked down at Ruthie. She stared at her little girl for a long time before she lifted her head and shook it once, tight-lipped. Whatever she needed to say, she wasn't going to risk frightening her daughter any more than she already had. "We should go."

They should. Getting the two of them to safety was Hayden's first priority. When he had the whole story, he might need to call the sheriff and Ross Hartnett, who owned the farm hosting the light show, to alert them if the threat turned out to be credible.

He was reluctant to leave without Rebecca and Gavin. His team would provide protection from the rear, watching for a tail as they headed back to his house. Although he had no idea what had scared Mia, the fear that they'd been found dominated his thoughts.

With one arm protectively around Mia and the other hand

on Ruthie's shoulder, he turned them toward the parking lot. He'd get them into the truck and—

"McGrath," Gavin called out as he jogged up with Rebecca. His grim expression confirmed the worst. "Whoever it was, they had a head start. This place backs up to a pretty dense wooded area. They could be anywhere or they could be long gone, but we're both pretty sure it was a female."

"Police?" Hayden reached for his phone.

"No." Mia was emphatic. "Technically, there's no crime, and we don't dare risk crying wolf."

She was right. There was no crime to report...yet.

Hayden herded everyone toward the truck, debating whether or not to make the call. Caution said he should, but raising a false alarm could slow the response if they really needed help in the future.

Fine. Until he got the whole story, they were on their own. Hayden kept walking as Gavin took up a position beside him and Rebecca moved around to walk with Mia.

Hayden took charge. "Follow us back to the house. Watch for a tail." He kept his voice low to prevent Ruthie from hearing. If she found out that her drive-through ice cream had been taken off the table, it might be one disappointment too many. While she was normally a well-behaved kid, the chaos around her had drawn out a rare irritability. It was better to deal with the emotional fallout at home.

He would have someone run to the store and buy every sprinkle on the ice cream aisle if he had to, but that wasn't his number-one priority.

Right now, he had to get his girls to safety and find out what had happened.

He ushered them into the truck and handed his phone back to Ruthie to distract her. They were on the road and moving along the miles-long line of cars that waited for admittance into the light show before he spoke. Glancing in the rearview to ensure Ruthie was sufficiently occupied and his trail vehicle was in place, he kept his voice low. "What happened?" It wasn't like Mia to scream.

Mia balled her fists on her knees and turned from where she'd been staring out the side window. Lines creased her forehead and dug trenches beside her mouth.

He'd seen this posture before. She was fighting a panic attack.

Times like this made him feel helpless. Sometimes she wanted to be comforted, but other times she wanted to be left alone as she went to war with her own mind and body. He never knew what to do until he tried.

Reaching across the console, he took a chance that she'd prefer to be comforted. He laid his hand on her clenched fist. "I'm here. Gavin and Rebecca are right behind us. You're safe right now. Let me handle the details. It's okay to let go."

Impossibly, her muscles tightened. One hand darted for the door, and she laid a finger on the button to roll down the window, seeking fresh air.

As suddenly as she'd tensed, her body relaxed. Her right hand fell to the seat beside her, and her fist relaxed beneath his grip. In the headlights of the vehicles lined up beside the road, tears glistened down her cheeks. "I'm not losing my mind."

"Nobody said you were." Was she doubting what she'd seen? Had she panicked and misread the situation?

He didn't want to think so. Even in the depths of fear, Mia managed to maintain a semblance of situational awareness. The things in her mind tended to frighten her more than the dangers she encountered in real life. "Can you tell me what happened?"

She relayed a stop-and-start story about Ruthie talking to someone at the door, but then she grew quiet. When she looked at Hayden, determination had set her jaw and had erased the lines that fear had etched into her forehead. "The woman Ruthie was talking to? I've seen her before." Mia leaned closer and lowered her voice. "Yesterday, at the café. She's the one with the backpack."

"The one who looked familiar to you?" This couldn't be a coincidence. Mia crossing paths with the same random woman twice in two different towns in two days was definitely odd. "You're certain?"

"Yes, Hayden." Her voice cracked like a whip. "I'm not losing my mind."

He winced, then reset his expression. Fear often lit a fire under Mia's anger. Volcanic emotions tended to erupt with various forms of lava. Sometimes it was hard not to take offense. It took restraint not to react, to step back and respond with kindness when he came under friendly fire.

Hayden kneaded the steering wheel as they reached the last in the long line of cars. He eyed the dark two-lane road ahead of them, where danger could be lurking.

In the rearview, Gavin's sedan kept pace about four car lengths back, standing between them and any threats from the rear. Several other vehicles followed them, likely other spectators who were making their way back to the four-lane state highway. Once there, it would be easier to determine if they had picked up a tail. He'd drive the exact speed limit, and most cars would pass them. After that, he'd take the most winding way home possible.

With Rebecca and Gavin watching the rear, Hayden could focus on Mia. He'd never been more grateful for his team. Their vigilance gave him time to pull away from the unfamiliar role of bodyguard into the more comfortable roles of friend and investigator.

If this woman had been able to flush Mia out of the restaurant in Wincombe and had also managed to find them near Elizabeth City, then… "I think we need to look at the possibility that the person who attacked you in Watchman's Alley might have been this woman."

Mia lifted her chin, staring at the ceiling of the pickup. "I've considered that. But did she purposely come into the café to unsettle me, knowing that I have panic attacks and she'd throw me off balance enough to make me run? Or did she randomly walk in, see me, then take her chances when I went into the alley? While a lot of people know what I'm going through emotionally, not a lot of people would know how to…" Her voice dropped. "How to pull my strings like I'm a puppet."

"Hey." He took her hand, needing to comfort her but also needing to watch the dark road ahead of them. "None of this is your fault."

Mia turned away. She pulled her hand from his, withdrawing into herself.

Hayden glanced at Ruthie in the rearview to make sure she was still engrossed in his phone, then turned his attention to the windshield. While the danger outside was very real, the bigger threat might be to Mia's mental health. If these attacks kept coming, she might turn completely inside to protect herself.

And that could be the most dangerous thing of all.

Mia sank onto Hayden's leather sofa and pulled a cream-colored throw pillow onto her lap, staring at the blank television screen above his fireplace.

The house was silent. *Finally.* Pumped full of holiday cheer, the Grinch cartoon and ice cream sprinkles provided by Hayden's boss, Ruthie hadn't settled down until nearly ten. Hayden had carried her up to the guest room, then disappeared while Mia had prepared her limp and exhausted daughter for bed. Ruthie had dropped off the moment her head hit the pillow.

Mia's ears were tired. Her body was tired. Her emotions were tired. All she wanted was to run until she couldn't run any more, until she finally felt safe.

At the moment, it seemed nowhere would ever feel safe

again. Not her hometown. Not her home. Not Hayden's house. The places she'd always counted on were all compromised.

Hayden's alarm keypad sounded a two-tone chime, and the door that led to the garage closed softly. A low rumble indicated that Hayden had pushed the button to lower the exterior garage door. Several beeps drifted from the kitchen as he set the alarm for the night.

Would it do any good? Her home had an alarm, but that hadn't stopped someone from trying to smoke them out.

When he walked through the kitchen doorway, he didn't seem surprised to see her on the couch. He looked slightly sheepish. "Sorry about Ruthie bouncing off the walls tonight. The sugar rush was totally my fault."

She actually smiled. "Yeah, I'm pretty sure her mother never authorized feeding her an entire container of ice cream sprinkles, but hey, you're here to deal with the consequences so I'm passing the torch." If Ruthie woke up crying with a stomachache, she'd gladly tell Hayden *I told you so*. "Still, it was worth it to see her happy. I think you might have successfully overwritten the memory of her mom freaking out at the bathroom door because she was talking to a 'nice lady.'" The words tasted bitter. While the grown-ups had to worry about threats, her daughter was still free to view life through a child's eyes. It was a blessing and a curse as Mia tried to teach her daughter to navigate a world that would gladly eat them both alive. The trick was guiding her toward wisdom while maintaining Ruthie's innocence.

And now that the hypothetical threats were real?

Mia drew her finger along the edge of the pillow. "I don't know how to handle any of this." She looked up at Hayden, who hadn't moved from the doorway. "Whoever thinks their husband is going to be murdered? That four years later, someone will try to hurt them as well? This doesn't happen in real life, does it?"

"You were a soldier and a law enforcement officer." He

walked over and sat on the other end of the couch, angling toward her. "You know the answer to that question."

It did happen. Every day. But it happened to other people, not to her. "This can't be my life. It's just not…real."

"You've told me before that anxiety makes you feel like you've taken a step back from reality. Maybe—"

Mia rocketed to her feet, the pillow dropping to the floor. "Why can't I shake this? Why does everything go back to the night Keith died? Why can't I just be…?" She threw her hands into the air, the words refusing to form. Since that awful night, nothing had been the same. The thing that had changed the most was the monster that lived inside of her mind, spinning frightening tall tales. It was never silent, at least not for long. It was always telling her that danger lurked around every corner, that something bad could happen to her or to Ruthie at any moment. Worse, it often told her exactly what that person had hissed hot against her ear in the alley.

That she was a terrible mother.

She wrapped her arms around her stomach and turned away from Hayden, looking up at the ceiling fan. It could use a good dusting.

Why was she noticing that now?

"I'm not losing my mind." Was she? Because the threat wasn't just being whispered into her brain this time. It was truly all around her.

Unless she was imagining everything.

The couch rustled behind her, then Hayden was there. He laid his hands on her shoulders and rested his chin on top of her head. "That's the third time you've said that tonight."

"Said what?" She wanted to step away, but she couldn't. The firm pressure of his hands on her shoulders and the warmth of his presence so close behind held her captive, but not in a bad way. It hemmed her in. Made her feel safe. Made her feel like maybe she wasn't about to drown beneath a wave of panic.

His chest moved against her back as he spoke. "You're not

losing your mind. Nobody thinks you are, least of all me."
He gently turned her to face him, then reset his hands on her
shoulders. "Mia, I know the hardest part of this isn't the fear
itself, the things digging into your thoughts. It's the ripple effect. You think people look at you differently. It's damaged
your entire life. You think you're weak, but in reality, you're
probably the strongest person I've ever known."

Mia shook her head. He had no idea what she endured every
single day.

"No, ma'am." His voice was gentle as he stepped around in
front of her. He tipped his head to try to catch her eye, but she
focused on the knit of his blue sweater where it stretched across
his chest. "Don't do this to yourself. A grenade got tossed into
the center of your world, and the damage was immense. Some
of it can't be repaired. Keith can't come back to life. Think
about it like combat. Explosions cause concussive injuries.
Some are temporary, others are permanent, but none are the
injured person's fault. They didn't pull the pin." He hooked
his finger under her chin and forced her to meet his eye. "Just
like soldiers have to do hard work to heal from physical injuries, it takes hard work to come back from mental and emotional ones. You're building something new, something that
won't look like the old way. You're recovering. That takes time
and energy and strength, and I admire you for it. I wish…"
His gaze slid from hers, lingering on something to his right.

Mia's mouth went dry. Something was…shifting. It was in
the feel of his hands on her shoulders. The deep rumble of his
words. The look in his eye. It reached into places in her heart
that had long been parched and dead, and rained new life.

Hayden was her friend. Her confidant. But could there be
something more? Because right now, more than she'd ever
wanted anything in her life, she wanted to close the distance
between them. She wanted to feel the full circle of his arms
around her, knowing if he held her close that she'd be warm
and safe and…

Whole.

Her lungs couldn't take in a full breath, but, far from the panic attacks that usually robbed her of air, this was different. This was something she hadn't felt since…since forever. Something that made her want to connect to this man in a way she'd never thought she would want to connect with anyone again.

Hayden's gaze returned to hers and lingered, searching. The longer he searched, the more she wanted to stay here forever. The more his expression softened, the more he looked like he wanted to—

His eyes dropped to her lips, then slowly scanned her face before returning, asking for permission.

Mia's heart kicked up to a dangerous pace. He had to be able to feel it.

But she didn't look away. Hopefully, he'd understand that—

His hands slid along her shoulders and up her neck, cupping her jaw. His thumbs stroked her cheeks. He leaned closer, raising her head slightly, and brushed her lips softly, returning to deepen the kiss before she could catch her breath.

Pulling her closer, his touch shattered her fear, reminding her what it felt like to be safe and sheltered and whole.

Chapter Ten

Hayden's knees went weak. He was pretty sure it was Mia holding the two of them up, because it certainly wasn't him. No woman had ever literally stolen his strength before. Not even when he'd been engaged to Beth had he felt his entire core so rattled, so—

Beth. Keith.

Mia.

Hayden inhaled sharply and backed away, his arms up and out to the sides as though he wanted to prove he was unarmed. "Mia, I am so sorry." He never should have kissed her. Never should have let himself get so caught up in a moment of admiration that he crossed a line.

She was his best friend. She was his best friend's wife. She was—

His head spun. But Keith was gone. Mia was a widow.

What was right? What was…what was anything? Mia talked so often about feeling detached from reality. He definitely felt like his life was not his own right now, as though he was watching it on a television screen.

Mia stumbled backward, her eyes wide. "I…" She pointed vaguely toward the stairs. "I have to go. Ruthie… I need…"

Shaking her head, her expression a mixture of confusion and pain, she practically ran up the stairs without looking back.

Hayden's heart fell as he watched her retreat. Yeah, he'd crossed a line. A big one. Worse, he couldn't even explain why. Sure, he'd been feeling…things…for the past day or so, but he hadn't realized…

Forget it. He scooped the discarded throw pillow from the floor, a "decorating touch" his mother had chosen, and sat heavily on the couch, letting the pillow drop onto his lap. His head fell to the back cushions. He wrapped his forearms over his face. He was an idiot, plain and simple. What kind of guy kissed his best friend, especially when her life was in so much turmoil that she'd confessed she had no idea which way was up?

Needing to move, he flung the pillow to the side and stalked to the back door in the kitchen. He turned off the alarm, hoping the chimes wouldn't frighten Mia, then stepped onto the patio, where two canvas beach chairs were the only furnishings. He dropped into one and turned his face to the stars, but no prayers would come.

He was an awful person. He'd failed to protect Mia and instead had selfishly taken advantage of both of their emotional upheaval. For what?

For a kiss.

A kiss that had been life-changing. Literally breathtaking. That had—

"You look like a man who regrets every single one of his life decisions."

At the deep voice from his left, Hayden jumped up and whirled, ready to fight.

It was Elliott, who'd switched places with Gavin for the night. His boss walked to the chair next to Hayden and sat, stretching his legs in front of him and crossing his ankles as though they were two buddies chatting after a cookout.

What would it be like to be as confident as Elliott? He was

unflappable, always analyzing, never "up in his feels," as he'd heard some of the younger members at church say. As much as Hayden hated that phrase, he definitely understood what it meant tonight.

"McGrath? You asleep over there?" Elliott's voice held the thread of sarcastic amusement that marked his personality.

"Deciding how much I want to say." He'd always been able to talk to his boss and friend, but this felt sort of like a high-school-crush problem and not an adult issue that needed to be analyzed.

"Hmm." Lacing his hands on his stomach, Elliott stared at the privacy fence at the back of the small yard. "I'm going to guess this is about more than figuring out who's hunting Mia and whether or not they've found you guys here." Without lifting his head from the back of the chair, he looked at Hayden. "And we're going to have to come back to that eventually, because even though I'm here watching the rear and Kelsie is keeping an eye out front, that may not be enough. If Mia's seen this woman twice, then it's pretty clear somebody knows y'all ran here. I'm going to recommend a safe house, even though you rejected the idea the first eight times I suggested it."

Would an unfamiliar place really be the best for Ruthie? "I don't know if—"

Elliott held up a hand to silence Hayden's protest. "That's a conversation for later. Right now, you've got some muck in your head that you need to clear out before we try to get tactical. Otherwise, you'll overwhelm and short-circuit. That's how bad decisions are made."

Hayden ran his finger along a rough spot in the plastic chair arm, ashamed that Elliott was right. He needed to release the valve on the thoughts and emotions he was desperately trying to cram into a pipe that had already burst. "It's Mia."

"I figured."

"Her husband and I were best friends our whole lives, and Mia was a part of that friendship almost as long." He wrapped his fingers around the chair arm. "How can I be feeling things for my best friend's wife? For my best friend now?"

"Well, first of all, we need to work on your terminology and maybe your slightly off-center sense of morality."

"What?" Hayden sputtered. "My off-center morality?"

"I said what I said." Elliott chuckled, then grew quiet. Long moments passed before he spoke again. "McGrath, as hard as this has been and still is, you and Mia both have to accept that Keith isn't coming back. While I'm sure Mia will always love him, he's no longer here. There is absolutely nothing wrong with having feelings for her."

The words hit so hard, Hayden flinched. He stared at the rarely used charcoal grill at the corner of the patio. It was the same kind his dad had used up until he'd passed away seven years ago from a sudden heart attack. Recognizing the childhood nostalgia that would link him to memories of his father, Mia had bought the grill as a housewarming gift when he'd moved in.

She was threaded through so much of his past and his present. Chances were high it would ruin him if he had to untangle her from his future.

Funny, but he couldn't see anything past today, had never let himself think about tomorrow. "After Keith died, I stopped caring about what came next. He didn't get another day. He had plans with Mia. They'd just adopted Ruthie. They had so many dreams, and every one of them was gunned down without warning." He continued to study the grill, draped in a canvas cover that kept it safe but attested to the little enjoyment he got out of it, since he never had the time to use it. "Just a few months later, Beth walked out. She took all of my dreams with her."

"Did she? Or did you lock them away from her?"

He ought to take offense at the insinuation that he'd destroyed his own relationship, but the words sank deep and heavy, dampening his anger.

Hayden pulled a piece of plastic from the chair. Had he pushed Beth away? He'd always assumed she'd been too weak to handle the grief they were walking through, had run at the first signs of struggle but... "I was spending a lot of time helping Mia with Ruthie. I was..." He clamped his back teeth together as memories shoved out of the closet where he'd locked them.

The arguments about setting a wedding date, picking a venue, finding a house...

In the wake of Keith's death, Hayden had stopped considering the future. The trauma of witnessing his best friend lying dead on the floor of a convenience store had shaken his life off its foundation. He'd fallen into a hopeless funk, unable to consider a future that might be violently ripped away. All of Beth's talk of weddings and houses had seemed trivial and foolish.

But they hadn't been trivial or foolish to Beth. The realization almost doubled him over. He pressed his hands against his stomach to keep it from making a run out of his body. Beth had wanted a future with him, had needed reassurance that he still wanted one with her, but he'd been so closed off in his grief, so focused on making sure his goddaughter and his friend were surviving, that he'd neglected the woman who loved him.

Then he'd blamed her when she'd chosen a life path that wasn't marred by his inability to love her in the way she deserved.

Sick pain muddied his veins. He'd hurt her so badly. How had he never seen it?

He should apologize, but there was no way to make this right. Beth had married a teacher in Dare County two years earlier and lived on Hatteras Island now, where she worked for a real estate company in Avon. She was happy with a man who'd made her his world and cared about her feelings, as she deserved. He'd have to pray about reaching out to her, but she definitely needed some form of apology, because he'd stopped considering her when he'd nearly drowned in his grief.

"It might be time to start thinking about what your future looks like. You're still here and breathing. So is Mia. Neither of you can close the book and call your story done. You say you believe in God, and you're always talking about Him like He's a part of you. Maybe you need to think about why the guy upstairs still has you here." Elliott had always scoffed when anyone spoke of Jesus, but clearly, he'd been listening.

Elliott pulled his feet closer and stood, looking down at Hayden. "Brother, let me tell you something. I know you're struggling with taking on Keith's case for the relook, but I think you're the exact right person. Maybe your closure is going to come when you face his death head-on and truly grieve it. You walked Mia through it, but you never felt it for yourself. You internalized it and you hid from it. Watch the video, McGrath. It won't be easy, but it's necessary." With a cuff to the side of Hayden's head, Elliott walked away, disappearing around the side of the house.

Hayden rubbed the side of his head, then slumped in his chair. This was too much revelation for one night. He'd kissed Mia, and frankly, he'd enjoyed it up until guilt took a baseball bat to the back of his head. He also needed to deal with the fact that they might have been tracked to his house, and now he was being asked to confront the past as well.

It was overwhelming.

He rocketed to his feet, restless and needing to move. He had to do something.

Maybe Elliott was right. Maybe he needed to stop hiding from the hard things. The only way to do that was to do the most difficult thing he could imagine.

To turn on his computer and watch his best friend die.

Mia bent forward on the carpet and wrapped her arms around her legs. Pressing her head against her knees, she rocked on the floor beside the bed, fighting tremors that threatened to rip her apart. Tonight had been too much. Everything was just...too...much.

Emotions swamped her. Her fingers and toes went numb. Her heart stuttered. Her mind raced even faster than her pulse. Her teeth knocked together as though she was freezing, yet her skin was hot. She couldn't function another second.

The walls were closing in.

The woman at the Christmas lights. The whiplash of feeling safe and then facing danger.

Kissing her best friend.

Mia whimpered and leaped to her feet, wobbling as her balance struggled to catch up. Grabbing the corner of the nightstand, she held on until the room stopped spinning. As soon as her feet felt secure, she paced the room, her arms wrapped around her stomach.

She had enough to process without diving into that kiss and the way it had made her feel. For a moment, she'd forgotten everything except Hayden, and it had been...freeing.

It had also been completely out of control.

Out of control was bad.

She needed to get out. To run. To breathe fresh air.

But Hayden's alarm system was even better than hers, and she'd heard him engage it a few moments earlier, when the keypad in his room down the hall beeped confirmation that he'd armed the system. Even opening a window could set off an alarm that would awaken Ruthie or bring Hayden's armed teammates on the run.

God, help me. It felt as though her skeleton was going to leap from her skin. She fought for breath, crying out silent prayers.

Please make it stop.

When she finally figured out her central fear, the cries of her heart poured forth. *Make it stop. All of it.* The panic attacks. The fear. The physical assaults on her family. *God, make it stop. You have the ability. You're God. All-powerful. All-knowing. Snap Your finger. Say the word. Just...make it stop.*

Once the words were out, the tears followed, and the tension in her body released. She dropped to the edge of the bed and fell onto her back, staring at the ceiling as tears ran into her ears. Anger replaced the fear, and the desire to pray evaporated. How mean was a God who could take away her pain but chose not to?

I don't want to talk to You. She felt like Ruthie in full hissy fit mode. If she crossed her arms and stomped her foot, the transformation would be complete.

She no longer cared if she looked immature or silly. This wasn't the first time she'd railed at God. It wouldn't be the last. Everything was so unfair. Hadn't they been through enough?

Rocketing to her feet, Mia headed for the door on autopilot. She needed water. Food. Anything to distract her from her thoughts. There would be no sleep anytime soon, even given how spent she was after a full-blown panic attack.

At the door, Mia stopped with her hand on the cool metal knob. If she went downstairs, she ran a 100 percent risk of seeing Hayden.

Could she face him?

Claustrophobia beat humiliation. She had to get out of this room, maybe talk Hayden into letting her sit outside for a few minutes. His friends would protect her. She just needed air.

She crept down the stairs, trying not to disturb him if he'd fallen asleep on the couch. Even if he hadn't, maybe she could sneak into the kitchen without him noticing. Given the house's open floor plan, that was likely impossible, but a girl could dream.

Could she handle looking him in the eye so soon after...? When she couldn't even articulate the feelings spinning inside of her? When she had no idea if that kiss had been a reaction to trauma or if it had been very, very real?

Because it sure had felt real.

When she reached the bottom of the stairs, the space was empty. Mia stepped into the living room, her brow furrowed. Every light in the downstairs was on, even the decorative lamp on the built-in bookshelf. It was as though Hayden had a compulsive need to dispel every shadow in the house.

The kitchen lights were ablaze as well. Her cheek twitched as tears stung her eyes. Sometimes she forgot that Hayden suffered, too. That he'd been present on the night Keith died. That he'd lost his best friend just as surely as she'd lost hers.

His amped-up alarm system was a silent testament to the inner turmoil he felt but rarely spoke. Maybe he normally kept all of the lights on, vainly trying to keep the darkness of night from creeping into his home.

But where was he? She'd heard him arm the alarm system, and he'd never come upstairs. His bedroom door was open, and the room had been dark when she passed.

She turned a slow circle and paused when she faced the front door. On the right side of the entry was an open dining room that he used as a man cave, where various military awards and photos were displayed. On the left side of the entry was a small office with French doors and built-in bookshelves. He must be in there.

The kitchen was behind her. Hayden was in front of her. She could easily slip in, get something to drink, hide until she regained her equilibrium, then sneak back upstairs. That would be taking care of herself, and no one would fault her.

Or, she could face her best friend despite the awkwardness and ask how he was doing. If she was spinning out of control, then he was likely feeling the vertigo of the past few days as well. That would be taking care of someone else.

For once, she needed to do the selfless thing.

Steeling herself against the sight of him, she pressed her fingers to her lips in a vain attempt to erase the sensation of his kiss, then walked toward the door.

When she peeked into the office, Hayden was sitting at

his oversize wooden desk facing the door, his head buried in his hands and his laptop open before him. It was a posture of hopelessness and defeat.

She'd done this to him. She'd dragged him into her world of fear and had forced him and his coworkers to protect her from a stalker... No, two stalkers.

Her heart ached. Maybe she should reach out to the police, although that would do no good. The crimes in Wincombe were under Tyrrell County's jurisdiction, and they were already being investigated. There'd been no actual crime tonight, although the woman was certainly suspicious and possibly dangerous. Still, there had to be some way to free Hayden from having to worry about her. Maybe she could take Ruthie to her grandmother's house in the mountains. Would they be safe there?

As she backed away from the door, the hardwood floor creaked.

Hayden's head jerked up, his hands rushing to close his laptop. "Mia." He exhaled roughly. "I didn't know what that noise was."

"Sorry. I didn't mean to scare you. I was feeling trapped upstairs and came down for some water. I shouldn't have bothered you." It was the last thing she'd wanted.

He slid the laptop aside, staring at it for a long time before he looked at her. "You can come in." He flicked his index finger toward one of the comfy leather chairs in front of the desk. "I'd rather not work tonight anyway."

Mia crept into the room and sat on the edge of the chair. *Work.* That meant... "Keith's case?" Until now, she'd forgotten he was heading up the reinvestigation.

His expression clouded, but he nodded.

She'd been right. He was suffering as much as she was, though his pain took on a different cast than hers. He wore the same veil of grief that he'd worn at her house the night before. Both times, he'd had his laptop in front of him.

Her eyes narrowed, and her stomach clenched. There was something about his laptop, something that disturbed him. "What files are you working on?"

He stared at her, his expression guarded. Deep lines furrowed his forehead. "I don't know that you want to have this conversation."

"Maybe it's not about me. Maybe you need to."

"I can't do that to you."

"You know, sometimes I get tired of being the weak one." A surge of strength charged through her. "You try to carry all of my hurts and fears as well as your own and...maybe it would be good for both of us if *I* took on some of what *you're* carrying for once. Maybe it would stop you from feeling so weighed down, and maybe it would stop me from feeling like such a burden."

"You are not a burden." His answer was quick and firm. "I have never once thought that. Being your friend is a privilege, Mia."

"Same to you. So let me share the privilege." She leaned forward, finding strength in letting go of herself to focus on him. "What's on the laptop?"

He shook his head.

"Hayden..." It was the same voice she used on Ruthie when her daughter was trying to tell a fib.

His shoulders slumped. "Elliott got the...security footage." It was clear the confession cost him.

That was it? They'd both viewed surveillance tapes dozens if not hundreds of times. Had watched so many hours of—

No.

The meaning of his words ran molten lead over her head, down her shoulders and to her feet.

Security footage.

Her gaze landed on the laptop and refused to break away.

On that machine were images of her husband's last breath.

Of their helpless baby girl in the carrier beside him. Of his blood. Of her first moments of grief.

Her breath caught. The moment her life had changed forever, had shattered into blood-spattered shards, was in the room with her, stealing the air.

She jerked her head, tearing her gaze from the laptop and landing on Hayden, who was watching her. The exact same emotions that ripped through her were plain on his face. They'd experienced that night together. Had suffered the tearing pain of loss together. Should they view that moment together as well?

Could she? If she fell apart now, she might never recover, and she'd be a burden to her best friend for the rest of their lives.

Hayden needed her, and she needed to be the strong one. If sitting beside him while he watched that footage would help him, she would. She'd do anything for him, just like she'd do anything for her daughter.

Just like she'd have done anything for Keith.

The realization settled like a warm blanket, something she'd always known but had never acknowledged.

Something that made their earlier kiss even more poignant.

Before she could make the offer, Hayden reached for the laptop, then pulled his hand away as though it was too hot to touch. "I've tried to watch it twice now, but I don't think I can."

If he was going to stay on this case, he'd have to face this. How could he—

Something thudded above her head in Ruthie's room.

Mia and Hayden leaped to their feet, and Mia whirled toward the door as Ruthie screamed.

Chapter Eleven

"Mommy!" Ruthie's terrified cries echoed along the hallway.

Hayden gripped the Glock he'd grabbed from his locked desk drawer and held it low, his finger down the side of the barrel. It was likely Ruthie had simply had a nightmare, though he was pretty sure she'd never had one before.

Given all that had happened, he wasn't taking any chances.

The door chime beeped, then the alarm blared, adding to the cacophony of sound both outside and inside of Hayden. Either Elliott and Kelsie had rushed in to help or someone was trying to escape.

No, it couldn't be an escape. If there was an intruder, the person would have had to pass them on the stairs.

But how did they get inside in the first place?

There was a series of beeps as someone keyed in the alarm's code, and the siren fell silent. It was definitely Elliott or Kelsie who had entered.

"Mommy!" Ruthie screamed again. Her bedroom door flew open, and a tiny rocket dressed in *PAW Patrol* pajamas streaked past him. His goddaughter threw herself into her mother's arms, sobbing.

At least she was safe.

Mia gathered the shaking little girl to her chest and whispered soothing sounds that had no actual words in them, just comfort.

Now wasn't the time to huddle in the hallway in the open. While it might have been a nightmare, there could also be an active threat.

Hayden hissed at Mia, "Get her downstairs and secured in the laundry room." The small space had no windows, and it was the best he could do for a safe room in a pinch.

Mia headed for the stairs with Ruthie, where Elliott and Kelsie pounded up, weapons drawn. By some unspoken conversation, Kelsie ushered Mia and Ruthie downstairs while Elliott approached Hayden and took up a position against the wall to his left. "Status?"

"Not sure, but I really hope we're overreacting to a little girl's nightmare." While Ruthie didn't typically have bad dreams, she'd been through a lot in the past thirty-six hours or so. Her emotions had to be overwhelmed.

In his pocket, his cell phone buzzed, likely the alarm company checking on the alert. He ignored it. If he didn't answer, they'd send the police, and that was just fine.

Hayden nodded toward Ruthie's door. "Let's go find out what we're dealing with." He crept along the wall as Elliott covered him, then entered the room, weapon raised.

Ruthie's night-light swept dots of light across the ceiling, mimicking stars. The shifting light cast moving shadows on the walls and floor, making it tough to discern what was real and what was a figment of his racing imagination. As his eyes adjusted, the shadows revealed no visible threat, although the room was unusually chilly.

He cleared the area and moved on to the bathroom as Elliott followed, checking the closet and under the bed.

No one was in the room.

But why was it so cold?

Hayden stalked to the window and jerked back the curtain.

The window was open. The screen had been removed and was leaning against the wall, hidden behind the floor-length curtains. The emergency fire ladder he'd anchored beneath the window was unrolled down the side of the house and was still swinging from the weight of a hasty exit.

"How?" He resisted the urge to shut the window, not wanting to mar any prints that may have been left behind. He closed the curtains and motioned for Elliott to flick on the switch, flooding the room with light. "How did somebody get past me? Past you? You and Kelsie have been outside the whole time, watching the front and back. There aren't any side doors. The only way…"

Hayden pulled his phone out. He texted Kelsie to shelter in place and to notify the police that this was not a false alarm. Pocketing the phone, he turned to Elliott, who watched from the bathroom door. "We have to clear the house."

Elliott offered a grim nod, then moved out, taking the two bedrooms on the left while Hayden took his bedroom on the right.

The only way someone had managed to get into Ruthie's room without being seen was if they had gained entry to the house while everyone was at the light show.

Hayden swallowed self-recrimination, forcing himself to focus on the job as he checked every possible hiding place. He followed Elliott downstairs, where they searched every nook, cranny and shadowy space.

Elliott met him in the living room, holstering his sidearm as he approached. "All clear."

Hayden lowered his Glock, then texted Kelsie to keep Mia and Ruthie in the laundry room a bit longer, not wanting the little girl further upset by the arrival of police officers.

From the laundry room, the sound of Ruthie's muffled sobs drifted into the den.

Hayden's heart tugged in that direction. He wanted to pick Ruthie up, cuddle her close and comfort her, but she was safe with her mother. Mia was the only comfort Ruthie needed, even though Hayden's heart ached to reach out.

He should secure his weapon before the police arrived, since he hadn't grabbed the holster. With Elliott and Kelsie both armed, he didn't need it for protection at the moment. Stalking into his office, he locked the gun in the reinforced top desk drawer and pocketed the key.

When he was done, he turned to find Elliott in the doorway, concern pouring off him. "What happened?"

"I don't know." Hayden sank into his chair, an adrenaline crash stealing the strength from his legs. "Somebody got into the house while we were gone."

"That's next to impossible." Elliott's dark eyebrows drew together, narrowing his brown eyes. "Your system rivals any bank's. Frankly, it's overkill, but I get it, after what you've been through."

Elliott was right. His alarm was a powerful system for a house that had little of value in it, but Keith's death had been a grim wake-up call that no place was truly safe. Frankly, after the past thirty-six hours, he felt like putting metal bars on the windows and never leaving again.

This must be how Mia felt every day. Like everything was a catalyst for fear. Like the world was out to destroy her.

Sympathy swelled in his chest, but he forced himself to focus. This mystery demanded answers. "My code's a meaningless series of numbers chosen by a random number generator. I know better than to use a birthday or something easy to guess."

Blue and white flashing lights reflected against the curtains, indicating the police had arrived with their sirens silent.

Hayden didn't move. He was empty. Exhausted.

Elliott backed into the entry, prepared to open the door when the knock came. "Any other way to shut the system off? Remote? Phone app?"

"I have an app on my phone, but..." Hayden stood as a horrible thought rushed in. "Maybe someone managed to hack my account. They could have downloaded the app and used it to disarm the system."

That would have required a sophisticated hack, but it wasn't impossible.

Had his first line of defense been compromised?

Mia was right.

Nowhere was safe.

Ruthie's arm rose and fell with her breathing, which had finally evened out after an hour of intermittent sobs.

Mia gently relaxed against the back of the couch, one hand resting on her daughter's arm where it was draped across her little stomach. Her other hand lay on top of Ruthie's head in her lap.

It was just after midnight. Dawn would come sooner than she wanted. As much as she was terrified of the dark, she hated to imagine what the coming day would bring.

She'd overheard Hayden talking to Elliott about moving to a safe house.

Mia bit down on what would surely be a harsh laugh. *Safe* was an illusion. That truth had hammered itself into her soul the moment Keith had breathed his last. Everything that had happened since she'd spotted the mysterious woman at lunch on Saturday only confirmed that danger lurked everywhere and could reach her whenever it chose.

The back door in the kitchen opened, then the alarm beeped as someone punched in the lock code. Hayden stepped into the arched opening quietly, obviously checking to see if she was asleep.

She offered him a weak smile, then tipped her chin toward Ruthie, whose quiet breathing was occasionally interrupted by an almost imperceptible snore that indicated she was down for the count. When she slept that hard, not even a hurricane could awaken her.

Boy, did Mia envy that kind of rest.

Hayden walked in, snagged a blanket off the back of his recliner and draped the covering gently over Ruthie before he sat down on the coffee table facing Mia. "You okay?"

"Did you really ask me a question you already know the answer to?"

"I did." He wrinkled his nose. "And yeah, I guess the answer is pretty obvious. You're no more okay than I am."

"What happens now?" The Elizabeth City police officers who had responded had taken statements from them all. One plain-clothed female officer had even sat with Ruthie over mugs of hot chocolate to talk in a gentle way about what had frightened her.

Ruthie's eyes had welled with tears as she'd shrunk against her mother. "A ghost. A shadow ghost." It had taken a bit more coaxing to get a firm description out of the little girl, whose senses had been hindered by her moving night-light and her fear. After a few more questions, Ruthie was able to articulate that the person in her room had been wearing dark pants and a dark hoodie. She had been unable to tell if it was a male or a female. The person had said nothing, had simply appeared in her doorway and approached her bed.

If Ruthie had been asleep instead of up playing with her night-light…

Mia swallowed a whimper. Had her daughter been asleep, then her would-be kidnapper likely would have had her gagged and out the window before Ruthie could have alerted them.

How close had she come to losing her daughter tonight—twice?

"Hey." Hayden's voice drew her out of her fear-soaked imagination. He leaned forward and rested his hand on her knee. "We're going to handle this."

Digging her teeth into her tongue, Mia forced herself to remain silent. So far, nobody had a *handle* on anything.

That wasn't Hayden's fault. Someone savvy was coming

after them, but she couldn't wrap her mind around the clues to discern who it might be. "I should be able to figure this out." She'd been a soldier and a deputy, yet any time she tried to think tactically, her mind turned to mush. It was further proof that she would never again be who she once was. She'd always be a hindrance and never a help.

It was also proof that the kiss with Hayden never should have happened.

"Hold up. This is not yours to *figure out*." Hayden pulled his hand away and rested his palms on his knees. "Your sole job in this moment is to be Ruthie's mother. Not a law enforcement officer. Not a soldier. You're the only one in the world who can do that."

"Not according to whoever tackled me in Watchman's Alley." The words slipped past the filter in her brain. Maybe she was failing as a mom. After all, she'd let her daughter be approached by a strange woman, had nearly let someone steal Ruthie right from under her nose, had—

"Whatever you're thinking, stop." Although he didn't touch her, Hayden leaned closer. "You're a great mom, and despite what you think, you're also a great friend. I wouldn't have made it through the past few years without you. You might think you need me, but I…" He looked away. His eyebrows drew together into a deep V, and he shook his head. "I'm sorry about earlier, between me and you. I'm not sure what happened, but it won't happen again." He abruptly stood, looking down at her. "You asked a couple of minutes ago what happens now."

The whiplash from the conversational turn threw Mia off balance, as though his words had affected her equilibrium. How had they moved from her being a mother to their friendship to the kiss to…? Was he talking about what happened next in their relationship or what happened next with the battle around them?

Clearly, his apology for the kiss meant this was about the

danger. As much as his regret over their kiss twisted her stomach into knots, she knew he was right. Ruthie's safety had to be their focus.

Digging deep, she sought the strength to move forward.

All she found was emptiness. She'd gone completely numb. That was worse than fear, but at least it allowed her to think. "We're leaving, aren't we?"

"Elliott's firming up arrangements for a safe house, and we're figuring out how to move the two of you without being tracked." He walked to the kitchen entry and stared in the direction of the back door. "They knew you were here. Worse, I talked to my alarm company. At shortly after five this evening, someone deactivated my alarm from a cell phone app and then reactivated it approximately one minute later. They hacked my house."

Mia eased away from Ruthie and stood, the law enforcement part of her brain engaged. She walked into the kitchen to avoid waking her daughter. "That means they were in the house for over an hour before we got home."

"Which means the woman you saw tonight wasn't the person in the house. We definitely have two people in play here, if—" He didn't look at her.

But she heard him loud and clear. "If I really did see the same woman from the café." His skepticism was understandable. If she was standing in his shoes, she'd feel it as well. Still... "I have no doubt she was the same person. The question is who she is and how she knew where to find us."

"And was she the person in the alley?"

"And who was in the house?" Mia slid onto the stool by the peninsula and buried her head in her hands. So much to consider. "I really don't want to move Ruthie to a safe house. It's technically Christmas Eve. All of her presents are here, and she's more concerned about Santa than anything else. This constant shuffling seems cruel."

When Hayden didn't speak, she lifted her head.

He was staring at the back door as though waiting for some-one to come through it. When he realized she was watching, he shifted his gaze to her without moving. "I get it, but…" He exhaled heavily, dragging his hands down cheeks thick with a couple of days' worth of stubble. "There's more."

Mia closed her eyes. She was pretty sure she couldn't bear the load of *more*. "Is it about Paige?"

"Not exactly." Hayden walked to the other side of the pen-insula and faced her. "Based on what you told me about your interactions with Paige's family yesterday, Javi and some of the other deputies have been looking into the people who were at the Crosby home who might have the most interest in you and Ruthie."

"Paige's father and her boyfriend." Cade had never been for the adoption, and Blake had acted so strangely, even though he'd signed away his parental rights. Maybe he'd changed his mind. "Who do they suspect?"

"Cade is still at the house. He's been there since he arrived after news of Paige's disappearance, and he was definitely in Wilmington when she vanished."

Mia felt a slight sense of relief. At least she could let go of any suspicion that Cade had killed his own daughter. "And Blake?"

"He hasn't been seen since he walked out of the house. His cell is off, and his vehicle didn't have GPS, so there's no way to track it."

Mia slumped in the seat. Blake had always been friendly. Had he been hiding dark motives? She couldn't fathom some-one who cared so much about Paige harming her. But… "Blake knows you and I are friends. He knows you were at the house with me. It wouldn't take much for him to figure out where we ran." It would also explain the comments from her at-tacker about her as a mother, particularly if Blake wanted to raise Ruthie.

"But it doesn't explain the mystery woman."

No, it didn't. "Maybe I really am so paranoid that I…" *No.* Surely her fear hadn't started causing her to hallucinate. As a law enforcement officer, she'd been trained to notice details about people. This woman had a scar on her temple and blond hair. Although it was full and clean now, her hair had once been—

Mia sat straight up. The scar. The hair. When the woman had walked into her memory just now, it wasn't with the lovely blond hair she had in the present. It was straighter. Stringier. And in Mia's memory, she was thin to the point of emaciated.

Mia gasped. "Hayden. I know who she is. I don't know how she found us, but I know who she is."

Tears pricked her eyes, and she pressed a finger to her lips, remembering that day. It had been her first week on the job as a deputy, and the Department of Social Services had requested law enforcement presence as they removed a three-year-old from the home of an addict who'd repeatedly been cited for neglect and abuse. The woman had grown violent, screaming and hitting anyone who came near as they carried her daughter, who seemed to have no emotional attachment to her mother, away from the home.

The woman had been handcuffed and arrested for her behavior, and as Deputy Anna Titus shut the car door on the woman, she'd turned to Mia, who'd been horrified by the scene, heartbroken for both mother and daughter. Anna had said, "That kid deserves better than her."

Mia related the story to Hayden. "She must have remembered me and blamed me for taking her daughter. Maybe she thought I said those awful things, then when she saw me at the café…"

Hayden reached for his back pocket, producing his cell. "Do you remember her name?"

Mia shook her head. "I only heard it once or twice. You'd think it would have been burned into my brain. It's in the reports. It was like my fourth or fifth day on the job." She tossed out a couple of dates. "Sheriff Davidson should be able to pull up the details."

Hayden dialed the phone and walked toward the back door, speaking in low tones, as Mia stared at her fingers, twined together on the counter. Was it going to be that simple? Was this all about revenge?

Chapter Twelve

"Her name is Jasmine Jarrett. I've sent her photo to each of you." Hayden pocketed the backup phone Elliott had brought him and looked around at his team, who had packed into his office. When Elliott had called Gavin and Rebecca, they'd returned. Along with Kelsie and Elliott, that made four extra sets of eyes and ears. Their unconditional willingness to protect him and the people he loved both warmed him and unsettled him.

They were rolling out in a few minutes for the safe house that Elliott had arranged. A buddy of his had a condo on the waterfront in Manteo, and, as long as they could get Mia and Ruthie there without detection, it should be difficult for anyone to locate them. He had the burner phone from Elliott, and Mia had already left her phone at her house. They'd moved Ruthie's car seat into a pickup they'd borrowed from Gavin. There should be no way to track them.

He'd made a tactical error in bringing them to his house when so many people knew he was linked to Mia. It was a mistake that could have cost them their lives.

As he glanced around the small circle, it was clear his friends and coworkers were as exhausted as he was. He honestly couldn't remember the last time he'd slept. Gavin and Rebecca had likely only gotten a couple of hours before Elliott had called them to see if they wanted to help, and there was no telling how long Kelsie and Elliott had been awake, given that they were already on night shift when everything fell apart.

Gratitude nearly knocked him off his worn-out feet. They'd sacrificed so much for him, and he was basically still the rookie on the team. He waited for everyone to check the photos he'd sent to their phones before he spoke. He had to clear his throat to get the words out. "I, um... Thanks. I know you could be anywhere else right now. I want you to know I appreciate you being here."

Rebecca bumped her shoulder against his. "My parents are in Hawaii on vacation. There is nowhere else I'd rather be right now than making sure that adorable little girl gets where we're going safely." They'd been careful not to mention their destination aloud, fearful of somehow being overheard.

"Ditto." Kelsie slid her cell into her hip pocket. Her brown ponytail fell over her shoulder with the movement. "I mean, my parents aren't in Hawaii, but ditto on the rest of that."

Elliott and Gavin grunted their responses.

"Still. It can't be—"

"Knock it off, McGrath." Elliott heaved an exaggerated sigh. "We get it. Now let's get this caravan rolling. Sooner we have everyone settled, sooner we can rest." He looked around at the assembled group. "Kelsie and I will take my truck and leave three minutes ahead of you, keeping an eye out for anything suspicious on the route and making sure it's clear. If you drive exactly three miles over the speed limit, we should maintain an even distance." He tipped his head toward Rebecca. "Rebecca, you and Gavin follow Hayden. Keep him in sight at all times, and watch behind you as well. We don't know how many bad actors are in play or how Jasmine Jarrett found Mia and Ruthie to begin with. We have no clue what might come at us next. All we know is that Jasmine's parole officer hasn't seen her in several weeks, and it's entirely possible she wants to take Ruthie as a way to punish Mia."

"Or to get what she feels she's owed. A kid." The thought turned Hayden's stomach. Whatever Jasmine Jarrett wanted with Ruthie, it wasn't good. He just hoped the BOLO they'd put out on her for parole violations would lead to a quick apprehension. "But why wait this long?" *And how did she know Mia had a daughter?*

"Too many questions, not enough moving toward the vehicles. Let's go." Elliott was in mission mode and ready to roll. Investigations could come later, when everyone was safe.

As the team headed out the front door, Hayden went into the den where Mia sat on the couch at Ruthie's feet, watching her daughter sleep. She'd packed their things, including Ruthie's Christmas presents, and Hayden had loaded them into the borrowed truck a few minutes earlier. All that remained now was to get Ruthie to the car and to get on the road.

Without a word, Mia gathered her sleeping daughter in her arms and preceded Hayden out the door. When she buckled Ruthie into her car seat and tucked Penelope into her arms, the little girl barely stirred.

Watching through the driver's side rear window, Hayden allowed himself a short moment for the scene to work its way into his heart. He couldn't deny that he loved Ruthie like she was his own daughter.

Could he deny that he loved Mia as though she was his own as well?

Shaking off the thought, he climbed into the front seat as Mia slid in and buckled up. No matter what Elliott said, the thought of being in love with Mia still felt odd.

Odd, but right.

It was also a distraction he needed to set aside if he wanted a future to contemplate.

As Hayden watched Elliott back out and drive up the street, the truck was silent except for the vents blowing warm air.

He waited three minutes before following Elliott. He knew the route to Manteo well, and he could practically drive it in his sleep.

Given that he hadn't shut his eyes in what felt like two years, he might have to. He was weary to the bone, yet his brain was amped and running through everything that could go wrong, all of the ways he could lose the people he cared about most.

"Are you going to watch the surveillance footage?" Mia's voice broke the silence so suddenly yet so softly, he almost wondered if he'd dropped off and was dreaming.

Long seconds passed before he comprehended her question. She was picking up their earlier conversation from the point when Ruthie's screams had interrupted them.

"Is this something we want to talk about now?" He'd prefer to save emotional discussions for another time.

"We have a long, dark drive ahead of us. Seems like as good a time as any. It's something you need to work through, and… I want to work through it with you. I don't want you to do this alone."

Her concern nearly unraveled him. He focused on the turn out of his neighborhood, considering what she was asking. The darkness and their inability to look each other in the eye as he drove lent a sense of anonymity to the moment, a detachment he wouldn't find anywhere else.

She might be right. This might be the best time to work through his emotions.

Did he want to watch the footage? The details were already seared into his brain and often plowed through his sleep, awakening him in a cold sweat.

Keith's motionless body, eyes wide and unseeing.

The metallic scent of blood.

Mia's cries as she held infant Ruthie and clung to Hayden.

The hopeless feeling of being too late, compounded by the sting of allowing Keith's killer to escape.

Did he really need the image of the bullet's impact imprinted on his brain?

"If I watch the video, it will add one more scene to my nightmares." He pulled his eyes from the dark road to look at her. "If I wasn't a factor, would you watch it?"

Mia's face was lit only by the dim lights of the instrument panel. Deep lines etched her forehead. Pain and fear had carved those lines.

He'd do anything to take them away.

Finally, she shook her head. "No." She offered no explanation.

She didn't need to. One word said enough.

At least for her. For him, the words bubbled up, needing release. "Elliott thinks I won't heal unless I watch it. And honestly, I'm the only one on the team who was there that night, who can give insight into—"

"Maybe Elliott's wrong."

The quiet words seemed to pick up speed, slamming into him at terminal velocity. His grip on the wheel tightened. Elliott...*wrong*? The man was a logical machine. One of the most well-thought-out people Hayden had ever known. His insights usually hit the mark, and his people trusted him for guidance. How could he be *wrong*?

"No offense to Elliott." Mia looked over her shoulder at her sleeping daughter, then turned her gaze to Hayden. "He's a great person, and he seems to care about all of you. I mean, how many people would do what he's doing for me and Ruthie, and he doesn't know us at all. But being a good person and caring about the people around you doesn't mean you're right a hundred percent of the time."

Maybe? But if that was the case... "Then who do I trust?"

"God first. And then, in a situation like this, yourself." She pulled one of his hands from the wheel and laced her fingers with his, resting on the console between them. "Hay, at some point, you have to stop second-guessing yourself. Maybe Elliott's path to healing is to know every detail, to file away every image so he has no questions. But you aren't Elliott. It would…" Her fingers tightened. "It would destroy me to watch what that camera picked up. My memories are bad enough. I think your memories are bad enough for you, too."

Hayden looked up in time to see the lights of a passing vehicle glisten in tears that stood in her eyes. The urge to pull off to the side of the road and hold her nearly overwhelmed him. He had to wrestle himself into submission to stick to the plan.

Mia sniffed, then swiped her eyes. "You're not solely responsible for bringing Keith's killer to justice, especially not if it's going to cause you harm. I don't think I could handle it if you watched the footage and it changed you."

His breath caught. Her words flowed on raw emotion.

"Hayden, you're human. One of the greatest guilts I carry is that you spend all of your time taking care of me and of Ruthie. I'm not sure you've ever really stopped to confront your own grief. You lost your best friend. You were a victim that night just as much as I was. You don't have to be the strongest man alive. You just have to be you, and you have to feel this in your own way or you're never going to heal."

The truth watered his dry spirit. The raging forest fire he'd felt for so many years was doused. His mind and emotions fell silent.

He was allowed to let go. Allowed to be angry and sad and scared.

He didn't need to power through. He didn't need to be the hero who saved the day. He was allowed to protect his own heart as well as Mia's.

The sense of peace that replaced the inferno within him was startling after so many years of smoke and flame. "I don't have to do this by myself." His left hand gripped the steering wheel tighter, and he tugged his right from Mia's grasp. That was something he hadn't meant to say aloud. While he didn't need to carry everything, neither did she. How dare he add to her burden?

"You were never supposed to do this alone. I mean, you have God. You have..." She looked away. Trees passed in the darkness as they left civilization behind. "You have me."

The tough cop, tough soldier, that lived deep inside of Mia cringed. *You have me.* She sounded like a sound bite from the trailer for a Christmas romance movie. They were driving through the darkness, fleeing for their lives, and she was talking like they were in a horse-drawn carriage on a snow-covered lane.

Thankfully the truck was dark so Hayden couldn't see the bright red glow that burned her cheeks.

She dug her teeth into her tongue to keep her from saying another word. Maybe he hadn't heard.

The problem was her brain. It had been running five hundred miles per hour for too long and was dangerously close to short-circuiting. The assault at Watchman's Alley, the arson attempt at her home, the breach at Hayden's... Everything increased the power until her system was running in the red.

And Hayden had kissed her. That event slammed on the brakes, though the engine still fired. With Ruthie's screams following so quickly after that brain-shattering moment, she had lost control of her feelings and her thoughts and the ability to censor herself.

She was out of control.

She had two choices. Either she focused on Hayden and his issues, or she popped the clutch and spun into a panic attack that might actually engulf her. She could feel it building, pounding, threatening.

The only way to stop it was to distract it with someone else's problems.

But she'd gone too far and inserted herself into the narrative. Now Hayden would know she'd been affected not just by his kiss but by every action he'd taken on her behalf in the past four years. She could see it all now, stretched out like a string of Christmas lights. Each act of careful concern, of quiet listening, of fierce protectiveness, added a bulb in the strand that led from his heart to hers. The lights had been there all along, but that kiss had finally provided the electricity, giving power to a glorious riot of colors.

How could she be thinking this way when her daughter was in danger? Shouldn't her focus be on getting them to safety?

Her head whipped toward Hayden, who gripped the steering wheel with both hands and seemed to be wrestling with the effect of her words. No, she didn't have to focus on safety, because Hayden was doing that for her. Just like always. He was there when she needed him, every single time.

"I'm not sure what to say right now." Hayden kept his eyes on the road. "It's a lot. There's…a lot going on. Paige is dead, and you're being hunted… Now Blake is missing, and… And then there's you."

She wished he hadn't listed everything that was happening. It brought to the forefront that there was an evil outside of this truck that was launching terror and harm at her family. The danger drew her focus away from him and back to the reason for this flight through the darkness. It reminded her that there were legitimate reasons for her to be afraid.

This fight wasn't against shadows in her head. This was real.

Mia shoved her hands under her thighs and dug her fingers into her jeans. She had to clamp down and hold on or she might fly apart. She had to focus on something other than the danger, and she had to do it quickly. "We should talk about what happened."

He stiffened, and the tension radiating from him was palpable. "I can't right now. I have to get you to the safe house. Everything else is a distraction."

Her eyes drifted closed at the pain his words knifed through her. She was a distraction.

No matter that she was feeling things she couldn't explain for him, he viewed her as a hindrance. "I understand." She had no doubt he could hear every crack that splintered through her heart.

"Wait. No." Hayden's words rushed forth. "That came out wrong. We do need to talk. It's just that now isn't the time. I'm exhausted, Mia. And, frankly, I'm scared of a lot of things. From what's happening around you to what's happening... Well, to what's happening between us. My brain can only handle one thing at a time. That's all I'm saying. When we get settled where we're headed, we can—"

A soft hum cut off the rest of the sentence, and Mia straightened, her emotions going numb as Hayden's phone lit up in the cup holder between them. They had planned to be radio silent unless there was an emergency, in case whoever was stalking Mia had gained access to their communications. If a member of Hayden's team was calling, then something terrible had happened.

Hayden picked up his phone and passed it to her. "Put it on speaker. The volume is low enough to keep from waking Ruthie."

A slight warmth broke through her fear. He always thought of Ruthie, of her, before anything else. As she swiped her thumb along the screen beneath Elliott's name and punched the speaker button, that warmth chilled. Her gut said she was about to hear something that would change her life...again.

She held the phone close to Hayden, who leaned toward it. "You're on speaker."

"Good. I want Mia to hear this. I just got a call from a buddy on the Elizabeth City PD. They picked up Jasmine Jarrett wandering down Halstead near 17. Apparently, she's on a stratospheric high, babbling about a lot of stuff no one can decipher. They're taking her to the ER in Elizabeth City."

The phone nearly fell from Mia's hand as relief ran through her, but she lifted it quickly as Hayden spoke. "Can we get someone there to talk to her?"

"You know we can't." Elliott's voice was clipped. "We're not law enforcement, and we're not investigating this. We're private citizens taking care of our own."

"Wishful thinking." Hayden tapped his thumbs on the steering wheel. "I say we stay the course, continue on to the safe house."

"Agreed. I'll let you know if anything else comes across." The screen went dark as Elliott disconnected.

Mia lowered the phone into the cup holder and leaned closer to Hayden after checking to be certain Ruthie still slept. "'Stay the course'?" She hissed the words, trying not to yell. "Jasmine Jarrett is in custody." Surely this was over. They could turn around, get some rest at Hayden's and be home in time for Christmas Eve dinner with her grandmother, who was driving in from Flat Rock.

"Mia, stop thinking with your emotions," Hayden snapped, then winced when she flinched. He lowered his voice. "Jasmine Jarrett isn't our only concern. We don't know if the person in Watchman's Alley was a man or a woman. I fought a *man* at your house. The only thing we have on Jasmine Jarrett is that you saw her in a café and Ruthie was talking to her at a light show. Neither of those things is illegal."

Resting her elbow on the console, Mia pinched the bridge of her nose. She knew. Oh, did she know. But she wanted so badly to pretend. She wanted to go home, pull the blinds, sleep in her own bed... She wanted to stop feeling hunted and vulnerable.

But Jasmine's arrest wouldn't make those feelings go away. Putting an end to this threat wouldn't change anything. She'd been locked in fear and anxiety for four years. They were magnified now that the threat was real, but they'd likely still haunt her even after she was supposedly safe again.

"I understand what you're feeling." Hayden's voice was

barely a whisper. "I want everything you're thinking about right now, too. I want to be home and safe and to have this all over."

He hadn't even had to ask. He just knew. "I'm scared." Not panicked. Genuinely scared.

"Me, too."

His quiet admission should have magnified the terror, but it had the opposite effect. The fact that he was frightened validated her emotions and made her feel...normal. She'd begged for *normal* for four years. Who'd have thought she'd find it in the midst of very real fear?

"Your lives are in my hands, and—" The phone buzzed in the cup holder.

Mia grabbed it and answered, turning on the speaker so Hayden could hear Rebecca.

Rebecca was midsentence when the call connected. "—got trouble. Someone is—" There was a screech and a shout, then silence.

Chapter Thirteen

"Call Elliott." Hayden rattled off the passcode to unlock the phone so that Mia could make the call. His heart rate picked up speed along with the truck as he pressed the accelerator to the floor. Behind him, Rebecca's car had fishtailed wildly before it disappeared.

Another set of headlights raced past the crash site, gaining fast.

Someone had run their tail off the road.

He had to catch up to Elliott and Kelsie before whoever had taken out Gavin and Rebecca could catch them. *Lord, let them be okay.* If a member of his team was hurt or worse because they were doing him a favor, he wasn't sure he could live with the guilt that would pile onto the load he already struggled to carry.

He glanced in the rearview as Mia dealt with the phone.

The headlights raced closer.

While he knew the road well, he didn't dare push the accelerator all the way to the floor. He couldn't risk outdriving his headlights. The darkness was complete, and it would be easy to misjudge a curve, doing the dirty work for whoever was behind them.

He slowed for a curve, and their pursuer gained ground.

Gavin's truck was fast, but there was no way to outrun the vehicle gaining on them.

He gripped the wheel tighter as Elliott's voice came through his phone's speaker. "What's going on?"

"Double back." Hayden barked the order. "Someone hit our trail car, and they're gaining fast."

"On the way."

The call ended, but Mia didn't release the phone. She stared at the screen, then turned to look at Ruthie, who slept on, clearly exhausted from her day. It was a small blessing. "Hayden..."

"I'm doing the best I can. I promise." The interior of the truck grew brighter as the car raced up on them. "As soon as we see Elliott's headlights, I'll hit the brakes. We'll confront whoever this is, and we'll make sure they're taken into custody so—"

The vehicle hunting them was only feet away.

Hayden held on to the wheel and lifted his foot from the accelerator. There was no way to avoid what was coming. He just prayed he could hold the truck on the road. "Hang on."

The command was torn by the sound of metal scraping metal as the car tapped his rear bumper, shoving the truck forward.

Hayden fought the wheel as the truck tried to fishtail, barely hanging on as the car dropped back and revved its engine for another run.

Mia covered her mouth with her hands, stifling a scream. Ruthie whimpered in her car seat, but she didn't fully awaken.

While everything in Hayden said to speed toward the help that was speeding toward him, the smarter move was to slow down. If the guy did manage to spin him, it would be easier to maneuver at low speed than at high speed.

His stomach swirled with sick indecision, but he kept his foot off the gas, letting their speed gradually drop as the car gained again. *Come on, Elliott.* While it felt like hours since he'd called, the reality was it had only been about thirty seconds. It would take Elliott a couple of minutes to arrive.

Minutes that might cost them everything.

The car charged up again, engine roaring. The driver acted as though he was going to pass Hayden and cut him off, but at the last second, he swung his front bumper into the back corner of the truck.

Hayden fought the wheel, but the truck whipped into a sickening spin.

Mia screamed.

Ruthie cried out in fright, ripping his heart in two.

Hayden turned into the skid, but he couldn't regain control. The tires caught loose dirt at the side of the road and traction disappeared.

Mia's scream abruptly shattered as the world exploded.

A force slammed him in the face, blasting him backward, then he slumped forward, the seat belt cutting into his chest. He couldn't see. Couldn't hear. Couldn't tell which way was up. What was happening?

From far away, through the ringing in his ears, he thought he heard a car door slam.

The truck rocked, and Hayden fought for clarity.

Mia. Ruthie.

Someone had run them off the road.

He had to know Mia and Ruthie were okay, had to get them to safety. Forcing himself to breathe, Hayden pressed the seat belt release and looked at Mia, who fought the airbag as she slowly sat up.

She shook her head as though she was covered in cobwebs.

He turned to check on Ruthie.

Her car seat was empty.

The back door hung open.

"Ruthie!" His voice was hoarse, his throat coated with dust from the airbags. Coughing, he sputtered her name again. "Ruthie!"

Turning, he tried to shove his door open but it was stuck.

Through the shattered side window, he saw a man shut the back door of a dark sedan, then slide in behind the wheel. The tires screeched as he roared away.

"Ruthie!" Mia screamed, then coughed, her voice jagged. "Ruthie! No!"

Mia screamed again.

Ruthie was gone.

She was dying.

Mia lay curled in a ball on Ruthie's narrow twin bed, her face to the wall and her arms wrapped around her legs. She couldn't remember how she got here. Everything was a blur of sirens and lights and movement.

Just like the night Keith had been murdered.

Her body ached with physical pain and grief. Her memories were a jumbled mess.

All she knew for certain was that the person who had her daughter had torn her heart from her chest and left her a hollow shell.

She pressed her forehead into her knees and dug her fingernails into her arms, desperate to feel something. In all of her worst nightmares, she'd always assumed that if something happened to Ruthie, she'd scream until her lungs collapsed. In reality, there was nothing but heavy, awful, suffocating silence. The weight was too heavy to allow her lungs to expand enough to whimper, let alone release the pain that was killing her.

In the distance, doors opened and closed. The door alarm chimed. Voices murmured in the makeshift command center that had been set up in her kitchen. Hayden was somewhere in the middle of the chaos, knee-deep in the search for Ruthie.

Her one clear memory since that car had struck the rear of their pickup was telling him to leave her alone after he'd helped her upstairs. She'd wanted to be in her own home. She no longer cared if she was safe. She needed to be in Ruthie's room, screaming silent prayers from the center of her being. Prayers that were sheer emotion, void of words.

The loose board in the hall creaked, but Mia didn't bother to acknowledge that someone was upstairs. Hopelessness flowed like thick sludge through her veins. Unless they were coming to say Ruthie was safe, she didn't care.

"Mimi?" The whisper from the doorway was reedy thin with an emotion that matched Mia's own heartbreak.

Mimi. Only one person called her that.

Mia rolled into a sitting position. The sight of her grandmother standing in the doorway with her hands clasped in front of her broke the dam around her emotions. "Noni." The name cracked on a sob,

Immediately, Noni was beside her, wrapping Mia in a familiar embrace. They rocked and cried together, Noni's chin resting on the top of her head. She had no idea how long she sobbed, but by the time the tears stopped, she felt like a limp dishrag.

But she had a clear head, and her lungs no longer felt as though they were clasped in a vise.

With a shuddered breath, Mia sat up and reached for her grandmother's hand. Holding it in both of hers, she sat quietly until she could form words. "I'm scared."

"As you should be." Noni squeezed her hand. "So am I. So is Hayden. So is everyone."

The truth that everyone who loved her daughter was terrified should have incapacitated her, but it did the opposite. It validated her feelings and made her somehow feel inexplicably stronger.

Swallowing the last of her tears, she looked at her Noni. She wasn't alone in this. Everyone who knew and loved her and Ruthie were right there with her, were already in motion to end this nightmare for both of them.

With her free hand, Noni swiped the tears from Mia's cheeks and then from her own. Her brown eyes were warm with compassion, but the deep lines on her face were furrowed with concern. Her shoulder-length gray hair was pulled back with a colorful cloth headband. Although she was nearly eighty, she could still pass for a woman in her sixties. Her days filled with hiking in the mountains and throwing pottery in her art studio kept her strong and full of life.

She squeezed Mia's hand. "I am so sorry this is happening to you, Mimi. You've already been through so much."

"It's not fair."

"No, it's not. It's horrible and unfair and wrong. All of it. If I could carry this weight for you, I would. You know that."

She did. With her parents constantly traveling the world for her father's job, Noni was her constant. Every holiday, every major victory, every crushing defeat, Noni was there. "How did you get here so fast?"

It had been four hours since the moment she'd heard Ruthie's screams from the back seat. At nearly five in the morning, there was no telling what time Noni had hit the road to reach them.

In fact, she'd have had to have left before Ruthie was even taken. "How did you know—"

Noni gave her a soft smile. "I didn't. I came in late last night and stayed at your parents' house, planning to surprise you this morning. I didn't know you'd left to go to Hayden's. I didn't know about anything that was going on."

Mia winced. Everything had happened so quickly that she hadn't told her grandmother anything, hadn't even been able to call her, since her phone was at the house to avoid being tracked. "I'm so sorry. Do Mom and Dad know?"

"I just got off the phone with them. They're doing their best to get here, but being on a cruise ship, it will take some time."

That was true. Given their trip, she hadn't even told them about—

Her stomach squeezed, and she faced her grandmother, holding her hand tighter. "Paige. Noni, Paige is—"

"I know, sweetheart. Hayden filled me in on everything. He called me and told me to come. He had no idea I was only a couple of miles away."

"And, Noni, Blake might be the killer." And the kidnapper.

Noni frowned. "Blake Darby? He's downstairs, and so are his parents. They came with Paige's family."

How? Why? Mia started to jump up, but Noni's grip on her hands stopped her. "Blake is here? Does he have Ruthie? Has he been arrested?"

"Why?" Noni's eyes narrowed.

"He's been off the grid. Vanished. Phone off. No trace of him. I thought... We thought..." Was it all a ruse to make them believe he was innocent?

"He was talking to Hayden when I came upstairs, but he didn't seem to be in any trouble. Hayden seemed to be sympathetic, and Blake seems to be as frantic as the rest of you."

"That doesn't make any sense." Was Blake a friend or the worst foe of all?

"None of this does, and rushing down to accuse Blake of something won't help anything. Hayden and the sheriff are handling it." Noni squeezed Mia's hand. "I'm so glad I listened to my gut and came early. When I was praying for you yesterday morning, something told me to get here quickly."

"Prayer." Mia bit her lip to keep more tears from rolling from her eyes. "I've been praying so hard, but..." She'd prayed for their safety. Had prayed every single day for her baby girl since Paige had asked them to consider adoption. Where had it gotten her?

Nowhere. In fact, she literally had the opposite of everything she'd ever prayed for.

"Don't you go questioning God, Mimi." Noni's voice grew stern, but then her expression softened. "Although if anyone has the right to, I'd say it's you. You've certainly known more than your fair share of heartache, and now this."

"Why?" She'd asked that question so many times since losing Keith, yet she never received an answer.

"We'll likely never know why, but we still have to trust Him. As unfair and horrible as all of this is, we were never promised fair or easy. If life were fair or easy, your grandfather wouldn't have died in Vietnam without ever getting to meet your mother."

"I know." They'd talked about Noni's heartbreak so many times. "You always tell me to pray, but… You knew Jesus for so long before he died that—"

"What?" Noni's head jerked back. "I had no idea who Jesus was when your grandfather died. You know I was steeped in a lifestyle that was nothing less than bohemian. I believed in everything except Jesus. I didn't know anything about Him until your grandfather had been gone for months."

Mia scanned her grandmother's face. "I always thought… You always talked about how Jesus carried you. How He was there through everything."

"Oh, I was no fan of His, especially not when I was left a widow with a toddler to raise. I'd never disliked another being so much in my life. But then I realized something… When I got angry and frustrated, it wasn't at anyone in the government or on the other side of the world fighting the war. It wasn't at any of the other gods I'd chased around or at the universe. It was at God. And that made me realize that He's real and He exists. So I told Him I knew He was real, but I was good and mad at Him. And after I did that? Mimi, I don't know how to explain this to you, but that's when I felt Him. I screamed and yelled at Him, and when I got it all out, He just kind of…met me with open arms. He didn't bring your grandfather back. He didn't change a thing about my situation, but He let me know He'd walk me through it, and He has. He's walked you through it, too. You've never been alone."

"I know. I've never felt alone, largely because of your story.

But I didn't realize you were in the midst of it when you found Him."

"He found me. I sure wasn't looking for Him." Noni smiled gently. "He's here now. I pray with all of my heart Ruthie is safe. I know God's with her, and He's here with us. I used to hold so tight to that verse in Isaiah, and I'm holding to it now."

Mia sniffed. Her grandmother had quoted Isaiah 43:2 to her many times in the past four years. "He's there when we walk in the fire and when we go through the flood." A sob clinched her chest, but she swallowed it. "I'm so tired of the flood."

"I know, baby girl." Noni wrapped a thin arm around Mia's shoulder and pulled her close. "Here's the other thing I know… You're a woman of action. Of movement. For the past four years, you've been standing still, and it's choking you to death." Mia started to protest, but Noni kept speaking. "I understand the kind of fear that's gripped you. It's real, and I would never diminish that. But I also know that you do best when you're helping others and when the focus is off of you. If you stay up here in this room, you're going to drown in the imaginations of where Ruthie is right now."

Noni was right. As much as she wanted to curl into a huddled mass of pain in the center of Ruthie's mattress, she'd die if she did. She was no help to Ruthie here. "I'm going to go downstairs and see if anybody's hungry or needs help or…" A new fire rose inside of her. Staying in the house wasn't doing anything. She needed to be out searching for her daughter.

Mia rocketed to her feet, dropping Noni's arm from her shoulder. "Or I might join a team that's going out." She'd been trained in search and rescue. If she could put her pain aside, she could help in the hunt for her daughter.

"Now, Mimi." Noni stood. "Let's think this through. I know you need—"

"Mia!" Footsteps pounded on the stairs, then Hayden appeared in the doorway, his hair wild as though he'd continually dragged his hands through it. His eyes were sparking with what might be anger or excitement or both.

Mia stepped toward him, her heart pounding from both his appearance and from the fact that he obviously had news.

He held his hand out to her. "We know who has Ruthie."

Chapter Fourteen

"That's when I knew something was horribly wrong." Eve Warner sat on the center of Mia's couch, flanked by her parents. Paige's older sister was pale and shaking, and her mother and father appeared to be equally stricken.

Hayden couldn't blame them. Their daughter had been murdered, their biological granddaughter had been kidnapped and now it seemed their son-in-law was the culprit. He couldn't imagine the pain.

He stood near the French doors with his arms crossed, watching the surreal scene unfold in front of him. Nothing about the setting or Mia sitting on a wingback chair beside him was right. Although the family had brought a lawyer and Eve had been walked through her rights, the whole thing was highly unusual. It would be better if this discussion was happening in a different place under more controllable circumstances.

But with Ruthie missing and the clock ticking, they had to move quickly.

When Blake had shown up with his parents a few minutes before Paige's family arrived with a lawyer, everything had kicked into high gear.

Paige's sister, Eve, had been sobbing about her husband Daniel's involvement in Paige's murder and Ruthie's kidnapping. While a detective had talked to her, Hayden had walked into the kitchen with Sheriff Davidson and Blake.

Given that the young man had initially been a suspect, it had been a shock to see him. He'd spilled a quick story that his parents had corroborated and could back up with their doorbell camera video. Blake had been home at the time of Paige's murder, and other than a trip back to Greenville that could be easily checked through credit card records and gas station security camera footage, he'd been with his parents. He'd initially believed that Trent Rhinehart, the husband of Paige's mentor, had something to do with her murder. Apparently, the man had made several unsuccessful passes at Paige over the years.

Blake had followed the Rhineharts back to Greenville when they'd left the Crosby home the day before, but when he'd realized he had no idea what he was looking for, he'd returned home and shared his suspicions with his parents. They'd agreed to call the sheriff this morning, but then news had come that Ruthie was missing.

And now they knew who had her.

Hayden looked around the room, needing a moment to catch his breath. Of all of the suspects they'd listed, Paige's brother-in-law, Daniel Warner, had been low on his list.

"When did you discover all of this?" Sheriff Davidson sat in one of the chairs at an angle to the couch. His fatherly demeanor lent an air of calm to the room, though the tension was thick enough to choke them all.

Eve swallowed audibly. "Daniel went out late yesterday afternoon, and he never came home. He had his johnboat on the trailer when he pulled out. I just assumed he…he…" She leaned against her mother's shoulder, and Sue wrapped her arm around her daughter. "I figured he was grieving Paige and needed…" Eve choked on the words.

Hayden looked away from her sorrow, overwhelmed by his own. According to Eve's first words when she'd walked into the house, Daniel had not only taken Ruthie, he'd killed Paige during an argument. Eve had used a phone app to show the sheriff footage from the video camera in their garage, but Hayden hadn't watched. He'd had his fill of death captured on surveillance cameras.

Elliott had filled him in, having stood over the sheriff's shoulder. In the audio, Daniel had railed at Paige, screaming at her for allowing Ruthie to be adopted "outside of our family." He'd grabbed her, shaken her, screamed at her for "giving away the daughter that should have been" his. When Paige had struggled, he'd shoved her.

She'd stumbled, the back of her head hitting the corner of the johnboat. Elliott said the location and force of the blow against the sharp angle of the boat had likely killed her.

"I never thought he'd take Ruthie. I never thought he'd…" Eve looked across the room at Mia. "I am so sorry. I wish I'd known sooner. I never knew he was feeling all of these things, that he was so angry. That…that he'd do something like this."

Mia stood and squeezed Hayden's hand as she passed. She sat on the table in front of Eve and pulled Paige's sister close.

Hayden watched, wide-eyed. In the midst of her fear and grief, Mia was comforting the wife of the man who'd stolen her daughter? He was pretty sure he was nowhere near that level of selfless.

Eve sobbed into Mia's shoulder. "We've had trouble getting pregnant. We've been through a lot of testing and a couple of rounds of…" She sniffed and sobbed for a long moment. "Last week we found out that Daniel is permanently infertile. He didn't take it well, but I never thought…"

Without warning, Eve sat back, swiping her face. After a deep breath, she seemed to find resolve. "If he's got the johnboat, he's headed for the waters around Alligator River. He knows that area well and fishes there a lot." She turned to

Sheriff Davidson and pulled something from her back pocket. "He didn't take his phone. There's an app on it that lets you mark your favorite fishing spots. I'd start there." She typed something onto the screen and held the device for a moment, staring at it. She hesitated, seeming to consider something before she passed it to the sheriff. "There's more that might... Well, there's also a bunch of texts between him and... Jasmine Jarrett."

Mia gasped. "What?"

At Mia's outburst, Eve flinched, but she recovered quickly. "We met her through a mutual friend, and we'd been talking to her about possibly being a surrogate for us until we found out that Daniel..." Tears welled in her eyes, and her face blushed a deep crimson.

The sheriff spoke as he scrolled through the phone. "Far as I can tell, he began texting her without Eve's knowledge about a week ago. He promised to help Jasmine get revenge on Mia, whatever that means. He's been keeping her updated on Mia's whereabouts, even drove her to Elizabeth City yesterday afternoon."

How had he discovered the connection between Mia and Jasmine?

Not that it mattered. It was clear Daniel had exploited Jasmine's pain to turn her into his puppet.

"Based on one of the early texts, he believed that if Mia was killed, he and Eve would get custody of Ruthie." The sheriff waved over an investigator and handed off the phone. After a low conversation, he stood. "I'll reach out and have ECPD ready to talk to Jasmine as soon as she's able." He turned to a small knot of deputies assembled near the kitchen. "Let's get Dare and Hyde Counties involved, and federal authorities as well. The wildlife refuge is their jurisdiction, and we'll offer to assist. Call in our volunteer search teams and redirect them to meet us there. I know the sheriff over in Dare will take all the help he can get."

The deputies dispersed, and Mia appeared at Hayden's side. "Your dad still has his skiff, right?"

Odd question. He looked down at her. "He does, but why would...?" The light bulb clicked on. "Mia, no."

Her upturned face held a determination he hadn't seen in a long time. There was no fear. No hesitation. She looked like the "old" Mia, the one who would stand tall against any foe. "Hayden, yes. I am going after my daughter."

He could forbid her, argue with her, try to reason with her, but he'd never win. He recognized the look, and if he was being honest with himself, the ferocity rising inside of her brought him joy, even in this dark time. At least for the moment, she'd successfully wrestled and won against everything that held her back.

He admired her strength. Her love for her daughter. Her willingness to sacrifice for others.

And he loved her for every bit of it and more.

He loved her.

For half a second, he forgot where he was, lost in the dawning of truth. He lifted his hand and trailed a finger down her cheek, pausing at the determined set of her chin.

The instant he looked her in the eye, though, he remembered what was at stake.

He'd take her wherever she wanted to go, would pilot his dad's boat to the ends of the earth if it meant finding Ruthie, reuniting the family he loved more than anything in the world...

And starting his future.

As the sun rose over the trees along the river at the Alligator River National Wildlife Refuge, the sky glowed in a riot of yellow, red and orange. The trees stood in silhouette against the dawn in the damp, chilled December air. On any other day, it would be a beautiful, praise-God-worthy sight.

Now, it was simply the start of a day on which her daughter was in danger and time to find her was running out. The wildlife refuge consisted of 152,000 acres of wetlands, wood-lands and waterways. That meant there were nearly 230 square miles where Daniel Warner could be hiding with her daughter.

And here she was on the water, doing her best to search as many of those miles as she could as the cold dawn broke.

Was she really doing this? For the first time in years, Mia's heart and mind had been clear when she'd forcefully told Hayden that she was joining the search for her daughter. But now?

Now it all felt surreal. She was in that horrible place of suspended reality, where her thoughts felt like they were two steps behind the scene around her.

They skirted the eastern bank of the river, the small out-board motor on the tiny skiff drowned out by the sounds of other, larger boat motors strung out along both banks. Smaller boats like theirs had been deployed in the shallower streams, creeks and canals.

So many boats of so many sizes. Mia couldn't count them all.

If she wasn't so numb, she'd cry. Dozens of first responders were out at dawn on Christmas Eve, braving the unseasonable cold to search for her little girl.

How could she not be out here among them, making the sacrifice herself?

Hayden and a score of other people had urged her to stay at the house and wait for news, but she couldn't. If she wasn't out here being active, she'd wither and die. She needed to be near Ruthie. If Daniel had taken her into the wildlife refuge, then the wildlife refuge was where Mia needed to be.

"You're awfully quiet." Hayden spoke from his seat behind her, at the rear of his father's small skiff, where he was direct-ing their course by turning the boat's motor.

There was too much to say. The thoughts in her head wouldn't sort into conversational pieces. Her daughter was missing. Ruthie's bio-mom was dead. Her bio-uncle was the killer and the kidnapper.

She scanned the bank, searching for the small inlet that would lead them to one of the fishing holes noted on Daniel's app. Apparently, there were a dozen places he frequented.

Hopefully, he'd taken refuge in one of them.

It was always possible he'd led them to believe he was out in the refuge when he was really on a plane to anywhere else in the world.

"Want to talk about it?" Hayden's voice was low, likely a response to the sunrise and the heavy air that hung over the river like fog. Hopefully, it would mute the sounds of the many searchers. If Daniel was alerted to their presence, there was no telling what desperation would drive him to do.

She couldn't think about that, though. "I just can't imagine Daniel doing something like this."

"Neither can I."

A helicopter roared overhead, getting into position to circle wooded areas that would be difficult to traverse on foot. Based on intel handed out at a safety briefing before they'd launched into the river, several more helos were on the way to set up search grids.

They'd find Ruthie. They had to.

Until then, she was left with her whys. "What makes someone steal someone else's child?"

"I don't know." Hayden navigated around a stump that jutted from the riverbank. "Grief? Entitlement? Fear? I can't answer that question."

At least they knew Daniel was seeking a child of his own, not looking to harm anyone, although he'd killed his sister-in-law in a fit of rage. Hopefully, he would be more gentle with a four-year-old.

Mia's hands started to shake. She gripped the sides of the metal skiff, rocking the boat slightly.

Their forward momentum slowed, and Hayden's warm hand rested between her shoulder blades. "Hey. We'll find her."

"We're not exactly quiet out here. All of these boats, helicopters, ATVs..." The sound of engines of all shapes and sizes as they fanned out into the preserve would surely tell Daniel that they'd figured him out. He could hop in that johnboat and go anywhere.

But if he did, surely they'd see him.

Unless he blended in with all of the other boats. It wouldn't be hard to simply join the search and vanish upriver.

But they'd all memorized the photos of Daniel's boat that Eve had provided. They were all on high alert.

God, let it be enough. Let Daniel hear the overwhelming size of our search team and give up.

She had little hope. He was a killer and a kidnapper. What did he have to lose?

"At least Ruthie knows him." Hayden pulled his hand from her back and gave the engine more power. "She won't be afraid of him. And he was apparently dressed as Santa last night. Likely, he's taking great pains to keep her calm so she doesn't alert someone to their presence."

He was just trying to make her feel better. Given his current mental state and sense of desperation, there was no telling what Daniel would do. "Where does he think he's going? Does he plan to live in the swamp with Ruthie forever? What's the plan? He can't—"

A low crackling sound broke through her spinning thoughts. From the walkie-talkie on Hayden's belt, Sheriff Davidson's voice rasped into the air. "Got word from Dare County. Daniel's truck was found on Buffalo City Road near the kayak launch. No boat on the trailer."

"That's not far from here." Hayden let the small skiff drift in shallow water near the bank, where a creek dipped into the trees and headed back toward the interior of the wetlands. He pulled the radio from his hip and spoke into it. "We've got several inlets over here. We'll take the one at…" He checked his GPS and read off the coordinates.

The sheriff relayed the coordinates, then ordered several other teams to head their way, both to search other waterways and to provide backup.

Hayden clipped the radio back onto his belt, then turned the craft slowly into the narrow creek that opened up into one of the kayak paddling trails.

Mia leaned forward. Somewhere in the shadows between the trees, her daughter was being held captive. She refused to let herself believe in anything but a successful outcome.

But, still…

Lord, let us find her before it's too late.

Chapter Fifteen

Hayden tried to keep an eye on the creek in front of him and also on Mia, who was strangely calm and quiet. Searchers had taken to land, water and sky to find Ruthie. Members of his Trinity team had taken off on foot, joining a search party that was working their way through the woods nearby. They had to succeed. If they didn't...

He didn't want to think about life if they didn't.

He navigated around a stump in the creek that wound away from the river. The narrow, shallow channel was more suited to a canoe than a skiff, though recent rains were helping them out. The app on Daniel's phone listed a site along one of the creeks near here as a place where Daniel liked to fish, so it was an area he was familiar with and might be comfortable hiding in.

But Mia...

When she'd informed him she was heading out on the search, he'd been so proud of her. But he'd also expected her to buckle under the weight of Ruthie's disappearance, especially after her grandmother had repeatedly suggested she stay at the house to wait for news.

He was kind of ashamed of those thoughts. How many

times had he told Mia he believed she was stronger than she thought she was? Now he was the one doubting she could handle the stress.

A kidnapped child was an extraordinary amount of pressure, though, the kind that could break even someone who wasn't struggling with PTSD the way Mia was.

Still, he knew from experience in both himself and those he'd served with that PTSD was a strange illness. It affected everyone differently, driving some to abuse substances, some to chase adrenaline highs and others to withdraw inside of themselves. He'd seen fellow soldiers completely change personalities, doing things they'd never dreamed they'd do. He'd seen others internalize their pain until they imploded.

And then there was Mia. In the moments when life was easy, fear hunted her and threatened to drive her to the ground. But when the danger was real and the threat was in her face? It was as though reality was less terrifying than the monsters that chased her thoughts.

He powered back the small motor on his dad's little fishing skiff as they eased deeper into the trees. With the sun just over the horizon, the wooded area around them still hung heavy with shadows where danger could hide. It would be easy to glide right past Ruthie and Daniel without ever seeing them.

As they made their way farther, the sounds of the other boats faded into distant mosquitoes, background noise that seemed to buzz through his ever-racing thoughts and prayers for Ruthie's safety.

The deeper the silence grew, the more he wanted to shatter it with a bloodcurdling scream.

Instead he reached out to Mia. "It's too quiet. Talk to me." If only she knew how much he needed to hear her voice. It had been that way for years—how was he just now seeing it?

How was he just now realizing that he'd fallen in love with her? He couldn't pinpoint the moment it had happened, and he couldn't have picked a worse time to uncover those emotions.

She looked over her shoulder at him, her ponytail falling down her back. "I'm doing a lot of praying, but I've been doing it quietly because I'm not good at doing it out loud."

"How are you holding up?"

Her chin tipped toward the ever-brightening tree canopy above them. "Numb. Scared. Overwhelmed. Lost. All of the things. I'm probably not doing as badly as I'd be doing if I was sitting in the house waiting for the phone to ring." She sniffed. "It's still hard. With me, it's tough to know what's normal and what's my brain going into overdrive."

It couldn't be easy to be trapped in her own mind. It wasn't easy to be in his own head most of the time.

He felt as though the engine in his brain had been stuck in high gear for years, but he'd become so used to it that he hadn't noticed. Now the roaring was about to swamp him.

But this wasn't about him. "I think feeling all of those things you said is normal right now. And, Mia? Just because your feelings are different than other people's, that doesn't mean you aren't normal. After all you've been through, you'd be abnormal if you weren't overwhelmed. I'd be worried about you if the world *didn't* scare you more than it scares other people."

Slowly, she tilted her head down. For a long time, she stared ahead of them, where the water broadened as they neared one of the larger creeks that ran parallel to the river. Ahead, the air seemed brighter where the trees thinned.

Finally, Mia braced her hands on the sides of the skiff and turned to look at him, rocking the small boat gently. Tears stood in her eyes. "You're right. My baby girl is missing. It's normal to be afraid. My husband was murdered, and I watched him bleed out in front of me while our baby was in her carrier beside him. Who's to judge what a normal reaction to that is? All this time…" Her gaze met his and held on. She blinked, and tears glistened down her cheeks. "All this time, I've been measuring my life against everyone else's. Everyone else hasn't been through what I've been through." She nodded, her ponytail bobbing as though it could express her resolve. "I have to heal in my own way. Who's to say what's *normal* when nothing about this is normal?" Looking away from him, she turned around as though she'd settled something in her heart.

He'd definitely settled some things in his. Watching the light dawn in her eyes, he'd felt his feelings settle into place, had heard Elliott's words all over again. Their lives weren't dictated by how anyone else lived. Everyone had their own story. He'd been her friend for years. Had been Keith's friend even longer. They were part of each other's histories.

There was a Psalm in the Bible somewhere that said God had written his days in a book before he was ever born. If that was the case, then He knew how it all started, how it continued and how it ended.

Keith's book had a start, a middle and an end. He'd lived his life fully, serving those around him and loving his wife and daughter for as long as he'd been able. There was no doubt in Hayden's mind that, given Keith's actions and his commitment to Jesus, he'd gone to be with Him when he died.

But Mia's book was still being written. So was his own. So was Ruthie's. One person's book being closed didn't mean that all of the other books simply ended. God continued writing chapters.

And maybe their chapters blended into a whole new book. Maybe there was a sequel.

A spiderweb brushed his forehead as they passed between two tree limbs. Hayden shuddered and swiped at the sticky threads. It felt like a hundred spiders skittered across his skin, but he shook off the sensation along with his shiny new thoughts about Mia.

Right now, finding Ruthie was the most important thing. They couldn't afford any distractions.

He scanned the trees and the water, throttling the boat's motor back, then shutting it off as they reached the wider creek. He didn't need to roar out of the trees with the engine humming. The sound would carry up and down the open stretch of water for a good distance. If Daniel was nearby, the last thing they wanted to do was alert him to their presence.

Hayden grabbed a low-hanging branch and held on, anchoring them against the gentle current that tried to push them back toward the river.

The morning air was quiet. The sound of the other boats on the river and in the various waterways had faded as they drifted deeper into the pocosin wetlands.

Actually...

He scooted off the small bench seat onto his knees in the damp bottom of the boat and leaned closer to Mia so he could whisper. "It's too quiet."

She held her breath, seeming to listen before she nodded. "No birds."

She had picked up on what he'd noticed. Not only were the birds in the nearby trees silent, but they were silent along the creek as well.

It could be because of their presence or because of the cold air, but even in the winter the birds in the area tended to greet the sunrise.

They weren't the only ones out here.

Had other searchers stumbled into their grid? Or was Daniel nearby with Ruthie?

Hayden reached for his radio, then hesitated. He couldn't call others away from their search areas on a hunch. To do so might mean they missed Ruthie completely and allowed Daniel to escape.

He'd already let one person who'd harmed the people he loved escape. He wasn't about to let that happen again.

Suddenly, Mia stiffened. She held up her hand before Hayden could speak and leaned forward, turning her right ear toward the creek.

As much as he wanted to ask what she'd heard, he kept his mouth shut, not wanting to cover another sound.

But then it came again, clearer.

"Now, Uncle Daniel!" It was Ruthie's voice.

And she was angry.

Mia nearly choked on her daughter's name. It rushed into her throat, begging to cry out.

"I want to go home!" The shout bounced off the trees and pierced her heart.

Only Hayden's hand on her shoulder kept her from leaping from the skiff into the shallow creek to rush through the water toward the distant sound of her daughter's ire.

Ruthie wasn't scared, but she was angry. There was no telling how long Daniel would deal with a temper tantrum before he snapped like he had with Paige.

Mia whimpered and struggled, and Hayden drew her back against his chest, covering her mouth gently with his hand. "Shh. I know. I know."

Every muscle in her body shook with tension and the screaming desire to charge forward. Her daughter was nearby. The longer they waited, the more likely it was that Daniel would pack her up and flee deeper into the wildlife preserve.

She had to go. Had to get to her daughter. Had to rescue her.

She could not be too late again. She could not lose her daughter because she arrived on the scene after the damage was done.

She couldn't.

Tears streamed down her cheeks as she struggled, the drops running between Hayden's fingers where his hand covered her mouth.

He continued to whisper words she couldn't quite make out, but they rose and fell with a cadence she recognized as his prayers. His chest pressed against her back, and his heartbeat raced along at what felt like the same speed as hers.

Hayden was as terrified as she was. He wanted to race in to snatch Ruthie back to them as much as she did.

He loved her daughter as much as she did. He would do the right thing.

She took a shuddered breath in through her nose, then exhaled slowly, forcing herself to relax.

The moment she did, Hayden slipped his hand from her mouth, but he didn't pull away from her. Instead, he whispered, "I'm going to text our coordinates to the sheriff." He moved away and secured the boat to a tree branch with a rope. As he shifted forward in the small craft, there was a soft click. He'd shut off his radio, not wanting to risk it going off and alerting Daniel to their location.

"Ruthie. Get in the boat." Daniel's shout knifed through the trees. They had to hurry. He was loading up to move. There was no doubt he'd heard the helicopters and the boats. It was possible he had a police scanner, and although they'd been careful about communications, he'd still be able to deduce that they'd figured out his location.

How did he expect to escape? The area was crawling with boats and with searchers on foot and in the air. Helicopters would easily track him.

But if he took off deeper into the preserve before they made contact, he could disappear once again.

"I want to go home. I want Mommy." Ruthie's anger carried, and her foot stomp was clear in Mia's mind, even if it wasn't visible in her sight.

Her heart shredded at her daughter's demands. Ruthie might be angry, but she was also scared. She needed her mother. Mia's breath stuttered, and she instinctively leaned forward to jump into the water.

She had to get to her little girl.

Hayden grabbed a fistful of her sweatshirt and pulled her to him. "Backup is on the way."

"If he gets her into a boat or he gets cornered..." There was no telling what Daniel would do if he was backed into a situation he couldn't get out of. He might hurt Ruthie. He was likely desperate enough to do anything at this point. "We can't wait."

"If you promise me you'll stay right here, I'll go see what we're dealing with." Hayden turned her to face him, gripping her shoulders to force her to look him in the eye. "Promise."

She nodded. While her impulses drove her to her daughter, her training and instincts planted her where she was. They couldn't go in without intel. That would only get one of them hurt, possibly Ruthie.

She had to think like a soldier. Like a law enforcement officer. Not like a mother.

Even if it ripped her insides apart.

When she nodded, Hayden slid his hand down to hers, then lifted her hand and wrapped her fingers around the branch he'd been holding. "Stay here." He laid his radio and cell phone on the bench seat, scanned her face, then grabbed the back of her neck and pressed a quick kiss to her lips before he turned away, gripping the side of the skiff. "Hold it steady."

Mia grabbed the rough branch with both hands, her mind and heart reeling. Her daughter. Hayden. The danger. That kiss. The other kiss. Her twisting, turning feelings.

It was too much.

The small boat rocked as Hayden stepped over the side into water that came just over his knees. Carefully, he made his way up the stream, avoiding the super-saturated ground along the bank that would suck his feet down and lock him into place.

He moved achingly slow, obviously not wanting to make too much noise as he waded closer to the larger creek. Once he reached the outlet, there would be no cover, and he had no way of knowing exactly where Daniel and Ruthie were or if Daniel was watching.

One move made too quickly could end everything.

Mia wanted to curl into a ball in the skiff. To press her face against the water puddled in the flat bottom of the metal boat, close her eyes and pretend that none of this was happening. Maybe she'd open her eyes to a different world, where she was at home in her own bed, with Ruthie safely tucked in down the hall.

Instead, her eyes dried out from not blinking as she watched Hayden's slow progress. If she looked away or let her attention lag, something horrible might happen to him.

She should pray, but the only prayers she could muster were jumbled silent screams from her heart.

That verse about God understanding even when she didn't have words had better be true.

Hayden stopped and grabbed the trunk of a tree that grew out of the water. He edged closer to the trunk, using the tree as a shield. Pressing as tightly as he could against the bark, he eased forward to look around the tree.

He jerked back, then looked directly at Mia. Deliberately raising his arm, he extended his left index finger, pointing in the direction he'd been looking, his thumb aimed at the ground.

It was a military hand signal. *Enemy in sight.*

Mia nearly collapsed into the bottom of the boat. Ruthie really was nearby, and Daniel had her. She wasn't sure whether to feel relief or panic, but she managed to lift a thumb in acknowledgment.

With grim determination on his face, Hayden lifted his arm again, this time bending his elbow and making a fist.

Freeze.

He expected her to stay in place.

There was no way she was going to give him a thumbs-up to that. If he thought she was going to stay here while he—

He shifted signals, holding his hand to his ear like a telephone.

Mia scrambled for the radio, then stopped. If Hayden wasn't speaking, then she didn't dare risk being heard. Following his earlier lead, she grabbed his cell phone and unlocked it using Ruthie's birthday, then texted Sheriff Davidson. Located Ruthie and Daniel at our last location.

The reply came quickly. Is he armed?

She had no idea.

Oh, Lord, don't let him be armed. She couldn't bear it if her daughter was being held captive at gunpoint. Guns had done enough damage to her life already.

She sent her answer. Don't know.

Headed your way on foot and by water. Don't engage unless necessary.

Clearly they hoped to rescue Ruthie by appearing in front of Daniel with overwhelming force.

Mia settled the phone onto the bench and lifted her hands above her head, crossing her wrists. *Remain in place.*

Hayden acknowledged with a raised thumb, then peeked around the tree, his hand at his hip.

Mia's spine stiffened. He wouldn't do that if Daniel was unarmed.

If she sat here any longer, she'd fly into pieces. Already, her heart was pounding and her skin was heating. Her mind raced, and her muscles ached to move. She was headed for a full-blown panic attack that would blow their cover if she didn't get moving.

This wasn't a mission, and Hayden wasn't her commanding officer. This was her daughter's life at stake, and she wasn't going to let him call the shots, even if his calls made sense.

She grabbed the branch above her head to steady herself, then slipped one leg over the side and stepped into the water.

Her running shoes sank into mud, but she moved slowly and deliberately through the water. She was halfway to Hayden, who glared at her with concern and anger, before she realized she'd left the radio and his cell phone behind.

She'd also misjudged how cold the water was. Her legs were freezing, and the shakes started almost instantly. Whether they were from cold or fear, she couldn't say, but she didn't dare stop moving.

She reached Hayden's side, and he glared in a way that made her glad she couldn't read his mind.

"What do you see?" She leaned against him and whispered directly into his ear.

He turned away, took a deep breath, then turned back to her. "Tent. Boat. Daniel. Ruthie's fine but not happy."

As if to punctuate his words, Ruthie cried out again. "Uncle Daniel! Take me home so Santa can find me!"

"Ruthie! Knock it off!" Daniel's voice roared across the space.

Mia swallowed a cry, but not fast enough. Her daughter's name was halfway out of her mouth before she clamped down on her shout.

"Mommy!" Ruthie's frantic voice cut through the morning, followed by a series of curses from Daniel.

They had no choice but to move.

Hayden stepped from cover, his hand on his hip, facing the right. "Daniel, you need to give up. Hand Ruthie over. There are reinforcements—" He jerked and reached for his hip, but before he could grab his gun, a shot cracked. Hayden grabbed at his face, stepped backward and stumbled, disappearing beneath the waist-deep water.

Mia's scream blended with her daughter's on the echo of the gunshot.

Chapter Sixteen

"No!" Mia's scream echoed off the trees. She lurched forward, her knees giving way, and dropped into water up to her stomach. Icy shivers ran through her.

Not again. Not again. Not again.

Keith.

Hayden.

Gunshots.

Death.

"No!" The word ripped from her throat, tearing at her vocal cords. She would not, could not, lose another man she loved. Not like this. Not to—

"Mommy!" Ruthie's cry was followed by a splash.

"Ruthie. Get back here!" Daniel's yell was hot with fury.

The same fury that had killed Paige.

Mia scrambled to her feet, the need to rescue her daughter breaking through the toxic fog of fear, shock and grief.

Ruthie needed her. That night at the Double R Convenience Store, Mia had frozen at the sight of Keith's body, leaving her daughter helpless in her car seat while someone else rushed in to save her.

Not this time.

Her daughter was in danger, and she would not fail her again. It was up to her, and with Hayden…

Swallowing a whimper, Mia stepped forward as the cold water on her body seemed to freeze in the icy air. If she didn't get to Ruthie quickly, her daughter would freeze in the water. She had no doubt the splash had been Ruthie diving in and rushing toward the sound of her mother's voice.

Mia waded the remaining few feet to the opening in the canal, heedless of Daniel's presence and unable to force herself to look toward where Hayden had vanished. *Dear Lord…* There were no other words. If she considered what had happened, she'd drop in her tracks.

A few bubbles surfaced where he'd vanished, and their trail seemed to move against the current. Was he hurt? Was he swimming to safety? How could she be facing this again?

She dragged her gaze to her daughter, praying for Hayden, for Ruthie, for herself.

Ruthie. She had to focus on Ruthie.

Clear of the overhanging trees, the sky above was bright with morning's light, though shadows overhung the creek and its banks.

On the other side of the wide creek, about forty feet away, Daniel had beached his johnboat. A small tent stood on the bank, and Daniel was splashing into the water, headed straight for her.

Six or so feet from the bank, Ruthie was wading into ever deeper water, nearly up to her neck already. Her hazel eyes locked on to her mother's. "M-M-Mommy!" The cry came through chattering teeth.

"Ruthie!" Only sheer determination kept Mia from collapsing with both fear and relief. Her daughter was safe at this very second, but submerged in frigid water with Daniel on her heels, that could change at any moment.

Daniel froze when he was knee-deep in the water, his expression registering shock at Mia's appearance. He was only a few feet away from Ruthie.

His hands were empty. He must have dropped the gun somewhere in his rush to reach Ruthie. Sure enough, he turned from Mia toward his boat, then back again. "Mia. You have no part in this. Don't make me hurt you."

She ignored him. Her daughter was her only priority. Let Daniel roar. She needed to get Ruthie back to the skiff. Back to where Hayden had disappeared.

Or she had to stall Daniel long enough for the cavalry to arrive.

Mia focused on her daughter, who was up to her neck as she tried to wade to her mother. Mia couldn't tell her to go back to shore, because Daniel was frozen in indecision near the bank. "Ruthie. You can get to me. I'll meet you in the middle." Ruthie had been swimming from the moment she could float. "It's too deep to walk. Swim."

"Cold." Even from this distance, it was clear that Ruthie's lips were turning blue. The greatest danger to her daughter right now wasn't Daniel. It was nature itself.

"I know, baby." They should have brought blankets, extra coats, something. Hopefully, the sheriff and his team had thought ahead. "Come to Mommy." She plowed through water that dragged her back. She was freezing where her wet skin met the air. Shivering. Weakening.

"Stay away from my daughter!" Daniel shouted and stepped deeper into the water. "I'm taking Ruthie where she'll be safe. Paige and Blake never should have—"

"I w-want to go h-home." Ruthie was close. Just out of arm's reach.

Mia reached over the water. "Come on, little fish." Her fingers brushed her daughter's, then she clasped Ruthie's cold wrist and pulled her into her arms, snuggling her to her chest. "It's okay, baby. Mommy's got you. We're going home. We're going to have hot chocolate and see Noni." She had to get back into cover and toward the river before Daniel could recover and react.

She had to get back to Hayden. Was he hurt? Alive? Was he...

There was no sign of him.

She turned to slog to the creek and the skiff, but splashing from Daniel's direction stopped her. Before she could look to see what he was doing, a gunshot cracked, and dead leaves rained down from above.

Ruthie cried out and tightened her grip around Mia's neck.

Mia froze. Gunshots. Daniel knew her trauma, her pain, her fear. Mia whimpered.

"Don't make me shoot you in the back, Mia." His voice was hard. "I've got nothing to lose." His voice cracked, then strengthened again. "Paige was an accident, but Hayden wasn't. If it means I take Ruthie and start a life with the daughter I deserve, the one Eve and I should have adopted, then I will do whatever it takes to leave with her."

Everything she feared most swirled around her. Ruthie in danger. The thought of leaving Ruthie as an orphan. Someone she loved injured or dead.

Injured or dead.

She stared at the spot where Hayden had been shot, where he'd disappeared into the water. She'd seen enough drowning victims to know that something should be visible, especially in water this shallow. His coat. His arm. Something.

Hope surged. Maybe she'd been wrong. Maybe Hayden was alive.

Then where was he?

In the distance, the low hum of boat motors surged.

Help was on the way, but would it be in time?

She looked over her shoulder, where Daniel aimed a double-barreled shotgun in her direction.

A shotgun. Two shells. Unless he'd reloaded, and she was

fairly certain there hadn't been time, then he had no more ammo in the weapon.

A shotgun also meant whatever Daniel had fired at Hayden had likely been shells filled with some sort of shot. From that distance, the damage would have been minimal. So where was he?

Behind her, a series of splashes indicated that Daniel was in pursuit. He'd be faster than her with Ruthie in her arms. He'd catch them. He'd drown her. He'd take Ruthie.

Where was Hayden? Would help arrive before it was too late?

She looked over her shoulder, and Daniel was gaining, cutting through the water faster than she ever could. She shivered as Ruthie shuddered.

She tried to gauge the distance to the skiff, then looked back again. Daniel was only twenty feet away. So close. So—

Something splashed between her and the skiff. She collided with something hard. A tree trunk. A—

An arm, dripping water from a heavy black work coat, wrapped around her and Ruthie, pulling them close and then moving them aside.

With water pouring from his hair and his coat and blood mixing with the water on his face, Hayden lifted his hand, his pistol aimed squarely at Daniel. "Stop now." He stepped in front of Ruthie and Mia. "It's over, Daniel."

With a sob, Mia leaned forward. She rested her chin on her daughter's shivering head and her forehead against the back of Hayden's soaking wet jacket, cradling Ruthie between them.

Behind her, shouts indicated that several other search teams were almost upon them.

It was over.

He'd better be right about Daniel not reloading.

Hayden held the pistol level, aimed at Daniel's center mass. The last thing he wanted to do was pull the trigger.

If he was right, he shouldn't have to.

Although Daniel stood about twenty feet away with the shotgun aimed at them, he didn't pull the trigger. He merely glared at Hayden as though he wished that first shot had killed him.

Hayden didn't want to consider how Mia must have felt in those long moments as he had maneuvered into position to end this fight. His heart had ached for her, his pulse throbbing in the small wounds that dotted his face and neck from the birdshot.

Keith had to be on her mind. She had to be reliving a nightmare. He'd wanted to cry out to her, to let her know he was safe, but then Daniel would have known as well.

He'd have had time to reload.

If Hayden was right, Daniel had no ammo. He had fired once at Hayden and once at the sky. That shotgun only held two shells. He hadn't seen Daniel reload, but it had also taken him some time to get from where he'd taken a dive under the shallow water to where he'd surfaced in the shadows.

Nothing else had gone to plan. Not getting peppered in the face with birdshot. Not surfacing to find that Mia had surged forward to confront Daniel unarmed.

She trembled against his back, shaking Ruthie's head against his shoulder blade. He was cold and numb, and surely they were, too, but he wasn't about to let Daniel Warner escape. As boat motors drew closer, he held his ground.

Red-faced and with a look harsh enough to drop a man in his tracks, Daniel tossed the shotgun into the water, then raised his hands.

At the same time, a helicopter roared overhead and hovered, stirring the trees and scattering dead leaves over water that whipped into small waves.

Daniel looked up, then ducked his head against the onslaught of rotor wash. There was nothing the aircraft could do, and he likely realized that. It couldn't land. It could only hover, letting the approaching water teams know their exact location.

Hayden reached behind his back and pushed Mia and Ruthie away. "Go. Get to cover. Now."

Mia wrapped an arm around his waist, her grip tight. No doubt she was overwhelmed and panicked.

Daniel saw his opportunity. He bolted toward the boat he'd beached on the narrow bank. The chances of him getting away were small, but the likelihood that he had another weapon stashed on the boat was large. If he reached it, it could lead to a firefight that endangered Ruthie, Mia and the searchers who had nearly reached them.

Hayden ripped Mia's hand from his waist, holstered his pistol and pushed through the water, desperate to reach Daniel before he reached the boat. Swimming would be faster, but the water was too shallow.

He had to get to Daniel. He didn't want a gun battle. Didn't want to pull the trigger. Didn't want Eve and the rest of Paige's family to live with Daniel's death the way Mia and he had to live with Keith's.

Just as Daniel reached the stern of the boat, Hayden pushed forward with one final lunge, knocking them both sideways into the knee-deep water.

Daniel rolled, seeking the advantage, but Hayden was faster. He came to his feet first and was already swiping water from his eyes. He eased around, putting himself between Daniel and the boat.

Scrambling to his feet with water dripping from his dark hair, Daniel backed a few feet away, eyeing first the boat, then Hayden, as though he was calculating his next move. He had to know he had a better chance of escape if he fled on foot deeper into the preserve, but his tenacious desire to get to the boat clarified Hayden's suspicions that he had a second weapon on board.

Gun or knife, it didn't matter. Hayden wasn't letting him

get past. His body ached and his face burned, but he held his ground.

The fear in Daniel's eyes was more frightening than any hatred could have been. The man knew he was backed into a corner, and corners made people desperate.

Without warning, Daniel whirled and fled onto the bank, stumbling toward the woods.

Elliott and Rebecca stepped out of the shadows, accompanied by two deputies who had their hands on their holsters.

Elliott offered a trademark grin. "Somebody call for the cavalry?"

Hayden could only nod, too cold to speak. He'd never been happier to see his teammates.

To the left, a boat appeared from farther up the wide, shallow creek, piloted by another deputy.

Hayden reached up and grabbed the side of the johnboat. It truly was over this time. His adrenaline ebbed, leaving him weak and shaky. The cold and the pain finally registered, and he sank to his knees in chilly water. Ruthie and Mia were safe. The threat was gone.

He turned as quickly as he could as the deputies took Daniel into custody, searching for Mia and Ruthie, but they were nowhere to be found. One of the skiffs that had entered from the direction of the river was powering away, carrying the woman he loved and the kid he adored to safety.

Without him.

Chapter Seventeen

Her home was safe once again.

Mia sat in the rocking chair in Ruthie's room and watched the rise and fall of her daughter's chest as she slept beneath the orange-and-pink-striped quilt. Ruthie's hair was a mass of tangles on the bright orange pillow, and she snuggled Penelope close. The doll had been left in Hayden's truck, but Elliott had proved to be the hero. He'd spotted Penelope in the wreckage and tucked the doll away in his own truck. Penelope had been waiting on Ruthie's bed when they came home from their short trip to the hospital ER, where they'd been evaluated for hypothermia and checked for other injuries before being sent home with a "prescription" for warm pj's, hot soup and a long rest.

Ruthie had been happier to see Penelope than she had been to see her mother. Almost.

Mia smiled. That was fine. Hopefully it was an indicator that she'd wouldn't suffer any lasting effects from her ordeal. A chat with a kind investigator had revealed that Daniel had not harmed Ruthie. She had, in fact, believed it was a grand adventure in search of Santa Claus, and had been more angry about not being allowed to go home than she had been afraid of what was happening. Only at the end, when they'd arrived to rescue her, had Ruthie begun to realize something was wrong.

There was hardship ahead of her, though. They had yet to tell her about Paige's death. Mia dreaded the moment when the truth was spoken.

For now, she was content to sit and rock and to watch Ruthie sleep, knowing that both Daniel and Jasmine were in custody.

Life would be good…if only Hayden would reach out to her.

The last time she'd seen him, he'd been standing in the water after help arrived. At that point, Gavin and Kelsie had hauled her and Ruthie away from the scene, rushing them to the river where a larger boat waited with blankets and dry clothes to combat the effects of cold water and colder air. They hadn't seen Hayden at the ER, nor had he called since.

Mia tapped her fingers on her knee. She had heard no updates. He'd been shot with birdshot from a distance, which shouldn't be too damaging, but still…

He'd been shot.

The truth sent a tremor through her, one she'd been holding back since the blast. Had Daniel been armed with a pistol or a rifle instead of a shotgun…

Mia stood so suddenly that the world tilted. She breathed deeply, trying to beat back vertigo and the panic attack that threatened to overwhelm her.

"He's okay." The low, deep voice from the doorway whirled her around, slamming the brakes on her fear.

Elliott held up his hands as if to show he was unarmed. The man who typically looked unflappable had a bit of a sheepish pink to his complexion, probably because he had invaded what he perceived to be "girl territory."

It was almost enough to make Mia smile.

He pointed toward the stairs and turned in that direction. "I know it's going to take a lot to get you away from your daughter, but can I talk to you?" When Mia's smile faded, Elliott shook his head. "Hey, I already told you Hayden's okay. So is everybody else. This is just a talk." Without waiting to see if she complied, he walked away.

A talk with Hayden's boss? A man who was clearly used to giving orders that were followed without question?

Since both the army and the sheriff's department had conditioned her to follow orders...

With one last glance at her daughter, Mia stepped out, pulling the door closed behind her. Knowing Ruthie, she'd nap until dinner. The kid slept like a champ.

In the den, Elliott was studying the Christmas tree when Mia walked in. He turned, shoving his hands into his pockets beneath his gray flannel shirt. "You go all out for Christmas?"

Mia wrapped her arms around her stomach and sat on the edge of the couch. The house was quiet. Her grandmother had run to the grocery store for dinner, the search teams had departed, and the Trinity team had scattered except for Elliott and Kelsie, who was nowhere to be seen. "It's for Ruthie. I'm not a fan, but she deserves the cheer. It seems like bad always happens at Christmas. That's when..." She looked toward the French doors, where the open blinds revealed Christmas Eve afternoon sunlight sparkling on the river. "Now this."

"You're a good mom."

She shrugged. "I try." When she looked at Elliott, he was still watching her. "Have you heard any more about what's going to happen to Daniel and Jasmine?"

"You and I both know any real answers will be slow in coming, but Daniel's revealed that he met Jasmine when they were looking for a surrogate, and it came out pretty quickly who you were and that Jasmine had some, well, hard feelings against you."

That was a gross understatement.

Elliott brushed a tree branch. "He'd never been happy with Paige about the way the adoption went, and meeting Jasmine was the match to that gasoline. His initial plan was to have Jasmine panic you into fleeing the café to make you vulnerable to attack, but that was obviously derailed. All of that was in the works days before his altercation with Paige, and once she was dead, he had no choice but to go all-in on getting Ruthie by any means necessary. With a confession like that, both of them are going to jail."

Barring a plea deal of some sort, Daniel's sentence could be for life. That poor family had been through far too much. It hurt her heart to think of it. When she looked up, Elliott was still watching her. "Did you have something else you wanted to say?"

"Probably not my place to say it, but I'm going to anyway." His grin lit brown eyes that were warmer than she'd initially thought. "I've never been one who kept my nose out of other people's business when I saw something that needed to be fixed."

Mia's forehead wrinkled. "Okay?"

Curling one side of his mouth, Elliott looked at the fireplace. "PTSD is a cruel companion, and it's something some of us have to live with. We learn to cope."

"It forces us into a new normal." Mia eyed Hayden's boss. Clearly, he was fighting his own battles. "I've started figuring that out the past couple of days."

"Good. Just know that having a new normal doesn't mean we stop fighting it or looking for ways to get better. It doesn't mean we stop living." Elliott finally looked at her. "I just want you to know I'm going to commit Trinity Investigations to this second look at what happened to your husband. We're going to find answers for you."

Gratitude warmed her. Someone outside of her small circle was fighting to bring Keith's killer to justice. "That means a lot. Thank you."

"And about that..." Elliott shifted from one foot to the other.

"Yes?" It was interesting to see him ill at ease. He was like a lost little boy.

Elliott lifted a slight smile, as though he'd read her thoughts.

"I'm going to tell you something I said to Hayden the other night. You're still alive. So is he. And I think the two of you need to have an honest conversation about—"

"You butting into my business, *boss*?"

Mia jumped up and turned toward the kitchen door.

Hayden stood there, a smile belying the tone of his voice.

"Hayden." He was here. Alive and walking. His face and neck were peppered with small cuts and a couple of bandages. His hair was a mess, and his face was drawn with exhaustion.

He'd never looked better.

She'd never loved him more.

He flicked a glance at her, then looked at Elliott. "I think Kelsie needs some help downstairs with the grill. She said something about hot dogs."

"Roger that, McGrath."

Mia didn't see Elliott leave, though she heard the front door close behind him. Her entire focus was on Hayden.

He was right, though. They had some talking to do, because the biggest thing she'd learned was something she'd known for months but had refused to acknowledge.

She loved Hayden. It was possible to honor Keith's memory while loving Hayden. She needed to be honest about her feelings, whether he reciprocated them or not, because she couldn't continue with the status quo. Not when her feelings had become very real and very obvious. Not when she wanted to spend the rest of her life with her best friend.

She had no idea where to start. "Are you okay?"

He stepped closer, slowly and deliberately. "Spent a couple of hours getting stitches and some IV antibiotics. Probably have a few scars. It'll be okay, though, if—" He reached the back of the couch across from her and stopped.

He was only a few feet away. She could reach out and touch him, but a sudden fear washed through her.

Not the kind of fear that had paralyzed her since Keith's death. This was different. She saw a new future laid out in front of her, one that involved her and Hayden and Ruthie as a family, but she was terrified he might not want the same.

She cleared her throat. "Ruthie is good. She's taking a nap. Noni went to get those hot dogs, and we're going to have a nontraditional Christmas Eve din—"

"I don't want to talk about dinner." His voice was deep and quiet, the tone one she'd never heard before.

It hit her spine and ran straight down to her toes, robbing her knees of strength. "What do you want to talk about?" The words were a whisper. Her breath was gone. Her heart was racing.

But this was no panic attack.

This was the exact opposite. It was…

It was everything.

Hayden extended his hands across the back of the couch. "Writing a new chapter."

Was he saying…? Mia rested her hands in his. His fingers were warm and slipped between hers like missing puzzle pieces.

He tugged gently, and she knelt on the couch, unwilling to take the time to walk all the way around it. All she wanted was to be in the protection of his arms. To know he was safe and she was, too…and that they both wanted the same things.

He slid his hands up her arms to her shoulders, then pulled her to him and wrapped his arms around her waist with the back of the couch between them. He nuzzled her hair until his lips were soft against her ear. "You know, don't you?"

"Know what?" Oh, she did, but she wanted to hear him say it.

"That I love you. Everything about you, Mia Galloway." He pulled away and slid his arms from her waist, cupping her cheeks in his palms. "The way you love Ruthie. The way you're always there when I need you. The way you need me. The way you're the bravest person I know. The way you honor Keith and yet…"

"And yet I love you." She wrapped her arms around his neck and pulled him close, kissing him in a way that said all of the things she couldn't. Giving her heart to the man God had given her for this moment, for this time, for as long as He allowed them to have.

She was going to grasp life again. To grasp joy again. To continue fighting...with Hayden by her side.

They could do this. Together.

She had a deeply rooted feeling that Keith would want them to take care of each other when he couldn't. That God had known the end from the beginning, and He'd given them each other to walk through the hard times together. Always remembering, yet always moving forward.

Hayden tugged at the hem of his blue sweater. Maybe he shouldn't have worn it. He was sweating to death.

Elliott, who stood next to him by the Christmas tree, elbowed him in the side. "Knock it off, McGrath. There's no way you're nervous."

"No. Just dying of the heat." Someone had turned on the gas logs, and Mia's living room was blazing hot. Sure, the ambience on Christmas afternoon was great, but it was stifling.

He was definitely not nervous. Marrying Mia on Christmas afternoon was the exact right thing to do.

Was it too fast?

Not at all.

In fact, according to Joann Hale at the Register of Deeds Office, who'd come in on Christmas Eve afternoon to issue their marriage license, they'd taken much longer than anyone had thought they would.

That same sentiment had been echoed by her parents and Noni, who stood by the kitchen door, by his family, who stood beside them, and Pastor Rollins, who stood next to him watching the stairs as they waited for Mia and Ruthie to come down.

Hayden smiled. When they'd told Ruthie that morning that

her big Christmas present was going to be her mother marrying her "Uncle Hayden," she'd been so excited that she'd forgotten to open the rest of the packages scattered under the tree. They were still there, wrapped in colorful paper and ribbons. She'd insisted they get dressed immediately, even though their impromptu ceremony wouldn't start until four.

He looked over at Pastor Rollins, who wore jeans and a forest green sweater as he clasped the small three-ring binder that held his notes for the service. "I'm sorry again that we dragged you away from your family's Christmas."

Pastor Rollins snorted. "Dragged me away? They've been waiting for you to marry Mia for a couple of years now. They practically shoved me out the door. Angela even sent me with a wedding present she bought for you guys last year." He gestured to a small gift bag that he'd set on the mantel when he'd walked into the room. "Believe me. The whole town would leave their Christmas dinners behind to be here if you'd invited them."

That might have been a little much, but the sentiment warmed his heart and reinforced the idea that they were doing the right thing. After talking, praying and stealing a few kisses before Ruthie awoke from her Christmas Eve nap, they'd decided not to wait, that a Christmas Day wedding in front of their families in Mia's living room was all they needed.

Everything had fallen into place in a series of answered prayers.

Once they'd talked through everything, they'd known they wanted to spend the rest of their lives with one another starting today, on Christmas. Building new memories of joy on top of the grief that had bonded them.

And they'd certainly received blessings from everyone involved.

His team had jumped into action under Noni's direction to make a huge Christmas dinner to be enjoyed after the ceremony. There was way too much food in the kitchen.

Mia had insisted that she needed no frills, just him.

Ruthie had insisted on dressing them both.

There was no telling what his two favorite ladies would be wearing when they came down the stairs in... He glanced at his watch. Well, right about now.

Sure enough, a rustle near the top step drew everyone's attention.

Ruthie descended, wearing a purple princess dress complete with a tiara. Strapped to her chest was Penelope, decked out in her own tiny pink princess dress.

Hayden choked, but he couldn't decide if it was a laugh or a sob. The precious little girl that he'd loved since the first time she'd grabbed ahold of his finger in her tiny hand was now so much more than his goddaughter. If she ever found out the hold she had over him, she'd be spoiled rotten.

She spotted him and rushed the rest of the way down the stairs, wrapping her arms around his legs and holding on tight. "Mommy's coming, Uncle Hayden, and she's so pretty. And I'm so happy. And so is Penelope."

Forget protocol. He reached down, swooped her up and snuggled her close, planting a kiss on the top of her head. Today could have gone so much differently. When he'd been swimming away from gunfire under swamp water yesterday, he'd never dreamed he'd be standing here just over twenty-four hours later.

There was another sound on the stairs, then Mia descended. She carried the fake flowers that usually sat in a vase on Ruthie's bookcase, a riot of pinks and oranges that the little girl had picked out at the holiday flea market the year before. She wore a pair of jeans and a bright orange T-shirt. A pink scarf was tied around her neck.

Yep, Ruthie had definitely chosen the outfit. It was a riotous blend of her two favorite colors.

Even in the clashing hues that ought to blind everyone in the room, Mia had never looked more beautiful.

When she reached him, she kissed his cheek, then Ruthie's. Threading her arm through his, she laid her head on his shoulder, pulling him tight to her side.

This was it. This was his family. This was where he wanted to be.

He held her close and shut his eyes, taking a moment to thank God for the man who had loved her and had been his best friend from birth, the one whose story had ended too soon.

And then he thanked God for another chapter, a different chapter, one that honored all that had been and all that was yet to come.

* * * * *

Romantic Suspense

Danger. Passion. Drama.

Available Next Month

Colton's Last Resort Amber Leigh Williams
Arctic Pursuit Anna J. Stewart

Mistaken Identities Tara Taylor Quinn
Kind Her Katherine Garbera

LOVE INSPIRED

Hunted On The Trail Dana Mentink
Tracking The Missing Sami A. Abrams

Larger Print

LOVE INSPIRED

Texas Kidnapping Target Laura Scott
Alaskan Wilderness Peril Beth Carpenter

LOVE INSPIRED

Ambush On The Ranch Tina Wheeler
Cold Case Disappearance Shirley Jump

6 brand new stories each month

Romantic Suspense

Danger. Passion. Drama.

MILLS & BOON

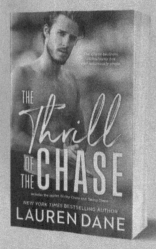
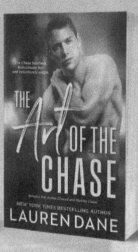

Subscribe and fall in love with a Mills & Boon series today!

You'll be among the first to read stories delivered to your door monthly and enjoy great savings.

WE SIMPLY LOVE ROMANCE

MILLS & BOON

JOIN US

Sign up to our newsletter to stay up to date with...

- Exclusive member discount codes
- Competitions
- New release book information
- All the latest news on your favourite authors

Plus...
get $10 off your first order.
What's not to love?

Sign up at **millsandboon.com.au/newsletter**

f @millsandboonaustralia 🐦 📷 @millsandboonaus